Lady of
Scandal

BOOK YOUR PLACE ON OUR WEBSITE AND MAKE THE READING CONNECTION!

We've created a customized website just for our very special readers, where you can get the inside scoop on everything that's going on with Zebra, Pinnacle and Kensington books.

When you come online, you'll have the exciting opportunity to:

- View covers of upcoming books
- Read sample chapters
- Learn about our future publishing schedule (listed by publication month *and author*)
- Find out when your favorite authors will be visiting a city near you
- Search for and order backlist books from our online catalog
- Check out author bios and background information
- Send e-mail to your favorite authors
- Meet the Kensington staff online
- Join us in weekly chats with authors, readers and other guests
- Get writing guidelines
- AND MUCH MORE!

Visit our website at
http://www.kensingtonbooks.com

Lady of
Scandal

TINA GABRIELLE

ZEBRA BOOKS
Kensington Publishing Corp.
http://www.kensingtonbooks.com

ZEBRA BOOKS are published by

Kensington Publishing Corp.
119 West 40th Street
New York, NY 10018

All Kensington titles, imprints, and distributed lines are available at special quantity discounts for bulk purchases for sales promotion, premiums, fund-raising, educational, or institutional use.

Special book excerpts or customized printings can also be created to fit specific needs. For details, write or phone the office of the Kensington Special Sales Manager: Attn. Special Sales Department. Kensington Publishing Corp., 119 West 40th Street, New York, NY 10018. Phone: 1-800-221-2647.

Zebra and the Z logo Reg. U.S. Pat. & TM Off.

ISBN-13: 978-1-4201-0848-4
ISBN-10: 1-4201-0848-4

First Printing: September 2009
10 9 8 7 6 5 4 3 2 1

Printed in the United States of America

For John,
my real knight in shining armor

For Mom and Dad,
my guardian angels

Chapter 1

London, April 1812

"Rumor has it he's returned from the dead."

Victoria Ashton frowned at the young woman by her side. Jane Middleton, a robust debutante in her fourth Season, was a notorious gossip.

Victoria remained silent, her eyes scanning Almack's crowded ballroom.

"I've also heard he has amassed a fortune and is quite handsome as well," Jane said. "Why, all the mamas of the ton are throwing their daughters before him!"

Victoria feigned interest and nodded at Jane's comments. Shifting to the side, Victoria peered around Jane and studied the faces of the couples as they danced past on the full floor.

Her eyes then wandered to the entrance of one of Almack's gaming rooms. A cold knot formed in her stomach at the thought that Spencer had already gone inside.

Jane stepped in front of Victoria and blocked her view of the card room. Raising her voice an octave, Jane continued, "Blake Mallorey's new country home is so extravagant that the Regent himself visited to obtain ideas for the next royal residence."

Something about Jane's last statement gained Victoria's attention. "Whose residence did you say?"

"Why, the Prince Regent's new residence."

"No. Whose home did the Regent visit?"

Jane stared at Victoria in confusion.

"Victoria, haven't you heard a word I've said this evening? I'm speaking of Blake Mallorey's—although I suppose I now should use his proper title, the Earl of Ravenspear—return to Town after ten years. You do recall him and his family?"

A sudden chill ran down Victoria's spine.

Did she remember Blake Mallorey?

The name brought back a flood of childhood memories. Some were sweet and poignant; most were not.

Jane touched her arm and smiled slyly. "Oh, Victoria. I'm sure you remember. Wasn't there some sort of scandal between your families?"

Victoria shook her head. "It was so long ago. I hardly recall him."

"Well, he was invited to Almack's tonight by Lady Cowper herself. Perhaps you will recognize him when you see him."

Victoria whirled toward Jane. "Blake Mallorey is expected here? Tonight?"

"Why, yes. The entire town is gossiping about him," Jane said. "He is so wealthy now and so well connected. There are rumors that he has even loaned the Prince Regent money."

Jane patted Victoria's arm as if to soothe her. "You must not fret over a past scandal between your families. With his new status, Ravenspear would hardly concern himself with such a trifling matter as to settle old scores."

Biting her lip, Victoria looked away. "Please excuse me, I must find my brother, Spencer."

Grasping the skirt of her silk gown, Victoria wove her way through the crowded room. Was Blake the only Mallorey to return? What of his mother and sister? Victoria forced a smile and proceeded past the refreshment table and the dance floor.

She glanced at a small circle of ancient society ladies gathered near a potted palm. Their wrinkled mouths frowned as they glared.

Dear Lord, did they all recall the scandal?

As soon as Victoria entered the gaming room, she spotted Spencer through a haze of cigar smoke. His thick crop of yellow hair stood on end as if he had run his fingers through it in agitation. His green eyes were feverish and glittering as he held a hand of cards.

Bloody hell! Victoria straightened her spine and headed toward her brother. Men and women moved fortunes over the tables, watching cards and dice with avaricious intensity.

Spencer sat at a table in the far corner of the room. As she neared, a tall man appeared next to her brother and handed him a glass of punch. Victoria halted, shocked. Her mind whirled as pulse-pounding recognition struck her.

Spencer turned from his cards and smiled up at Blake Mallorey. Victoria watched in amazement as Blake grinned in return and slapped her brother heartily on the back at something he said. They rocked with the laughter of revelers and longtime friends.

Her mouth dropped open.

Blake leaned against the table and lazily picked up a hand of cards. He casually studied his cards before discarding one in a haphazard manner.

Her eyes were drawn to his face. She would have to be blind not to acknowledge he was a startlingly attractive man. As a boy, Blake had been a good-looking youth on the pretty side of handsome.

But as a man . . .

His features were rugged and tanned. He had a straight nose and a chiseled jaw. His hair, dark as a raven's wing, was cut neatly to reach his collar. He was very tall and muscularly built, with deep-blue eyes. His clothes were impeccable and obviously costly, but his taste for decoration was moderate, unlike most of the male members of the ton. His dark-blue velvet jacket was stylish and perfectly tailored to fit broad shoulders, and was devoid of any lacings or silver brocade. His only jewelry was a diamond pin in his crisp knotted cravat.

Although he would be twenty-seven now, the same age as Spencer, Blake appeared older, more powerful. There was something dangerous and sinister about him that added to his attraction. A certain hardness to his features, an arrogance in his stance, proclaimed to all that this was a man who would not be dictated by society's rules, only his own.

Cobalt eyes rose to meet hers and she realized with dismay that she was standing still, staring openly at him.

Looking away abruptly, she feigned interest in an elderly man's cards sitting at the table before her. She slowly circled the card table twice before daring another glimpse beneath lowered lashes.

She drew a swift breath.

Blake Mallorey studied her as intently as she had him moments earlier.

As their eyes met and held across the room, a flicker of faint amusement crossed his face, and he nodded his head in greeting.

He recognized her!

Spencer sat beside Blake, engrossed in his cards, oblivious to Victoria's presence and Blake's interest.

Blake pushed himself away from the table, and with a pang she realized he intended to approach her. He moved without haste but with purpose, his gaze never leaving her face.

Her heart thumped madly, but she remained where she was, squaring her shoulders and raising her chin.

Halfway across the room from her he was overtaken by an eager crowd of females. Victoria observed with an odd bitterness that they were women of all ages, from society's latest crop of debutantes to the older patrons of the ton, all vying for his attention. He was politely attentive, but his eyes simultaneously roamed the room.

Victoria ran to her brother's side.

"Spencer!" She touched his shoulder. "Do you realize who you've been speaking with?"

Spencer turned bloodshot eyes toward his sister. The strong smell of alcohol wafted from his skin. "Vicki! You're ruining my concentration."

Victoria plucked the cards from her brother's hand and threw them on the table. "The gentleman folds," she announced to the wide-eyed dealer and the other startled players at the table.

Grasping Spencer's arm, she led him toward the opposite end of the room, where large French doors that led onto a terrace were open.

Spencer snatched his arm free. "Now why did you have to go and do that? I was ahead one hundred pounds."

Victoria glanced from side to side to ensure they were alone on the terrace. "One hundred pounds!" she whispered vehemently. "Wherever did you get the money to join a game with such high stakes?"

Spencer grimaced and rubbed his red eyes. "Damn, Vicki. I don't recall."

"That's because you arrived drunk," Victoria spat, "and why are you speaking with Blake Mallorey?"

Spencer's face lit up. "Why, now I remember. I borrowed the money to play tonight from Blake."

She gasped. "What? He loaned you money?"

"Of course. We've been out on the town all week together, and he has been enough of a gentleman to get me into both White's and Waiter's. I haven't been on the guest list at either establishment for over two years."

"You've been socializing with Blake Mallorey for over a week? Have you lost your wits? Have you forgotten the horrid scandal?" Glancing sideways, she lowered her voice further and added, "or the suicide?"

Spencer swallowed hard. "But that was so long ago, over ten years now. Blake is now an earl, and he has assured me that his wealth and status are secure. He has no interest in digging up old grudges."

"And you believed him?"

He shrugged dismissively. "Why not? I haven't had this much fun since I came into my inheritance from Aunt Lizzy at twenty-one."

Victoria reached out and clutched his hand. "It might have been ten years, but I have not forgotten, and I'm sure Blake's memories are stronger than mine. We must keep our distance from him. What would Father say if he learned you owed Blake Mallorey money?"

Spencer paled at the mention of disciplinarian Charles Ashton.

"Vicki, I owe Mallorey more than just the hundred pounds for tonight. He's been lending me money the entire week, and he has even purchased some of my outstanding markers."

Before Victoria could respond, the scrape of booted feet on the terrace cobblestones echoed through the night air.

Forcing a smile on her face, Victoria turned to greet the intruder as if she hadn't a care in the world. She stiffened.

Blake Mallorey's tall figure headed toward them, his eyes on her face. "I wondered what could be so appealing to lure you away from the tables, Spencer. Now I know."

Victoria's eyes met Blake's as he approached, and a shiver of apprehension coursed through her. She was keenly aware that he watched her with all his attention.

"How are you, Victoria?"

"Well, sir. Thank you," she said with rigid formality, refusing to use his deceased father's title.

His dark eyebrows arched mischievously. "Is this proper lady the same girl that followed me around and kicked the back of my heels to gain my attention?"

Victoria felt her face burn. "That was a long time ago. Children grow up."

"Ah, yes, they do. And you have grown into a stunningly beautiful woman. You have the same jade-colored eyes and sable hair that made you an adorable child, but as a woman your features are quite ravishing."

"We had heard you were killed at sea," she said, tossing her hair across her shoulders. "Some wicked, adventurous pirate story, as I recall, right, Spencer?"

Spencer coughed. "Vicki! That was just pure gossip. No truth behind it at all, I assure you, Blake."

An easy smile played at the corners of Blake's mouth. "I wouldn't want to discourage such rumors if they enhance my reputation."

She met his gaze without flinching. "In that case, there are numerous stories you may be interested in that I have overheard about you over the years."

"Vicki!" Spencer's face was bright red now.

"Perhaps," Blake said, "we could stroll the gardens and you could tell me all about these stories."

"I must decline." Victoria touched her temple with two fingers. "I seem to have developed a headache."

She swiveled quickly, turning her back on Blake. "Spencer, I'd like to leave now."

Spencer's mouth opened and closed like a fish's, then he merely nodded.

"Another time, then?" Blake pressed.

"I doubt our paths will cross again. Good night." Victoria entwined her arm with Spencer's and nearly dragged her brother from the terrace.

Victoria waited until they were safely seated inside a hackney cab, before she breathed a sigh of relief. She rested her head against the side of the padded coach and closed her eyes.

"I'm surprised at your rudeness," Spencer said, breaking the silence. "I consider Blake my new friend."

Victoria's eyes flew open. "Friend? He could cause the family a considerable amount of trouble should he choose to use his newly acquired wealth and power to do so. Don't forget that Father was recently appointed a Junior Lord Commissioner of the Treasury for the Regency and he would not want any blemish to tarnish his reputation."

"Blake's harmless, I tell you," Spencer said.

Harmless.

A picture of Blake Mallorey's face flashed before her. His wolflike grin, intense blue eyes and powerful build.

She shivered.

"Harmless" was the last word she would choose to describe him.

She had an odd premonition that he would indeed seek retribution for the wrongs he believed were done to his family, and that, worst of all, her life would never be the same once he chose to do so.

Chapter 2

"Devil take it, Blake. You're six months ahead of schedule," Justin Woodward said.

Blake Mallorey flashed his friend and man of affairs a smile and propped a booted foot on top of a massive oak desk in the library of his London town house. He watched as Justin read the latest accounting ledgers while pacing back and forth on the thick Aubusson carpet.

"Did you ever doubt me?" Blake asked.

Justin stopped pacing and looked up from the papers. A slender man of substantial height, with brown eyes and flaxen-colored hair, he had a youthful appearance.

"Charles Ashton has no idea how swiftly his life is about to change, does he?" Justin asked.

"None at all."

A feeling of satisfaction surged through Blake. Destroying Charles Ashton had been Blake's reason for living for so long, it was hard to believe his carefully laid plans were finally coming to fruition. And tonight at Almack's a most pleasant surprise had crossed his path that would make revenge even sweeter.

A vision of creamy skin, a cloud of dark hair and

bewitching green eyes singed his memory. He would never have guessed that young Victoria Ashton would become such a beautiful woman.

He remembered seeing her at her home when he visited with her brother while his father conducted business with Charles. An imp as a child, she had loved to meddle in Blake and Spencer's affairs. She had a crush on Blake and had often followed him around. He had dismissed her childhood fascination as more humorous than annoying.

That was ten years ago, so she would be near twenty now.

To his surprise, he had recognized her instantly tonight. The mischievousness in her jade eyes as a child had since turned into fiery challenge.

He hoped her adolescent infatuation remained.

Justin dropped the papers he was studying on the desk. "You're distracted. What are you thinking?"

"That I've been on English soil for nearly six months and have yet to arrange a mistress for myself."

"A mistress?" Justin's lips curled into a smile. "You've only been back amid society for a month now. Surely you've noticed the throng of women that flock around you? Not all are virginal debutantes. Plenty of married or widowed women would proposition you for the type of relationship you desire."

"Ah, but there is a certain lady I have in mind."

"And who might this mysterious lady be?"

"Victoria Ashton."

Justin straightened, an incredulous look flashing across his face. "Victoria Ashton! Are you serious?" After studying Blake's expression Justin said, "Blast. The lady will never consent."

"You know her, then?"

"Yes. I haven't been out of town that long."

Blake rose and walked around the desk. "I met her last night at Almack's. Of course I knew her as a child when our families were on good terms, but as a woman"—Blake arched a brow—"she caught my attention."

"She's well known among society," Justin said. "Her family holds no title, but Charles Ashton's appointment as one of Prinny's Lords Commissioners of the Treasury enhanced her family's status. Her coming out in society was a while back and there was gossip as to why she had not married. But then I had heard she is to be engaged to Ashton's newest business associate—Mr. Jacob Hobbs, I believe."

Blake frowned. He knew of Hobbs. He knew everything there was to know concerning Charles Ashton's personal and business affairs. Hobbs was nearly twice Victoria's age. She seemed too spirited, too independent, to marry such a man.

"The lady will never consent to becoming your mistress, no matter how charming or rich you are. It would ruin her reputation. A marriage proposal would be more appropriate."

"Marriage? To an Ashton? I thought to destroy the family name, not marry into it." Blake walked to a tall window and stared at the busy street below. "But then, I've always had a soft spot for Victoria. I'm not wholly opposed to marriage, but I'd prefer not to pay such a hefty price to have the lady. I'd rather entice her to accept my offer of mistress."

"What if Charles Ashton refuses?" Justin asked.

Blake chuckled. "It's not the father's consent I'm worried about but the daughter's. Knowing Ashton, when I explain his situation, he will hand Victoria over to me quite willingly under *any* terms."

"You plan to attack Ashton socially as well as financially? Your conscience may bother you where the lady is concerned."

Blake's eyes were like chips of stone. "I lost my conscience years ago when I killed a man to escape the same poorhouse I saved you from."

Victoria stretched on her bed and studied *The Times* with concentration.

Stock prices were high this month. Based on her calculations, they would rise even more. Investing in companies that traded sugar, tea and spices from the East Indies had proven to be lucrative. But the new London Bank and several other money-lending businesses caught her eye. Such investments involved risk but offered the opportunity for large returns. No doubt the Prince Regent's outrageous spending habits, resulting in the Crown's enormous debt, were a major factor in the recent success of such lending establishments.

"Are you going to make as much money as I need, Vicki?"

Victoria's brows knit at Spencer's interruption. "I don't know. You've accumulated more debt than ever before. Investing takes time to turn a profit. You cannot become rich overnight."

Only Spencer knew her secret, and at times like this, she regretted sharing it with him.

Spencer sighed and fell into a chair in the corner of Victoria's bedchamber. "I know. I'm just desperate to keep my debts from Father."

Victoria rubbed her eyes with the palms of her hands and returned to the paper before her. She wondered for the hundredth time that evening how she had become her brother's salvation.

A knock on the door startled Victoria. She had just

enough time to hide *The Times* beneath her pillow before the door opened and her mother entered.

"Your father requests your presence in the library, Victoria." Mary Ashton stood in the center of the room. A petite woman with dark hair and assessing green eyes, Victoria had inherited her mother's physical traits. The black velvet of her mother's dress heightened the translucence of her face and neck. Her hands were folded in front of her and her wrists were small, her fingers slim. She appeared delicate and dainty, the epitome of a lady.

A sense of uneasiness swept over Victoria. "Is Jacob Hobbs downstairs?"

Mary looked first at Spencer, then at Victoria, a frown marring her features. "You know better than to question your father's request. You're a constant worry to him . . . near twenty and no closer to being married. You have done yourself and this family harm by refusing every decent proposal of marriage. You have earned your reputation as difficult. No man will risk rejection by offering for you now. You should be thankful that your father has your best interests at heart."

Victoria sat on the edge of the bed. "I hardly call Jacob Hobbs in my best interest. Such a match would benefit only Father by keeping the business profits in the family."

Her mother raised trembling fingers to her temple. "Whatever am I to do with you, Victoria? You know a daughter must obey her father, just as I must obey my husband. Men provide for us and in return we must follow their dictates. It's nature's course for women. Just ask your brother."

Spencer rose from his seat and took their mother's arm, a sympathetic expression on his face. "Of course, Mother. A woman is not capable of earning money for herself, and thus a man must provide for her."

Victoria almost choked in rage at the twinkle of mischief in Spencer's eye. She jumped to her feet and confronted her mother. "All I want is the freedom to choose my own spouse!"

"You cannot. You know very well that women of our station seldom pick their husbands." Mary sighed and continued to rub her temples. "I don't like to argue, Victoria. Such discussions always bring on a terrible headache."

Victoria swallowed her disappointment. Mary Ashton was never able to deal with her headstrong daughter, and guilt washed over Victoria for upsetting her mother's fragile disposition.

"Don't fret, Mother. I'll go downstairs right away."

As soon as Victoria opened the library door, Jacob Hobbs was on his feet to greet her.

He raised her hand to his lips and bowed formally. "My dear Victoria, you look lovely, as always."

Before he straightened up she observed the top of his head where his hair was thinning. He looked in her eyes. Jacob was not unattractive, with silver hair, pale-blue eyes and his expensive choice of dress.

But she was not in love with him.

"You flatter me, Mr. Hobbs."

Jacob's brows drew together. "Please call me Jacob. We have known each other for some time, and I'm certain your father would approve." Jacob glanced over his shoulder at Charles Ashton, seated behind a large desk.

Victoria turned to her father, who looked up from his papers to study her. For a man who recently celebrated his sixtieth birthday, he appeared much younger, with a full head of steel-gray hair and a stocky, muscular build.

"I gave Jacob my permission to take you for a carriage

ride in Hyde Park this afternoon, Victoria," Charles said, his mouth spreading into a thin-lipped smile.

This afternoon? she thought. *However will I get to Capel Court to place my stock order for the month?*

"But Spencer is to take me shopping at the new silver-smith's in Town—"

"You can go another time."

Victoria gazed at her father's starched cravat and forced a smile. "Spencer and I shall go tomorrow, then."

"Of course you will, my dear."

The cynical tone in her father's voice and the glint of satisfaction in his eyes grated on her.

She clenched her fists, her nails forming crescent shapes in the flesh of her palms. The same physical reaction arose whenever her father forced Jacob upon her. She had escaped the marital web so far, but she knew her time was expiring.

For the rest of the meeting, Victoria sat in the rear of the library while the men discussed their joint ventures.

On many previous occasions her father had summoned Victoria while he talked of business affairs with Jacob. No doubt Charles Ashton had seen these times as opportunities to put his strong-minded daughter and Jacob in the same room.

Victoria stirred in her chair and feigned interest in a porcelain figurine of a shepherdess which stood on a nearby bookshelf. It was during these meetings that she had discovered she had a head for figures.

At first Victoria had been bored and confused with the talk of profit margins, price fixing and dividends. But as time went by, she had begun to listen and learn how to invest. She had started to predict which stocks would earn money, and she had known she had a gift when she had been correct more often than both her father and Jacob.

With her newfound knowledge came enlightenment, and she had realized that the wealthy men in society held the power that enabled them to control their own fate. Wives were dependent upon the charity of their husbands and could not spend a shilling without their spouse's permission. Such was the situation between her parents. Only the widows whose deceased husbands had left them fortunes were free to choose how to spend their own money and, more importantly, that of their second spouse.

Her father grew impatient, and Victoria knew her true desire in life—to marry a man for love, a man who would recognize her intelligence without crushing her independent spirit—was unrealistic. By creating an income stream for herself, Victoria hoped to gain a bit of freedom from the oppression of a loveless marriage.

At the end of the meeting, Jacob stood and took Victoria's hand.

Careful of her father's close scrutiny, she smiled as she rose from her seat.

"I apologize if our talk bores you," Jacob said.

Victoria lowered her lashes. "Oh, I think of other things. I don't pretend to understand business matters, and anything to do with the Stock Exchange confuses me."

Jacob patted her hand like one would a small child. "Women aren't expected to comprehend even simple money matters."

He escorted her out of the library and paused by the front door. Jacob looked down at her in the dark hallway, a serious expression on his face. "I intend to handle the finances and provide for my future wife. It's no secret that I wish that woman to be you."

Victoria stiffened, her arm still resting on Jacob's sleeve. "I don't know what to say, Jacob."

"I've already discussed my proposal with your father and have his consent."

She stared up at him, her heart pounding. "I'm not sure I'd make you a good wife."

"Your father has spoken with the church to arrange the reading of the banns next month."

A soft gasp escaped her. "But I must consent! My father cannot take the marital vows for me."

"You must obey your father, Victoria. We have decided what is best for you."

Her vision blurred with the desire to lash out at him.

He dismissed her by turning his back and opening the door himself, not waiting for the butler. "I'll arrive later in the afternoon for our ride in Hyde Park. Be ready, Victoria."

She shut the door behind him. Leaning her back against the frame for a moment, she tried to gather strength. She had not expected things to progress with Jacob with such speed. She hated the way he treated her like a child and never considered her own intelligence or desires.

Victoria jumped at the sound of a knock on the door.

Whirling around, she yanked open the door, expecting to see Jacob, returning perhaps for his hat, cane or some other personal item he had left behind.

She instead discovered Blake Mallory standing on the porch.

"Good afternoon, Victoria."

She merely stared, tongue-tied.

He leaned to the side and looked around her. His dark hair was ruffled by the breeze in the doorway, and he smiled, showing even, white teeth that contrasted pleasingly with his tanned skin.

"Do you always answer the door so quickly, or were you expecting me?"

Without waiting for her response, he haughtily walked past her and into the house.

Stunned at his forwardness, she rushed to catch up with him and grasped his forearm.

"What do you want?" she blurted out.

He looked at her hand, then arched his dark eyebrows. "I'm here to speak to your father."

She pulled away. "My father?" she asked, surprised.

Biting her lip, she looked up at him with an effort. "Does this have anything to do with Spencer?"

"Your family owes me quite a bit of money."

There was a cold edge of irony in his voice which increased her uneasiness.

"Spencer is good for every shilling," she said. "There's no need to speak with our father."

He ignored her and strode forward as he studied the interior of the house like an appraiser at a foreclosure sale.

Victoria watched him, acutely conscious of his tall, well-muscled body. He carried himself with a commanding air of self-confidence that added to his arrogance. He looked stunning in his finely tailored clothes, and the broad outline of his shoulders strained against the fabric of his coat.

Blake turned toward her. His gaze met hers, then moved over her body lazily. "I find that my patience with your family has worn thin, and I've come to collect what I'm due."

Her blood pounded; her face grew hot. Her mood veered sharply from unease to anger.

"A true gentleman would give my brother more time. Had you not loaned him the money, he never would have gambled for such high stakes. You seduced him by acting as his friend. My father was right. Your father was deceptive, untrustworthy and a coward to kill himself after—" She stopped suddenly as she realized with dismay that digging up the past could only hurt her brother's situation.

"Forgive me." She backed up a step. "I'll tell Father you are here to see him now."

His fingers wrapped around the dark fabric of her sleeve, stopping her. "Do you always speak your mind so freely?"

She tried to remove his hand, but when her fingers brushed against his she froze. He stood so close she could feel the heat from his body and smell his masculine scent. Her heart thumped erratically at an unknown emotion that rose within her.

She boldly met his eyes. "I believe in speaking my mind."

His lips twisted into a cynical smile. "Good. It shall provide endless hours of entertainment."

She glared at him, baffled. "What do you *really* want?"

His cobalt eyes were dark and unfathomable. "I'm glad you asked. Let there be no lies between us. I want you, Victoria."

Chapter 3

"What?"

Blake watched as all hint of color drained from Victoria's face. "It will be a mutually beneficial arrangement."

"I'm not sure what arrangement you speak of. But I'm certain you're insane."

"You hold in your hands the power to save your family, Victoria."

"I told you Spencer is good for every last shilling."

"It's not Spencer to whom I refer."

She raised her chin. "Then you are mistaken. My father is an established businessman and paid well as one of the six Lords Commissioners of the Treasury."

Blake gazed down upon her face. He reached out to touch a loose tendril of hair brushing her cheek. Its silky texture mesmerized him. She appeared momentarily stunned when he grazed her face.

Emboldened, his fingers fluttered to her neck.

As if coming to her senses, she moved away. Nervously she moistened her dry lips. "You presume much, my lord."

"You cannot deny the attraction between us. Do you feel the same when Jacob Hobbs touches you?"

She looked at him in surprise, and then her breath burned in her throat. "Your arrogance is astounding. I'll tell my father you're here to see him."

Victoria hurried to the library door and knocked.

A moment later, the door jerked open. Charles Ashton looked down at his daughter, a frown on his face.

"What is it? You know not to disturb me unless I ask for you."

"There's, uh—"

Blake cleared his throat. "I requested Victoria to fetch you."

Charles's head snapped up. At the sight of Blake standing in the vestibule, he inhaled a deep breath. His features smoothly transformed from astonishment to masked indifference with the skill of an experienced politician.

"I had heard you had returned," Charles said. "How many years have passed?"

"Ten, to be exact."

Charles stood tall and rigid in the doorway. "I've also heard you've done quite well for yourself."

"The Indies proved quite profitable. Which is why I decided to visit. I'm here to discuss a business proposal."

Charles's eyebrows lifted.

Blake read curiosity warring with caution behind his enemy's hard eyes until inquisitiveness and greed won, just as Blake had anticipated.

"Do come inside, then." Charles stepped aside and opened the library door wide. "I have excellent brandy we can share before we discuss your proposal."

Blake stood still. "Victoria should be present as a witness."

Charles's eyes darted to Victoria. "I do not involve the women in my household with business affairs."

"Perhaps you will make an exception today."

Without waiting for a reply, Blake entered the library and strode to a bay window overlooking the gardens. Behind him, he heard Charles usher Victoria inside and close the door.

Charles poured a glass of brandy and handed it to Blake. "What type of business do you have in mind?"

Blake accepted the drink and sat in a leather chair. "Tobacco."

He watched Victoria sit on the edge of a chair across from him. With what he suspected was great effort, she avoided meeting his gaze. Her breathing was rapid, and her breasts rose and fell temptingly against the low neckline of her gown. Her eyes shone like emeralds, and the ivory skin at her throat contrasted with the inky darkness of her hair.

He felt the stirrings of desire, and annoyance rose within him.

He needed to have his wits about him for the initial meeting with Charles, to set the trap. He could not allow his enemy's daughter, no matter how desirable, to distract him.

"Tobacco?" Charles asked. "You're mistaken. The market is currently flooded. I have a warehouse stacked to the rafters with the weed. I can't find a shipping company willing to transport it. Even Crown Shipping, London's largest company, refused."

"I know," Blake said. "I own Crown Shipping."

Charles looked at him with surprise. "You understand tobacco is perishable. I would consider it a good faith gesture for any future business relationship if you would reconsider. As I said, other shipping companies have refused me."

"I know. I instructed them to do so."

Charles's face reddened. "You haven't forgotten the

past, then. And you're here on some crusade to avenge your father's—"

"I didn't come here to discuss how you would ship your tobacco but how you will pay for it."

"How I afforded the crop is none of your concern."

"Oh, but it is."

Blake rose and stepped forward until he towered over Charles who was seated behind his desk. "I now happen to own the bank you borrowed from to purchase that crop. A little over one thousand pounds, correct?"

"Don't look so smug." Charles jerked to his feet. "I will have the full balance of the loan available on time."

Blake held up a hand. "That's not all of your debt. You owe a considerable sum to other banks for other investments. It appears that you've overextended yourself, Charles."

"What I owe those banks are my private affairs."

"Unfortunately for you," Blake said, "I purchased those notes. According to my solicitors, you owe me fifteen thousand pounds, and you have thirty days to pay."

"Bastard!"

Sweeping an outstretched hand across his desk, Charles sent papers flying and knocked the crystal decanter off the table. Amber-colored liquid spilled across the carpet and splashed onto the hem of Victoria's gown.

Victoria remained seated. Her eyes widened like saucers in her pale face at her father's display of temper.

Blake felt a thrill course through him at Charles's distress. He had waited an eternity to bring his enemy to his knees. But this was just a lure into a much larger, deadlier trap, just a tease to reel Charles in. Blake would allow himself to enjoy the moment, but would not let it overwhelm him, not until Charles Ashton was completely destroyed.

"I'm willing to extend the terms of the loans under specific circumstances." Blake waited, watching as

Charles clamped down on his temper and looked at him with interest.

Blake turned his gaze upon Victoria. She lowered her head, inadvertently presenting him with a view of her full cleavage.

For a brief, heart-stopping moment, he felt a stab of pity, but the emotion was so foreign, so deeply buried, it was easily crushed.

"I want Victoria in exchange for leniency on the loans."

Charles looked confused. "Are you asking for my daughter's hand in marriage?"

Blake laughed. "Marriage? Good Lord, no. I was proposing a more loose arrangement."

"Your mistress!" Charles hissed, outrage written across his pinched face.

"In return, I'll extend the terms of your loans for one year without interest. That should give you sufficient time to get your affairs in order."

"Victoria is a lady, not the type of woman that would be any man's mistress. Her reputation would be ruined, and any chance of a respectable marriage destroyed."

Blake turned to leave. "Then I withdraw the offer. I'll instruct my solicitors to start collection proceedings for the full fifteen thousand pounds by the end of the month. Your position as a Junior Lord Commissioner of the Treasury will surely be terminated. I'll see to it that your entire family is sent to the poorhouse."

"Wait!" Charles choked.

Victoria stood, straightening her shoulders and clearing her throat. "There's no need to negotiate as if I weren't present. I will not, nor would I ever, become your mistress. I'd rather starve in the poorhouse."

"Speaking from experience, Victoria," Blake said dryly, "life with me would be much more desirable."

"How long would you require her . . . services?" Charles asked.

Victoria turned to stare at her father, an incredulous expression on her face. "I told you, I refuse to—"

"How long?" Charles repeated.

"One year. The same amount of time we spent in the poorhouse."

"I said *no!*" Victoria's voice was shrill.

Charles ignored his daughter. "I'll need time to decide."

"You have until the end of the week."

"Damn you to Hell, Ravenspear."

Blake's lips twitched. "I've already been there and back. It's your turn, Ashton."

Chapter 4

"Open the door, Victoria."

Inside her bedroom, Victoria's jaw clenched as she sat on the side of the bed.

Spencer stood watching her, his back to the window. Shock and sympathy were written on his face after listening to her story of what had occurred in the library moments ago.

The rapping started again, this time louder.

"Open the door *now,* Victoria."

Tears welled in her eyes.

Spencer knelt and clutched her trembling hands. "You'd better let him in, Vicki. No sense rousing his foul temper further."

She rose and unlocked the door.

Charles Ashton burst in and towered over her. Father and daughter eyed each other warily until Charles turned away, his spine rigid. "You have to go with him." His voice was flat, emotionless.

Victoria blinked. "I refuse. I cannot believe you would ask it of me. To be his . . . his mistress."

Charles spun around and took an abrupt step toward her. "Our predicament is entirely your fault. We would not be in this position if you had not refused numerous marriage offers from eligible men."

"My fault?" Shock yielded quickly to fury. "You blame *me* for your bad business decisions?"

Charles's expression turned thunderous; his cold eyes sniped at her.

Victoria's breath stalled in her throat, and she feared she had gone too far. But instead of the explosion she expected, he swallowed hard and moved to sit in the sole chair in the room.

"There is no need to lose our tempers, Victoria," Charles said, smoothing imaginary creases from his trousers. "There is a practical solution to our problem, but you must be less selfish."

She sat stiffly on the edge of the bed and faced him. "He wants me to be his *mistress,* Father. Not his wife. My reputation would be in tatters after such a scandal and any future marriage prospects ruined. Even Jacob would not have me afterwards." She swallowed against the fresh rise of tears. "How am I being selfish by refusing such an offer?"

"Have you ever been inside the poorhouse, girl?" Charles asked. "The conditions are filthy and squalid. You work twenty hours a day to earn three potatoes. You know how frail your mother is. Do you honestly believe she would survive such hardship? And what about Spencer?" He glanced at his son for the first time since entering the room. "If I had to wager, I believe your mother would outlive your brother in such an institution."

Spencer remained silent and scurried farther to the back of the room.

Charles's hard stare pinned Victoria to her seat. "You won't have to worry about your reputation then. Our entire family would be destroyed." Leaning forward, he glared at her intently. "Your only choice is to agree to his demands now with some pride, or to wait a few months, completely devalued. Only then you would not be a coveted mistress, but nothing more than a street prostitute begging for whatever handout he would throw your way."

Victoria closed her eyes and shuddered inwardly at the thought. The truth of her father's words, however vulgar, cut deep. If she refused Blake's offer, they would surely end up in debtors' prison. Her family's good name would be destroyed. Her father would lose his position with Prinny.

She thought of her mother's ill health and chronic headaches. She considered Spencer and, if she was honest, admitted that her brother did not have the strength or disposition to last in such conditions.

As for herself, how long could she endure debtors' prison?

Victoria was a realist and knew what happened to young, unmarried women in London's infamous institutions. They ended up abused, pregnant and in poverty. Most were forced into prostitution.

Her father's words rang true. She would be at Blake's mercy if such a fate befell her.

So what did it matter if her reputation was shredded? Her concerns over becoming a mistress and creating a scandal paled in comparison to such a dire outcome.

Victoria took a deep breath before looking her father in the eye. "Is there not another way?"

"Yes and no." Charles put up a hand at the sight of optimism in her eyes. "I will attempt to borrow money from another source, but it will most likely not cover the full amount of the loans, only a portion of the interest, and will take me months to obtain such a sum. In the meantime, you must go with him."

She exhaled as short-lived hope petered out and died

like an extinguished flame. Gathering her courage, she asked, "What did occur between you and the late Lord Ravenspear to make Blake hate us so?"

Charles sat very still, his eyes narrow. "Talking about the past will not change your circumstances."

"If I have to sacrifice myself, then I deserve the truth."

Charles jerked to his feet. "You know the most of it. Malcolm Mallorey"—he paused and gave a bitter laugh— "Lord Ravenspear, he was an earl after all, although it seemed ludicrous to address him by his title when we were equal partners. Our business was import and export of an amazing variety of goods—English tea, fine china, furniture, clothing, even animals. We were successful at first, but as tensions grew with France and war became imminent, trade slowed to a trickle.

"Malcolm had lavish spending habits, and soon he was in debt. Out of desperation, he arranged to export guns and ammunition to France for enormous profit despite the Crown's embargo against its longtime enemy. Malcolm kept his treasonous arrangements secret from me. When I discovered the truth, I had no choice but to sever business ties and liquidate all assets. Malcolm accused me of taking more than my share of the profits."

Charles hesitated, then continued in a harsh voice. "Such accusations were entirely unfounded, of course. Eventually, Malcolm's debtors came calling. After covering up for his traitorous actions, I refused to loan him money, and we had a terrible row. Months later, I heard that Malcolm had lost his entire estate and his family was headed to the workhouse. Malcolm killed himself to avoid such a fate. Unfortunately, his wife and children did not escape so easily. Last I heard, his wife and daughter died of consumption in the institution. I had thought Blake had died as well."

Biting her lip, Victoria looked away. "I had heard about Lord Ravenspear's suicide, but I had no idea Blake's mother and sister had died so tragically."

"By the time we had learned of their fate, it was too late," Charles said.

He stood and opened the door to leave. "The past does not change the present. Mother will help you pack your things. I'll send a note to Blake advising him you accept his proposal."

"I have a plan, but we have to move quickly." Victoria jumped out of a hackney cab and walked briskly down Threadneedle Street.

Spencer rushed to keep up. "I still can't comprehend how Father expects you to go with Blake. A mistress! You were right about him. I stupidly thought him my friend."

They continued past a dressmaker's, a silversmith and a bakery before coming upon the Bank of England. To the immediate east of the bank was their destination: the London Stock Exchange. The massive building was built of stone and white brick, and occupied a large triangular area in the city. Built in 1802, the impressive structure was only ten years old. Prior to its existence, dealers in stocks and shares of trading companies used to meet at Jonathan's coffee house in Change Alley.

They headed for the main entrance of the Exchange, known as Capel Court, in Bartholomew Lane. A doorman in a crisp red uniform, complete with a black top hat and gloves, opened the heavy oak doors.

Victoria swept inside. The smell of cigar smoke and expensive whiskey immediately assailed her nostrils. As she walked across the bare lobby, the heels of her shoes tapped on the marble floor and echoed off the stone walls.

A servant rushed to greet them. "Miss Ashton," he acknowledged with a genuine smile.

The man turned toward Spencer and his smile vanished. "Mr. Ashton." He nodded.

Victoria guessed Spencer's reputation for reckless drinking and gambling preceded him.

The servant returned his attention to Victoria. "I presume you wish to see Mr. MacDonald?"

Victoria nodded, and with a wave of his hand, the man indicated where they should sit and then rushed off.

She chose a chair opposite a pair of swinging doors that led directly into the heart of the Exchange. As they waited, Victoria marveled that the large lobby, devoid of luxury or decoration, was where clients consulted with their brokers each day, where millions of pounds exchanged hands.

The doors suddenly swung open, and she caught a glimpse of the ongoing activity on the trading floor. The hall was packed with men carrying on business. They ran around the trading floor in a frenzy, all fluttering trousers and jackets, yelling and gesturing wildly at one another to be heard above the crowd, the noise level deafening.

Always thrilled to be this close to the action, Victoria's pulse quickened at the mere glimpse of the hall.

A group of well-dressed men left the floor, exiting through the swinging doors. They chattered about the day's business deals.

Victoria lowered her head demurely so as not to draw attention to herself.

The London Exchange was a male domain. It was widely assumed that women did not have the intelligence to comprehend economic matters, let alone invest with the intent to earn money. So Victoria had cleverly devised a way to operate in their world.

Once again the doors swung open. Victoria's head

snapped up and the blood rushed through her veins. Numerous jobbers, who bought and sold shares for the stockbrokers, scurried about carrying sheets of paper to place the day's trades.

Watching the flurry of activity, she felt excited, fully alive.

Fifteen minutes later, a short, portly man with wire-rimmed glasses and thinning hair arrived. "Miss Ashton! What a pleasant surprise. Has your ill uncle sent you to place another trade on his behalf?"

Victoria stood and smiled tentatively at the oldest stock-broker at the Exchange. "It's a pleasure to see you too, Mr. MacDonald. Unfortunately, Uncle Sheldon seems to have taken a turn for the worse."

Victoria blinked as if holding back tears. "He asked us to find out the balance on all his accounts." She choked and dabbed at her eyes with a handkerchief before continuing, "Just in case, you understand."

Mr. MacDonald clasped her hand and helped her retake her seat. "I'm terribly sorry, Miss Ashton. I'll . . . I'll be right back," he mumbled, obviously uncomfortable with her tears, and disappeared through the lobby doors.

Spencer grinned. "Shame on you for upsetting the old man."

"It's the only way I can continue to place my trades. Need I remind you women aren't allowed to trade, and you are not sufficiently established to gain membership. So imaginary Uncle Sheldon from France must suffer a few health setbacks, but he shall survive them all, I assure you."

Mr. MacDonald returned and handed Victoria a folded sheet of paper. "All your uncle's assets are listed. After you speak with him, I'll buy or sell whatever stocks he desires."

She waited for the broker to leave before unfolding the paper.

"Only five hundred pounds," Spencer said. "Father owes Mallorey fifteen thousand pounds, and that doesn't even include what I owe him."

"Blake never mentioned your debt to Father." Victoria's fingers tensed in her lap. "I wonder why. As for 'Uncle Sheldon's' money, I had hoped the sum was sufficient to make one month's payment so that Father could borrow from the source he mentioned."

She looked at Spencer. "What am I to do? The thought of going to Blake Mallorey terrifies me."

Spencer sat upright. "Give me the money."

"What?"

"I want to help you, Vicki. Give me the money. I'll go to White's tonight and gamble. There's a chance I can double, maybe triple it. We may be able to buy you more time."

Victoria shook her head. "It has taken me years of investing to earn five hundred pounds. You have had bad luck at the tables lately."

"What do you have to lose?"

Yes, what did she have to lose?

Only her reputation, her future and her freedom if she was forced to go to that dark-haired devil.

A thought occurred to her, and she jumped to her feet. "No, Spencer. If anyone is going to gamble tonight, it's going to be me. It's time I paid Lord Ravenspear a visit."

Chapter 5

That afternoon, Victoria set off for Blake's town house. She had heard from Jane Middleton that the location was St. James Street, a most prestigious address. It was a mild April afternoon, and she instructed a hackney cab driver to drop her off a mile away and ignored the stares a lady walking alone received.

As she stood on the porch, her courage wavered. Her hand felt heavy as she lifted the door knocker.

A butler with a strained face and tight-lipped smile opened the door and stared at her.

Her face grew hot. "Miss Victoria Ashton to see Lord Ravenspear."

He nodded and opened the door wide for her to enter. "I shall inform his lordship."

Blake came to the top of the stairs, and when he saw who it was, rushed down to meet her. "Welcome to my home, Victoria."

Blake removed her cloak and handed it to the servant. He took her arm and led her into a formal receiving room, then closed the door. "You should not be visiting me alone. Although I would be lying if I said I wasn't pleased."

"You worry about my reputation while you force me to become your mistress?" she asked, incredulous.

"You agree, then? I received your father's note today advising my terms are acceptable. I responded that I wanted to hear it directly from you."

"Why? So you can humiliate me as well as my father?"

"It was never my intention to humiliate you."

"My father, then?"

His eyes darkened. "Yes. I told you before, let there be no lies between us."

"By destroying my reputation, you think to bring scandal upon my father?"

"I won't deny it."

"Have you no conscience, no forgiveness in your heart?"

His eyes never left hers for an instant. "I lost my conscience years ago. As for forgiveness, Charles Ashton deserves none." His voice sounded empty, emotionless.

"What about me? Is there no sympathy for the child you once knew?"

Blake's expression softened, and Victoria sensed she had touched upon a nerve. Maybe an inkling of kindness existed in his heart for the girl he had once liked and often teased.

Determined to make the most of the moment, she stepped forward and said softly, "I have plans for my life and becoming a mistress is not one of them."

"Do such plans include marriage to Jacob Hobbs?"

"Jacob?" she asked, confused.

"Do you love Jacob Hobbs?"

"Would it matter if I did?"

The tenderness in his expression vanished along with her advantage. Back was the hardened, angry man.

"Despite what you think of me, I would not destroy a love match." His look turned intense. "Do you love him?"

Victoria opened her mouth to speak, then stopped. For a heart-stopping moment she knew he read the truth in her eyes. Anyway, she could not bring herself to lie—to tell him she loved Jacob.

Blake nodded. "I did not think so. From what I've learned of Mr. Hobbs, he would not make you happy."

She pierced him with a hard stare. "And you believe you could?"

He stepped closer and touched her arm lightly. "Yes. You wanted me once, remember? You used to follow me around and kick the back of my heels to gain my attention."

Her cheeks burned in remembrance. "I was a child then."

"You swore you knew what you wanted. You were quite rude about it too. Remember the stables? You stood there demanding Spencer and I go back to the house at once, leaving our lady friends behind."

His gaze stayed on her, reminding her . . .

Victoria had searched the entire house for Blake, and the stables had been her last resort. Throwing open the stable doors, she had found Blake and Spencer in the hay, with a farmer's daughter beneath each of them. The shock of discovery had hit her so hard she was momentarily unable to move. But then her temper had flared at the sight of Blake, *her Blake,* touching the blond-haired girl. Rage had consumed Victoria, and she had stomped her little foot until the girls had fled out of fear of discovery.

Yes, as a child she had been as temperamental as a ball of fire, and she was helpless to halt her embarrassment at the memory.

"I would make a horrible mistress," Victoria said, returning to the present.

"Is that so?" He crossed his arms.

"Yes. I have little experience . . . pleasing men . . ." she said. "And I think I'm frigid."

He raised an eyebrow. "Frigid, you say? How would you know if you have no experience?"

"I dislike kissing."

"Really? I find it difficult to believe a woman with a temper such as yours lacks passion."

"It's true," she insisted. "And that's why you would be most dissatisfied with your decision and should find someone more . . . qualified for the . . . position."

"I'll make you a wager, my dear. I'd like to kiss you and find out if what you say is true. If you don't respond, then I won't force you to fill the position."

Her heart lurched, and she grew suspicious. His offer sounded too easy. "Just one kiss?"

He put his hand under her chin and turned her toward him. Dipping his head slightly, he said, "Just one."

She nodded in consent, then watched in fascinated horror as his mouth lowered. His lips, gentle at first, became more insistent, and he pulled her against him. Victoria felt herself engulfed. Overcome by his masculinity, her soft body molded against his hard chest. The heat from his body seeped into her own, cascading down her limbs. His lips were not demanding but seductive, urging and coaxing a response.

Her eyelids fluttered closed; her lips parted. She grasped his forearms, but resisted the temptation to slide her hands up his arms around his neck. She stopped herself just in time. This wasn't a lover's kiss but a game he was playing. If she lost control to him so soon, he would swallow her whole.

She pushed against his chest. Stepping back, she raised trembling fingers to her lips.

He took a deep breath. "Just as I thought, Victoria. You are far from frigid."

"You're wrong. I felt nothing."

He laughed. "Hardly. If the kiss continued, we would have gone up in flames. Besides, even if you didn't respond, I would not have let you go free."

"Your word as a gentleman means nothing, then."

"I never said I was a gentleman. Your father made sure of that years ago."

She wasn't sure how to respond so she did not.

"I'll make you a promise, Victoria. I won't touch you unless you ask me to."

"I don't understand. Is this a trick?"

"I assure you that I'm serious. My vengeance is directed at your father, not you. Only if you ask will I touch you. The choice is yours."

"After going through such lengths to force me here, you now claim that you won't expect intimacy from me?" Disbelief ran through her.

"Having you with me is enough punishment for Charles Ashton. I've never forced a lady into my bed. I only ask that you live here. Do you agree?"

Victoria struggled to comprehend Blake's astonishing offer. Her mind raced like quicksilver, considering her options. Her dreams of financial independence and marrying for love did not have to be sacrificed. If she became Blake's mistress, eventually he would tire of her and she would be free. Such an arrangement offered more independence than would marriage to someone like Jacob Hobbs.

Marriage was forever.

Divorce was extremely difficult to obtain.

But a mistress offered much more flexibility. And if Blake never shared her bed, then she had nothing to fear.

After their affair ended, Victoria would not be shackled with an unwanted husband. She would be free to pursue her goals. Of course, her prospects would be limited after her reputation was ruined. But Victoria was familiar with the men of the *beau monde*, and she was not interested. No, she would travel in search of her perfect mate. Maybe even go to America, where titles were less important than a man's character. Surely she would find a man she could love and who would overlook a scandal.

After reasoning with herself, she came to the conclusion that Blake's offer was not such a bad one after all. It would free her of her father's tyranny and of society's demands.

"I accept your offer, but do not think I will ever willingly come to your bed."

He grinned mischievously. "We shall see."

Spencer Ashton's pulse quickened as he entered the gaming hall known as the Cock and Bull. Thick swirls of smoke wafted through the air and disappeared into the tobacco-stained rafters. Buxom barmaids scurried about delivering heavy tankards of cheap ale to their customers. The tables were full tonight, the stench of unwashed, perspiring bodies as overpowering as a pile of horse manure in the heat of summer.

Spencer eyed a gaming table in the back of the room with a mixture of excitement and apprehension. The familiar thrill of the game coursed through his veins, blaring like a trumpet in his brain, urging him on.

But tonight was different. He wasn't playing for himself. He was playing for Vicki, for her honor.

His gut clenched at the thought of his sister. She had been right about Blake Mallorey; Spencer had acted the fool. Vicki was the only person he could count on in this world. She understood him, accepted him, weaknesses and all.

And faults Spencer had. He drank too much; he had a compulsion for gambling; he was a failure in their father's eyes. Worst of all, he had shamelessly taken advantage of his sister time and again—for Vicki's secret investing talent had saved his neck from the noose of several of London's greedy moneylenders.

Which brought him here, to the Cock and Bull. He fully intended to win Vicki's freedom from Blake Mallorey. Luck was with Spencer tonight. He felt it deep in his bones, and his fingers itched to hold a hand of cards.

But first he needed money to enter a high-stakes game, and since Victoria hadn't been willing to give him her savings, he was left with one choice.

Spencer took a breath and headed for the back table where the city's most infamous moneylender sat.

Slayer.

He was a massive man, who appeared to weigh well over twenty stone, with beady black eyes in a fleshy face and sagging jowls. A throng of men surrounded Slayer, and Spencer was reminded of a feared dictator holding court.

When Slayer raised cold eyes toward him, Spencer felt as if a hand had closed around his throat. For a heart-stopping moment, doubt flooded through him, but an inner voice burst forth, propelling him forward.

Luck is with me tonight, he thought. *I will amass what I need and pay Slayer back in the same night.*

After all, what could go wrong?

Chapter 6

Victoria arrived home from Blake's town house to find Jacob waiting for her.

He rushed at her and tugged at her cloak, nearly ripping the sleeves. Throwing the garment at the closest servant, he pulled her through the vestibule into the library.

"Where have you been?" he demanded. "I arrived hours ago for our ride in the park, only to learn from your father of Lord Ravenspear's outrageous proposition."

Victoria met Jacob's angry gaze. After her encounter with Blake Mallorey, she was weary and drained. The last thing she desired was a confrontation with Jacob.

"I needed solitude so I took a walk," she said.

"Alone?"

She brushed past him and sat on a chaise longue. "Yes."

Jacob snorted. "I suppose your reputation does not matter henceforth."

She leapt to her feet to face him. "How dare you! Do you think I asked to become Ravenspear's mistress?"

Jacob stalked forward, his face twisted in annoyance. "You must have done something to encourage him. A man does not return from the dead and seek out a child he barely knew ten years earlier to become his paramour."

Victoria felt her cheeks burn. "I assure you, sir," she said, her spine stiff in angry outrage, "I did nothing to *encourage* his attention."

Jacob grasped her upper arms, squeezing the tender flesh until she grimaced. "Are you sure? I wonder if you enticed him so as to escape marriage to me. I have recognized for quite some time how you act agreeable towards me only when your father is near. I suspect your true feelings are far from amicable. A flirt you are, Victoria Ashton."

She opened her mouth to protest but was stopped short by her father's arrival.

Charles Ashton strode into the library and closed the heavy doors. "Do not say something in the heat of anger, Victoria, which you will undoubtedly later regret."

He continued past the argumentative couple, poured himself a generous brandy and sat behind his massive desk. "I've done nothing but think of Ravenspear's demands since his 'visit' and I've thought of a way to use his thirst for revenge to our advantage."

Victoria recognized the gleam in her father's eye. She had seen it a thousand times before when Charles Ashton had clinched a business deal. She had never approved of his questionable or ruthless methods.

The thought that she now was involved firsthand was unnerving.

Holding her breath, she waited.

Her father turned his gaze upon her. "Victoria is going to Ravenspear as his timid, obedient mistress. As far as he will know, she has every intention of keeping her promise of one year of servitude to save her family's fate. But what the blackguard will never suspect is that Victoria will be spying for us and learning all there is to know about

Ravenspear's businesses and stock purchases. I will then use such information to procure a profit, pay off the bloody loans and then destroy him."

Jacob jumped to his feet. "But you promised Victoria to me. We are to be engaged."

Charles downed his brandy in one swallow and slammed the glass on the desk. "Don't be a fool, Jacob. Ravenspear holds the notes on all *our* loans. If he chooses to call any of them in, it won't only be me that's headed to the poorhouse, but you as well."

Jacob paled. "I had not thought of that. Workhouse conditions are notoriously abominable." He turned to look at her. "Victoria must go."

Victoria shook with impotent rage and fear. They cared nothing for her, only for themselves, willing to sacrifice her to avoid debtor's prison. They were no better than Blake Mallorey himself.

She sat forward, fingers curling around the chair's arms, digging into the soft velvet material. "How do you expect me to spy on Lord Ravenspear? Do you honestly believe that he'll allow me to roam his home and rummage through his sensitive business documents?"

Charles arched an eyebrow at her tone. "As a matter of fact, I do. He'll not suspect a woman capable of espionage."

"And you think me intelligent enough to sort through his papers and interpret which ones are important?"

Charles chuckled. "Of course not, my dear. I wouldn't dream of expecting a mere woman to understand even simple business affairs. But you can report conversations you overhear and steal specific documents."

Clenching her teeth, she was furious with his assumption regarding a woman's intelligence. It was on the tip of her tongue to blurt out that her latest investments had been more successful than his.

With great self-control, she kept her expression impassive. "How would I gain his confidence to get access to his papers?"

"Ah, my dear. You hold more power over him than you think. He must desire you badly for him to demand you for an entire year."

She swallowed hard, trying not to reveal her anger. "He desires nothing but revenge . . . revenge against you."

"You're wrong, Victoria," her father said. "He could have easily destroyed me by calling in my loans. No, I'm certain he wants you. I realize in your innocence you may not recognize his intent, but we can undoubtedly use it to our advantage."

Victoria's stomach churned in anxiety. Her own father spoke of crude male lust as a weapon for her to wield. The thought sickened her. She wanted to tell him that Blake vowed not to rape her, but sought to ruin her father by destroying the family name. Victoria remained silent, not trusting her own parent. She was still stunned that her father expected her to succumb to Blake's demands and become his mistress. Now her father demanded she spy as well.

Were all men such selfish, hedonistic creatures?

She glanced at Jacob with the hope of finding some sort of protest against her father's suggestions. But Jacob looked off in the distance, no doubt still contemplating his future in the workhouse should he be forced into servitude.

"It's the perfect opportunity for us to disarm Ravenspear," Charles said. "You can weaken him with a mere smile, all the while gathering the information we need to pay off the loans. I'm sure you have no fond feelings toward the man?"

"Of course not," she said.

"It's settled, then," Charles said. "Keep your eyes and ears open, Victoria. Jacob and I will do the rest."

The wheels of the coach rolled through another rut in the road, and Victoria bumped her head against the buffed leather interior.

Blake had spared no expense, and had sent the opulent vehicle for her journey. She had been agog when the black-lacquered coach and team of six had stopped in front of her father's town house. The large, impressive carriage was emblazoned with the Ravenspear crest. The matching team of horseflesh had stood obediently, and their sleek muscles had gleamed beneath the afternoon sun.

When the footman had opened the door, Victoria ascended into the most magnificent coach she had ever traveled in. The interior was luxuriously padded with hunter green leather the identical color of the window shades and carpet.

The road they traveled was in such disrepair that, without the comfort of the padded coach, she would have been black and blue by the time she arrived at her destination.

When the coachman informed her that she would be traveling not to Blake's town house but to his country estate in Sussex, she was too surprised to do more than nod.

She had been convinced that Blake would take her to his London town house on St. James Street for all of society to learn she had become his mistress. With the arrival of spring, the Season had just begun, and all the members of the ton had returned to London from the country.

The scandal would have been instantaneous. The gossip would have destroyed her reputation overnight.

But to her disbelief, she was on her way to his reclusive country manor, Rosewood, far away from such a fate.

What plan was he hatching? Was he prolonging her humiliation until the height of the Season?

Victoria raised the tasseled shade to gaze out the window of the swaying coach at the green countryside. The sun shone brightly, and she could feel the warmth on her face through the glass. It was a glorious day, in direct contrast to her black mood.

Her father's instructions echoed in her head.

Sheath your shrewish tongue, Victoria. Act submissive, obedient. Gain his trust, then rummage through his papers and eavesdrop on his conversations. Jacob and I will contact you to obtain the information you gather.

Could she do it? Spy on Blake with the specific intent to bankrupt him? Destroy him?

Much as she tried to deny it, part of her childhood fascination remained. It was too easy to forget the past and imagine that Blake desired her presence at Rosewood out of love, not revenge.

The memory of his kiss flooded back, heating her blood. She shook herself mentally, forcing herself to concentrate on the task she was ordered to accomplish.

Would she be able to steal the information her father wanted?

Blake hardly seemed like an amateur businessman who left sensitive documents lying around. Her father had no idea the extent of her knowledge when it came to stocks and the London Exchange.

No doubt her experience would prove invaluable to Charles Ashton should she chose to use it for the sole purpose of espionage.

She would wait and see how Blake treated her, what his true motives were. Even though she was naïve when it came to men, she sensed a softness in him when he kissed her. Perhaps he harbored kind feelings for her.

Why else would he agree not to touch her, not to bed her, unless she consented?

And consent she never would, no matter how many fond childhood memories remained. Victoria considered herself a lady, and even if her reputation was soiled she would still remain a virgin for her husband. Once Blake realized she would never bend, he would surely tire of her and return her to London. Perhaps there would be no need to steal his secrets or eavesdrop.

The coach turned onto a long, winding driveway. Victoria gazed out the window at the tall trees on both sides of the road and acres of well-tended lawn beyond. She gasped as a huge lake came into view, the water's surface as calm and clear as fine Italian glass. Pure-white swans sunbathed at the center of the lake, their long, graceful necks curved like ballet dancers. The coach passed boxwood hedges in the formal gardens, where rose bushes and flowering shrubs of every color bloomed and filled the air with their heady fragrance.

Victoria strained to see up ahead, when suddenly a manor home came into view. Her heart skipped a beat at her first sight of Rosewood's size and beauty. Blake's home looked like a castle, with white stone walls and four miniature turrets. A fountain in the courtyard surrounded by marble statues welcomed visitors.

The coach rolled to a stop. She heard springs squeak as the coachman jumped down from his high perch. The latch clicked and the door swung open wide.

The coachman extended his hand. "We have arrived at Rosewood, Miss Ashton."

Gathering her skirts in one hand, she leaned on his arm as she descended from the vehicle, all the while gazing up at Rosewood's magnificent architecture.

"I'm still impressed by its beauty," the coachman said

as he studied her face, "and I've been employed here since Lord Ravenspear renovated Rosewood."

Victoria nodded and followed the servant up stone steps into a brightly lit entrance hall.

An enormous chandelier holding at least a hundred candles drew her attention. Sunlight from the open door bounced off the chandelier's crystal prisms, creating a magnificent image on the marble floor. A lavish floral arrangement of long-stemmed roses in every hue occupied the center of the vestibule.

Beyond the flowers, a winding staircase led to a second-floor balcony. But before Victoria could observe further, a heavyset woman of about fifty, wearing a black dress with a starched white collar and cuffs, approached.

The woman smiled at Victoria in welcome. "I'm Mrs. Smith, Lord Ravenspear's housekeeper. Ever since His Lordship told the household you were visiting, we have been looking forward to your arrival."

Victoria wondered precisely what Blake had told his household her 'visit' entailed. Or perhaps the staff came to their own conclusions regarding a young, unchaperoned woman's stay at a bachelor's home.

Despite her efforts, Victoria's face grew hot with humiliation.

Mrs. Smith gave her a kind look. "Would you like some tea, Miss. Ashton? You must be tired from your travels."

Victoria nodded. "Thank you, Mrs. Smith. You are most considerate."

The robust housekeeper bobbed a curtsey and led Victoria into a spacious salon. A large wire ring of keys at Mrs. Smith's waist clinked as she walked.

Victoria's eyes widened. At least fifty keys hung on the housekeeper's key ring.

Just how many rooms were there in this mansion?

The salon at Rosewood was grandly furnished with cherry furniture and priceless artwork on the walls. Even the ceiling was decorated with a delicate fresco of partially nude goddesses and playful nymphs.

She sat on a red velvet settee as Mrs. Smith served her tea and scones. Victoria raised her teacup to her lips, savoring the fine English brew.

The housekeeper placed the silver serving tray on a dainty end table. "I would show you to your room, but Lord Ravenspear gave strict orders that he wanted the duty himself."

Victoria set down her cup and saucer with a loud *chink*.

The nerve of the man! She wondered if the rogue would escort her directly to his own room.

"Is Lord Ravenspear present?" Victoria asked with a strained voice. "I would like a word with him."

"Good afternoon, Victoria. I see you've arrived safely," a masculine voice spoke behind her.

The tone, deep and sensual, sent a ripple of awareness through her. Victoria's head snapped to the doorway.

Blake stood tall as a towering spruce, arms crossed over his broad chest. He was dressed simply in fawn-colored breeches with polished black Hessians. A stark-white shirt contrasted with the bronze skin at his throat. Even though his clothes were devoid of lace or decoration, the fabric appeared expensive and tailored to perfection for his lean frame.

He looked every bit the mighty lord of the manor.

She was struck by the knowledge that the power he wielded in his own domain would be unchallenged. She had effectively relinquished all control by crossing the threshold of Rosewood.

A wave of apprehension swept through her, and she

realized just how vulnerable her new position was in his household.

At her continued silence, he walked forward, stopping in front of her. "Welcome to Rosewood. I trust your journey was comfortable."

Victoria stood, lifting her chin and meeting his gaze straight on. "Yes, but I'm sure my return travel home will be much more enjoyable."

Blake grinned. "And how were your parents this morning? Did they send their regards?"

She smiled sweetly, hoping to wipe the grin from his face. "My mother sends her regards and has confidence in your newly established reputation as a gentleman and lord of the realm. My father and brother both pray that you contract a painful, mortal ailment in the near future."

Victoria heard the rattle of fine china on a serving tray behind her. She had forgotten that Mrs. Smith was still in the room.

The housekeeper curtsied and excused herself from the salon, nearly tripping in her haste to leave.

Damn. He had made her lose her temper, and she hadn't been in his house or in his presence more than ten minutes.

Her father's instructions rang in her head. How was she supposed to act sweet and docile and gain Blake's trust?

A wry but indulgent glint appeared in Blake's eyes. "Careful, Victoria. It's in your best interest to be very nice to me."

"Why should I? Your offer made no mention of how I should behave, only that I come."

"Self-preservation, my dear. You're not in London anymore. You're at Rosewood, where I'm the master and my word is law." He raised her chin with his finger to look into her eyes. "I have the power to make your stay quite enjoyable or wholly unbearable. It's best if you not forget that fact."

Victoria bit her cheek to keep silent, then nodded. Now was not the time to challenge him.

He took her arm. "I'll show you to your rooms, my dear."

As they walked out of the salon toward the stairs, she was conscious of his hand touching her sleeve. The scent of his cologne reached her nostrils . . . sandalwood and cloves, distinctly male.

They reached the top of the stairs and passed one door after another in the long hallway. She wondered which room was his.

"There are two wings," he said as they walked. "An east and a west. The west is unoccupied at the present."

They stopped in the middle of the paneled hall. He swung open a door and extended his hand. "After you, my dear."

Victoria walked forward, her eyes taking in where she was expected to reside for the next year. She need not have worried about Blake leading her to his room.

The chamber was exceedingly feminine and decorated entirely in rose-colored hues. From the plush pillows and down coverlet to the curtains and carpet, the shade was everywhere.

"It's beautiful," she said honestly. "Did you choose the color rose for Rosewood?"

"No. I had it decorated especially for you since it's your favorite color."

Stunned, Victoria turned to face him. "How did you know?"

He shrugged nonchalantly. "I looked into a few matters before you arrived. I want you to be comfortable here."

He pointed to a door in the corner. "The dressing room

and sitting room are through there. Your trunks have been brought up. Mrs. Smith will help you unpack."

She was taken aback at his thoughtfulness. He inquired into what she liked, her favorite color? He had the room furnished to suit her tastes?

It was a beautiful room, nothing that she had expected. No wonder Mrs. Smith thought she was an honored guest.

Her mind spun with confusion. His consideration seemed out of character for the bitter, vengeful man he had become.

Victoria turned to face him. "Where are your rooms?" She couldn't help herself from asking, then regretted the question immediately.

He arched an eyebrow. "Are you considering a visit? I'd gladly let you in."

She felt her face grow hot. "You flatter yourself, my lord."

He walked to the window and drew aside the pink curtains to gaze at the gardens. "My rooms are directly across the hall."

"So close?" she blurted out. "You said the west wing is unoccupied. I'd be perfectly content to occupy a room there."

He let the curtain fall and turned to face her. "I'm sure you would, my dear, but I want you close by."

Victoria's hand fluttered to her chest. "You promised not to force me . . . not to bed me without my consent."

"Ah, but I never agreed not to *try* to seduce you, my dear."

Chapter 7

"Seduce me?" she asked, aghast at the thought.

"Yes. I'm sure you're aware that I'm attracted to you. If my instincts are correct, I believe remnants of your childhood infatuation for me remain."

Victoria shook her head. "Your instincts are wrong, my lord."

He reached out to trace her cheek with a finger. "Are they? No sense claiming you're frigid again. We both know that's false."

A shiver of excitement ran down her spine at his mere touch. The intensity of his blue eyes captivated her.

Why did he have to be even more devastatingly handsome than she had remembered?

Suddenly she recalled a childhood memory when she was about eight years old, and he had taught her how to overcome her fear of horses. He had been so patient and gentle, letting her set the pace at first, and soon she was riding with confidence.

She could not lose what little power she came here with. Her pride was already bruised, but she had her integrity. She must resist his magnetism.

"My reaction to your kiss was but a weak moment for me. I won't respond like that again."

"Then you won't mind if I keep trying?"

"Suit yourself, my lord. I'm quite immune to your charms," she said with false bravado.

"We'll be spending a significant amount of time together. I'm anxious to see how long you can hold yourself aloof."

"I doubt we'll see each other that often. You have quite the reputation as an innovative businessman after all, my lord. I'm sure your days are kept busy expanding your vast empire."

"Ah, so I see you've thought of everything, my dear. But I plan on having you with me, even when I work."

She contemplated this news. If she was with him during the day, there was a possibility she could watch his private dealings. It assured her easy access to everything her father and Jacob Hobbs desired.

But at the same time, the more hours she spent with him, the harder she would have to fight herself not to succumb to his planned seduction.

The irony was not lost on her that if Blake had been as attentive toward her ten years ago, her heart would have burst with joy.

Victoria turned to face him squarely. "It won't work, you know." When he raised an eyebrow as if to ask what she was talking about, she rushed on. "I suspect what you're planning. You think by forcing me to spend time with you, old feelings will resurface, and I'll tumble into your waiting, open arms."

Her stomach knotted in agitation, and she pointed her finger at his chest. "I'm telling you right now, your efforts will fail. I was a child then, but I'm a woman now, in case you haven't noticed."

Blake cocked his head to one side, and his gaze slid lazily down her body. "Oh, I've noticed."

Victoria's cheeks burned. "What I'm saying, my lord, is that whatever feelings I had for you as a child are long dead."

She stomped to the dressing room and jerked open the door. "Now, if you'll please leave, I want to change."

He chuckled behind her. "Of course. Dinner is at seven."

She stood still, her back to him, until she heard the door close behind her.

Hours passed before Victoria gathered the courage to venture out of her bedroom. She took a deep breath and tried to relax as she reached for the doorknob. Her first challenge awaited. She must explore Rosewood and locate the most important chamber in the manor: the library—for most businessmen, including her father and Jacob Hobbs, conducted their business in their library offices.

She opened the door, half-expecting to be run over by a servant, but found the hallway empty. Passing bedroom after bedroom, she wondered why Blake had purchased a massive estate like Rosewood. His home was more suitable for a large family who frequently entertained than for a bachelor.

She smiled as a thought occurred to her: he probably acquired the showpiece to feed his already-inflated masculine vanity.

After discovering there was nothing on the floor other than bedrooms, two linen closets, and a cleaning closet complete with mops, buckets and rags, Victoria decided to search the main floor.

Her footsteps were silent on the carpet runner as she descended the stairs. She expected to encounter many servants here but was surprised to see only a few. She poked her head into a music room, a dining room and a grand ballroom before finally finding the library.

It was a grand library, with an impressive collection. Row after row of mahogany shelves stacked with books from floor to ceiling covered each wall of the enormous room. Two tall wheeled ladders hung on runners, which could be pushed back and forth, assuring access to all the high shelves. The comforting smell of books and well-oiled leather furniture lingered.

A massive desk in front of the window caught her eye. Neat stacks of paper beneath polished stone paperweights covered the surface of the desk.

Victoria's breath quickened. Good. He did conduct his business here, and it looked like he kept many documents out in the open. How convenient.

Despite her earlier decision to wait and see how Blake behaved, she had an overwhelming urge to rummage through the papers. Clenching her fists at her sides, she turned away from the desk and temptation. There was no time now. She couldn't risk getting caught on her first day at Rosewood. Where would that get her?

Her father would be furious at her failure, and he would still be in debt to Blake.

Walking briskly from the library, she entered a long corridor. The passage was empty. Several portraits hung on the papered walls. She was certain they were paintings of past Ravenspear earls, their wives, children, horses and dogs. She assumed Blake had acquired the paintings after his return to England, since his father had sold every last possession before the family was condemned to the poorhouse.

The thought made her steps falter, and she braced her arm against the wall. No sense thinking about the past. She was paying for other people's sins right now, and she had to keep her mind focused more on the future.

She continued on, suspecting the passage led to the unoccupied west wing that Blake had mentioned. As she walked, the sound of voices began to drift down the hallway.

At first the voices were distant, but as she progressed, they became more audible.

Male voices. Yelling. Guttural sounds.

Strange animal sounds.

Her breath caught in her throat.

Reaching the end of the corridor, she peered around the corner to see a large empty room, the hardwood floors gleaming from a recent polish. She tiptoed past numerous chambers, finding each barren.

The west wing was indeed unoccupied, and except for the male voices she continued to hear, she would have turned around and headed back to the main part of the house.

The noise grew louder, and she swore she heard a fight. The dull *thud* of a fist hitting flesh.

The noise was distinct; she had heard it before, when Spencer started a fight at the tables after a rival accused him of cheating at cards. Her stomach churned with anxiety, just as it did the second before Spencer's opponent had smashed his fist in her brother's face.

Even though the hair on her nape stood on end, her curiosity would not allow her to retreat. She pushed forward, searching for the source of the disruption.

Blake had been quick to quash her suggestion that she reside in the unoccupied west wing. His message had been clear: he didn't want her to wander here.

Why? Was he hiding something? Something she could use against him?

She came to a doorway and pressed herself flat against the wall. They were inside. More specifically, Blake was inside. She recognized the deep timbre of his voice. At least two other men were present; one was issuing words of encouragement as the beating continued.

Half in anticipation, half in dread, she pushed away from the wall and stepped into the doorway. The sight that met her eyes was quite unexpected.

They were fighting, all right. But not brawling as she had suspected. Bare-knuckle boxing instead.

She froze in stunned tableau.

Dominating the large room was a square ring roped off with stakes at each corner that were anchored to the floor. In the center of the ring, Blake and an opponent circled each other, rocking back and forth, their nimble footwork catching her eye.

Each man was bare-chested and bare-fisted. Both combatants were slightly bent over, head and shoulders pressed forward, knees slightly bent, and with their fists balled up. They jabbed and punched as they moved around the ring in a well-practiced athletic dance. They appeared well-matched, and the scraping of their shoes on the hardwood floor echoed off the walls as they fought. A third man, presumably the trainer, stood outside the arena, his arm resting on the rope, his voice shouting instructions to the combatants.

They had not yet noticed her. She watched, fascinated, as the sweat poured off the men's foreheads and ran down their chests, stopping at the waistband of their trousers.

Her eyes were drawn to Blake's form. She had never seen a man naked from the waist up before, but she suspected Blake's torso was impressive by any standard.

The muscles in his arms bunched as he surged forward, hitting his opponent squarely in the gut. A sprinkling of dark hair covered his chest, and his stomach rippled with corrugated muscle. His powerful body moved with an easy grace as he balanced himself on the balls of his feet. He reminded her of the statues of the Greek gods on display at the British Museum. Blake could have been the sculptor's model.

She had no idea how long she stood in the doorway watching the fight. It was the instructor who noticed her first.

"Stop. A lady is present," he shouted to his pupils in the ring.

The instructor, a massive man with the broadest shoulders she had ever seen, advanced upon her. He had a protruding forehead, bushy eyebrows, and a crooked nose that she suspected had been broken numerous times.

Her first instinct was to turn on her heel and flee, but she refused to look like a coward on her first day at Rosewood.

The imposing man winked when he caught her eye, then bowed before her. "Allow me to introduce myself. Mr. Tom Cribb, at your service, my lady. It isn't often that a beautiful woman watches my lessons."

Victoria was taken aback. The man's proper manners certainly were at odds with his rugged appearance.

"Did you say Cribb?" she asked. "As in Killer Cribb, the famous boxing champion?"

Cribb's chest puffed with pride. "The one and only. And what is your name, my lady?"

"This is my houseguest, Miss Victoria Ashton," Blake said, coming up to Tom Cribb.

Blake had donned his shirt, but the material clung to his moist flesh like a second skin. The top button was undone, revealing the corded muscles of his neck and the hair on his chest. A cotton towel, which he had used to wipe the sweat off his forehead, dangled from his fingers.

In this male arena, after such physical activity, he exuded a potent masculinity that drew her like a lodestone. After watching the brutality of two men fighting, she should be repulsed, but instead she secretly found it exciting, exhilarating—they were so unlike the painted popinjays of her acquaintance.

She dared not look at Blake, afraid he would see the attraction in her eyes.

"You're well known, Mr. Cribb," she said. "Even I have heard of you and I have never attended a boxing match. After my brother took lessons at Gentleman Jackson's, all he could speak of was how you dominated your opponent in your last fight."

Mr. Crib grinned, revealing two missing front teeth. Probably another hazard of his profession, she thought.

"I'm honored you know my name. Many women do not approve of the pugilistic sport."

"I have nothing against boxing as a means of exercise, Mr. Cribb, but I do believe the laws against prizefighting should be enforced."

Victoria was aware of the popularity of boxing. Many wealthy men invested in personal trainers to teach them the art. A strong and manly figure was prized and a key to attracting the opposite sex, especially since men's jackets were cut so scandalously short that they revealed everything from the waist down.

Prizefighting, on the other hand, was technically illegal, even though highly popular, and fascinated men of all classes.

Blake crossed his arms over his chest and leveled his gaze upon Victoria. "It seems the lady has a strict interpretation of the law, but has no qualms about wandering where she is uninvited."

Alarmed, she parted her lips to speak, but then hesitated, unsure how to respond.

How dare he admonish her in front of a stranger?

Mr. Cribb must have sensed the rising tension within her, for he spoke first. "Lord Ravenspear hired me to train him in the sport. He's turning out to be an apt pupil."

She shot Blake a withering glance. "Yes, beating a rival into a bloody pulp does seem his style."

Blake abruptly caught her by the elbow and firmly escorted her away from the doorway farther into the room. Over his shoulder, he said, "Excuse my guest's rudeness, Mr. Cribb. If she could enter the ring, her shrewish tongue would surely slay any opponent before the first punch could be swung."

Mr. Cribb laughed and tipped his hat on his way out. "It was a pleasure, Miss Ashton. I hope to see you again soon."

"Let go." Victoria pulled against his viselike hold on her arm.

He released her, then bent down to whisper in her ear. "I told you that it's in your best interest to be nice to me. Throwing insults in my face in front of my friends is not a good start of our one-year relationship."

His breath brushed against her ear, and the feelings that rushed through her were unwelcome. She refused to succumb to his magnetism, or be attracted to him in any way. She had to fight her own battle of personal restraint and remember that he was not the Blake of her childhood, that he had changed, and all he wanted now was to ruin her family.

Blake straightened and looked behind her. She realized the reason he had whispered: there was yet another person in the room.

Whirling around, she watched as the man Blake had been sparring with in the ring approached.

"Lord Ravenspear has spoken of your visit, Miss Ashton, and it is a pleasure to finally meet you. I'm Justin Woodward, his lordship's assistant."

Justin Woodward was attractive, with warm brown eyes and a quick smile. A swath of blond hair fell casually on his forehead, giving him a boyish appearance. Like Blake, he had donned his shirt before approaching her. He was as tall as Blake, but not as broad shouldered and on the thin side.

Something about the fair-haired man was vaguely familiar. "Have we met before, Mr. Woodward?" she asked.

A momentary look of discomfort crossed Justin Woodward's face. "It's possible you knew someone from my family, but we left England years ago. I've only recently returned with Ravenspear."

"So you've spent time in the Indies together?" she asked, keenly aware of Blake's scrutiny.

He nodded. "I've worked for him for some time now."

"Justin and I are good friends, and you will see him frequently at Rosewood, my dear," Blake said.

If Justin Woodward was going to offer more about the time the pair spent in the Indies, Blake's smooth interruption stopped him. Still, she was fairly certain she had met, or at least seen, Mr. Woodward before.

Blake took her elbow, gently this time, and escorted her from the room. Justin Woodward trailed behind.

"Justin and his lady friend will be joining us for dinner tonight," Blake said.

Victoria's step faltered. "I had planned to eat alone in my room. I'm fatigued after my trip here."

She wanted to spend as little time as possible with Blake. She knew he intended to force her to frequently accompany him so that he may charm her into his arms. But she was certain that if she could stay to herself, he would soon tire of the chase.

Entertaining his friends was definitely not in her plans.

"Nonsense, my dear," Blake said, dismissing her concerns. "You must eat, and I insist. You will like Lady Devon, I assure you."

Without waiting for a response, Blake began to walk, his firm fingers cupping her elbow.

Victoria rushed to keep up with his long strides. The portraits in the corridor she had previously stopped to admire were a colorful blur as they raced by.

Leaving the west wing, Blake guided her back to the main part of the house.

Once in front of her bedroom, Blake stopped and swung open the door. "Don't try to evade me by making excuses in the future, Victoria. I won't be dissuaded." He put his finger under her chin and forced her to meet his eyes. "If you'll allow yourself, you'll acknowledge the attraction between us."

"I don't know what you're talking about."

Amusement flickered in his eyes. "Liar. I saw the way you were watching me in the ring. Studying my body, comparing it to others in your mind. You looked excited, eager, *hungry*."

She swallowed hard, her senses leaping to life as he traced her jawline with his finger, then down her neck and along her exposed collarbone.

"No," she croaked, but her voice sounded weak, unconvincing even to her own ears.

"Oh, yes. It took all my self-restraint not to swing you up into my arms, carry you away and have my way with you in the closest private corner I could find."

She felt her face redden. "Don't speak to me that way."

No man had ever spoken to her so brazenly. Not Jacob. Not any of her prior suitors. A lady should never hear such shocking words, not even if there was a hint of truth to them.

His eyes traveled to the wildly beating pulse at her neck. "There's no reason to deny our feelings over the course of the year. We can share great pleasure, Victoria, if only you will allow it."

His gaze lowered to her mouth and lingered, and she sensed he intended to kiss her. She should have slammed her bedroom door in his face. But when his eyes darkened with desire, when his head lowered, and when she felt his breath against her lips, she didn't turn away. Didn't protest. Didn't move.

The touch of his lips was a delicious sensation, whisper-soft at first, then firmer, more persuasive. When she sighed and parted her lips, he took control of the kiss, exploring the recesses of her mouth with his tongue.

She stood on her toes to move closer, and he gathered her into his embrace and ran his hand down the hollows of her back to press her more tightly against him. Her heart hammered at the unfamiliar hardness of his solid chest and manly scent.

He was everything she had ever dreamed about as an infatuated girl. All muscle and sinew, so different from her own soft curves. Dark, dangerous and exciting. Her mind told her to resist, but her body refused to comply.

Raising his mouth from hers, he kissed the pulsing hollow at the base of her throat. "There can be so much more between us. Let me show you."

A delightful shiver of wanting ran through her. Her knees felt weak, and she feared falling. In the dark recesses of her mind, she knew she must resist, must stop him, or he would steal all her resolve on her first day here.

His hand lowered to trace along the edge of her bodice with his fingers. When his thumb brushed against her sensitive nipple, she jerked backward. As if she was plunged in a bucket of cold water, she came to her senses.

What was she doing?

"Blake, stop."

He stepped closer to keep her near, his head lowering to once again kiss her.

Victoria jerked her head to the side, and his lips brushed her cheek.

"Don't be afraid, sweet. I won't hurt you," he said, his breath warm against her face.

"Blake, stop!" she cried. Desperate to put distance between them, she shoved against his chest with both hands.

He took a step back.

She kept her features deceptively composed. "Remember your promise, my lord, for I shall never forget mine. I'd die before I will ask you to bed me."

Blake stiffened. The familiar mask of coldness descended once again. "My apologies for misreading your response," he said, his voice harsh. "Dinner is at seven. Don't make me fetch you."

Chapter 8

Victoria's eyes widened in wonder at the ostentatious display on the laden table.

She had entered Rosewood's dining room expecting an intimate dinner with friends, only to find a feast that should have been served at the grandest of parties.

At the end of the dining table were the meats: saddle of mutton, lamb, fowls, tongue and ham. There were a dozen vegetable dishes, each served from gold-rimmed chafing dishes bearing the Ravenspear crest. The crowning centerpiece, a large salmon with its head intact to show its freshness, was surrounded by scallops in a butter sauce.

A liveried footman carved ham for her and placed it onto her plate. With a nod of her head, she indicated which vegetables she desired, and the servant placed them neatly next to the meat.

Expensive sherry flowed freely, and numerous footmen assured that the guests' glasses were never empty.

The amount of food on Blake's table could have fed a poor London family for a month. The entire meal, in Victoria's opinion, was excessive and gluttonous and orchestrated for the sole purpose of showing off Blake's wealth.

She observed Samantha Heron, properly known as the Baroness of Devon. A wealthy widow in her thirties, Lady Devon was striking with blond hair, blue eyes, and a willowy figure. She was dressed in silver satin with a heart-shaped neckline, exposing a décolletage that would draw any man's eye. Blond curls were piled on her head in an elegant coiffure with stray wisps brushing her high cheekbones.

She was beautiful, but it was her air of self-confidence that intrigued Victoria.

Justin Woodward was clearly younger than his companion, and Victoria wondered what had brought the unlikely pair together.

Victoria had worried what Blake's friends would think of an unchaperoned lady residing in a bachelor's home, but neither Justin Woodward nor Lady Devon hesitated when Victoria was introduced as Blake's houseguest.

A disturbing thought flashed through Victoria's brain. Just how many other unchaperoned women had Blake brought into his home and introduced to his friends?

Lady Devon rested a silver fork on her plate. "Are you enjoying Rosewood, Miss Ashton?"

Victoria blinked, then focused her gaze. If there was a hint of sarcasm in the woman's question, Victoria didn't hear it.

"I've only just arrived today," Victoria said. "Although, I have uncovered vigorous activity while exploring the house." Her eyes darted to Blake.

Confusion crossed Lady Devon's features, and she turned toward their host.

Blake tipped his wineglass, draining it. "Miss Ashton wandered into the west wing."

"Ah," Lady Devon said. "So you've discovered their pugilistic pastime. I've never watched them practice with

Mr. Cribb. I know the sport is quite popular, but I find it brutal."

Victoria should have found the viciousness of the sport revolting, but she had been fascinated instead. The image of Blake bare-chested and sweating, muscles rippling, had left a burning imprint on her mind.

What did that say about her morals?

As the meal drew to an end, Victoria toyed with the crisp napkin in her lap, twisting it this way and that with nervous fingers. She thought of excuses to take her leave. The day's travel had made her weary, after all, and she longed to rest her head on the feather pillow in her rose-colored room and succumb to sleep. Maybe then she could escape her problems for a few blissful hours.

But manners prevailed, even at this bachelor home, and the women were expected to leave the table to allow the men to drink their port. Justin held Lady Devon's chair for her as she rose. Blake followed suit by pulling out Victoria's chair so she could stand.

His fingers brushed the tops of her naked shoulders and lingered.

"Justin and I will join you shortly, my dear."

She was conscious of Lady Devon keenly observing the exchange. Heat stole into Victoria's face at Blake's intimate touch, and she hurried from the dining room into the parlor.

A welcoming fire burned, a large log crumbling in the hearth. Victoria stood before the marble fireplace when she heard Lady Devon enter behind her.

"Now that we're finally alone," Lady Devon said, "we can speak openly."

Victoria spun around. "I suppose you're curious about the circumstances behind my arrival at Rosewood."

Lady Devon shook her head, and the movement of her

silver gown made it shimmer in the firelight. "Heavens, no. Mr. Woodward tells me everything."

Victoria chewed on her lower lip. "So Ravenspear has started my humiliation already, telling others the truth behind our arrangement."

"Nonsense," Lady Devon said. "Ravenspear confides in Mr. Woodward, and I would not betray my Justin by gossiping. Ravenspear knows the secret is safe with me, of course. That's why I was invited here tonight."

The baroness slid gracefully onto the red cushions of the settee. Her blue eyes pierced the distance between them. "Never mind what brought you to Rosewood, Miss Ashton. My question for you is what are you going to do about it?"

Victoria hesitated, blinking with bafflement. Whatever did the woman mean? What could she do? Box Blake in his own ring? "I fear I don't understand."

A thoughtful smile curved Lady Devon's mouth. "Of course you do. I'm asking how you plan to even the odds."

Victoria stared at Lady Devon in astonishment. If anything, the woman was direct.

"Ravenspear holds all the power," Victoria said. "I'd be happy to survive the year."

Lady Devon threw her head back and let out a great peal of laughter. "Ha! Such poppycock! When it comes to power between a man and a woman, an attractive female always holds the upper hand."

Lady Samantha Devon was turning out to be a complete surprise. Was it possible that this experienced, sophisticated woman could become her ally?

Victoria sat down beside the baroness and looked at her intently. "I know little of men."

"Can I be honest with you, Miss Ashton?"

"Please." Victoria thought the woman had already been speaking plainly.

"When I first learned the truth about you coming to Rosewood from Justin, I was stunned at Blake's actions. The thought of him using an innocent woman in such a manner seemed out of character for him, and it sickened me. But then I agreed to dine here tonight, and I observed the way he watched you. There's something there, in his eyes, and a smart girl could use it to her advantage."

"With all due respect, you're wrong," Victoria said. "When he looks at me, all he sees is a convenient means to ruin my father. Why else would he force me here?"

With her hands folded in her lap, speaking to this stranger about the twisted events that forced her to leave her home, Victoria's composure was as fragile as an eggshell.

Lady Devon reached out to touch her hand. "My dear Miss Ashton, settling a score may have been an outward excuse for bringing you here, but a man of Ravenspear's wealth has many means at his disposal to harm an enemy. No, there must be more. He would not bring a woman he did not have feelings for into his home."

Victoria's head dropped to look at the smooth hand holding her own. "He may have felt something for me when I was a child, but no longer."

"You'll see. In the meantime, we will socialize frequently as my country residence is near Rosewood, and I visit Justin often. If you ever seek advice about men, I hope you will come to me."

Victoria raised her eyes to study Lady Devon. Hope blossomed in her chest. "Can you speak to Mr. Woodward? Perhaps he can talk Ravenspear out of this mad scheme."

A genuine smile curved Lady Devon's lips. "I fear it will do no good. When Ravenspear has set his mind to accomplish something, he cannot be dissuaded. All I can say is this: I have seen the way he treats Justin and others in his employ. He is not a cruel man, but fair and honorable, even overly generous. I don't believe he would harm you or ill-treat you." Squeezing Victoria's hand, she said, "A smart woman can turn a man's desire into more."

"But how?"

Footsteps in the hallway alerted them to the men's presence.

Lady Devon held a finger to her lips, signaling Victoria to keep quiet.

Victoria was bursting with the need to ask more questions.

How could she turn Blake's base needs into something more, something that could tip the scales in her favor in this twisted game?

Blake and Justin, port glasses in hand, entered the parlor.

Blake strode to the fire and placed his glass on the mantel shelf, then studied the two women. His sharp gaze seemed to miss nothing, the way the women sat facing each other, closer than required for mere casual conversation.

"How have you ladies been faring?" he asked. "I trust we have not kept you waiting for too long?"

Not long enough! Victoria wanted to shout. She needed more time, and perhaps pen and paper, to quiz the older, wiser Lady Samantha on all the aspects of male manipulation.

She must have glared at him, for he smiled at her a bit too cheerfully.

"I believe Miss Ashton is exhausted, Lord Ravenspear," Samantha said smoothly. "She has had a long day traveling, and I fear I have kept her awake." The baroness rose to depart.

Justin Woodward set his glass on the closest table and took her arm. "I'll escort you to your carriage."

The couple departed, leaving Victoria alone with Blake.

An uncomfortable silence stretched between them. Blake rested his arm casually on the mantel, fingers brushing his glass, and Victoria sat awkwardly on the edge of the settee.

She had done as he had asked and dined with his friends. The day's travel and the tension of arriving at her new home for the next year had taken their toll. She was so tired her temples throbbed.

Rising from the cushions, she clasped her hands before her skirts. "I'd like to retire if you are finished with me."

Blake's look was one of faint amusement. "Your choice of words are intriguing, my dear."

Victoria blushed. Why did he have to interpret an innocent comment in such a vile manner? "You're showing your coarse upbringing in the poorhouse, my lord."

"Careful, Victoria. All that keeps me from honoring my promise not to visit your chamber tonight is my good temper."

The blood drained from her face. She dared to shoot him a scalding look before fleeing to her room.

Chapter 9

"I don't remember how to ride," Victoria insisted.

"Once you learn, you never forget," Blake said. "I taught you how to ride before, and I'll give you a quick refresher course now."

They were in the stables, and Victoria nervously eyed the animals in the stalls.

That morning, after a small breakfast, Blake had asked her to accompany him on horseback to inspect his country estate. Trying to avoid spending time together, Victoria had protested.

When she was a child her family had resided in the country, and she had ridden often. But there was never a need for her to ride after they had moved to London, and it had been over ten years since she had sat a saddle.

Victoria chose a small white horse. The mare nuzzled her hand with its velvety pink muzzle. Its rough tongue tickled her palm as it licked a sugar cube she offered, and she giggled.

"See. I remembered you were a natural with animals."

With false bravado she strode to the mounting block, lifted her skirts and swung her leg over the palfrey's back.

She mounted successfully, but her skirts were tight and restrictive.

"This gown wasn't made for riding."

"Then we'll have to get you riding clothes."

Her lids slipped down over her eyes, avoiding his gaze. It was easier to resent him when he acted arrogant and combative. She did not want his kindness to touch a nerve.

Raising her chin a notch, she asked, "What do I do next?"

"Put your boots in the stirrups, and grip the reins loosely in your hands. You must be ready to tighten them if need be."

She followed his instructions and then looked at him expectantly.

Blake mounted his own horse, a large black stallion, and rode to her side. "Remember, the horse will respond to the pressure from your knees, and you can guide her by pulling on the reins. Go slow and follow my lead."

For the first two miles, they walked their horses at an easy pace. Soon Victoria gained more confidence as her memories of riding astride returned. She relaxed, and began to enjoy the fresh country air and magnificent scenery.

With the arrival of spring, the sky was a brilliant blue, and the morning sun warmed her cheeks. As they crossed an open field, she breathed in the fragrant scent of the wildflowers that dressed the landscape with wild abandon. The splashes of vivid color reminded Victoria of a classical painting.

Suppressing a fanciful impulse to stop and pick handfuls of the delicate-looking blooms, she turned her attention to her mount. "It's coming back to me now. Can we go faster?"

Blake grinned in approval. "Grip your legs tighter and ease up on the reins."

The small horse began to canter, then gallop. Blake rode beside her.

A cool breeze blew through Victoria's hair, and she reveled in the freedom that riding astride made her feel.

As they approached a copse of trees, Blake said, "Pull back on the reins and slow her down."

Victoria did as he instructed. She glanced at the thick saddle muscles on his thighs as he gripped the powerful stallion and brought it to heel. His shirtsleeves were rolled up, and his big hands held the reins skillfully. His fingers, tapered and strong, appeared calloused from hours of labor.

Hardly the hands of an earl, she thought. But then, nothing about Blake Mallorey was similar to any of the nobility in her acquaintance.

She remembered what his fingers had felt like when they traced her lips, her cheek, her collarbone, and, heaven help her, her breast.

Her eyelids fluttered and she trembled.

"Are you all right? There's a stream up ahead where we can rest."

Victoria stiffened, momentarily abashed. He mistook her physical reaction for fatigue.

God forbid he suspected the real reason behind her shivering.

He drew rein beside the stream, beneath a large oak tree, and helped her dismount. He did not tether the stallion but allowed him to wander to the water and drink.

Victoria followed his lead, and the smaller palfrey roamed to the water.

Blake withdrew a canister from his saddlebags, knelt by the water's edge and then filled the container. He offered the fresh water to her first.

She eyed the canister, unsure how a lady should drink from it. Not wanting to appear timid, she drank the water, throwing her head back for the last few drops, then handed the canister back to him.

He nodded in approval, refilled the canister, and then imitated her actions.

Watching the white horse, she asked casually, "What's my mount's name?"

"Persephone."

"The daughter of the Greek god Zeus and goddess Demeter? I had no idea you were knowledgeable of the Greek classics."

Her tone sounded condescending to her ears, but it was not her intention to appear superior.

Blake's eyebrow rose a fraction. "Don't you mean to say that you're surprised a poorhouse boy would have learned the classics?"

She swung her head around to look at him. "I didn't mean to insult your education, my lord. I was just . . . genuinely surprised. Not many men call their animals by names from mythology."

Turning back around to look at his enormous stallion, she asked, "What's his name?"

"Pluto."

She chuckled in disbelief. "According to the myth, Persephone was abducted by the god Pluto to rule with him over the underworld."

"I know."

The sudden realization dawned on her that Blake was Pluto and she his Persephone, captured by him to stay by his side and endure his seduction, his dark underworld, for an entire year. Their horses' names seemed an uncanny coincidence.

Momentarily speechless, she looked up at him.

His mouth quirked with humor. "You picked the horse, my dear, remember? I can hardly control your thoughts."

She eyed him suspiciously, not entirely certain that he had no mystic powers. If he could wield control over her physical reaction toward him, against her wishes, what else could the dark devil do?

Blake raised a forefinger and pointed. "All the land you see to the hill beyond belongs to Rosewood."

She cupped her hand over her eyebrows to shield the sun from her eyes and surveyed Blake's property. "I had no idea your estate was so extensive."

"Six thousand acres."

Six thousand acres!

She couldn't fathom one man owning that much land. She wanted to ask how much he had paid for Rosewood, but at the same time, she didn't want to hear the gross figure from his arrogant lips.

If he could afford so much real estate without strapping himself financially, then her father's fifteen-thousand-pound debt meant nothing to him. Blake could have easily extended the terms of Charles's loan.

But it isn't about the money, she reminded herself. *It's about revenge.*

They remounted their horses, and Blake led her toward the tenant farms. First they passed acres of orchards, where the sweet smell of apples, pears and peaches hung in the air. Then they rode through grazing pastures of horses, lambs and sheep.

Victoria spotted the dwellings of Rosewood's tenant farmers. As they approached, families came out of their homes to greet them. Children ran forward, smiling and happy, to welcome their lord and pet his horse.

Blake laughed and reached down to ruffle the hair on the youths' heads.

To her astonishment, Blake knew all their names and recalled a personal fact about each man, woman and child.

The birth of a babe, the death of a distant relative, the dates of upcoming nuptials and the accidental injury of a son were all familiar topics of conversation between master and tenants.

Victoria realized that he regularly patrolled his property and took a keen interest in the people working the land.

Looking into the eyes of these hardworking families, she saw their respect and admiration for Ravenspear.

Two farmers with calloused hands and bronzed skin conversed with Blake regarding several fallow fields Blake and Victoria had previously passed. The rough-hewn men suggested rye and barley be planted on the land set aside for next spring.

Blake agreed with his tenants' plans and recommended hops be planted as well.

Victoria had never heard of a master taking an interest in the crops on his country estate, only in the money the land would yield to support a gambling habit in London.

On their way back to Rosewood, Blake guided Pluto through an unkempt path in the woods. Brush grew in abundance, scraping the soft leather of her riding boots and snaring the hem of her light-wool gown, and Victoria wondered where the untraveled road led.

They entered a clearing, and a small cottage came into view. The dwelling was dilapidated, unlike the tenants' homes they had just visited, with a patched straw roof, a shutter dangling from its hinge and a garden full of weeds.

Blake dismounted, removed a package from his saddle-bags and proceeded to the front door.

Victoria followed, curiosity aroused.

A woman opened the door and upon spotting them, curtsied immediately.

"Yer lordship. I wasna expecting yer visit."

She appeared middle-aged with equal parts of gray and brown hair. Crow's-feet lined the corners of her eyes, and deep creases around her mouth made her lips look permanently puckered. Her gown, navy in color but faded in most places, was fraying at the hem.

From what Victoria could see and smell, the interior of the cottage was dingy, damp and dirty.

Blake reached down and raised the frail woman from her knees. "How are you and little Simon faring, Maggie?"

The woman's eyes remained respectfully downcast, and she twisted the worn material of her skirt with gnarled fingers. "We are gettin' by, me lord."

"My housekeeper, Mrs. Smith, arranged a package of food for you. She tells me Cook prepared enough fowl and biscuits that will last you and little Simon a week."

Tears welled within Maggie's eyes as she reached out to take the parcel. "God bless ye, me lord. Before my William passed, he always said ye becomin' the new master of Rosewood was the best thing to happen here."

Victoria heard the patter of little footsteps behind Maggie a moment before a red-haired boy of no more than five peeked behind Maggie's faded skirts.

Blake bent down on one knee and looked into the child's round eyes. "Hello, Simon."

Simon smiled, revealing two missing front teeth. He looked up at Victoria, a glint of wonder in his eyes. "She's pretty."

Victoria knelt eye level to the boy. "My name is Victoria."

Simon turned to Blake. "Yer wife?"

Victoria flushed. "No. We are not married."

"Simon!" Maggie admonished as she pulled the boy tightly against her side and shot him a stern look.

Victoria recognized the look of horror on the boy's face at the possibility of insulting his master.

"We are just friends, Simon," Victoria said.

Simon offered a small, shy smile. "Well, yer a pretty friend."

Maggie handed the package of food to her son and pushed the boy behind her. "Take this inside, Simon."

The boy rushed to do his mother's bidding.

"I apologize fer my boy, Lord Ravenspear." She shuffled her feet and lowered her gaze. "I also apologize fer this month's rent."

Blake took Maggie's worn hand into his own. "Nonsense, Maggie. I told you I don't expect anything from you and Simon. I spoke with Tanner and he will fix the leak in your roof this week."

A tear rolled down her wrinkled cheek. "I donna know what to say except to thank ye."

"That's plenty, Maggie."

As they rode back to Rosewood, Victoria could not get the image of Maggie and the adorable red-haired Simon out of her head. "What is Maggie's story?"

"Her husband, William, passed away four years ago, right after Simon was born. Maggie has been struggling to support her son ever since. Apparently, the former master of Rosewood did not give a fig for their tragic circumstances and gave them no rent relief. I learned of their plight soon after I purchased Rosewood. Maggie's pride won't allow me to move them into a habitable cottage. So with Mrs. Smith's and Cook's help, we make sure they have sufficient food."

Victoria's heart ached at the unfairness of Maggie's situation and the cruelty of the former owner.

She recalled her conversation with Lady Devon—that Blake was not a cruel master but fair and honorable, even overly generous. This part of him—compassionate, caring, kind—reminded her of the Blake Mallorey of her youth.

"Maggie seems old to have a son as young as Simon," she said.

Blake turned toward her. "Maggie's your age, Victoria."

She looked at him with surprise, remembering the deep creases around Maggie's eyes and lips, her head of gray hair, the knotted fingers. "But she looks so old."

His mouth was tight and grim, his hands clenched the reins. "Poverty and hardship will age a person," he said, a cold edge in his voice.

In an instant, gone was the pleasant gentleman she had spent the day riding with, and in his place was the bitter, cynical earl. She knew he was thinking of his time spent in the workhouse as a boy.

The experience had not aged *him* but rather had honed him into an avenging demon.

His sharp change in mood caused the anger to rise within her at the unfairness of her own situation. The urge to lash out at him was insuppressible.

"I'd take any amount of poverty over forced servitude to you," she said in a nasty tone.

His eyes slightly narrowed. "I think not, my dear. Females that look like you never go hungry for long in the poorhouse or on the streets. They quickly find a lucrative means by which to support themselves."

"Are you insinuating I'd turn to *prostitution?* How dare you!"

"I'm not insinuating anything, I'm merely stating fact."

They arrived at the Rosewood stables. Blake slid from the saddle and held up his arms.

Victoria slapped away his hand and leapt down, careful not to brush against his hard body.

The line of his mouth tightened a fraction more. "Dinner is at seven, my dear."

This time, she knew better than to argue with him about sharing every meal. Tossing her hair behind her shoulder, she sauntered past him with the regal bearing of the Queen of England.

Chapter 10

Blake strode into the library, his booted feet muffled by the thick Aubusson carpet.

Justin's head snapped up, and his hands clenched the sheath of papers he had been studying at Blake's desk. "You startled me."

"Not my intention, Woodward."

Dropping the papers, Justin stood and moved away from the desk. "You look bloody miserable. I take it you didn't have a pleasant ride with Miss Ashton?"

Blake fell into the chair Justin had vacated. He leaned back and rested his boots on the edge of the desk. "Things were progressing nicely, until our pasts interfered."

"That serious?"

"She'd rather become a prostitute than spend the year with me."

Justin burst out laughing. "That qualifies as quite dastardly."

Blake sat forward. "She feels something for me. I can see it in her eyes, the softening of her facial expressions, every time she recalls a childhood memory. And there's sexual attraction too. I'm no longer an inexperienced boy, and I clearly recognize it."

Justin picked up a crystal decanter resting on an end table and poured two glasses of brandy. He placed the drink before Blake. "She is very beautiful."

Blake swirled the amber liquid in his glass. "She is, isn't she? Who would have thought?"

"Send her back to her father, Ravenspear."

Blake's eyes snapped to Justin's. "Let her go? I can't."

"Then you are torturing yourself."

Blake laughed bitterly. "If the thought of Victoria under my roof makes Charles Ashton lose even one night of sleep, then any suffering her presence causes me will be well worth it."

"Have you thought of the lady's feelings?"

"Too often. However, I promised myself a long time ago that I would allow nothing to get in the way of my vengeance."

Blake swallowed the last of the brandy and then slammed the glass on the desk.

Justin shrugged and said offhandedly, "Samantha likes her. It puts me in an awkward position."

"Since when have you allowed your cock to rule your brains, Woodward?"

"Don't worry, Ravenspear. My loyalties lie with you. I wouldn't be here today if not for your actions."

Blake raised a hand. "Please spare me any gratitude." His eyes dropped to the papers on his desk. "What are these?"

Justin strode to the desk and jabbed his forefinger at the papers. "These are a way to trick Charles Ashton into doing business with you."

"Why would I want to do business with the whoreson?"

"We need something he has. Your investment in the

latest technology, high-pressure steam engines, requires steel pistons that can handle enormously high temperatures. The only company that produces such pistons in England is co-owned by Charles Ashton and Mr. Jacob Hobbs."

"I'll be damned," Blake said. "Neither will ever willingly sell me the parts."

"Not to *you,* but they will sell them to Illusory Enterprises."

"And whose company is that?"

"Your new subsidiary. I've already spoken with your solicitors. It's perfectly legal."

Blake hooted with laughter. "Your genius never ceases to amaze me, Woodward! I'll be buying the equipment I need right under Ashton's nose. And I approve wholeheartedly of the company name." He rubbed his chin with his thumb and forefinger. "Give the lawyers permission to proceed, but tell them to keep our actions strictly confidential."

Justin touched his forehead in a mock salute. "Yes, sir."

Over the course of the following week, time passed at a snail's pace for Victoria. A pattern was established where Blake and Victoria would share two meals a day: breakfast at sunrise and the evening meal at seven sharp.

In addition to dining together, Blake insisted she accompany him during the majority of his daily tasks, whether he rode out to inspect his property and visit his tenants or studied his papers in the library.

Because he often worked at home, she spent a significant amount of time in the library, surrounded by the finest collection of books she had ever seen, and read as he silently buried himself in mounds of paperwork.

She frequently pretended to read, watching him

unobserved beneath lowered lashes. His appearance fascinated her, and she marveled at how much he had changed
from a good-looking youth to a darkly handsome man.

There was no trace of boyish softness in his face, rather
all hard and chiseled angles, and blue eyes so compellingly
direct she shivered. He was the most handsome male she
had ever seen, and her unbidden physical response to him
was immediate and overwhelming.

At times she was so absorbed with watching him work
that she had no idea of the title or author of the novel she
was reading and wouldn't have been the least bit surprised
if she was holding the pages upside down.

On one instance, he glanced up from his papers, caught
her staring and grinned.

Swiftly averting her eyes, she had the uncanny feeling
that he knew her thoughts.

He was a rare type of male, one that possessed an irre-
sistible combination of masculine confidence infused with
a streak of dangerousness. Such an amalgamation in a man
could easily lure a woman to her doom.

Victoria had always considered herself a practical
female, but Blake Mallorey seemed to cause all common
sense to fly from her head.

Her frustration mounted daily because he did not speak
out loud of his business transactions and, because she was
rarely alone, she had no opportunity to rummage through
his business documents. When he did meet with Justin
Woodward to talk business, she was excused.

Blake's behavior added to her exasperation. He never
mentioned the cross words they had exchanged during their
first tour of Rosewood. He was polite, suspiciously so, and
she wondered at his change in tactics. Yet he continued to
find excuses to touch her—acting the gallant gentleman.

When he held out her dining chair, his fingers would

brush the sensitive skin of her collarbone above her neckline. As he escorted her from a room, he would stroke her elbow. Lifting her like she weighed no more than a grain of salt to place her on her horse, his strong hands would hold her close to his hard body and linger on her waist.

The time they spent together brought forth unwanted memories of her childhood infatuation and made her mindful of her sensuality.

She recalled his kindness to Maggie and her son, Simon. Blake was respected and admired by his tenants.

Both instances softened her anger, and her feelings toward him became confused.

She feared for her sanity, wondering how she would survive the year. She wanted to hate him and tried unsuccessfully to suppress her girlish crush. Yet she was physically attracted to and sensually aware of the attractive man he had become.

Just when she thought she would scream from frustration, the Baroness of Devon paid a visit to Rosewood.

Lady Devon swept into the parlor, took one look at Victoria's ashen face, and said, "Has he treated you that badly?"

Victoria's smile did not reach her eyes. "I'm glad for your visit, Lady Devon."

"It's Samantha, darling." She approached Victoria and touched her shoulder. "We will have time to talk after dinner."

The evening meal progressed much like the last she had shared with Justin Woodward and Lady Devon. The food was plentiful and delicious, the sherry expensive and selected to enhance the flavor of the dishes.

After dinner, the women retired to the parlor. The men did not keep them waiting long, instead choosing to drink their port in the ladies' presence.

Victoria's agitation surfaced at not having any time to speak with Lady Devon in private.

She grit her teeth when Blake and Justin entered the parlor. "We expected you would take longer," she said, a note of impatience in her voice.

Blake, ignoring her tone, smiled merrily. "Do you enjoy playing cards, my dear?"

Victoria knew society was obsessed with gambling. Every successful party, ball or masque ended in the card room these days. She hadn't thought Blake shared the fascination.

"I'm familiar with the rules of whist," she said.

"Good," Blake said.

He walked to a dainty end table, opened a slim drawer and pulled out a deck of cards.

Lady Devon's blue eyes widened and she sat forward. "Whist is my favorite, but it requires four players, two against two as partners, so we seldom play."

Rising from her seat, Samantha rubbed her hands with excitement. "Let's play gentlemen versus ladies!"

Two chairs were pulled up to the table. Justin sat next to Victoria on the settee, Samantha moved to a chair across the table, and Blake took the chair across from Victoria.

Blake shuffled the deck with nimble fingers, and Lady Devon cut the deck. He then dealt the cards with the faces down to each player in clockwise rotation, until he came to the last card, which he placed with the face up on the table.

"Hearts are trump," Blake announced.

Samantha placed a sharp pencil and a piece of paper next to the cards.

Realization dawned on Victoria. "I have nothing to wager."

"Please forgive us if we made you uncomfortable, Miss

Ashton," Justin Woodward said. "It's true we usually play for stakes. But we may play purely for pleasure tonight."

"Yes, of course," Samantha agreed.

"Forget the money," Blake said tersely.

A sudden daring thought occurred to Victoria. Lifting her chin, she met Blake's hard gaze straight on. "A side bet between me and Lord Ravenspear, then. If I win, I'll wager fifteen thousand pounds, my father's entire debt, on one hand."

A hush descended, and Jacob and Lady Samantha turned toward her.

"Assuming the fifteen thousand is yours to begin with, what will be my prize if I win?" Blake asked.

The couple's heads swung toward Blake.

Victoria's hand rose to her throat, fingering the diamond necklace she wore. It had been a gift from her parents when she was a debutante. Hardly worth fifteen thousand, it was still an expensive piece with exquisite workmanship. Loath to give it up, her fingers trembled as she reached behind her neck to unclasp the gold hook.

Setting it on the table between them, Victoria took a card and threw it with the face up on the table. "I believe I go first."

She held her breath as she watched Blake, afraid he might reject the bet outright.

Blake picked up his cards, glancing at them in a cursory fashion before looking back at her and nodding. "First team to earn seven points wins."

The game progressed in silence, the tension in the room palpable.

Blake played casually, Justin more seriously and the women intently. The teams earned tricks, or points, in an alternating fashion, until they had six each. The next hand would determine the winner.

Excitement mounted within Victoria as she studied her cards. The Queen of Hearts, her remaining trump card, seemed to quiver in her hands.

The probability of her and her partner winning the game was good. The only two cards that could beat her trump card were the Ace of Hearts and the King of Hearts.

Victoria struggled to remember if either card had already been played, knowing that if they both had, the women were certain to win.

But counting cards was Spencer's forte, never hers.

"Queen of Hearts." She smiled as she placed the card down.

When it was Justin's turn, he bit his lip and said, "I'm sorry, Ravenspear. I can't beat that."

Lady Devon discarded her unwanted card in a trice. "I don't need to defeat my partner!"

All eyes turned to Blake, waiting for him to discard the card that would break the tie.

There was a lethal calmness in Blake's eyes, and with a flick of his wrist, his card landed on top of hers.

She stared in disbelief at the King of Hearts that had won him the game. The irony was not lost on her that her submissive Queen of Hearts was beaten by none other than his dominant King.

"Congratulations," she whispered huskily, biting back tears of disappointment. A heaviness centered in her chest as she slid her treasured necklace toward him.

He made no move to take the necklace but sat motionless, his flat, unspeaking eyes watching her and prolonging the moment. "You should have agreed to play for fun."

Not trusting herself to speak with the lump that lingered in her throat, she did not.

Samantha must have sensed Victoria's inner turmoil, for she stood abruptly and broke the awkward silence.

"You have the Devil's luck, Ravenspear. You play like a professional gambler."

Victoria smiled weakly and rose from her seat on shaky legs to join Lady Devon by the dying fire.

The urge to flee to the privacy of her room and succumb to the sobs she held in check was overwhelming. But she refused to give Blake the satisfaction of seeing her cry.

She wasn't a child but a woman full-grown, who made a wager in a card game and lost, knowing full well the consequences of gambling.

No one died. No one was bleeding. She would survive the loss of her necklace.

Lifting her chin, Victoria straightened up with dignity. She talked with Samantha for the remainder of the evening, careful to avoid eye contact with Blake.

To her relief, the men conversed and drank their port in the corner of the room, away from the fireplace.

A quick glance at the table revealed her necklace still lying upon the surface. The brilliant diamond sparkled in the firelight, teasing her.

So close, yet no longer hers . . .

Her head ached from the effort of holding her rioting emotions inside. She lost track of the conversation, unsure what Lady Devon was speaking about.

Samantha looked at her with understanding. "We'll talk another time, Victoria. I see you are preoccupied with your thoughts."

Victoria nodded and excused herself. She held the banister tightly as she climbed the stairs to her room.

Closing the bedroom door, she leaned heavily against the frame before the first blinding tear rolled down her cheek.

Chapter 11

It was no use. She was never going to fall asleep, no matter how comfortable the four poster or how soft the coverlet in her rose-colored room.

Throwing off her blankets, Victoria swung her legs over the side of the bed, stuffed her feet into slippers and impatiently donned a silk wrapper. Then she took a candle from the mahogany night table, lit it, and carried it with her from the room.

She tiptoed along the second-floor hallway to the top of the grand staircase leading down to the main floor. As her slipper touched the last step, she paused to look around.

Lamps glowed faintly, casting eerie shadows on the satin wallpaper, but all was silent.

Confident the residents of Rosewood had retired for the night, she ventured forward.

Thoughts of the night's card game flickered through her mind for the hundredth time.

She had behaved like a fool.

What had seemed like a flash of genius was in hindsight nothing more than sheer lunacy.

She should never have wagered her necklace. She had

succeeded in putting Blake in a position of superiority over herself once again.

Seeking solitude, she wandered past empty rooms until coming to the music room at the back of the house. Slowly opening the door to ensure no one was inside, she crept forward. Carefully, so as not to make a sound, she closed the door.

The dying embers in the fireplace radiated little light. Her single candle was not sufficient to illuminate the length of the room, but she remembered a long window in the back overlooking a portion of the gardens.

A full moon dominated the night and beamed a ray of light through the window across the polished hardwood floor.

Victoria walked to the window and pressed her hand against the cool glass, mesmerized by the luminosity of the moonbeams streaming from its mass.

She turned away from the lunar sight to study the instruments in the room.

A glossy black pianoforte with its stark white keys rested in one corner, a violin and music stand close by. Sheets of music lay open on the stand in disarray, and a bow rested across a chair.

A musician must have practiced recently, for Victoria found it difficult to believe Rosewood's servants would overlook any lack of order in the immaculate manor.

Setting her candle on top of the pianoforte, Victoria wondered which occupant of Rosewood played the instruments.

Surely not Blake Mallorey? When he entertained, he probably hired musicians to amuse his guests.

An intricately carved harp caught her eye. The gold ornamentation on the arched neck and post was breathtaking.

She flitted to the instrument, her nightgown and wrapper

flowing about her ankles, and ran her fingers upon the harp's design. Smooth to the touch, the craftsman's work was exceptional, and she wondered the cost of the magnificent piece.

Gently plucking the strings, a harmonious lyric penetrated the silent room.

She sighed, enjoying the soft melody, and touched the strings again. The night's tension eased from her shoulders, and she knew she could relax here amongst the moonbeams and instruments such that she could not in her own room. After an hour or so, she would be able to fall asleep, problems temporarily forgotten.

"I wasn't aware your talents included music."

At the sound of the masculine voice, Victoria spun around. She had heard the voice, more specifically *his* voice, yet she saw no one.

Her stomach clenched tight. "Where are you?"

"Here," he said, stepping into the room. "It wasn't my intention to interrupt, my dear."

Blake's face and figure were half-concealed by darkness and half-illuminated by moonlight. He walked stealthily forward until he stood a mere foot away.

Dressed in black, with the top buttons of his shirt undone, he reminded Victoria of a wild animal stalking its prey.

"I couldn't sleep so I came here to relax," she said. "I shall leave at once so as not to disturb you."

She made to brush past him, but he caught her arm.

"Don't go. Please."

Victoria looked up into dark, compelling eyes. The tentative, almost-imploring tone of his voice surprised her. Her gaze dropped to his fingers holding her arm.

Releasing his grasp, he asked, "Why couldn't you sleep?"

She shrugged. "Sometimes sleep eludes me when I have things on my mind."

"What's on your mind tonight?"

She ignored the question and pulled her silk wrapper tight around her body as if to shield herself from his penetrating gaze.

"I shall retire," she said. "I'm sure I won't have problems sleeping now, and you may have the music room to yourself."

"Nonsense. I interrupted you."

"I didn't hear you enter the room, and you carry no candle."

He smiled. "Years in the crop fields of the Indies at night, far away from civilization, taught me how to find my way around without much light. Besides, I'm quite familiar with the layout in my own home."

He took a step closer and the moonlight highlighted the handsome features of his face. His distinctive masculine scent filled her senses.

"You still haven't answered my question," he said.

She studied the lean, sun-bronzed face and wondered what question he referred to. His closeness made her mind spin, leaving her dazed.

He arched a dark brow. "Well? What's on your mind?"

"Nothing of consequence."

If the harp was not touching her spine, she would step backward. But she didn't want to appear the coward, and God forbid he discover his effect on her.

Reaching into his shirt pocket, he produced her necklace. The gold chain dangled from his fingers, and the small diamond sparkled.

She bit down hard on her lower lip. "It's bad sportsmanship for a winner to flaunt his victory."

"You misunderstand, Victoria." He extended his hand, palm upward, offering the jewelry. "I'm returning your necklace."

She took a quick breath of utter astonishment. "Why? You won fairly."

"I have no need of a ladies' necklace. It would look ridiculous on me, and I have no one to give it to. Besides, you should not have placed it up for stakes. I never knew you shared your brother's habit for gambling."

"I don't," she blurted out, then frowned at her admission.

He was ruffling her composure. Always one to think things thoroughly through, like she did before choosing a stock to invest in, Victoria found herself acting spontaneously and impulsively around him, and blurting out whatever was on her mind.

He was maddening.

She stared at her necklace in his outstretched hand. She wanted to grasp it and run without contemplating the cost of his generous act, but her suspicious nature stopped her.

He waited, watching her.

"I don't understand," she said.

Dark blue eyes probed to her very soul. "Because it angered me that you recklessly sought to escape our agreement. And because even if you'd won, I had no intention of letting you go."

Her brain was in tumult. She should be outraged that he had led her to believe the wager was good—that she actually had a chance of winning her freedom—but at the same time, she respected his honesty. She had lost the necklace, and he did not have to admit that he never intended to release her had she won.

And now he was offering to return her jewelry.

She started to reach for the gem, then hesitated. "What do you want in exchange?"

"I want only to erase the sad expression from your face. And I want you to be able to sleep soundly in my home."

Surprised at the sincerity of his tone, she was speechless.

"May I?" he asked, holding up the necklace.

She nodded, and he turned her by her shoulders so that her back faced him. Strong fingers entwined in her hair as he pushed the dark mass to one side.

He brushed her neck, and she felt a lurch of unwelcome excitement. With his arms around her, he secured the clasp. The diamond felt cool against her suddenly heated flesh. His touch lingered, his thumbs stroking the sensitive skin behind her ear, down the column of her throat.

She froze as her senses leapt to life. "Ravenspear," she said, barely above a whisper. "This cannot continue."

Leaning down, he whispered in her ear. "Why not?" His teeth grazed her earlobe. "You're so beautiful."

Victoria's legs weakened, her stomach felt like jelly.

His finger stroked her cheek, down her jawline.

Her eyes fluttered close. "We must stop."

He laughed. "Who would have thought this is the same woman who followed me as a child and begged me to spend time with her?"

Turning in his arms, she raised her eyes to his. "That was long ago, my lord. Much has happened since then, and my feelings have changed."

"Have they? I believe only that they have grown from a child's crush to a woman's desire."

"You're wrong . . ."

Blake bent his head, his eyes dropping to her mouth.

"I don't think . . ." She struggled to gather her frazzled thoughts beneath his heated gaze.

"*Shh,* my sweet Victoria." His mouth covered hers.

Surprisingly gentle and whisper-soft, his lips brushed back and forth as he spoke. "So responsive to my touch."

His lips recaptured hers, more demanding this time. His tongue traced the soft fullness of her lower lip, then gently sucked on the sensitive flesh.

Victoria grasped a fistful of his shirt, kneading the hard slabs of muscle beneath the thin material.

Was she pushing him away? Or trying to get closer?

She didn't know. Her senses reeled, her body ached for his touch.

"You struggle against the inevitable, my love." His voice was husky. "Do not deny yourself. Give in to what you need, what you *crave*."

As though his words released her, she allowed his hands to explore the hollows of her back, then clasp her tightly to him. The heat of his body coursed down the entire length of hers.

Where her thin night rail brushed against his chest, her breasts tingled. Victoria closed her eyes and leaned fully against him.

"That's it," Blake whispered against her ear. "Your body cries out for my touch, for more."

He kissed her again, this time more thoroughly, exploring the recesses of her mouth.

She moaned and squirmed in his arms, rubbing her swollen breasts harder against him.

"Yes," he said, hoarsely. "You learn quickly, my beauty. Let me show you more."

He opened her wrapper and slid it down her arms. The silk pooled at her feet. She felt his hand cup her breast over her nightgown, then his thumb flick back and forth over her nipple. Pleasure radiated outward from the hardened tip, and she moaned softly.

"Yesss," he hissed, as if he knew how sensitive her breasts were to his fondling.

His thumb dipped beneath the silk bodice to graze the swollen nub. Shivers of delight followed his touch, and she breathed heavily through parted lips.

"If you like that, you'll love this." His head lowered, and

his moist breath dampened the sheer fabric covering her breast. Slowly, he sucked the entire crown into his mouth, molding the material to her skin. Peeling down the wet silk, his tongue explored the rosy peak of her breast.

Her head fell back; she gasped in sweet agony.

He moved to capture the other breast with his lips and sucked her nipple with tantalizing possessiveness.

Passion inched through her veins, heating her thighs and groin.

His rock-hard thigh pressed at the junction between her legs. She willingly parted her thighs for him, and he pulled her up until she squirmed against him. Delicious sensations radiated from the soft core of her body.

Her head fell back, her nails buried into his shirtsleeves. "Please," she whispered.

He froze suddenly and stepped away, taking his body heat with him. His fists clenched at his sides, his breathing was labored. "I apologize, Victoria. It was not my intention to force myself on you. I only wanted to return your necklace."

She looked up at him, her mind cloudy with desire, trying to figure out what he was talking about. She had no wish to back out of his embrace. He had interpreted her eager response as a plea to stop.

Her senses returned, and as her passion cooled humiliation took its place.

The night air against the wet bodice of her gown made her shiver. Glancing down, she was shocked to see what his lips and tongue had done. Through the wet silk, her breasts were fuller, her nipples pebble-hard.

Bending to retrieve the silk wrapper, she was thankful the moonlight hid the extent of her embarrassment. "Thank you for returning my necklace. Good night, my lord."

Resisting the urge to look at his face, she fled the music room before he could stop her.

·Chapter 12

Blake watched Victoria escape the room.

Cursing beneath his breath, he ran his fingers through his black hair in agitation.

A battle raged within him. Sexual and vengeful needs combating ruthlessly against the urge of tenderness and protectiveness.

Seduction had not been his intent this evening. The sad expression on her face after she had lost at whist, the manner in which she had said good night to Lady Samantha and Justin and had excused herself early to retire, had bothered Blake more than he cared to admit.

So he had sought her out tonight for the sole purpose of returning her necklace.

But when he saw her, standing before the window in the music room dressed in white silk awash in moonlight, he wanted a taste of her.

Just a taste.

But her eager response, the longing in her eyes, her sweet-tasting kisses, had inflamed his passion.

Damnation.

He cursed himself for allowing his enemy's daughter to

affect him this way. She turned his insides into chaos. His heart hammered foolishly, and the pit of his stomach churned whenever she was near.

Where was his cold, cruel logic, his unwavering determination? His thoughts turned to the demise of his family. His father had shot himself in the head and left his family alone to face the horrors of debtors' prison. Consumption had been rampant in the poorhouse, and his sheltered mother had contracted the disease almost immediately upon entering the prison. And his sister, beautiful, kind Judith, had suffered worst of all in her vain attempts to spare Blake and their mother from further suffering.

As for Victoria, she was supposed to be a ploy, nothing more. He had to stick to the plan, or all was lost. The chit, no matter how beautiful, or how intelligent, could not interfere with his quest. Justice would be done, even if the cost was high, and even if he lost part of his soul along the way.

"He insists you stay with him *all* the time?"

At the incredulous expression on Lady Samantha's face, Victoria nodded vigorously.

"I'm even expected to sit and read in the library as he works at his desk," Victoria said. "Only when Mr. Woodward needs to speak with Ravenspear am I excused."

Samantha leaned back on the settee, settling into the deep-red cushions. "Oh, my. The situation is more serious than I had initially thought. What you're describing is odd behavior indeed for Ravenspear. I've never known him to be so possessive of a woman."

Victoria poured tea from the sideboard, handed a cup and saucer to Lady Devon and then sat across her in a wingback chair. "I feel fortunate he allows me to escape his presence long enough each day to have tea with you."

Over the course of the past week, Victoria had invited Samantha to Rosewood for daily afternoon tea. It was the only opportunity for Victoria to socialize with a woman, other than the servants, since her arrival at Rosewood a month ago.

To Victoria's growing annoyance, the staff idolized their employer and never spoke an ill word about him.

Victoria needed to learn everything she could about the man Blake had become, and she knew befriending the baroness was an excellent decision.

Victoria eyed her new friend over the rim of her raised teacup. "He seemed wary when I first told him I had invited you to Rosewood."

Samantha's gentle laugh rippled through the air. "That's because Ravenspear knows me, and he's worried what I might tell you."

Setting her cup and saucer on an end table with a loud *chink,* Victoria sat forward and looked at Samantha expectantly. "That other night after dinner, before the men interrupted us in the parlor, you mentioned how a smart woman could turn a man's desire into more. Into her advantage . . ."

Victoria felt her face grow warm just mentioning the subject of male manipulation.

Samantha's lips curled into a smile. "Ah. So you do admit Ravenspear finds you desirable."

"Desire is not love."

"You're right to say that a man does not have to love a woman to lust after her, but it is unusual that he would bring you to his home to live with him and then insist you spend your days together. His feelings must run deeper than mere desire."

"The only reason he has forced me to reside at Rosewood is for retaliation," Victoria said.

Samantha leaned forward and clasped Victoria's hand.

"Like I said before, a man as wealthy as Ravenspear has numerous means at his disposal to gain revenge." Her clear blue eyes dropped to Victoria's neck. "I've noticed you're wearing your lovely necklace. Did he return it after you recklessly gambled it away, or did you have to steal it from him?"

Victoria's hand instinctively rose to touch the diamond's familiar smoothness, and her lips quirked at the thought of anyone stealing anything from Blake. "No, he was gracious enough to give the necklace back."

"What did he ask for in return? A kiss perhaps? A nightly visit to his bedchamber?"

If Victoria had been holding a hand mirror, she was certain she would see that her face was flushed crimson.

Even after a week of socializing with the outspoken baroness, Victoria still felt awkward openly discussing such topics. Her proper mother would faint if Victoria so much as uttered the word "kiss" or raised the topic of a bachelor's bedchamber in her presence.

Yet Victoria knew taking Lady Samantha's advice and learning from her life experiences were crucial if she was to survive a year in close quarters with a male as powerfully attractive as Blake Mallorey.

At the stunned look on Victoria's face, Samantha prompted, "Well? What did he do?"

"He made his feelings clear, but he has not forced himself upon me."

Memories from the night Blake had come upon her in the music room lingered around the edges of her mind. From the recollection alone, her senses leapt to life, and she vividly remembered the moonlight, his masculine scent, the feel of his powerful arms around her, the softness and hardness of his lips on hers, the wet roughness of his tongue on her breast, her nipple . . .

Samantha gave her a knowing look. "Ah. There is nothing quite like the first time a virgin is sexually awakened. I'm surprised he has restrained himself thus far."

"I don't want to be awakened, at least not by him. I despise my weakness."

Indeed, Victoria had hated herself ever since that night. Still shocked at her own sexual response toward him, she was grateful that he had misinterpreted her plea when she had begged him to continue touching her. He had thought she had pled for him to stop, and if he had not released her, she had no idea what she would have done, how far she would have gone.

"Do not be so hard on yourself, my dear. Many a female has nearly swooned when he enters a room."

"But I'm not just any girl! I'm not sixteen, but a mature, full-grown and independent woman." Victoria spoke with her hands, accentuating the annoyance she felt with herself. "I'm a thinker and a planner and I used to consider myself quite intelligent."

"But Ravenspear is a very masculine man. Living with a beautiful woman such as you, it is only a matter of time before he knocks on your bedroom door one night."

Victoria shook her head decisively. "That will *never* happen."

Samantha arched a well-plucked brow. "How can you be so certain?"

"He swore not to lure me into his bed, unless I invite him to share it with me."

Samantha's jaw dropped a notch. "Oh, that's rich! I cannot imagine Ravenspear promising any such thing. Don't you see, Victoria, how deep his feelings for you are? He must have wanted you badly to agree to such absurd terms."

A heaviness centered in Victoria's chest. "All he wants is to humiliate my father by destroying my reputation."

"Then why bring you to his reclusive country estate? Why not flaunt you in London during the height of the Season?"

Why indeed?

The same thought had occurred to Victoria many times. The only answer that came to mind was that Blake sought to prolong her father's misery, give him false hope, before crushing her family name and jeopardizing Charles Ashton's position on the Treasury Commission.

"Ravenspear seeks to torment my father for the years he spent in the poorhouse, and for his mother's and sister's unfortunate deaths," Victoria said.

"Then it makes no sense for him to wait. The sooner the scandal, the faster the retribution. He may want your father to spend sleepless nights worrying about your treatment, but I'm convinced that Ravenspear doesn't want to hurt you."

"I do not trust him. And I despise being so powerless."

"Powerless?" Samantha looked astonished. "You make me want to pee! There is nothing more powerful than a beautiful woman."

"What should I do?"

"Tease him, my girl!"

"Tease him?"

"Resist his charms, yet tantalize him at the same time. Make him regret his ludicrous promise."

"I cannot. That would make me no better than a true mistress. My reputation may be in tatters soon, but deep in my heart I still have my dignity. I hope to marry someday, and the least I can give a future husband is my innocence."

"Marriage is not everything," Samantha said. "I spent my youth in a loveless marriage under the thumb of a domineering, elderly husband and bound by society's rules.

Only in my widowed status am I finally free to seek out Justin—a man ten years my junior—a younger son with no inheritance who was expected to marry for title, money or preferably both."

"I envy your freedom." Victoria realized that the death of the baron gave Lady Samantha the wealth and title Justin Woodward sought.

"Don't you see? You have the same freedom now."

At the look of confusion on Victoria's face, Lady Samantha explained. "You have the opportunity to experience the man without binding yourself to his side for all eternity. It is the same type of freedom that a mistress has."

Giving Lady Samantha a skeptical look, Victoria asked, "Even if I secretly want to know Ravenspear, how do I give myself to a man I don't trust? A man who may have already spread rumors of my ruin?"

Samantha shook her head. "I attended Lady Cameron's ball in London last week, and not a word has been uttered about you. The fact that he agreed not to coerce you into his bed tells me that he cares for you more deeply than he wants others to believe."

"But to tease and tantalize him? I don't know how!"

"He is a good man; you must trust him and your heart. When you are ready to be with him, I'll tell you how to go about seducing an earl."

Chapter 13

"None of this is necessary, my lord."

"Of course it is, my dear. You said yourself that your skirts were too tight to ride astride." Blake's face creased into a sudden smile as his eyes roamed down her skirts. "I spend a significant amount of time in the saddle when in the country, so new riding clothes are a necessity for your stay at Rosewood."

With a firm touch on her elbow, he guided Victoria inside Madame Fleur's shop.

She bit her cheek to keep from arguing that just because he enjoyed riding didn't mean she did as well. He assumed she would join him outdoors whenever the inclination suited him, and that was the reason he had dragged her to the dressmaker this morning.

Tiny bells chimed as the door opened and closed behind them, alerting the shop owner to their presence.

A short, fashionably dressed woman approached them, a frown marring her features. "Do you have an appointment, monsieur? I have numerous fittings lined up for today."

"I am the new owner of Rosewood, and we've come to browse," Blake said, his tone chilly.

He measured the portly woman with a cool, appraising look that would alert any merchant to the presence of wealthy aristocracy.

Upon learning the Earl of Ravenspear graced her shop, the dressmaker's demeanor altered drastically. Stumbling over a nearby easel crowded with drawings of gowns, she rushed to assist them.

"Lord Ravenspear, what a privilege. I had heard you renovated Rosewood to surpass even its former glory."

Blake nodded. "Madame Fleur, may I present my cousin, Miss Ashton."

The Frenchwoman's mouth twitched, insinuating that she knew exactly what type of relationship the pair shared, but she quickly spoke. "I am honored to make your acquaintance, Mademoiselle Ashton. You are very beautiful."

Victoria stiffened, too startled by Blake's comment to respond.

His cousin!

What a ludicrous explanation. Why in the world would he lie to the dressmaker? If the woman's expression was any indication, then she already suspected they were not related. Besides, any matisse-maker worth her salt was skilled in discretion, from vast experience in dressing the mistresses of countless wealthy men.

Blake stepped forward into the store, leading Victoria with him. "My cousin must be fitted for numerous dresses suitable for riding, Madame Fleur."

"*Oui,* my lord, of course. Please look at my materials, and I shall measure mademoiselle," she said, rushing toward the back of the store for her measuring tape.

Victoria spun to face Blake, her green eyes wide with astonishment. "Your cousin?"

Blake shrugged nonchalantly, his gaze lazily roving the store's merchandise before coming to rest on a specific dress. "It's hardly any of the woman's business who she serves. All that seems to concern her is profit."

Victoria turned her head to look at the gown hanging on a nearby rack that held Blake's attention, and she knew he was basing his opinion on more than just the dressmaker's attitude.

Gazing at the dress, she noticed the high waist, but plunging neckline and tight-fitting sleeves, which a woman of loose morals might wear. The gown confirmed her earlier suspicions of the shop's customers.

She looked up from the gown to find Blake watching her. "Your money can't buy everything, my lord."

His expression stilled and grew serious. "I'm quite aware of that fact."

His steady scrutiny was unnerving, and Victoria walked away to study the vast array of materials Madame Fleur offered.

Bolts of fabric stacked on shelves soon seized her attention. Silks, brocades, crepes, satins and velvets in every color of the rainbow vied for space on the shelves and spilled onto the floor of the crowded shop. Every shade was represented, from bright jewel tones to pale pastels.

On impulse, Victoria reached out to touch several swatches and was instantly awed by their texture and softness. She had never been obsessed with fashion and clothing like many females of her acquaintance, but at the same time Victoria did enjoy shopping for new gowns. The thought of a custom-made outfit thrilled her.

So engrossed did she become that she nearly tripped over a bolt of fine black silk. She grasped at air to catch herself, but a strong hand caught her elbow, steadying her.

"What is it about women that makes their heads spin whenever they shop?"

Rising to her feet, she ripped her arm from Blake's

grasp. "This may shock you, but not all women are brainless creatures."

He gave her a smile that sent her pulses racing. "I was only teasing, Victoria."

Heavy footsteps behind Victoria alerted them to Madame Fleur's return.

"If you would both please follow me to the fitting room, we can begin measuring mademoiselle."

The dressmaker led them into the back of the store, past more bolts of fabric and dresses crammed onto racks, and finally into a narrow chamber.

A round pedestal was positioned in the center of the room before a cheval glass mirror, and mounted brass hooks lined the perimeter of the walls. Mounds of sewing cluttered the corners of the fitting room, attesting to the shop's large volume of business.

Madame Fleur walked behind Victoria. "Mademoiselle, I will unhook your gown so that I may take your measurements."

Victoria whirled around. "Wait!" Her eyes darted nervously back and forth between the woman and Blake. "I want Ravenspear . . . I mean I want my *cousin* to leave. It's not appropriate for him to see me undressed."

The woman's eyes widened in astonishment, and she stared, speechless. The dressmaker's response reaffirmed Victoria's beliefs that she had never believed her customers were cousins.

Blake arched an eyebrow, and his eyes sparkled with humor. "It appears my cousin is prudish."

Victoria felt her skin grow hot, and she wanted to fly across the room and smack the mocking expression from his handsome face.

Prudish!

What did he expect? That she allow a strange woman to strip her naked in his presence so that he may ogle her?

Blake spoke up before she could respond. "Is there a place I can wait in comfort?"

"Of course, my lord. I'll have my assistant bring a chair outside the fitting room."

The woman clapped her hands and called out for help. Almost immediately, a young man appeared and Madame Fleur gave instructions to him in rapid French.

To Victoria's enormous relief, Blake followed the assistant out of the room, through a set of red curtains into the hallway.

The dressmaker watched Victoria with a keenly observant eye. "Now I can measure you, *oui?*"

Victoria turned her back, and the woman unfastened her gown and hung it on one of the brass hooks on the wall. Returning to her customer, Madame Fleur was all business as she handled her measuring tape.

Victoria squared her shoulders, straightened her spine, sucked in her stomach and stuck out her chest at the dressmaker's instructions.

"I have walking dresses in your size on the rack that you can try on now, mademoiselle. For any others you desire, I have sketches you may select from."

At Victoria's nod, the woman hurried from the room and returned with the clothing.

Victoria donned a dress and stepped onto the pedestal before the mirror to view her reflection. The dress was lovely, made from a spotted muslin fabric, with three rows of frills at the hem, and was accompanied by a green spencer. Satin frogs clasped across the bosom on one side and buttons on the other. A matching satin bonnet with a plume of green feathers shading one side of her face completed the ensemble.

"Oh, what a beautiful dress," Victoria whispered.

Her female vanity bubbled up inside her, and she spun around admiring her reflection in the cheval glass.

"Mademoiselle wears my clothing well. You are a stunning woman with your dark hair and green eyes. No wonder monsieur fawns over you."

Victoria stood still, unsure how to respond to the Frenchwoman's comments.

Madame Fleur walked around Victoria, tucking, pinning and smoothing her skirts, and fussing over her like a mother hen would a chick.

"I shall go and get the sketches now," the woman said as she hurried out of the fitting room.

Once alone, Victoria turned again on the pedestal, more slowly this time, enjoying the brush of the airy muslin against her legs. Smiling to herself at her impulsiveness, she stopped before the cheval glass and ran her palms down her skirts.

She looked at her reflection, only to discover herself being observed in the mirror by Blake.

He stood tall and proud in the doorway, his one hand pushing aside the curtains, the other resting on the doorframe. Their eyes met and held, and she shivered beneath the intensity of his gaze.

How long had he been standing there watching her? Had he witnessed her spin before the mirror like an excited schoolgirl?

His eyes lowered to her body, missing no detail, as she stood poised like a prized statue before an art fanatic. Tilting her head to a flattering angle, causing the plume of feathers on her bonnet to bounce saucily, she posed for him. She found herself flattered by his unwavering attention.

His eyes raised and swept over her face approvingly. "You are a beautiful woman, Victoria."

A warm glow flowed through her. She lowered her thick black lashes, trying to mask the pleasure she felt from his compliment. She dared not let him learn how much his opinion mattered to her, or how attracted she was to him.

In a respectful tone she said, "Thank you. The dress is flattering."

He took a step into the room, and the curtains closed behind him. "It's not the dress but the woman that wears it that attracts me."

Blake walked forward, stopping in front of her, until he could reach out and touch her should he wish to do so. Standing on the foot-high pedestal, they were eye level.

He reached up to lightly touch a green plume, then lowered his hand to finger a loose curl at her nape. "The clothes are enchanting, but the essence of you is what is so compelling, what draws me inexorably."

Taking her hand, he spread her fingers open and kissed the sensitive flesh of her palm. He looked into her eyes and asked, "What are you thinking behind those emerald eyes?"

Victoria swallowed, her throat suddenly gone dry like ashes in the wind. Emotions coursed through her with startling intensity. The grazing of his lips on her hand disarmed her, and she struggled to grasp her senses. She lowered her gaze, trying to gain her composure.

Whatever did he mean that her essence drew him to her?

She wanted so much to believe that he cared for the woman she was and not the daughter of the man he held responsible for his demons.

He had yet to release her hand, and his thumb now rubbed her palm with slow, circular strokes, causing her body to tingle from the contact.

"The essence you speak of is nothing more than what attracts all men—the conquest," she said. "Because I reject your advances, you are compelled to continue your pursuit."

"I may have thought so in the beginning, but no longer."

Victoria held her breath, waiting for him to explain, wishing feverishly he would confess his feelings were of love, not revenge.

The rustle of skirts alerted them to Madame Fleur's return to the fitting room.

The trance broken, Victoria pulled her hand from Blake's grasp.

The dressmaker dropped a pile of drawings on a nearby table. "These are the latest fashions. After mademoiselle selects the dresses she likes, we can choose the fabrics and accessories."

Victoria stepped down from the pedestal and approached the pile of sketches. The dresses were all in good taste and many appealed to her.

Making a mental note of how much each garment would cost, she realized she could afford to purchase one dress, plus the one she was wearing. She had brought money with her that she had earned from her investing activities, but she knew it was not sufficient to buy the amount of clothing Blake insisted she order.

Selecting her favorite sketch, she presented it to the dressmaker. "I like this one the most."

Madame Fleur looked puzzled. "Does mademoiselle find nothing else to her liking?"

"The others are lovely, but I must consider the cost, madam."

The woman glanced at her in utter disbelief.

Blake stepped forward from where he stood behind Victoria's shoulder. "Nonsense, my dear. I insist on paying for your clothing while you are staying at Rosewood. In fact, while you are looking at the drawings, you should purchase new evening gowns as well."

"I prefer to pay myself," Victoria insisted.

"I will not hear of it. Your cousinly companionship is worth much more to me," Blake said, a glint of humor in his eye.

He was teasing her again, affectionately, not maliciously, and Victoria felt a ripple of mirth.

He insisted on continuing the charade that they were related, even though it was obvious Madame Fleur knew otherwise. Victoria had a good deal of pride and wanted to pay for her own dresses, and she didn't want to feel obligated to him in any way. But his jesting manner was contagious, and there was more than a grain of truth to his logic.

If the reason she needed new clothing was because he insisted she accompany him everywhere, then shouldn't he pay to dress her?

She brought her hand up to stop him from arguing. "All right, my lord. Just a few dresses."

The next hour was a whirlwind of activity as sketches Victoria liked were studied and others tossed aside. Materials were selected and adornments of silk flowers, ribbons, laces, feathers, fringes and furs chosen. Chemises were ordered from bolts of superfine muslins and linens to wear beneath the new clothes. Matching shoes and gloves of kid leather were picked for the evening gowns and boots, bonnets and parasols for the walking dresses.

Initially hesitant at the large amount of items Madame Fleur encouraged her to purchase, Victoria looked to Blake to gauge his reaction.

He appeared relaxed at the dressmaker's suggestions, and nodded his approval for everything.

Victoria hadn't expected him to be so free with his money, and the fact that he was spending it on her, his sworn enemy's daughter, was indeed stunning.

"You have excellent taste, mademoiselle," Madame

Fleur said. An expression of satisfaction at making such a large sale showed in her eyes. "You will have to return for your final fitting in two weeks."

On the way out of the shop, Victoria felt compelled to acknowledge his generosity. "Thank you, my lord."

He stopped suddenly, looking down at her. "It is I who should thank you, Victoria. You believe it's the conquest—the chase—that attracts me, but I'm certain it is not. I have come to look forward to the time you spend with me. As for the clothing, it's a small gift in exchange for your companionship."

Her breath caught in her lungs at his admission. For the second time that day, he had surprised her.

Weaving their way through the country folk that crowded the streets and shops of the small town, Blake led Victoria to a tiny store nestled between an apothecary and a jeweler.

Victoria was perplexed at the goods displayed in the window, and she stopped to read the sign. "Children's Toys," she read out loud.

"That's right." Blake nodded with a grin and led her into the shop, crammed from floor to ceiling with toys.

He chose a hand-carved wood train with colorfully painted railroad cars and held it up for her inspection. "Do you think Simon will like this?"

A picture of the small boy with unruly red hair hiding behind Maggie's worn skirts flashed through her mind.

Victoria stepped forward and took the toy from Blake. Running the tiny wheels back and forth on her palm, she studied the train's workmanship. She raised her eyes to find Blake watching her, a boyish look on his face that increased his attractiveness.

"It's a wonderful little toy. I'm sure Simon will love the gift."

Blake smiled broadly and, train in hand, turned to pay the merchant.

During the transaction she observed Blake's broad shoulders from behind, and was once again amazed at his attention to the destitute boy that came with Rosewood.

What kind of man would show kindness by buying a poor child a gift yet force his enemy's daughter to live with him out of vengeance?

Blake was an ever-changing mystery.

Returning to her side with the toy tucked beneath his arm, Blake escorted her back to the street.

"We should return to Rosewood. I've kept you out all day. Are you tired?"

"It was a lovely day. I feel wonderful."

With a pang, she realized she meant her words. The quaint country town held a charm that was lacking in the overcrowded shops of London. But it was Blake's companionship that she enjoyed most of all, and the thought made her stomach clench tight.

A row of carriages stood waiting on the curb. The black lacquered coach with the Ravenspear crest stood out from the rest.

Just as the footman lowered a step for Victoria to ascend into the coach, a loud cry pierced the air.

"Miss Ashton! Miss Ashton, is that you?"

Victoria, with a foot perched on the step, glanced uneasily over her shoulder.

A stout woman dressed entirely in black waved vigorously and hurried toward the carriage.

"Miss Ashton! It must be you. It's Lady Taddlesworth."

The woman reached them and positioned herself between the coach and Victoria. "I recognized you from afar."

With a deliberately casual movement, Victoria turned to face the middle-aged woman. Her nerves tensed immediately.

Of all the people to run into while shopping in this small town, Lady Taddlesworth was the most destructive.

As a titled lady, Lady Taddlesworth was an influential chaperone to many of the wealthy, untitled heiresses, and was paid only when one of her young charges made a successful match in the marriage mart. It was common knowledge that the woman's wagging tongue about numerous debutantes had destroyed their chance for a husband and instead secured her own charges those coveted prizes—and Taddlesworth a fat purse.

Victoria smiled, feeling as if the effort would cause her face to crack. "Lady Taddlesworth, what a pleasure to see you."

The woman's beady eyes darted curiously back and forth between Victoria and Blake.

With a feeling of dread, Victoria realized that Lady Taddlesworth was waiting for Victoria to introduce Blake.

Turning stiffly toward him, Victoria said, "May I present the Earl of Ravenspear."

Blake smiled charmingly and inclined his dark head. "I believe we met briefly at Almack's, Lady Taddlesworth."

"Yes, of course, my lord. I never forget a face."

"What brings you to the country during the Season?" Blake asked.

"My uncle's funeral, my lord. A great tragedy."

As if on cue, Lady Taddlesworth pulled a black handkerchief from her reticule, sniffled and then dabbed at the corners of her dry eyes.

"Our sympathies," Blake said, eyeing the severe cut of her mourning gown.

Lady Taddlesworth's dead relative appeared to be suddenly forgotten, for the woman stuffed her handkerchief back in her bag, then craned her neck to look inside the coach for, Victoria supposed, a chaperone.

Victoria imagined the scandalous thoughts that were churning through the nosy woman's mind at discovering an unchaperoned, unmarried woman alone with the realm's most eligible bachelor.

"Miss Ashton, I was not aware your family maintained a country residence," Lady Taddlesworth said, a devious smile curving her thin lips. "You must be Lord Ravenspear's guest, then. Is Rosewood as lavish as they say?"

Victoria clenched her hands by her side until her nails dug into her palms.

So the time has come for my ruin. She had envisioned the humiliation a thousand times since her arrival at Rosewood, but now that it was here, she felt a momentary rush of panic.

All practiced responses flew from her head, and her thoughts scampered like dry leaves in a strong breeze. When she opened her mouth to speak, her voice wavered, then cracked, then was gone altogether. Swallowing the lump in her throat, she tried again. "I uh . . ."

Blake's smooth voice intruded. "Miss Ashton is a guest of my neighbor, Lady Samantha Devon. You are familiar with the baroness?"

His voice was confident, insinuating that anyone worth their title would be personally acquainted with the Baroness of Devon.

Lady Taddlesworth appeared taken aback. "Yes, of course. How is Lady Devon faring?"

"Not so well at the moment, I'm afraid. She has a terrible cold and is sleeping in my coach as we speak."

"Oh, dear, how awful," Lady Taddlesworth said as her

neck stretched to an unhealthy proportion to glimpse inside the dark carriage.

"We must be off. Lady Devon needs to be home in bed."

"Yes, of course." Lady Taddlesworth barely had time to blink before the unlikely pair stepped into the coach and the door slammed in her face.

Chapter 14

The wheels of the coach hit a rut in the country road, causing its occupants to bounce on the padded leather seats.

Blake sat across from Victoria, his long legs brushing her skirts. She looked out the window, her posture stiff, her slender fingers tense in her lap. Even though she remained silent and kept her gaze averted, her anxiety was tangible, as if he could reach out and touch it across the seat.

Studying Victoria's profile, he found her captivating. Her facial bones were delicately carved, her lips full and rounded over straight teeth. Thick lashes fanned the greenest eyes he had ever seen.

It was pointless to deny his attraction to her. Even after all the time he insisted she spend with him, the emerald eyes and raven hair drew him to the point where he found himself devising still more excuses to keep her close.

A mounting frustration grew within him, and he felt like a caged beast within the confines of the coach. Her beauty was a drug, clouding his brain, stealing his logic, destroying his plans.

Since her arrival at Rosewood, nothing had gone as planned. He had intended to flaunt her as his mistress and shame Charles Ashton into social ruin. The perfect opportunity had presented itself this afternoon with the arrival of the notorious gossip Lady Taddlesworth.

But did he take advantage?

When the moment had come, a surge of protectiveness so strong rose within him at the thought of sacrificing Victoria to the malicious woman that he had itched to reach out and choke Lady Taddlesworth by her scrawny neck.

A smooth lie had spurted from his lips, and he found himself tossing Victoria inside the coach and slamming the door in Lady Taddlesworth's pinched face.

The carriage struck another hole in the dilapidated road.

Victoria lurched forward, her hand grasping Blake's thigh for support. All color drained from her face, and she immediately pulled her hand back as if it was scalded, then returned to stare silently out the window.

Every muscle in Blake's body tensed, and beads of perspiration formed on his brow. He cursed himself for allowing his enemy's daughter to affect him so.

He was entranced to the point of distraction. One innocent touch of her hand on his thigh, and he was aching for more, as eager and erratic as a randy schoolboy peeping into his first whorehouse. The feelings were foreign and uncomfortable for a man who had never needed to seduce women into his bed and had parted easily from them without a backward glance.

In his arrogance, he had been convinced that he could overcome her innocence and get her to come willingly to his bed.

But his attempts at seduction, at insisting she spend hours by his side, had served only to drive *him* wild with need.

He was more uncertain now than ever, at a time when he needed to stick to his well-laid plans. Charles Ashton had to be destroyed, had to pay for his past sins—and by Blake's own hand.

Grinding his teeth, Blake was overcome by self-disgust. Where were his sharp and calculating wit, his brutal efficiency?

He had endured a vicious taskmaster and near starvation in the poorhouse, had witnessed his mother's gruesome death in filthy conditions and had toiled beneath the blistering sun in the Indies. Now that he was finally in a position to seek justice, just the sight of Victoria's distress made his gut clench tight and guilt stab at his chest.

He rubbed the back of his head, feeling the throb of a beginning headache.

"Why did you not tell Lady Taddlesworth the truth?"

Blake's head snapped up to look at Victoria, startled by her question as much as by the broken silence. He frowned, not knowing how to answer when he wasn't sure of his own motives.

She stared at him, waiting for his response, her eyes wide as disks, her full lips slightly parted.

Uncomfortable beneath her gaze, he blurted out the first thing that came to mind. "I want to choose the moment, not have it chosen by some annoying gossiper."

She nodded curtly as if his ludicrous explanation made perfect sense. "I would like some warning, my lord."

"Warning? Of what?"

"Of when you do chose to reveal our . . . our arrangement," she stammered.

His fingers ached to reach over and reassuringly smooth her tense hands in her lap. His jaw clenched instead.

"I do not wish to speak of Lady Taddlesworth or our so-called 'arrangement,'" he answered in a tense, clipped voice that warned against further discussion.

She chewed on her bottom lip. "You're angry with me. Why?"

His headache began to build in intensity and pound in the base of his skull. He longed to tell her that he was angry at himself, not at her, but the words died on his lips. He had his pride, after all, and he needed to regroup his thoughts in private and plot his next course of action.

He sighed, and shook his head, letting her know he didn't intend to speak further.

Victoria leaned forward, touched his hand and raised thick lashes to look up at him. "Thank you for misleading Lady Taddlesworth, my lord. You could have easily told her the truth, and even though you had reasons not to reveal our arrangement, I'm still grateful."

At her gentle touch, Blake felt the blood drain from his head and surge in his groin. His heart hammered erratically as sexual arousal and tenderness raged within him.

She had thanked him, by God, and all he wanted to do was straddle her on the leather seat, strip her naked and make love to her the entire journey home.

All that stopped him was the knowledge that she was a virgin and deserved better than a quick toss in a carriage on a bumpy country road . . . and that damnable promise—not to force her into his bed—which he had come to regret ever making.

He lied, Victoria thought to herself, *I don't believe his excuse that he wants to choose the moment of my ruin. I must mean more to him than he cares to admit.* Victoria was gathering her thoughts while pouring tea.

Lady Devon and Victoria were in the parlor at Rosewood. Victoria had told Samantha to arrive when she knew Blake would be occupied with Justin.

"I knew it," Lady Samantha Devon said. Sitting forward on the edge of her chair, she accepted the teacup and saucer. Excitement shone in her eyes ever since Victoria described Blake's odd behavior during yesterday's country outing. "What did I tell you, my girl?" Samantha asked. "I am an excellent judge of male character."

Victoria set down her own saucer and teacup and sat across from her friend.

"No matter his actions yesterday, I'm still convinced that he seeks to destroy my father and plans to use me in some way for that purpose."

"He is not acting like a man who intends to hurt you."

"I cannot allow myself to trust him," Victoria insisted, "no matter how many new gowns he buys me, how generous he is with his money or even how kind he is to his tenants."

"But he protected your reputation not once but twice in the same afternoon. Why would he do that?"

"I have no idea why he lied to Madame Fleur. Perhaps he believes the seamstress will sew better for a man's cousin than for his mistress. As for Lady Taddlesworth, he told me his reasons."

Samantha rolled her eyes. "You don't honestly believe either explanation, do you? Ravenspear wouldn't give a fig what the seamstress thought. He'd accept nothing but exquisite workmanship from her. The only explanation I can think of for his behavior towards Lady Taddlesworth is that he must have been truly concerned for your feelings."

Victoria pinched the bridge of her nose with her thumb and forefinger as she searched the recesses of her mind for a plausible explanation.

Lifting her head, she looked at Lady Devon. "It does seem foolish that he failed to use Lady Taddlesworth's wagging tongue to his advantage. He could still gain satisfaction by bragging about our arrangement at any gentleman's club."

Raising her cup to her lips, Samantha blew on the hot brew. A teasing smile curved her painted lips. "Has he kept his promise not to break down your bedroom door at night?"

Victoria was conscious of the heat stealing into her face. "Yes, although it does not dissuade him from touching me under false pretenses."

"I should hope not, darling. Now do you finally acknowledge that you have power over him?"

"I acknowledge no such thing," Victoria said, shaking her head vigorously. "He has all the power. There is a brick dangling above my head, and I'm to wait until he decides to let it smash down upon me."

"Don't be so dramatic, Victoria. You are to act the coquette like I told you and encourage his feelings for you. That is how you can protect yourself and gain influence."

That's not the only way, Victoria thought. *I can spy and steal his innermost business secrets. And then, one stock at a time, I can punish him.*

Victoria had yet to rummage through Blake's books, and she dared not look within herself to find the true reason.

At first she had told herself it was because she lacked opportunity since Blake insisted she continually stay by his side. Thereafter, she reasoned it was because her father and Jacob Hobbs had yet to contact her with their demands.

But the longer she stayed at Rosewood, the more she discovered about its owner, and the more she admired.

The servants adored him, his tenants respected and admired him, and he cared enough to buy an impoverished boy a toy. She grudgingly admitted that she was better fed and dressed at Rosewood than under her own father's roof.

And as far as she knew, not an ill word had been uttered about her in society.

Perhaps he intended to make her father suffer just from the knowledge that she was living under Blake's roof for an entire year.

Maybe if she could encourage—no, exploit—Blake's feelings for her, then a one-year sentence would satisfy his need for vengeance. If tormenting her father with her absence would suffice, then she need not spy, and Blake need not destroy her reputation.

She was startled at the lurch of excitement she felt by the mere idea of nurturing Blake's affection.

He had once told her that her childhood infatuation had grown into a woman's desire. She had vehemently denied the statement. But nothing could change the fact that he was the most compelling male she had ever encountered. Not only was she battling her fond adolescent memories, but his honorable character traits she had discovered of late made her firm resolve to stay cold toward him begin to melt.

Being forced to spend a year in close quarters with the grown Blake Mallorey would surely strain her self-control.

If Lady Samantha's instincts were accurate—that Blake was truly concerned for her feelings—then there was hope. If Victoria could fan his interest like a slow-burning flame, then perhaps he would grow to care enough for her to not shame her in public.

But could she make him fond of her without ending up in his bed? She was certain that he intended their relationship to expire at the end of the year, and if she allowed him to make love to her, then she would be exposing her heart to devastation.

Victoria looked at Samantha. "How can I make Ravenspear care for me so as not to carry out his mad plan? How can I encourage him, yet keep him at a safe distance?"

"Ah, so you do not intend to sleep with him?"

Would she ever grow accustomed to Lady Devon's directness? "He has no intention of offering marriage and plans to discard me in a year's time."

"But you seek my advice to soften his heart . . . to manipulate him."

"At least then my father will have a chance to keep his commission and pay off the dreaded loans. And I will escape this lunacy with my reputation intact."

"I see." Samantha plucked a grape from a fruit bowl and popped it into her mouth. She cocked her blond head to one side as she chewed, appearing to contemplate the situation. "It may not be as easy as you think despite his recent thoughtful behavior. I don't think Ravenspear is a man you can toy with yet keep out of your bedroom."

Victoria realized her lack of experience could be her downfall, and she immediately said, "Lady Samantha, I'm ignorant on the subject. Please tell me what to do."

"I'll give you a few tips, darling. But first you have to believe in yourself, in your femininity. A woman's power is as old as time itself. It's so strong that men are merely pawns, waiting for the opportunity when a woman's defenses weaken or she chooses to lower them."

Victoria's brows drew together in confusion. "I don't understand. Am I expected to obey his every command with the hope that one day his resolve will weaken, and he will consider my needs?"

"Not at all!" Samantha said. "I want you to do the complete opposite. Men, especially dominant males like Ravenspear, love a challenge. The harder they have to work, the more infatuated they become. Make him exert great efforts for your affections."

"How?"

"Keep him off balance," Samantha said. "Act warm and inviting one minute, then cold as ice the next."

Victoria sat back, taking mental notes of everything the experienced baroness said.

"Flirt with his closest friends beneath his nose. It makes all men raving mad with jealousy. In your case, you have my blessing to trifle with Justin."

Lady Devon's advice sounded contrary to common sense. Wouldn't a man despise and distrust a woman who flirted with his friends?

"You must exude confidence at all times," Samantha said. "A man is drawn to a woman's aura as much as, if not more than, her beauty. And never tell him your true feelings, especially if you love him. If you keep him guessing, he will spend many sleepless nights with his insecurities until he is driven mad with his need to mark you, to possess you, as his own."

"Oh, my," whispered Victoria, sitting motionless. "I had it all backwards."

"Use your sexual power to entrance and arouse him. Find false excuses to stroke his arm, his chest, even his thigh."

A hot shiver rippled through Victoria at the thought of purposely touching Blake in an intimate manner. "More, tell me more."

Samantha shook her head. "I planned on giving you detailed instructions—from what a man looks like naked to what he will do to a woman in bed, to how best to pleasure him—but I've changed my mind. Please do not be angry. My reasons are simple. Your virginity is an extraordinary prize. It is also a lure that gives you enormous power over a man that an experienced courtesan only dreams of attaining."

Victoria held her breath as the idea sent her spirits

soaring. She would love to have enormous power over Blake Mallorey.

Samantha leaned forward. "Men have killed for innocence, have paid treasures to possess it. A dominant male like Ravenspear is a natural-born hunter, impulsively enticed and aroused by the scent of untouched flesh."

Victoria's pulse quickened at the thought, and her fingers fluttered to her lips.

"It is a dangerous game you play with an experienced man like Ravenspear, a man you already have feelings for. Are you certain, darling?"

The warning in Samantha's tone was clear as day.

The true question was: could Victoria lure Blake to her side without losing her innocence, her very soul along the way?

Chapter 15

Victoria's hand trembled as she knocked on the library door.

"Enter," a deep male voice responded.

Victoria swept gracefully into the room. Gifting Blake with an inviting smile, she asked, "If your work permits, my lord, would you like to play chess tonight?"

An expression of pleasant surprise crossed his face. Dropping the papers in his hands, he was up at once and headed for her.

"I'd be delighted, my dear," Blake said. "I'm working on a new company Justin and I have established, but I always have time for you."

With a light touch at her elbow, he led her toward the chess table and held out a chair.

Victoria sat, arranging her flowing skirts. She had taken great care with her dress this evening, choosing to wear one of the new gowns Blake had purchased for her. It was her favorite, made of white silk. Adorned with pink crepe trim and heart-shaped silk buttons, it had puffed short sleeves, and a low, rounded neckline.

She had arranged her hair in the Grecian style with the

front parted, falling in loose raven curls down her back, with a small jeweled comb on one side—another costly gift from Blake. Opals and pearls in the comb enhanced the pure whiteness of the silk gown.

The color of her dress was virginal, and Victoria had selected it with Lady Samantha's speech in mind.

Would Blake's base masculine nature to hunt untouched flesh spring forth at her display of innocence?

More importantly, would it give her enormous power over him?

Blake sat in the opposite chair, and his blue eyes darkened as he gazed down at her. "You look beautiful in white, Victoria."

"You work long hours, my lord. It becomes lonesome in such a large home by one's self."

He reached across the table to grasp her hand, an intense look on his face. "You are never alone here, all you need do is summon me."

She leaned forward, tilted her face toward his and squeezed his hand.

A strange, faintly eager look flashed in his eyes.

A tremor of excitement ran down her spine at his fervent response. Samantha's instructions echoed in her mind—a light touch, a coquettish glance, an inviting smile—they seemed to work so far.

"I'm pleased you came to me, Victoria. Even when you are not near me, you are never far from my thoughts."

Her heart thumped uncomfortably at his smooth words. *Careful, Victoria. You are playing a calculated role. You must not let him entrance you.*

She was convinced he was attracted to her appearance, and only then because she had refused him and pricked his masculine pride. If she ever gave her body to him, the prize would be seized and its value tarnished and diminished. His ego would inflate at the knowledge that Charles Ashton's daughter had thrown herself at Blake Mallorey.

No, she had to keep her wits about her and remember what she wanted, had always wanted—a man that appreciated intelligence before beauty. Such a person was rare indeed, and Ravenspear did not fit this description.

"Would you like wine?" he asked.

At her nod, Blake rose and opened a liquor cabinet in the corner of the library.

Victoria fidgeted with a pawn on the chessboard and stole a sideways glance at his back as he poured two glasses. She wondered how many men were jealous of him. She knew firsthand that the cut of his jacket over his shoulders was not artificially padded to appear broad like many other men's jackets were.

He returned to his seat and raised his glass. "A toast," he said, "to the loveliest chess companion I've ever played."

"To a challenging game," she added as she raised her wineglass to his. "I'm quite good, you know."

"I never thought otherwise, my dear."

After playing for an hour, it was evident they were evenly matched. The flowing wine heated her blood, and Blake's steady conversation calmed her nerves. He talked about the improvements he planned for Rosewood's tenants and mentioned his idea for updating the kitchens for Cook.

Remembering Lady Samantha's advice, Victoria set out to listen attentively as he spoke, but she soon realized there was no need to feign interest. He did not speak extensively about himself like Jacob Hobbs did. Rather, Blake discussed the needs of the people who depended on him for their livelihood and care.

She grudgingly admired his driving intelligence and creative solutions to improve the lives of his tenants and servants. She made suggestions of her own, and to her surprise, he did not dismiss her ideas outright but agreed with several of them.

Blake then turned the topic of the conversation to her childhood.

Victoria, suddenly uneasy, toyed with a marble chess piece in her hand, turning it this way and that.

"Forgive me if I made you uncomfortable," Blake said. "I meant only to learn what happened to you and Spencer after I left. Spencer and I were boyhood friends, remember? I have no interest in ruining an unexpectedly pleasant evening by resurrecting our fathers' past."

Raising her eyes from her lap to look at him, she saw the sincerity in his expression, and his tone soothed her. The tension eased from her shoulders, and she returned the pawn to its position on the chessboard.

"We moved to London on my twelfth birthday," she said, "two years after you left. By then, father had officially gained membership in the Stock Exchange and he needed to be in the city. At first, Spencer and I missed country life terribly, but we soon realized the advantages London has to offer and adjusted to city life."

"I take it Spencer did not waste time in immersing himself in London's pleasures."

She eyed him warily. "You're already aware of his preferences for gambling and drinking."

"I'd be lying if I said I wasn't disgusted by Spencer's lack of discipline. I suspect he is capable of much more." Blake leaned slightly forward, his blue eyes intense. "But I'll say this, I have no intention of calling in the debts Spencer owes me. I never have."

"I feared you had brought Spencer's markers with you when you came to our town house that morning. I thought you were going to tell Father what Spencer had done."

"Your father doesn't know?"

She shook her head. "Not the extent of Spencer's habit."

"Then he shall never learn of it from me. I promise you. My quarrel is not with Spencer."

Relief flooded her at the knowledge that Blake had no ill feelings toward Spencer. Her irresponsible brother had his fair share of creditors hounding him without his having to also worry about his significant debts to Ravenspear.

"Let us continue playing," Blake said, offering her an arresting smile, "although I'm enjoying the conversation as much as the game."

"Me too," Victoria said, and she realized she spoke the truth.

They played until the hour grew late, yet there was still no clear winner. They agreed to leave the pieces untouched and return to the game another night.

Blake carried their wineglasses to a table close to the fireplace, and she joined him on a sofa.

Sitting side by side, she found herself extremely conscious of his virile appeal. His familiar cologne, sandalwood and cloves, stirred her senses. She stole glances at his handsome profile and couldn't help thinking that she would have given anything to spend a similar evening with him in her youth.

If only their circumstances were different . . .

Blake passed her wineglass to her, and she drank deeply. It was an unusually cool summer evening, and a low fire burned in the fireplace.

"Is there anything you need, Victoria? I want your stay at Rosewood to be comfortable."

"Mrs. Smith sees to everything. She is quite competent."

"I apologize if my selfishness in forcing you to stay by my side has grown tedious. If you are bored during the day, you may ride the grounds or visit Lady Devon at any time."

Watching you will never become tedious. Blurting out the first thing she could think of to cover her wayward thoughts, she said, "I miss Spencer and my mother."

"I can arrange for them to visit."

Victoria knew her father would never permit either to visit without him accompanying them. And she doubted Blake would allow Charles Ashton to cross Rosewood's marble threshold. Yet, she found herself saying, "I'd like that."

The warmth from the fire combined with the heady effects of the wine caused a tingling in the pit of her stomach.

He set down his glass on an end table and turned to look directly at her. His expression stilled and grew serious as he studied her face unhurriedly, feature by feature.

She tried to quench the dizzying current racing through her at his intense perusal. *Control yourself. This is a tactic, not a lovers' tryst.*

Edging closer, he trailed a finger down her cheek. "Never before have I been attracted to a woman's intelligence and wit as much as her beauty. You are a rare treasure indeed."

Her heart hammered at his admission. It was as if he knew exactly what she was thinking, what she wanted most of all, and delivered the smooth words at the precise moment.

Plucking the wineglass from her limp hand, he set it next to his, then returned to her side. He leaned forward slowly, his gaze dropping to her lips, and she knew he meant to kiss her.

"I'd like to kiss you, Victoria."

She froze as his mouth came coaxingly down on hers. His lips feather-touched hers with tantalizing persuasion. She released a pent-up sigh and rested a quivering hand against his warm chest. Feeling the solid power of him beneath her palm, she sat with eyes half-closed and kneaded the rock-hard muscle beneath his shirt.

He groaned and, putting a large hand to her waist, drew her close to him. The pressure of his kiss increased, and her mouth parted beneath the domination of his lips. When his rough tongue brushed against hers, an unbidden shiver of wanting coursed through her. She kissed him back, lingering, savoring every moment.

Blake's insistent fingers splayed through the hair at her temples and held her captive for his mouth's plundering. His lips seared a path, seeking the sensitive skin of her eyelids, behind her ear and down her neck. His moist mouth reached the low neckline of her gown, and her nipples firmed instantly in response. When he gently nipped at the swell of a breast, she gasped in surprise, and liquid heat pulsed between her legs.

All her inhibitions dissipated beneath a smoldering need that begged for satisfaction. Her head fell back of its own volition, her hands reached up to clench his shoulders, and her spine arched forward in submissive offering to his continued ravishment.

Blake stopped suddenly, breathing heavily. His expression was strained, passion burning in his blue eyes. "Tell me you want me, Victoria. That you don't want me to stop."

"What?"

"Tell me," he demanded. "I need to hear you say it. That you want me to touch you."

Her mind fuddled. His words were slow to penetrate the haze of passion that threatened to overwhelm her. What was she doing?

Her plan to soften his attitude yet keep a safe distance had been easily unraveled by his skillful fingers. It was clear that she could not be in close proximity to him and still keep her senses. In the back of her mind was the nagging truth that all that kept her from lying with him tonight was *his* self-control in keeping his promise not to force her into his bed.

She pushed weakly against him. "I cannot."

Easing back to study her face, Blake rubbed her trembling bottom lip with the pad of his thumb. "I promised not to force you, swore that you would come to me as a woman full-grown, embracing your sexuality. The intense attraction between us is rare between a man and a woman. It should be appreciated, explored and savored. Even in your innocence, you recognize the heat when we touch. Your body cries out for more, is begging for release. All that keeps us apart is foolish stubbornness."

Victoria touched her swollen lips with cold fingers. Could she lie with this man, give him her innocence, knowing his true motive was pure revenge? More importantly, knowing there was no future?

"I'm sorry," she whispered. "It is more than just stubbornness. I cannot give freely the part of myself I value most."

She rose on shaky legs and left the library, knowing a night of restless sleep awaited her.

Blake watched her leave, his body tightly coiled and tense, ready to explode into a thousand pieces. He must have her soon. She responded with fire to his touch, like a ripe fruit begging to be picked.

Only honor and his wretched promise had stopped him from pushing her back onto the soft cushions and raising her silk skirts. Even though he felt she would not have protested, would, rather, have urged him on eagerly, his pride demanded that she ask him to make love to her—or, at the very least, acknowledge her own passion.

He took a deep breath, focused on his labored breathing, and counted to ten. His body was slow to calm, his arousal that strong.

Tonight, he had jumped at her offer to spend time together, never once searching for the true meaning behind her invitation.

Not true, he thought.

The moment she stepped into the library looking like a virginal temptress come to rob him of his mind and his senses, disbelief and suspicion had clouded his brain. But as quickly as those thoughts developed, they vanished beneath a need so great it made his mouth water. Unbelievably, as he roused her passion tonight, his own starving need grew stronger.

"Christ," he swore out loud as he ran his fingers through his dark hair. Starting to rise from the sofa, his palm pressed a hard object deep into the red cushions. Glancing down, he picked up a marble queen and frowned. It was the piece she had last moved. She must have dropped it when he had first kissed her.

It had not surprised him how adept she was at chess. A complicated game, he enjoyed strategizing his next move against a worthwhile opponent.

And she was a challenging player. With the wine flowing freely, she had played passionately, enthusiastically, and her eyes had shone with excitement. It was in the middle of the game, when she had chewed her lower lip as she contemplated her next move, that he was struck with the realization that he admired her intelligence even more than he enjoyed her beauty.

A combination that could easily unman him and deter him from his purpose.

Every moment they spent together made it more difficult to focus on the reason he had brought her to Rosewood.

Reaching for the pillow she had leaned on, he raised it to his face and inhaled her unique fragrance. As the sweet scent of lavender tickled his senses, a picture of long raven curls contrasting against flowing white silk flashed in his mind.

How much could a man take? How much longer could he live with her, have fantasies about her, and not bed her?

He now wanted much more than avenging the greedy, traitorous enemy whose selfish deeds resulted in the ruin of the Ravenspear family.

The simple had now become complex. His goals were changing—to seduce her, for sure, yet shelter her from her father's rage afterward.

Chapter 16

Victoria stared at a note in her trembling hand, her brain in tumult. "What did you say?"

A disheveled boy, who had popped out of a nearby alley to hand her the note, looked at her as if she were an idiot.

"'Tis from a gent who paid me to deliver it to ye. He said you'd be expectin' him to contact ye."

Beneath the torn brim of the hat that the boy wore pulled down to his ears, greasy brown hair hung down and framed his dirt-smudged face. His skinny bare ankles protruded from ill-fitting trousers, reminding her of some of the street urchins she had often seen scurrying about London.

Victoria looked about on the crowded street, bile rising in her throat. "Is my father here? Now?" Her voice sounded strained to her own ears.

She turned back to the boy, but he was gone, disappeared in the throng of shoppers and street peddlers.

Clutching the note in a tight fist, she hurried back to the spice shop she had walked out of when the boy had startled her by grasping her arm and thrusting her father's message in her hand. Glancing into the establishment's bay window, she searched until she spotted Lady Devon sniffing samples of tea leaves in the back of the store.

After last night's encounter with Blake, Victoria had gladly accepted Samantha's invitation to go shopping this morning. She desperately needed time away from him to clear her thoughts.

The crumpled paper grew damp in her sweaty palm. The urge to reread the missive, to study it line by line, was overwhelming. But she was determined to keep its contents private. Only after Samantha started haggling with the shopkeeper did Victoria feel confident to unfurl the paper and reread it more carefully.

I will send Spencer next week to collect what you have gathered. Do not disappoint me.

Charles

He hadn't even signed it "Father," but "Charles" instead. It sounded as if he was giving orders to one of his underlings in his official capacity as a Junior Lord Commissioner of the Treasury. The cold tone of the letter, combined with its content, sent a chill down her spine.

The fact was, she had gathered nothing. There had been little opportunity and even less desire to spy.

But the time had come for her to make a decision.

Just then, bells jingled behind her, and Samantha exited the spice shop.

"Victoria, where have you been? I found the most amazing chamomile-and-mint tea." Samantha proudly held up a tin of tea leaves. "It's said to miraculously ease abdominal pain during a woman's monthly courses." Cocking her head to one side, her eyes raked Victoria's face. "What's wrong? Have you been crying?"

Victoria, as nonchalantly as possible, pulled out a

handkerchief from her reticule and at the same time pushed the note to the bottom of the bag, hiding it from Lady Devon's view.

"'Tis nothing," Victoria said, dabbing at the corner of her eye. I simply have something in my eye."

Victoria hated lying to her friend. But if Samantha knew the truth, then her loyalties would be torn—and she would have to choose between maintaining Victoria's secret and confiding in Justin Woodward. Victoria did not want to come between the two lovers.

Samantha looked at her curiously. "You're certain? You're not still thinking of last night, are you?"

Victoria had told the baroness about last night's debacle in her attempt to soften Blake yet keep him at a distance—minus a few heated details.

"I can't seem to forget how easily I lost my focus," Victoria said. "I must seem like a failure to you."

"Nonsense, my darling. I told you that you didn't fail, but to the contrary, you have him eating out of the palm of your hand. You just don't see it yet."

Taking Victoria's arm, Samantha guided her to an awaiting coach. "You do not look well; we should return to Rosewood."

As the coach pulled into Rosewood's white stone driveway, Victoria's tension mounted. She had been unusually quiet on the drive home, and, thankfully, Lady Devon did not question her.

Her friend believed she was reliving a kiss from Ravenspear, when in truth, she was deciding whether to steal from him instead.

Unsure whether the master of Rosewood was out of the house, Victoria tiptoed across the marble vestibule and up the staircase. She hoped to reach her room unnoticed, but to her dismay, she heard a bedroom door open and close. She hadn't yet reached the top step, and she froze as Blake met her at the landing.

Clutching the polished banister, her eyes moved upward from his shiny black Hessians to his broad chest before meeting his gaze.

They had not seen each other since last night's chess game. Blake had departed early in the morning with Justin to ride the estate. Victoria had burned her tongue drinking her morning cup of tea in her haste to leave before Blake had returned.

And now, as she stared into his compelling blue eyes—the color even more intense in his bronzed face—she was reminded of her sleepless night, tossing and turning in bed, thinking of his touch, his embrace, his heated kiss.

She couldn't deny the truth any longer.

There was strong passion within her, and Blake Mallorey had the power to unleash it at his whim. Her vow to entice him without succumbing to his masterful touch could shatter beneath his persuasive lips.

He watched her with a curious intensity, like a predator would its prey.

"I missed you this morning, Victoria," he said. "I left very early, and when I returned, Mrs. Smith advised me you had departed for the day."

"I decided to listen to your suggestion and spend more time away from Rosewood with Lady Devon."

Blake moved aside, allowing her to step up to the landing. With quick strides, she hurried to her bedroom door, all too aware of his long legs keeping him easily beside her.

As her hand touched the brass doorknob, she hesitated. Was he going to follow her into her room? She opened her mouth to protest, then closed it, unsure what to say.

"I wanted to ask you if . . ." Blake faltered, looking about as if to find the right words in his head. "Would you like to attend the theater with me this evening? The town has a good production and the actors are quite talented and have received good reviews by the critics. Of course, it's not as exceptional as London's Drury Lane Theatre, but good nonetheless."

If Victoria didn't know any better, she would swear he sounded nervous.

Blake Mallorey, fifth Earl of Ravenspear, apprehensive?

She turned to face him squarely, her back to the door. "Are you asking me to attend a public event with you unchaperoned?" she blurted out.

Had the time finally come for him to reveal their relationship? Then why ask her permission?

"You misunderstand," Blake said. "My intentions are only to enjoy your company for an evening and see a fine show. I have a private box at the theater, and we don't have to arrive until the lights are dimmed and the production begins. It will be difficult for anyone in the general audience seated below to see us together."

When Victoria shot him a doubtful look, he rushed to continue. "If it makes you more comfortable, I shall request Justin and Lady Devon to join us. To all appearances, Samantha will be your chaperone."

The idea of attending the theater sounded wonderful to Victoria, but she was still hesitant.

Then she recalled her conversation with Samantha. Maybe all wasn't lost after last night? Perhaps Blake's attitude had softened—just a touch—toward her already.

"I'd be delighted to go if Mr. Woodward and Lady Samantha agree to accompany us."

A shadow of disappointment crossed his face but was

quickly masked with a contented look. "Wonderful. Can you be ready by seven?"

"Don't you need to speak with Mr. Woodward first?"

"Of course. But I'm certain Justin and Lady Devon will be pleased to accompany us. I'll come for you at seven."

He offered her a charming smile, then turned on his heel and strode down the hallway, his confidence obviously returned.

Shaking her head in disbelief, Victoria opened her bedroom door, turned the key in the lock and collapsed in a wingback chair by the window. Minutes passed before she felt secure enough to pull her father's note from her reticule.

Her stomach still churned with anxiety over the surprise delivery. The large hearth in the corner of the room caught her attention and, jumping to her feet, she threw the dreaded paper into the vacant fireplace. Lighting a match, she touched an edge of the note, and then watched as the corners curled and blackened as it burned.

What choice am I going to make? she wondered.

If she listened to her father, then she had not one second to spare, for rummaging through Blake's voluminous papers would take hours, days, even.

A picture of his massive library desk, piled high with dense files, flashed through her mind. No, she would have to search the recesses of her mind to recall bits and pieces of conversations she had overheard while Blake and Justin had talked business in the library, over dinner, during cards and wherever else they had spoken in her presence.

The note had completely burned, no evidence of its existence except the tiny pile of ashes that remained, and still there was a terrible tenseness in her body. If only Victoria could deal with her father's plans as easily as she had with his missive.

There was no doubt in Victoria's mind that Charles Ashton would soon seek her out through an emissary—either Spencer or Jacob Hobbs would do his dirty work. He would never jeopardize his position on the Treasury Commission.

But no matter whom he sent, Charles would demand results.

Victoria paced her bedroom, then entered the sitting room and walked around aimlessly, her mind racing. Her father didn't know of her investing ability or knowledge. Only Spencer knew the extent of her activities, and her brother would never reveal her secret.

She could lie to Jacob and her father by telling them she rummaged through Blake's documents but couldn't make sense of anything. If she put on a convincing act—the helpless, flustered female—they would believe her. They would never imagine a woman capable of understanding the complexities of the London Exchange, let alone earning money investing in it.

And the truth was, she didn't want to spy on Blake Mallorey. He had kept his word not to force her into his bed, had seen to her every care and need, had even gone to lengths to protect her reputation—most notably from the malicious gossip Lady Taddlesworth. And, lo and behold, Victoria's conscience was bothering her. Even though he had forced her to reside at Rosewood, she fought a daily battle to maintain her resentment toward him.

She could live like this for a year, and then return home with the yoke of Blake's debt lifted from around her father's neck. Maybe then her life could return to her normal, predictable routine.

But deep down inside, she knew she would never be the same after living with Blake Mallorey. How could she forget such a powerfully attractive male that she had feelings for as far back as she could remember, and who could send her insides aflutter with no more than a sideways glance? She knew that any man she encountered in the future she would compare with Blake Mallorey. She had no doubt that all others would fall far short.

With sudden clarity, Victoria knew what course of action she would take. She smiled a secret smile and opened the doors of her wardrobe, intent now on choosing a gown to wear for tonight's theater outing.

"You can lie to Father," she mumbled out loud. "You've been doing it for years, and he's never suspected a thing. Why worry now?"

Chapter 17

When the Ravenspear coach and team of six stopped before the Berry Street Theatre, Victoria felt excitement bubble up inside her.

Ever since Blake had mentioned the theater tickets this morning, she had looked forward to the play. A frequent attendant of London's Drury Lane Theatre, she hadn't realized how much she had missed the experience.

Leaning forward in her seat, Victoria raised the tasseled window shade of the coach to get a better look. Through the building's large bay windows, she could see the well-dressed gentlemen and ladies parading around the lobby while they sipped glasses of bubbly champagne.

Much like London, she mused, *the mingling is just as important as the quality of the production.*

"If it would make you more comfortable," Blake said, "we could wait inside the coach until the play starts and everyone is seated."

Victoria met Blake's gaze, taken aback at his remark. He mistook her curiosity of the crowd for anxiety. He had been considerate all evening, informing her that Justin and Samantha agreed to accompany them and ensuring that his private box was high enough and sufficiently dim to keep curious eyes at bay.

His good manners had made her even more fretful regarding her father's demands.

She was aware of Blake's stare as he awaited her response, and, once again, she swore he appeared uneasy.

Is he worried I'll change my mind and not enter the theater? Where is the calm, collected and composed earl?

"Waiting is not necessary since Mr. Woodward and Lady Devon are with us," Victoria said, looking at the attractive couple seated across from her.

Samantha smiled and reached across the seat to squeeze Victoria's hand. "To anyone that asks, Victoria is a dear friend of mine who has come to enjoy the fresh country air and escape the oppressive London gossipers."

Blake cocked an eyebrow at Samantha's dramatics, then opened the coach door and hopped out. Holding out a hand to Victoria, he asked, "Shall we, then?"

She placed her hand in his, and his long, tapered fingers grasped her firmly as she stepped down. With just one touch, she was instantly aware of his strength and dominant masculinity.

As the two couples walked into the lobby, they drew attention. Stealing a glimpse at Blake's devilishly handsome profile and commanding manner, Victoria understood the crowd's fascination.

Tonight Blake wore light brown trousers that hugged his flat stomach and thighs. His double-breasted jacket, a darker shade of brown than his trousers, was perfectly tailored to accentuate his broad shoulders and tall, lean frame. A crisp, snowy-white cravat was tied at his throat, and superfine linen ruffled down the front of his shirt and at his shirt cuffs.

After observing Blake's meticulous attire, Victoria was

relieved she had dressed with care. She had chosen a gown of pale-pink silk with full short sleeves, adorned at the bodice with crystal beads that shimmered in the candle-light. Her raven tresses were piled high upon her head, with loose curls framing her face, exposing her neck and low-cut neckline.

Almost immediately, people came over to greet them. Most sought to acquaint themselves with the newly re-turned Earl of Ravenspear, and it became apparent that Blake did not socialize frequently enough to satisfy the curiosity of his country neighbors. Many shot curious glances toward Victoria, and she began to have doubts about her decision to accompany Blake in public.

Lady Samantha must have sensed her tension because she edged closer to Victoria in silent support.

Several young gentlemen elbowed their way through the crowd to stand before Victoria. They bowed gallantly as they introduced themselves.

One, Nathan St. Bride, was more daring than the rest, and his lips lingered a moment too long on the back of her hand. A wiry man of average height, he had an aquiline nose, straight forehead, and dark, observant eyes. His thick, tawny-gold hair curled around his ears and matched the twirled tips of his mustache. Strong cologne wafted from his body, overpowering the perfumes of the women surrounding her.

"Lady Devon, where have you been hiding your rav-ishing friend?" The man spoke to Samantha, but his gaze never left Victoria's face.

"Hiding?" Samantha asked coyly. "We've been out and about town all week long, Mr. St. Bride. Where have you been, sir?"

Nathan St. Bride smiled broadly at Victoria, revealing

pearly, even teeth. "I must socialize more if I'm missing such beauty."

From a sideways glance, Victoria was conscious of Blake's watchful glare. A muscle near his eye twitched, and his fists balled at his sides.

An unexpected thrill ran down Victoria's spine at Blake's jealous response. She recalled Lady Samantha's advice about flirting with other males to inspire jealously and rivalry in Blake. She had doubted the wisdom of the baroness's odd advice, but Victoria was beginning to see its usefulness.

She smiled sweetly at Nathan and laughed at one of his jokes.

Behind St. Bride's shoulder, Blake's nostrils flared, and his jaw clenched, hard as a lump of granite.

"Will you allow me to call on you, Miss Ashton?" Nathan asked.

"I don't think that's possible, Mr. St. Bride," Victoria answered, alarmed at his forwardness. "Lady Devon keeps me busy, and my time in the country is limited."

She was willing to flirt with St. Bride in the safety of a public place, but she had no desire to further acquaint herself with him in private.

Nathan leaned forward and whispered so that only she could hear. "Ah, I understand. You're with the earl and can't talk freely in public, can you?"

Stunned, Victoria stepped back. How did he know? She was spared from having to answer when Blake approached her side.

Blake touched her elbow lightly, urging yet protective. "The play will start soon," he said, shooting Nathan St. Bride a stern look. "We should take our seats."

Allowing Blake to lead her away, they made their way to his private box. She had little time to think about

St. Bride's remarks before the curtain opened and the production began.

As the actors played their parts, Victoria sat mesmerized, absorbing every word, lost in the story. Only when the curtain fell, signifying the interval, did she turn her head. Samantha and Justin then excused themselves to seek refreshments in the lobby, and Victoria was left alone with Blake.

She turned to look at him and found him studying her.

"That was beautiful," she said. "Thank you for bringing me."

"I enjoyed watching you more than the play itself. I had to drag my eyes from you, afraid that others would notice. You look lovely tonight."

She sat as still as a mouse, and her heart turned over in response to his eloquent words. She was flattered by his interest despite herself, and was highly aware of his dark sensuality. Everything about the man attracted her tonight, from the one lock that fell a little forward over his dark brow, to the distinctive muscle of his thigh pulling against his trousers, to his familiar cologne.

"I have something for you." He reached into his double-breasted jacket to pull out a red velvet box. "It reminded me of you, and I hope you like it." Placing the box in her hand, he coaxed, "Go on. Open it."

Victoria's heart beat fast as she lifted the lid. Her throat went dry at the sight of an exquisite emerald necklace nestled inside folds of red velvet. The size of a pigeon egg, the green gem was surrounded by brilliant diamonds and glistened in the candlelight.

She had never held, let alone worn, such a costly piece.

"It's beautiful," she whispered, awed by the gift. Raising her eyes to meet his, she searched his face for an answer. "Why? Why would you give me this?"

"When I first saw it, I was drawn by its emerald beauty, but when I studied it up close, when I touched it, I was enchanted by its fire and its depth and knew I had to possess it, for it had completely captivated me."

The double meaning of his words blared like a trumpet inside her head. He alluded to the effect she had on him, not only to the necklace she currently held in her limp hands.

Entirely caught up in a wave of emotion, she tried desperately to throttle the dizzying currents racing through her.

"I cannot . . ." she began, looking down at the jewel in her lap. "Thank you, but you know I cannot accept it." She snapped the lid shut and handed back the box to him.

He stopped her in midmotion. "Please. It would give me great pleasure to see you wear it."

A frown creased her brow. "But it's such a lavish gift, and the reason I agreed to come to Rosewood for an entire year is to pay off my family's debt. It makes no sense for you to give this to me."

"It's your father's debt, Victoria, not yours. Besides, my motives are not entirely selfless. I receive just as much pleasure from seeing beautiful things on you as you do wearing them."

Reaching for the box, he lifted the necklace from the velvet folds and leaned close.

She raised a hand. "A man would only buy his wife or a kept woman such a costly gift. Despite what you would have my father believe, I'm *not* your mistress."

He arched a brow. "No one is more aware of that fact than I am, my dear. But unlike such a man, I do not expect anything in return. Do you believe me?"

She did. He had not yet made any sexual demands on her other than a few stolen kisses which she had more than encouraged him to take.

"I believe you," she said, "but I'm not certain . . ."

"I am."

He unhooked the clasp and reached around her neck. His fingers barely grazed her skin, yet her flesh tingled from the contact. Her lids fluttered, and she inhaled his masculine scent. The M-cut collar of his jacket tickled her nose as he leaned forward, and she suppressed the urge to rest her cheek on his shoulder.

Blake sat back. His eyes clung to hers and then lowered to her neck. "As I thought, the emerald matches your green eyes exactly. Beautiful."

She swallowed hard, once again stunned by his sweet flattery. The emerald lay between the valley of her breasts, the gem heavy, yet cool. With trembling fingers, she touched the large stone. "You must stop, you know. It's madness, really."

"What must I stop?"

"The things you say to me . . . the way you look at me when you say them . . . it's all inappropriate."

"I speak the truth." He reached out to tuck a loose curl behind her ear, and her skin prickled at his touch. "Would you have me lie?"

"What of the items you've already purchased for me? The clothes and accessories. This necklace."

"I promise," he said earnestly, "I expect nothing in return. You can take everything with you when you leave Rosewood."

Her heart fell at the finality of his words. Why should she care if he talked about her departure after a year? Isn't that what she longed for?

She hesitated, torn by conflicting feelings. "I suppose I could use the necklace when I return home."

A flicker of emotion passed over Blake's face before he hid it with a smile.

What had she seen? Regret? Disappointment?

Just then the heavy curtains in the rear of their private box parted, and Lady Samantha and Justin entered.

"We brought you champagne," Samantha said, handing Victoria a bubbly flute.

The baroness sat, adjusted her voluminous skirts and then turned toward Victoria. "Oh, my!" Samantha gasped as her gaze dropped to Victoria's neck. "How stunning! No wonder you didn't join us in the lobby." Her wide blue eyes swung from Victoria to Blake. "What has transpired between you two since our brief fifteen-minute break?"

Blake gave Lady Samantha an exaggerated wink. "I gave Victoria a gift. Does it not match her green eyes to perfection?"

Samantha laughed richly. "You charming devil, Ravenspear."

Heat stole into Victoria's face. "I have not yet decided to accept such an expensive gift."

"My darling girl," Samantha said, leaning close to whisper into Victoria's ear. "Have I not taught you anything? Only an infatuated man would give a woman he has sworn not to coerce into his bed such a costly jewel. You are exceeding my wildest expectations. Of course you will accept it."

The lady leaned back, a wicked smile on her face as she turned toward Justin. "I hope you follow Ravenspear's lead, my love. I'm particularly fond of rubies."

Justin kissed the back of her hand. With a twinkle in his eye, he said, "I refuse to be outdone by my rogue employer."

Samantha giggled as the curtain rose once more, signaling the start of the second act.

Victoria sat still through the rest of the play, but this time, she was more entranced by the man by her side and

he emerald nestled between her breasts than by the actors
on the stage.

After the play, she sat in the coach listening to Samantha and Justin discuss the performance in animated detail.
Victoria stole sideways glimpses at Blake's rugged profile.

He was an ever-evolving mystery, an enigma she feared
she would never begin to comprehend. A man sworn to destroy her father, yet a man she found irresistibly attractive.
A man who had forced her to leave her home and threatened
her way of life, yet a man whose consideration, charm and
generosity heightened her girlhood fascination to a woman's
obsession.

She remained unmoving next to him, aware of the heat
from his hard body coursing into hers. A war of emotions
raged within her. She was unwilling to face him directly,
yet unable to turn away completely.

When she was finally alone in her bedroom at Rosewood, she allowed her false composure to unravel. Sitting at her dressing table, she plucked the pins from her
hair and dropped her head in her hands. She massaged her
scalp with rigid fingers, hoping to ease the tension that had
built inside her skull.

Totally bewildered at his behavior tonight, a tumble of
confused thoughts and feelings assailed her. She felt like
a sailor lost at sea, treading water and barely holding his
head above the waves.

For a woman who had always had a plan, had always an-
alyzed things with remarkable detail, Victoria's swirling
emotions paralyzed her to the point where all logical decisions and actions were impossible.

Chapter 18

The following morning, Rosewood's coachman dropped off Victoria at Lady Devon's country estate. The baroness's country home was not as large as Rosewood but was still an impressive piece of property, with acres of landscaped grounds and a white stone mansion which boasted twenty bedrooms.

As soon as Victoria stepped over the entryway, Lady Samantha flew down the curved staircase to greet her.

"My darling girl, tell me you wore the necklace so I can get a closer look."

Taking Victoria's cloak and tossing it to a servant, Samantha whirled Victoria around by the shoulders and peered at her neck.

As if on cue, the emerald sparkled in a ray of sunlight that beamed through the windows.

"Magnificent," Samantha said, her eyes as round as saucers. "I all but fell off my chair last night when I set eyes on it. I was dying to count the diamonds surrounding the piece, but had to force myself to stay seated."

"Ten," Victoria said, her voice flat, emotionless.

"Ten what?" Samantha's brow furrowed in confusion, and her eyes never left the necklace.

"Diamonds. Ten brilliant diamonds surround the emerald."

The gleam of excitement was back in Samantha's eyes. She reached out to run a finger across the stone's smooth facets. "It must have cost Ravenspear a small fortune."

"Exactly. And that's why I hate it."

Samantha's head snapped up to study Victoria's face. "You're upset." Her shrewd gaze traveled over Victoria's fatigued features, the dark circles beneath her eyes.

The baroness took Victoria by the arm and led her through the house. "My butler, Samuel, has arranged tea outside by the gardens. I've always believed fresh air helps with anyone's troubles."

Tea service was on a charming patio overlooking immaculately tended lawns as far as the eye could see. Large pots of blooming flowers lined the perimeter of the brick patio, and the air was as fragrant as a heady perfume.

A cup and saucer were placed before Victoria as she gazed at the chirping birds splashing gaily in the birdbath. She felt a flash of envy at the birds' carefree display of happiness.

"I don't understand him," Victoria said. "The angry earl that came to my father's house and threatened to send us all to the poorhouse is not the same man I have lived with for the past two months."

"You care for him," Samantha said matter-of-factly.

"I don't want to. I hate myself for it. What kind of woman am I to have feelings for a man bent on ruining my father?"

Samantha sighed. "A flesh-and-blood woman with a pure heart."

"But I *desire* him. What does that make me?"

"A better person than me, my darling. If I was in your situation, I would have left my bedroom door ajar a month ago."

At Victoria's scowl, Samantha cocked her head to one side. "Have you ever considered that what Ravenspear says your father has done in the past is true?"

"No," Victoria blurted out, but she knew it was a lie. "I suppose," she mumbled, then finally whispered, "Yes."

The truth was she had thought about it incessantly since Blake Mallorey had returned into her life, his youthful smile gone, replaced with a hard man's bitterness.

Victoria had witnessed her father in business, had seen his ruthlessness. Hadn't he been willing to give her to Jacob Hobbs against her wishes, only to turn around and sell her to Blake Mallorey without even a word of apology to her?

Yes. She had contemplated Blake's version of the truth. It would explain many things, such as Blake's honorable behavior since her arrival at Rosewood versus his cold-hearted attitude toward her father.

But could Charles Ashton have sent his former partner, his closest friend, along with an innocent family, to the poorhouse all those years ago?

Yes, she thought. *If there was profit or position in it for him.*

A man clearing his throat drew the women's attention. Samuel, the butler, stood in the doorway, his stance rigid and his face impassive, as if he had not overheard the topic of the ladies' conversation.

"You have a gentleman caller, Lady Devon." Raising a gold-embossed calling card, Samuel read, "A Mr. Nathan St. Bride awaits in the parlor."

"Well, well." Samantha looked at Victoria. "It seems

you made quite an impression at the theater, and eager St. Bride has come to call."

Pushing back her chair, Samantha rose and motioned for Victoria. "Come along, darling. We must be sure Ravenspear hears about this visit. I enjoyed the dark scowls he threw Nathan's way last night as much as you did, I'm sure."

As soon as the shock of the butler's announcement subsided, Victoria jumped to her feet and grasped Lady Samantha's arm. "Wait! I do not wish to see Mr. St. Bride. What shall I tell him if he inquires further about my circumstances?"

Victoria was astonished that Nathan St. Bride would be so forward as to call on her when she had made it clear she was not interested.

Samantha patted her hand reassuringly. "You have nothing to worry about. He already believes you are my guest, and it's quite convenient that you are presently under my roof. We need not make excuses regarding your whereabouts. Your reputation is quite secure. Besides, amorous attention from an attractive man is always good for a woman's self-esteem."

But as Victoria followed Samantha through the house, her misgivings increased.

When they entered the parlor, St. Bride had already taken advantage of the baroness's hospitality and sat in a leather chair to drink a hefty glass of port despite the early hour.

He jolted upright when he spotted them, sloshing a good amount of the amber-colored alcohol on his buff-colored trousers. He dabbed at the stain with a kerchief, then straightened his shoulders and cleared his throat.

"Lady Devon," he said, bending over her hand. "It has been too long since I paid my neighbor a visit, and seeing you at the theater last night reminded me of my lack of good will."

"Oh, nonsense!" Samantha laughed. "You're here to see my lovely guest, Miss Ashton."

St. Bride's meticulously trimmed mustache twitched in amusement. "Ah, you were always perceptive in matters of the heart, Lady Devon."

He turned toward Victoria and smiled. "I confess. I found myself entranced, Miss Ashton, and I wanted to see you again."

The strength of his cologne was as overpowering as she had remembered, but now mingled with pungent alcohol, the scent assailed her nostrils.

Nathan was not an unattractive man—most would consider him handsome in an effeminate way—but the depth of his stare unnerved her and alerted her to tread with care.

Victoria remained standing, not wanting him to sit and get comfortable. "I'm flattered by your visit, sir."

Samantha stepped forward. "Would you like some refreshments other than your port, Mr. St. Bride?"

"I would love some, Lady Devon." Nathan smiled, revealing straight, white teeth.

"No doubt," Lady Samantha said, a mischievous twinkle in her eye as she turned to leave. "Good help is difficult to find these days, so I'm certain I will be a while," she announced over her shoulder.

Don't leave us alone! Victoria wanted to cry out, but the baroness had already departed. No doubt Samantha's intentions were to inflate Victoria's self-worth by putting her in the same room with the smitten man. Samantha may even have Ravenspear learn of the encounter with the hope that Blake would become jealous. Either way, every fiber in Victoria's body warned her against Nathan St. Bride, and she regretted flirting with him.

He stepped closer and touched her hand. "Your hostess is very generous to allow us time alone together."

Victoria resisted the urge to snatch her hand from his, and instead pulled away politely. "I do not wish to mislead you, Mr. St. Bride. But as I told you last night, my time as Lady Devon's guest is limited."

He laughed softly and took a step closer. "Now, now, Miss Ashton. There's no need to continue the charade when we are alone."

Victoria felt a stab of annoyance at his forthright behavior. "Whatever do you mean, sir?"

"Don't be coy, Victoria. I saw the way the earl looked at you at the theater, the way his hand lingered at your waist under the guise of escorting you to your seat. Such intimacy between a man and woman cannot be feigned."

Her shock yielded quickly to fury. "You're out of place to speak so inappropriately." She stepped back until her thighs brushed the settee. Unwilling to sit with him towering above her, she raised her chin in defiance. "There is nothing between the earl and me but friendship. You have an overactive imagination to believe otherwise."

Nathan continued to advance, causing Victoria to bend backward at a precarious angle. Her arm flailed for support, grasping the back of the settee.

"Mr. St. Bride!" she protested indignantly.

He leaned forward, his expression lustful. "An overactive imagination?" He shook his head curtly. "I don't think so. I know that I did not conjure up Ravenspear's possessiveness toward you. But at the present, with you so close, my imagination is running wild."

With a large hand against her shoulder, he pushed her down onto the couch and was on top of her in an instant. He pressed his lips against her ear as he leaned his weight upon her. "How did a man with such a sordid past get a mistress as beautiful as you?"

"How dare you!" Victoria screeched. She struggled violently, beating against his chest, but he was not to be dissuaded.

He pushed her deeper into the cushions. "Don't worry," he rasped. "Ravenspear never need find out."

"Get off me!" she demanded.

"Quiet," he admonished. "I must have a taste, sweet Victoria. I can't control myself. Surely if you're so generous with Ravenspear, you can spare me a scrap of affection."

He smothered her lips with his in a forceful kiss as he moved his hands downward from her bare shoulders to the rounded neckline of her gown. Squeezing her breasts roughly through the thin silk fabric, he plunged his hand beneath to pinch a tender nipple.

Victoria squirmed and bucked beneath him and opened her mouth to scream, but his cruel mouth smothered her cry. His mustache scraped against her sensitive skin a moment before he bit down on her lower lip.

A sharp pain pierced her lip, and the metallic taste of her own blood filled her mouth. Panic engulfed her, and she knew she had to alert Samantha or another to come to her aid. When St. Bride laid his full weight upon her and continued to stifle her cries with his mouth, she felt as if her breath was cut off and feared passing out.

Suddenly St. Bride was seized from behind and ripped off her, and he yowled in protest.

Blake's face was a glowering mask of rage as he threw St. Bride across the room.

The man landed hard on his backside against an oak bookcase, toppling leather-bound volumes on his head. The heavy bookcase teetered on its edge until gravity prevailed, and it came crashing down beside St. Bride, causing a cacophonous noise. Clearly dazed, St. Bride struggled fitfully to rise. Blake grasped the back of his collar and threw him headlong toward the door.

"Out! Before I change my mind and dismember you."

St. Bride scrambled to his feet and ran out of the room as if pursued by the Devil himself. His footsteps echoed down the hall, and, seconds later, the front door opened, then slammed shut in his haste to leave.

The tight knot within Victoria began to ease, and she collapsed on the settee.

Blake rushed forward and kneeled before her. "Are you all right? Did he harm you?" His brows drew together in an agonized expression, his features tense.

"I . . . I'm fine now," she said, her voice wavering.

He reached up and brushed her swollen lower lip with the pad of his thumb. He withdrew his hand, stared down at the smeared blood on his finger, and his mouth clenched tight.

"The bastard," Blake hissed. He withdrew a kerchief from his waistcoat and dabbed at the bruised flesh.

"Thank you," she said, taking the kerchief from him to press it firmly against her lip.

The floorboards creaked behind Blake. Victoria leaned aside to see Justin Woodward standing awkwardly by the door. She hadn't realized he was in the room but assumed he had entered with Blake.

What was either of them doing at Lady Devon's home?

Justin came forward to touch her hand, his kind brown eyes filled with worry. The familiar lock of blond hair fell on his forehead, giving him a youthful look despite his years.

"Is there anything I can get you?" Justin asked. "Shall I summon Samantha?"

Just then light steps could be heard on the hardwood

floors, and Lady Devon burst into the parlor. She halted, shocked at the scene of the tumbled bookcase and dozens of books scattered across the floor. Her wide eyes traveled to Blake kneeling before Victoria and Justin holding her trembling hand.

"Whatever happened?" she asked. "Where's Mr. St. Bride?"

Blake rose to his feet. "Gone for good, if the man has any brains."

Justin quickly stepped forward to stand beside Samantha. "We arrived just in time to find St. Bride mauling Miss Ashton. Ravenspear took care of the man."

"Oh, my poor darling!" Samantha cried and ran to sit beside Victoria. "Will you ever forgive me for leaving him alone with you?"

Victoria managed a shaky, reassuring smile. "I'm truly fine. Nothing happened."

"Nothing happened, madam!" Blake roared. "I had to pry that groping defiler off your body, and you call that 'nothing'?"

Victoria was caught off guard by Blake's flare of temper.

Samantha's hand flew to her mouth. The lady appeared as if she was on the verge of tears for placing her friend in such a vulnerable position.

Justin's lips thinned with anger as he gazed at Samantha in disapproval for her apparent role involving St. Bride.

A tense silence enveloped the room, adding to Victoria's uneasiness.

"If you'd leave us," Blake said, addressing Justin and Samantha, "I'd like a word in private with Victoria."

Lady Samantha opened her mouth to protest, but quickly shut it when Justin shot her a cold look of warning.

The couple wordlessly exited the room, and Victoria was left alone with Blake.

Immediately she rose, and sensing his bridled anger, sought to soothe his temper. "Thank you for your help. Neither Lady Samantha nor I could have possibly suspected his behavior."

Blake whirled around, towering above her. "It's no wonder that dainty dandy behaved the way he did after the way you displayed your wares for him last night. A man can only stand so much taunting from a beautiful woman."

"What?"

"I decided to accompany Justin to Lady Devon's house to escort you back to Rosewood myself. Imagine my surprise when I found you reaping the rewards of your flirtatious efforts."

"You blame me?" she asked incredulously. "You think I somehow encouraged St. Bride to attack me?"

"Didn't you?"

"You're mad!" She turned her back quickly, her skirts swooshing around her ankles, fully intending to leave the room.

His hand shot out to grasp her arm and spin her back around, his fingers steel bands encircling her flesh. "Had I not shown up when I did, you'd be lying on that couch"—he jerked his head toward the settee—"with your skirts up to your neck, and a fop fumbling with his breeches on top of you."

Victoria felt her stomach flip-flop as the horrible image his words evoked flashed through her mind.

She tried to pull her arm from his viselike grip, suddenly desperate to be away from him, from his penetrating gaze. "Let me go."

Dragging her close instead, his face was mere inches from hers. His eyes were black and dazzling with fury. "You belong to me, Victoria. You're bought and paid for this year, and no one will touch your body but me."

She felt her face drain of color. How dare he! Her mood veered sharply from fear and anxiety over escaping rape to fury over Blake's cold remarks.

"You are insane!" she screeched. "You're angry because a man treated me like a woman of loose morals when that is exactly what you set out to accomplish from the beginning. It would destroy my father to have society learn that his daughter had become a whore."

He released her arm, and glared at her with burning, reproachful eyes. "Not a day goes by, my dear, that I don't reconsider my strategy and have my justice swiftly by challenging Charles Ashton to a duel. No matter what weapon he chose, I could end it instantly once and for all."

The hair at her nape rose on end at the finality of his tone. "Then why don't you issue your challenge?"

"I prefer to prolong his suffering."

Like a pair of scorpions with their tails raised ready to sting, they circled each other dangerously.

"You unfairly blame my father for everything done to you," she said, "yet no jury or judge has ever issued a guilty verdict."

"You defend him like a doting daughter, blinded by loyalty to his true character, never considering the possibility that he is capable of betrayal."

Victoria felt like laughing at that. Her a doting daughter? Never. More like a child whose behavior vacillated between defiance and fear while growing up with such a disciplinarian for a father.

"You cannot possibly hold Charles Ashton responsible for your father's . . . your father's . . ."

"Suicide?" Blake finished, his voice curt. "I know full well that my father put a pistol to his head and blew his brains out. That is a fact I have to live with all my life. But what you don't understand is that a man can be forced into such dire circumstances where he truly believes there is no other alternative."

"I find it difficult to believe my father could push yours into taking his own life."

"What could you, a mere woman, know of business dealings?"

It was on the tip of her tongue to tell him she knew more than most men, that she, a mere female, was a talented investor, who, with enough time, hoped to support herself in style one day *without* a man's assistance. But she bit her lower lip to stay quiet.

Her knowledge was an ace up her sleeve, one she may need to protect herself from the ruthless men threatening her way of life.

At her silent glare, Blake continued. "You refuse to believe the possibility that Charles Ashton is capable of evil."

"Whether he did what you say is irrelevant," she snapped. "Perhaps your anger is misdirected at my father instead of at yours for killing himself and leaving your family alone. You should consider *that* possibility."

A shadow of grief crossed Blake's face before the familiar mask of bitterness descended once again. "That does not excuse the fate that befell my remaining family thereafter. I can forget what I endured, but I can never forgive my mother's and sister's suffering."

Some of the fight left Victoria at the mention of the demise of the Mallorey women. Though Blake tried to conceal his sorrow, she clearly recognized the fleeting emotion on his face.

His grief was deeply buried beneath layers of hatred, which over the years had seeped into his bloodstream, spread like pestilence and poisoned his being.

"I am sorry. I had heard your mother died of consumption from the workhouse's poor conditions, but I never knew what happened to your sister, Judith." His sister had been the eldest child in Blake's family, and from what Victoria remembered Judith had been softly feminine and reserved.

Blake exhaled through clenched teeth. "The specific facts of her death are of no consequence."

Sensing she evoked painful memories, Victoria touched Blake's arm. "It was long ago. Perhaps it's best if we all forgot."

Blake's head snapped up, his nostrils flaring like a provoked beast. "There is no doubt in my mind that Charles Ashton is responsible, and I will see justice done. Our short discussion today has reminded me that I have been dallying from achieving that goal. Simply put, my dear, you have distracted me. But no more."

Victoria stood stunned as he dropped her limp hand from his sleeve and turned and strode away.

Chapter 19

"Fill it to the brim."

Justin raised the crystal decanter once again and filled Blake's glass with the expensive brandy. "At the rate you're drinking, why not bring out the cheap liquor?"

Blake laughed and leaned back in his chair. "Because there isn't any inexpensive alcohol in Rosewood's cellars."

Justin rested his elbows on the table and studied his longtime friend and employer. After they had returned from Lady Samantha's, Justin had followed an irate Ravenspear directly to his rooms.

Victoria arrived home much later, insisting on having the coachman drive her back separately to Rosewood—a wise choice, in Justin's opinion.

Both Justin and Samantha had overheard the loud row between Ravenspear and Victoria that had obviously put Blake in such a foul mood. The master of Rosewood had immediately requested a glass and decanter as soon as he stepped foot in his house. He was determined to drink himself senseless. It wasn't beyond Justin to provoke his friend when he believed it was deserved.

"I take it that this afternoon you destroyed the headway

you had worked so hard to achieve with Miss Ashton?" Justin asked, a mischievous glint in his eye.

Blake frowned. "Don't be so cocky, Woodward. From the looks of it, you and Lady Samantha weren't getting along very lovingly."

"Checkmate," Justin said, raising his own glass in mock salute. "I wasn't pleased with Samantha's involvement with Nathan St. Bride. If I know my scheming woman, she arranged to have Victoria and St. Bride alone to prick your jealous nature. But then when things spun out of control, she did regret her actions."

Blake drummed his fingers beside his glass on the table. "We argued about her father. I suppose you overheard. She had the audacity to insinuate that my anger is misdirected at Charles Ashton instead of at my own father for committing suicide."

Victoria's words continued to replay in Blake's mind. The truth was, she had touched a nerve, and Blake did not want to consider any possible accuracy behind her statement. If it wasn't for Ashton's betrayal, his father would not have been driven to take his own life, and his mother and sister would be alive.

Blake made a look of disgust, then said, "She blindly defends him."

"Do you blame her?" Justin asked.

"Her opinion matters naught to me," Blake said tersely. "As I told her, I can forget the hell I went through, but never that of my mother and sister."

"Does she know?"

"Of my mother's sickness only. Not Judith."

"Perhaps you should tell her about Judith," Justin suggested.

"What good would it do? The details would sicken her,

and in Victoria's naiveness she may misunderstand, or worse, compare herself with Judith."

"Then you are back to the beginning of your wooing."

Blake tipped his head back as he drained his glass and then slammed it on the table. "Damn, I've been a fool. I've allowed her to weaken my resolve, to distract me from the one thing that has burned in my belly and kept me alive all these years."

Justin shrugged a shoulder. "She is a very beautiful woman. And she's living under your roof, sleeping across the hall. As a further temptation, even a blind man can see that she is drawn to you."

Blake cursed in frustration. "I should be able to break down her bedroom door, strip her naked and throw myself on top of her. Then, after I have sated this damnable hunger, I should feel no remorse in using her humiliation to destroy her father."

"Ah, but you must not be the savage you thought you were. And I don't think you can use her as casually as St. Bride intended himself."

At the mention of Nathan St. Bride, Blake's gut clenched. His mind burned with the memory of the eager fop straddling Victoria.

A blinding fury had nearly knocked Blake off his feet at discovering the pair. Then a stark fear that Victoria had been hurt, or worse, violated, panicked him into violent action. Both emotions were unwelcome and frighteningly unfamiliar.

What had come over him?

Yes, he wanted her in his bed, wanted to make love to her. He imagined daily every position and way he could take her. How much longer could he bear having her near, sleeping mere yards away, without tossing her on the bed and burying himself deep within her?

But what would his lust cost him?

Cockiness had made him swear not to force her into his bed, so confident was he that he could resurrect her childhood infatuation and inflame her woman's sensuality. That vow now taunted him—as if when he promised never to treat her as a mistress, then knowing he was forbidden to touch her, she had become the woman he must possess.

Each night as he lay in his large bed alone, he desired to go to her. It would be so easy, to cross the hall and unlock her door. But his damnable pride would not relent.

How could he beg any woman, let alone his enemy's daughter, to have him?

Blake jerked his fingers through his hair, pulling the roots away from his forehead until his scalp stung. Exhaling slowly, he dropped his hand. "She is ruining my plans."

Justin chuckled. "Hardly. You may have temporarily lost your head by a pair of pretty emerald eyes, but I assure you, as your bookkeeper, everything is precisely on schedule. I reviewed the ledgers yesterday, and you will sleep soundly when I tell you how successful Illusory Enterprises has become. Who would have thought that high-pressure steam engines would have become England's most valuable technology, and that thanks to Charles Ashton, your investment would become your most lucrative so far."

Blake cocked an eyebrow, his interest clearly piqued. "I had thought our luck had run out when you told me the only company in all of England that manufacturers the steel pistons that can handle such enormously high temperatures was co-owned by Charles Ashton and Jacob Hobbs."

"Ah, but our subsidiary has been quite successful. Illusory Enterprises has been buying the parts we need directly from Ashton and Hobbs for two months, and the high-and-mighty commissioner has been none the wiser."

"Hah! Freeing you from that workhouse was the wisest decision I've ever made. Ashton would choke on his own bile if he knew."

"There's more," Justin said, his eyes twinkling with mischief. "Our spy on the Treasury Commission says Charles has been 'borrowing' money from the Treasury for personal use and replenishing the 'loan' before the accountants have noticed."

Blake's pulse pounded as he leaned forward. "Just as we expected—his greed shall be his downfall."

Long before Blake set foot in London, he had carefully concocted Charles Ashton's ruin. Blake knew that his enemy's avaricious nature would result in his own demise. By stealing from the Crown, Charles Ashton had committed treason and had cinched the rope around his own neck.

"Deceiving the old bastard thrills me," Blake said with a hard, cold-eyed smile. "Invest more money in Illusory Enterprises' activities. Increase our orders from Ashton. After all, how will he ever know?"

I must do this. He leaves me no choice.

Victoria's hands trembled as she fumbled with the locked desk drawer. Scanning the surface of the crowded desk, she spotted a shiny silver letter opener. The handle was engraved with a fancy *R* for Ravenspear, probably a costly trinket from one of his admirers, but the sharp tip was what interested her.

Grasping the device with a sweaty hand, she inserted the tip into the lock and gently tried to pry open the desk drawer. A bead of perspiration dripped down her forehead into her brow, and she wiped it away impatiently with her free hand.

After a minute of twisting and turning, it became evident that the letter opener would not work unless she broke the lock, which was not an option.

If the slightest suspicion was raised, all would be lost.

She glanced nervously at the closed library door. She prayed Blake and Justin were long into the bottom of their brandy glasses and had no intention of visiting the library tonight.

After returning to Rosewood from Lady Devon's, Victoria had overheard Mrs. Smith talking to Cook about the master's unpleasant mood and coarse demands for alcohol and privacy. Victoria had seized the opportunity, knowing that after their heated argument in Samantha's parlor, she must act to protect herself.

Despite Blake's past kindness and quizzical behavior, he had made no declarations of love. To the contrary, he had been brutally honest with her this afternoon about his goals of vengeance and her usefulness in attaining them.

So she had snuck past the servants unnoticed and shut herself in the library.

If she had learned anything from growing up beneath her father's roof it was that information was power, which could be used to hurt an adversary or to defend yourself. With no other means at her disposal, she concluded that she had to learn as many of Blake's secrets as possible. What she did with the information afterward was an entirely different dilemma she would worry about later.

But her plans would fail if she couldn't open the file drawer containing Blake's most sensitive documents.

Feeling overheated, not knowing if it was from the sun beating down on her back through the large window behind the desk, or from her nervousness, Victoria pushed damp tendrils of hair behind her ears that had escaped the knot at the base of her neck.

Her fingers brushed against a hairpin, and she felt a rush of excitement as a solution came to mind. Plucking the pin from her hair, she stuck it in the lock and went to work.

Within seconds the lock sprung free and the drawer rolled open.

It was a large drawer, more than a foot deep and two feet long. Rows of brown folders, with hand-printed tabs identifying the contents of each, were filed in alphabetical order.

She recognized Justin Woodward's meticulous block handwriting on the tabs, each letter capitalized in bold black ink. Every piece of paper in the folders was clean, unwrinkled and stacked evenly. Not an edge was curled or earmarked.

She stared in amazement. It seemed the loyal and intelligent Mr. Woodward wore many hats—Blake's man of affairs, bookkeeper, accountant, friend and confidant being just a few.

Starting at the letter *A* and quickly thumbing through the alphabet, Victoria was amazed at the vast array of stocks Blake owned and the numerous lucrative businesses he had started.

He owned stock in Russian and Baltic companies which imported timber, oil, tallow, hemp and seeds. He imported wines from Southern Europe, mahogany from West Africa, and rare carpets from Armenia, India, Persia and China. He was a member of the Society of Lloyd's which collectively underwrote marine insurance. He had an arrangement with the East India Company to store goods in his riverside warehouses—tea from India and Ceylon, pepper, snuff, saltpeter, furniture made from exotic woods, embroidered hangings, ivory, silk, brocades, arrack, spices, cloves, nutmeg and mangoes. There were also receipts for purchased Treasury bonds—a stack two inches thick.

The list went on. Blake even owned old ships that sailed to Barbados and Virginia with any cargo they had need of.

To the inexperienced eye, his investment choices seemed haphazard—a mix of small and large corporations, with a sprinkling of bonds.

He was exceptionally diversified, and she wondered at his strategy. She had thought the extent of his business involved sugar, rum and coffee from the West Indies. But the more she studied his records, it became clear that Blake Mallorey may have earned his initial money in the Indies, but that he had amassed his fortune by more diversified means.

Her father's and Jacob Hobbs's investment plans were much simpler. Based on the current market, they would pick a stock that was presently a moneymaker, and sink all their capital into it in order to gain as much profit as quickly as possible.

The concern with such tactics was that one had to be ahead of other investors in anticipating the peak before the stock became inflated and its value depreciated before it could be sold. Their methods involved high risk but high profit as well, if one predicted the market accurately.

Victoria had long suspected that her father's position on the Treasury Commission ensured him access to confidential financial information that other members of the Exchange lacked. She knew that Charles Ashton would not hesitate to use such information to make money—even if he had taken an oath of office not to do so.

Unlike her father's investment, many of Blake's appeared to yield relatively low profits initially but had the potential for huge returns.

Flipping open files, Victoria discovered numerous stock

picks which had enormous monetary returns. The figures were astounding, proving once again that her father's debt was a measly sum, a drop in the bucket for the fabulously rich Earl of Ravenspear.

A pen and piece of paper caught Victoria's eye. She dipped the quill in an inkwell and set to furiously jotting down the stocks Blake had owned for more than a year. These were his income producers—his bread and butter. Next, she recorded his newest investments—some subsidiaries of existing corporations—all with a higher level of risk.

One of Blake's companies caught her eye, initially because of its unusual name, Illusory Enterprises, but then because of its primary product.

High-pressure steam engines.

Victoria had read about this revolutionary new technology in the *The Morning Post* and *The Times* over a year ago. She had been surprised when her father and Jacob Hobbs had purchased the sole manufacturer in all of England of certain parts for such engines.

Her memories of Hobbs bragging about such a fact were pure and clear.

So where was Blake getting his parts?

An inkling of suspicion heightened her senses.

The second hand of the longcase clock ticked on, an ever-nagging reminder of her limited time. But with abrupt clarity, she knew she had stumbled onto something important.

Shifting through a stack of invoices, her hands so sweaty now she feared leaving splotches on the paper, she finally found what she was searching for.

There, in the purchase column were prior orders for high-pressure steel pistons from her father and Jacob to Illusory Enterprises.

Blake was buying parts from her father and Jacob without their knowledge!

It was then that the real purpose behind the subsidiary name, Illusory Enterprises, became clear. It was just an illusion to trick her father into selling Blake what he needed most. She should be offended, but instead was awed by Ravenspear's creativity and craftiness.

Heavy footsteps down the hall caused warning spasms of alarm to erupt within her. Thrusting the invoices back in their file as orderly as her shaking hands would allow, Victoria pushed the file down in place and slammed the drawer shut. She folded the piece of paper and thrust it in her skirt pocket.

As she hurried around the desk, the library door opened.

Blake entered, taking several strides forward before noticing Victoria standing in the middle of the room.

"What are you doing here?" he demanded.

His speech was slurred. His normally immaculate attire was in disarray. The jacket and cravat were gone, and the top three buttons of his shirt were undone, revealing the corded muscles of his throat and mat of hair on his chest. His dark hair was ruffled as if he had run his fingers through it over and over, and his normally piercing blue eyes were bloodshot and red as if he had spent a month in a smoky pub.

Victoria's nerves were so frayed that it took her a moment to comprehend that Blake Mallorey was stinking drunk.

"Well?" he asked.

At his gruff tone, she instinctively took a step back. "I . . . I came here to read . . . to be alone."

Blake swaggered forth. "Then you should have chosen your own bedroom, my dear. There isn't a more quiet or lonely chamber in this entire mansion."

Standing less than an arm's length away, he reeked of alcohol and cynicism.

"Is your sarcasm necessary?" Victoria raised her chin a notch and faced him squarely with false bravado.

She was perspiring as if she had run the perimeter of Rosewood at full speed. The incriminating paper she carried felt like it had burned a hole through her skirt pocket and singed the flesh at her waist with a capital *T* for thief. Her composure, which she usually prided herself on, was now a fragile shell around her. Her stomach churned with anxiety from the need to escape from his disturbing presence before her crime was discovered.

"I apologize, then, if I disturbed your solitude. But we ran out of brandy," Blake said.

He bowed mockingly, then went to a tall cabinet, opened the doors and withdrew a crystal decanter full of amber-colored alcohol.

He turned around, brandy in hand, and walked behind a leather chair. He rested his forearms on the back of the hammerhead chair, leaning forward, letting it support his upper body. The decanter dangled from his right hand, the liquor sloshing within it. His tailored cotton shirt, no longer starched stiff, was stretched tightly across his broad shoulders and emphasized his sinewy strength.

He held up the decanter. "The closest stash to my room, you see."

She shifted uneasily from one foot to the other before finding her voice. "Now that you've found me, I'll leave you to your drink." She turned to escape.

"Wait."

Victoria's hand froze before it could touch the door-knob.

"Have a drink with me."

"I don't think—"

"Just one drink."

She turned to face him. He held up two glasses, and she wondered how he could move so swiftly, as intoxicated as he was.

Blake poured her two fingers' worth and filled his glass to the rim.

Victoria hesitantly accepted the drink.

"A toast," he said, raising his glass.

"There's nothing to celebrate."

Glassy blue eyes shone like cobalt. "Of course there is. What about my rescuing you from the overly amorous Mr. St. Bride?"

Her heart skipped a beat. "I'd rather not drink to that."

"Then what?"

"A truce," she offered expectantly.

"Ah. You'd prefer to forget what was said this afternoon and go back to the way things were between us."

"Is that such a bad idea? If we are to spend a year under the same roof, can we at least be civil?"

"Civil?" he repeated, arching a dark brow. "Just splendid," he said in a voice that suggested he was anything but pleased. Some of the alcohol from his glass spilled onto his lace cuff, staining the white fabric. Blake was oblivious as he finished the brandy in one swallow.

Mimicking his actions, Victoria raised her glass to her lips and swallowed. The potent alcohol burned her throat and every inch of her esophagus, all the way down to her stomach, and she coughed. The effect was instantaneous, warming her blood and taking the edge off her frayed nerves.

Blake laughed. Stepping close, he plucked the empty glass from her hand and set both his and hers on the end table. Returning to her side, his gaze dropped to her mouth, and his eyes darkened. He raised a finger to trace her full bottom lip.

"Although I drank to your suggestion, I can think of many other words to describe what I'd prefer our relationship to be other than *civil*."

The pad of his forefinger on her mouth made her pulse skitter alarmingly. He stood so close she could feel the heat from his body. Her fingers ached to stretch forth and caress his lips. Instead, she grasped his wrist and removed his hand.

"Stop."

His eyes shuttered and his expression hardened. "Unfortunately for you, there is no going back, no possible truce. What was said, in anger or not, was the truth. You have succeeded in reminding me I have been delinquent in carrying out my plans."

"What do you mean?"

"I've been far too lenient for too long. Pack your bags, my dear. We're returning to London."

Chapter 20

Footsteps echoed down the city street. Breathing heavily, Spencer turned down a dark alley and spurted recklessly forward.

His eyes were blinded by the darkness, for the light from the city gas lamps did not illuminate the narrow alley. He felt his way along the wall's bricks as fast as he dared, scratching his hands on the rough surface as he moved.

He ran headlong into a solid object, and pain burst through his skull like a firecracker. Precious seconds passed before he realized he had collided with a large iron box. The foul smell of rubbish that assaulted his nostrils alerted him that he had smashed into a trash receptacle for the nearby building's tenants.

Gasping, he rested his hand against the box until his head cleared.

Footsteps splashed through a puddle at the entrance to the alley, then stopped.

Panic welled in his throat. His pursuer suspected he was in the alley.

There was nowhere left to run. He had to act fast.

Without further thought, Spencer scrambled into the iron box and buried himself in the refuse.

The stench was overpowering. Bile rose up in his throat, and he gagged. He thrust his fist in his mouth and bit down hard on his knuckles to prevent himself from vomiting and alerting his pursuer to his location. All manner of putrefaction touched his skin—rotten food, sewage and even a decomposing dog.

The scrape of booted feet came close, and then stopped. Two men. Slayer's enforcers.

Spencer ceased to breathe. He wondered wildly how he had gotten himself in this predicament. He had felt confident when he had entered the Cock and Bull and struck a deal with Slayer. But Spencer had lost heavily at the tables that night. His losses had been so sweeping and great that he had later suspected Slayer had stacked the deck.

Ever since that night, Spencer had been looking over his shoulder—for as soon as he had failed to make Slayer's payments, including the outrageous interest, Slayer had sent his lackeys after him.

Slayer's message was clear: pay up or he would take in flesh and blood what was owed him.

Spencer's legs became numb in the cramped space. His misery was like a steel weight crushing his chest. The only person he could confide in, who could help him, was out of reach to him.

Vicki. For the first time in his miserable life, he had tried to help *her,* and he had once again made a mess of things.

One of Slayer's men cursed. "The weasel got away."

"He must have turned down another alley," a gruff voice answered.

"We'll find 'im, we will. He may be the commissioner's son, but he don't have much of a brain."

"Aye, I'm lookin' forward to beating the rat to a bloody pulp, I am."

Coarse laughter echoed off the alley walls, and then the departing footsteps of the two men.

Heart beating frantically, Spencer eased his cramped limbs out of the receptacle. Malodorous waste clung to his hair, face and clothes.

He wondered how long he had to live.

I cannot believe I'm back in London.

Victoria looked out the window at the people scurrying about the street. A powerful storm was brewing, and the crowd below rushed about for cover. The wind howled, blowing leaves from trees and swirling debris from the street into the faces of pedestrians. Well-dressed men clutched the collars of their frock coats tight about their necks in an effort to keep the wind at bay. Those with tall-crowned hats pulled their curled brims down over their ears to shield their ruddy faces.

As the first fat raindrops fell from the sky, the gas lamps hissed and steamed in the street like angry dragons.

Despite the warmth and dry air inside the room, Victoria rubbed the goose flesh on her arms. Stepping away from the window, she let the lace curtains fall back into place.

She was in Blake's London town house on St. James Street. The popular address, as attested by the view from the street, was mostly inhabited by wealthy bachelors.

All one had to do was drive by to see the establishments that lined the street—White's, Brook's and Boodle's being the most famous. So much was it a male magnet, that if a

woman was observed in an open carriage or walking along
St. James after dusk, she was labeled of questionable character.

Victoria dared not analyze the real reason Blake had
brought her here.

Wandering about the room, she studied her surround-
ings. Gone was the delicate rose-hued wallpaper with
matching bedspread and quilt. Her new bedroom was decorated in peach tones with dark mahogany furniture.
A large four poster with a superfine gauze canopy dominated the room. On one side of a fireplace was a tall chest
of drawers and on the other side stood a sturdy wardrobe.
Through a set of double doors was a small sitting room.

It was tastefully done, and Victoria could find no fault
with her accommodations. But at the same time, the dark,
bold furniture was obviously masculine and, in contrast,
the peachy color very feminine.

The room smelled and appeared freshly painted. Victoria could imagine the servants scurrying about in haste to
transform a masculine guestroom into a suitable lady's
suite in order to meet their master's demands on short
notice.

It was clear that Blake's bringing her here was not expected or planned.

Slipping from her room, she stopped to listen. She
hadn't seen Blake or Justin since her arrival this morning.
Back at Rosewood, Blake had advised her that she would
be traveling to London alone and that he would arrive by
separate coach thereafter. He had been short with her since
their quarrel at Lady Devon's. Their altercation in the library had not improved his mood.

She had no desire to run into him, and she looked about
the empty hallway to ensure she was alone.

Her stomach growled noisily, reminding her that she

hadn't eaten since leaving Rosewood. Creeping down the hall, she descended the grand staircase to the main floor before Mr. Kent, Blake's ever-present butler, intercepted her.

"Would you care for luncheon, Miss Ashton?" Mr. Kent asked.

Victoria's stomach rumbled at the mention of food. Cheeks flushing, she said, "Lunch sounds lovely."

The butler nodded and motioned for her to follow. "This way, Miss Ashton."

Mr. Kent was tall and paper thin, with a perpetual bloodhound expression, and had impeccable manners and a discreet nature, which was an invaluable characteristic for a bachelor's butler. He had been respectful since her arrival, seeing to her every need.

If he was curious about an unmarried lady's presence in the household, he did not show it. Mr. Kent's polite demeanor reminded her of Mrs. Smith, Rosewood's heavy-set housekeeper, and Victoria wondered what orders Blake had given the head of both households.

She followed the butler through the vestibule just as the front door burst open, and a gust of wind blew loose tendrils of hair in her face.

"What a God-awful storm." Blake's voice boomed above the howling wind.

Brushing her hair from her eyes, Victoria saw Blake and Justin, cloaks billowing around them, dripping wet in the entryway.

Mr. Kent rushed forward to close the heavy door. "It's wonderful to see you back, my lord." Taking Blake's and Justin's sodden cloaks, Kent continued, "And you as well, Mr. Woodward. Will you be spending the night?"

"Just tonight," Justin said.

It was then that Blake noticed Victoria standing behind

Mr. Kent. A fleeting expression of relief crossed his face before the corners of his mouth curved into a smile.

Why? Did he think she would have fled to her father's home the moment she returned to London?

Blake peeled off his damp leather gloves and handed them to the butler. "I take it our guest has been shown to her rooms and her every comfort seen to?"

Mr. Kent nodded. "Of course, my lord. I was just escorting Miss Ashton to luncheon."

Blake's blue eyes traveled from Victoria's face down to her feet. "I'm famished. I shall join Miss Ashton."

Justin chuckled behind Blake. "I'm not as famished as Lord Ravenspear and would rather change clothes before I eat."

Justin winked at Victoria, then followed Mr. Kent up the staircase.

Stepping forward, Blake took Victoria's elbow and led her through a set of French doors to the dining room. The sideboard was laden with steaming dishes, and the delicious aromas made her empty stomach growl once again.

His head snapped to her face. "Have you not eaten?"

"There was no time on the journey."

Blake frowned. "The coachman should have stopped at an inn."

She ignored his brusque tone and, not seeing any servants, picked up a plate on the end of the sideboard and helped herself.

· "Eat more," he growled, grabbing the plate from her hand and spooning an enormous portion of eggs on it. "There's very little to you as is, and I'll not be accused by your family of starving you."

Victoria glared at him. "Of all the things they fear I will endure at your hands, I doubt starvation is one of them."

She plucked the plate from his hand and sat at the table.

Snapping open a starched white napkin, she spread it across her lap. He had arrived at his town house only ten minutes ago, and already his high-handed behavior irritated her.

She waited until Blake filled his own plate and sat at the table before raising the topic that had been on her mind since he announced they would be returning to London.

"You do realize, my lord, that bringing me back to London puts me in close proximity to my family."

Blake set down his fork and met her eyes. "Do you miss them, Victoria? If you do, I can arrange for them to visit. I extended the same offer to you once at Rosewood, but you never mentioned it. I'm speaking of your brother and mother, of course." He cocked his head to one side, then laughed ruefully. "But not your father. I cannot allow that man in my home."

Victoria was taken aback by his earnest tone. While at Rosewood, she had wanted to take him up on his offer, but she knew her father would never allow Spencer or her mother to visit Blake's country residence. But now that she was back in London, things had changed, and she needed desperately to see her brother.

She cast her eyes downward and then gave Blake her most innocent look. "I do miss Spencer terribly and would love to see him, but I do not feel comfortable having my brother visit me here . . . at a bachelor's home. I'd like to see him elsewhere."

"Of course. I shall accompany you. There is an inn with a private dining room that serves excellent fare. I know the owner."

Victoria's brain worked feverishly. She didn't want Blake present when she met Spencer.

How would she pass her brother the information she had gathered?

"I'd prefer to meet Spencer alone," she said.

"Are you worried about your brother's temper?"

"Not Spencer's, but yours."

"I told you before, I have no hard feelings toward Spencer."

"You may change your mind when he accuses you of acting the whoreson for what you have done. I do not desire fisticuffs between you two."

"I see," Blake said, his posture stiff at her choice of words. "And do you think I've acted so cruelly towards you?"

She regarded him thoughtfully across the table. "You've made your intentions clear, my lord. I'm not an idiot to assume we are back in London simply because you've missed the social whirl."

His handsome features hardened like granite. "I've never doubted your intelligence. Go alone, then, and give my regards to your brother."

Blake rose abruptly, tossed his napkin on the table and left the room.

Victoria waited until she heard his booted feet cross the marble vestibule before summoning Mr. Kent for a coach.

"Vicki! I've missed you so much!"

Victoria returned her brother's warm embrace and buried her face in his collar. The coarse wool scratched her cheek, but she didn't care. "It's good to see you again too, Spencer."

Spencer held her at arm's length and studied her from the tips of her shoes to the top of her head. "How awful has it been? Has Ravenspear harmed you in any way?"

Victoria quickly shook her head. "No, Spencer. You must believe me when I tell you I am fine, and that he has behaved as a gentleman."

"I don't believe you," Spencer said, his brow furrowing. "Why are you protecting him?"

"I'm not."

"Are you telling me that he did not touch you inappropriately . . . did not bed you?" he asked, his eyes downcast, clearly uncomfortable.

Victoria felt her face burn. She didn't want to discuss such a humiliating topic with her own brother, but she sensed that it was critical that Spencer understand she had not been assaulted.

"Blake has not touched me," she said. "I swear it."

"You're still a virgin? But why?" Amazement flickered across his boyish features. "I know he is attracted to you. The day he came for you, I saw the lust in his eyes when he looked at you."

Again, Victoria struggled to overcome her embarrassment. "Up until now I thought he was using me simply to hurt Father. Blake believed that the mere fact that I was under his roof night after night would be sufficient to torture father."

"Up till now?"

"He seems to have reached the end of his patience. I believe we've returned to London so he can publicly reveal my disgrace."

Spencer clenched his fists at his sides. "I'll kill him with my bare hands. I was hoping the coward would accompany you today so I could beat him to a bloody pulp."

Victoria was momentarily speechless. The notion that Spencer could best Ravenspear was ludicrous. She vividly recalled Blake's pugilistic pastime and ability, but she would never hurt her brother's feelings by telling him what she thought.

"There is a better way. Violence is not necessary to hurt

him." Victoria pulled the piece of paper she had secreted in her reticule and handed it to Spencer.

He unfolded the paper and scanned the contents. His brows creased as he read her notes about Blake's investments. Comprehension dawned, and he looked at Victoria in amazement. "You're joking. The arrogance of the man."

"Give it to Father. He'll know what to do."

"In the past I've always hated the way Father and Jacob Hobbs have conducted business. But this is one time I'm grateful for their ruthless business practices. I'll gladly help them any way I can."

"Then my work is done," she said. "Father should be satisfied."

Victoria studied her shoes as an uncomfortable emotion flooded her.

Shame?

Disappointment in herself?

She wasn't sure what she felt, but she had not expected such a heavy sense of dread after following through with her father's plans. She had told herself a hundred times that she had to protect herself.

Wouldn't Blake do the same if their situations were reversed?

Spencer raised her downcast chin with a finger. "I'm sorry, Vicki, for not considering what you must have suffered to obtain this information. Come with me now. You do not have to return to him."

"Where would I go? I doubt Father or Mother would allow me to return home."

"We can leave London together," Spencer said, gripping her limp hands. "It would take Blake months to find us, and by then we could set sail for America."

"Oh, Spencer." Victoria reached out to touch a lock of

blond hair that had fallen over his forehead. Spencer had always been a dreamer—the free spirit and easy-loving brother of her youth.

"Where would we go?" she asked. "How would we survive? What funds do we have to even purchase our fare on a ship?"

"You think too much, Vicki. We'll find a way. I can earn our fare at the tables."

"Gambling? Have you been successful lately?"

There was no need to even ask if Spencer had been gambling since her departure. She suspected that without her guidance, he was more drawn to the cards than before.

A sad expression crossed his face. "Alas, no. My luck turned when you left."

What luck? she thought to herself. "How bad?"

He shrugged. "Not too much."

"How bad?"

"Slayer's men have been hounding me."

"Slayer!" Shock flew through Victoria at the mention of the infamous moneylender's name. Rumors of his barbaric tactics, of physically assaulting desperate borrowers who could not repay his exorbitant rates of interest, raised the hair on her neck. "How have you been able to avoid Slayer's lackeys?"

It was then that she noticed Spencer's appearance, really noticed it. In the unforgiving light of the afternoon, her older brother appeared gaunt, much thinner than she recalled. His clothing hung loosely on his frame, the heavily padded jacket appeared ill-proportioned on his slender torso. His classically handsome features were now fine-boned, his green eyes glassy and his fair hair dull. Fine lines creased his forehead and the corners of his eyes.

Victoria reached out to touch his arm. "Oh, Spencer.

They have been after you, haven't they? And I haven't been here to help you."

A strange choking sound came from Spencer's throat, and he raised a hand to cover his eyes. Victoria suspected it took great control for him not to cry.

Spencer took a shuddering breath. "The truth is I'm in trouble, Vicki. I'm glad you're back in London now, even if you can't stay at home."

"We shall visit the Exchange. It's time Uncle Sheldon checked on his investments."

Spencer looked up, his eyes watery with unshed tears. "Thank you. It seems my younger sister is constantly rescuing me."

That's because I am. Victoria frowned at her thoughts. "Pass the information I gave you on to Father. We shall meet at the Exchange in a week."

Blake was sampling his second brandy while gazing out the bay window of White's when Justin found him.

"You won't believe what has occurred," Justin announced. Out of breath and obviously frazzled, Justin collapsed in an empty wingback chair across from Blake.

Blake set down his glass. "Whatever it is, it doesn't sound good."

"It's not. Charles Ashton and Jacob Hobbs have abruptly stopped selling to Illusory Enterprises."

"What items precisely?"

"Everything," Justin said, leaning forward. "No high-pressure pistons, no piston rods, no replacement parts. Every future order has been spit back in our faces."

"Damn," Blake cursed. "How much is this going to cost me?"

"Like I said before, Ashton's company is the only

manufacturer in England of the steel pistons we require. We can order from other manufacturers in Europe, but there would be weeks of delay plus the exorbitant cost of shipping and tariffs. The loss in profits will be high, but fortunately you are diversified enough to survive. The bulk of your wealth will not be affected."

"Why?" Blake growled. "Why would that greedy cut-throat stop selling to Illusory Enterprises? There was sufficient profit in it for him. He must have discovered the truth, the sham behind the company name. And the only way that could have happened is if there is a spy amongst us."

"A spy?" Justin asked, frowning. "But who?"

"Who else knew of the deal?"

Justin rubbed his eyes as he struggled to recall. "Other than you and me, only your solicitors that filed the legal documents to create the company."

"I have used the Weinstein and Brooks firm at the Inns of Court for years. Our dealings have always been strictly confidential. It makes no sense for them to steal this infor-mation and risk ruining their reputation and losing one of their clients," Blake said.

"Perhaps it was one of the firm's clerks or secretaries."

"Highly improbable."

"Then we need to retrace our steps," Justin said. "The only other opportunity a spy would have had to steal such information is if they found where the documents them-selves were stored."

"You think one of my servants is guilty?"

Justin shrugged. "I'm at a loss."

A sudden anger lit Blake's eyes. The thought of some-one in his own household stealing from him made his temper flare, but the knowledge that the stolen information benefited Charles Ashton caused Blake's anger to singe the corners of his control.

Blake stood abruptly and reached for his jacket. "Whoever the traitor is, I will hunt him out. God help the Judas when I catch him."

Chapter 21

A town house is much smaller than a country estate. It made the search for a spy easier.

Blake's eyes adjusted to the darkness as he watched Victoria, dressed in a white nightgown and satin slippers, tiptoe down the hallway into his library and quietly shut the door.

The maid's utility closet at the end of the corridor, with the door cracked slightly open, provided a perfect view of the hallway, specifically the entrance to his library office. But the space was tiny, crammed with cleaning supplies, and made Blake feel like a thief in his own home.

He sighed and leaned his forehead against the doorframe. His elbow knocked aside a broom, and the handle bumped his head. He nearly laughed out loud but caught himself.

He still couldn't believe Victoria was the spy, the traitor who had cost him thousands of pounds and helped enlighten his greatest enemy.

He had been observing her for a week now. Always she waited until nighttime, until she was certain the household was asleep, before venturing out to conduct her activities.

At first he had been livid. After all, his temper when crossed could be almost uncontrollable. He attributed his short fuse to the years he spent as an abused laborer beneath the cruel taskmasters in the poorhouse. It had taken all of Blake's control not to confront Victoria that first night she had slithered down the hallway into his office.

But then cold, calculating logic had cleared his brain of anger. His books and files were a complicated matter, and the fact that Victoria had been able to sort through the voluminous documents and discover not only that Illusory Enterprises was Blake's subsidiary, but also that the sham company was buying steel pistons from her father and Hobbs, was stunning.

He had come to recognize her intelligence over the past months she had been with him, but her latest ability was even more enlightening. It meant she had business exposure, specifically dealing with companies, their subsidiaries and the London Stock Exchange.

The shock of this discovery dulled some of the fury he had felt, and he grudgingly admitted that he admired her for her savvy and her guts. He wanted to confront her and demand she explain how she had such knowledge, but something held him back.

Victoria had already revealed his biggest secret to her father, yet she still visited Blake's library every night. There was something else she was searching for, and Blake needed to learn what that was.

His gut told him to remain silent and follow her closely to see what she was up to. Then he would have the satisfaction of a face-to-face reckoning.

He knew he should be furious. She had fooled him, sneaked through his most private papers and helped her father harm his interests. All the while, she had sat with him over meals and smiled sweetly, innocently, duping him into thinking he held the upper hand. The urge to tear her apart should be there. But it was not. The answer to one nagging question quenched such a need.

What would he have done if he was in her position?

The same or worse, he mused.

So instead of an uncontrollable rage, he felt an uncontrollable lust.

The library door opened and Victoria peeked out. Looking both ways to see if anyone was about, and once convinced she was alone, she ventured forth. She held a single candle and, combined with the candles in the wall sconces, her path was illuminated.

She stood still as she slowly closed the library door behind her so as not to make a sound. The lace-trimmed satin nightgown hid little of her form. The glimmering candlelight made it look sheer.

He could make out her profile—a slender leg, the curve of a tempting buttock and a trim waist. Her long dark hair was loose and curled around a full breast. She was as close to naked as he had ever seen her and yet, the fact that she was not only excited him more. His blood flowed hot in his veins, and he felt himself swell and harden with desire.

The outline of her enticing buttocks through the silk as she walked down the corridor made beads of perspiration form on his brow.

He was stuffed in the damn utility closet, hard as a rock, sweating like a pig, and anger was the last thing on his mind. All he could think of was tasting, touching and teasing the one woman he had foolishly sworn not to.

Blake opened the closet door and stretched his cramped muscles. He needed a good stiff drink, then laughed out loud at the mere notion that anything "stiff" was what he needed.

Climbing the main staircase two at a time, Blake shut his bedroom door and stripped off his damp shirt.

One thing was certain: she was up to something more.

The damage had been done regarding any dealings he had conducted with Ashton and Hobbs.

So what else are you looking for, sweet Victoria?

His pulse pounded with anticipation, and he looked forward to outmaneuvering her this time.

The truth was he couldn't wait to discover all her secrets.

By the end of the week, Victoria had gathered everything she needed and met Spencer in the lobby of the Exchange.

Unlike her previous visit, it was busy today, and brokers and their clients crowded the lobby. Many businessmen stood, since the sparsely furnished area had limited seating.

An older broker with graying hair and a matching-color beard eyed Victoria curiously before standing so that she could sit.

Uneasy with the crowd, Victoria eyed Spencer nervously. She normally loved the Exchange, loved the excitement humming within its walls, but not on a busy day like today. And it was not the type of arena where she desired to attract male attention.

"This shouldn't take long," she told Spencer. "I have a list of stocks I want to buy that I can hand to Mr. MacDonald. Then we can be on our way."

"Are you sure the stocks are winners?" Spencer asked.

"I'm certain."

Spencer hesitated a moment before realization crossed his features. "Ah, they're Ravenspear's picks."

Victoria hated to admit that she hadn't chosen the stocks herself, and that she had stolen the tips from Blake. She had always taken great pride in researching and selecting her own investments, unlike her father and Jacob Hobbs, who sunk their money in the current hot pick, whatever that might be.

"You said you needed money fast, that Slayer's men were hounding you," she snapped. "I did it for you."

"I apologize, Vicki. I do need money quickly."

Just then, Victoria spotted Mr. MacDonald approaching. So nervous was she to hand the elder broker the list and depart the overpopulated building, it took her longer than it should have to register that Blake Mallorey himself had approached the broker and was engaging him in conversation.

Mr. MacDonald smiled up at Blake, revealing they were on familiar terms.

Blake laughed at something the broker said, then looked up to meet Victoria's stunned gaze. Blake's lips curved into an all-knowing smile.

Sheer black fright swept through her. With pulse-pounding certainty she knew he had discovered all. The impulse to turn and flee the building like a madwoman from an asylum was overwhelming.

Blake's hard eyes never left hers as he spoke with Mr. MacDonald and the pair wove through the crowd toward her. The confident smirk on Blake's face and the gleam of warning in his gaze spoke as loudly as a blast from a trumpet.

He knows everything and is going to make me pay.

"We have to leave, Spencer. *Now.*"

"What are you talking about, Vicki?"

Spencer had yet to see Blake approaching. "It's Raven-spear," she said breathlessly. "He's here . . . with Mr. Mac-Donald."

All hint of color drained from Spencer's thin face, making him appear like an ancient mummy in a museum.

Too late. Blake was before them, a smiling Mr. MacDonald by his side.

"Miss Ashton, how wonderful to see you again," Mr. MacDonald said, taking her hand. "Mr. Ashton," he said, and nodded toward Spencer, who stood unblinking. "I've had the immense pleasure of meeting Lord Ravenspear. When I told him I had an appointment to meet with you this morning to handle your sick uncle's affairs, Ravenspear told me he was a close acquaintance of Uncle Sheldon. Imagine that! In all the time we have been meeting, I have never met anyone who has known your uncle."

Victoria blinked rapidly. *Spencer and I are going to prison for fraud!*

Her brother said nothing, just stood completely still, as if frozen to the spot. She glanced at Blake, and the fierce anger that lit his eyes made her stomach clench tight.

"I explained that dear Uncle Sheldon's health has been improving," Blake said, "and that soon he may visit the Exchange and conduct his own affairs."

Blake's voice was absolutely emotionless, and it chilled her. Only the cold gleam in his blue gaze directed at her revealed his wrath.

Victoria swallowed hard, feeling a pang of loss as Blake destroyed her indispensable alias. Of course, Blake knew very well that without the imaginary Uncle Sheldon, Victoria's investment career was over. She shook herself mentally. No, it had nothing to do with that, really, for as soon as Blake Mallorey had discovered her secret all had been lost. It mattered naught whether the broker thought her "uncle" had recovered.

Mr. MacDonald stood patiently, awaiting Victoria's response to Blake's "wonderful" news.

She opened her mouth to speak, and then closed it as

thoughts flitted through her mind. Feeling like a fish on a fisherman's hook, she looked to Spencer for help.

Stiff as a corpse, her brother looked worse off than she felt. *No help from him,* she thought.

"I . . . I had heard Uncle Sheldon had traveled to Bath and that the springs had helped his chronic cough." Looking at Blake, Victoria continued, "But one never knows if my uncle will feel well enough to return to London for business."

Mr. MacDonald patted Victoria's hand. "We can only hope, Miss Ashton. What can I help you with today?"

Again Victoria glanced at Blake's stern features, and then lowered her eyes.

How could she hand the broker the list of stocks she had stolen from Blake when he was standing before her?

"I uh . . . I seem to have misplaced my uncle's instructions," Victoria said. "I fear I must leave and will have to reschedule our appointment. I do apologize."

Mr. MacDonald's bushy eyebrows met as he frowned. "Another time, then?"

"Please excuse us," Victoria said, already turning to flee the building and Blake Mallorey's overwhelming presence.

Not waiting for the broker's response, Victoria wove her way through the crowd in a mad rush for the street. Pushing through the doors, not waiting for the doorman to open them, she ran into Capel Court. She hesitated long enough to make sure Spencer was behind her.

"He would not dare confront us publicly, Spencer."

"Wrong again, my dear," said a familiar, deep-timbered voice beside her.

Victoria stiffened in shock and whirled around to find Blake at her right side. "How did you follow so quickly?"

"I can move fast when I need to." Blake stepped forward and his fingers clamped around her wrist.

Victoria looked around nervously. Businessmen mingled in Capel Court, and the doorman opened and closed the door to the Exchange for a steady stream of patrons. No one paid her and Ravenspear any attention.

"Don't touch her!" Spencer stalked forward. "You're the worst type of defiler, Ravenspear," he hissed. "You're foul and immoral and don't deserve her."

Spencer stood, feet braced apart, fists clenched at his sides.

Victoria feared her brother would attack Blake. Without a doubt, she knew Spencer would get hurt if he acted rashly.

"Spencer, no." She tried to go to Spencer's side, but Blake refused to release his grip on her wrist.

"And you, a reckless gambler, deserve her?" Blake asked, his voice heavy with sarcasm.

"Whoreson!" Spencer yelled, attracting a few raised eyebrows in the court. "My sister is coming home with me." Spencer reached for Victoria.

Blake's eyes narrowed dangerously as he pulled Victoria behind him, and his broad shoulders blocked her from her brother.

"She's not going anywhere with you because she is leaving with me," Blake said. His voice, though quiet, had an ominous quality.

Spencer's face reddened, mottled with rage. "With me she'd be safe from your lust."

"Safe with you? When Slayer's men are lurking about to break a leg or two to get you to pay your debts? That vicious moneylender would not hesitate to hurt you or anyone you cared for to get his money. I suspect you are all too aware of Slayer's barbaric tactics. That's why you used Victoria to steal confidential stock information and risk herself by coming to the Exchange just to bail you out of debt. It's time you stopped taking advantage of your sister."

Victoria's eyes widened at Blake's knowledge.

How on earth did he find out about Spencer borrowing from the unscrupulous Slayer?

"Perhaps I'm no better than you, Ravenspear," Spencer spat. "You're using Vicki for revenge against our father, and I need her to help me. But at least I don't seek to destroy her reputation, her future."

"No? Shall we call the magistrate and see? Breaking locks to steal private papers and fraudulently investing in the London Stock Exchange could get one thrown into Newgate for twenty years. But prison wouldn't damage her reputation any, would it?"

Spencer's shoulders slumped slightly. He could not rebuff Blake's logic. He had put Victoria in grave danger. He had manipulated her with his desperate plea for help, knowing she would risk herself to aid him as she had always done in the past.

"I do not trust you, Ravenspear," Spencer said.

"It doesn't matter. She goes with me." Blake pulled Victoria with him as he turned to leave.

Victoria allowed Blake to lead her away. She glanced back once to see Spencer standing still, looking defeated and miserable.

They reached Blake's coach. He helped her inside, then sat across from her, his long legs brushing her skirts. His nearness in the confines of the coach was overwhelming.

Feeling the need to explain her actions before his wrath was unleashed, Victoria blurted out, "I agreed to come with you only because I don't want Spencer hurt."

"You would come with me nonetheless."

She looked up, and his fierce blue eyes made his face look stark. He wasn't just angry, she realized, but furious. She shivered.

"You have learned everything, then?" she asked, fearful of his expected response.

Blake leaned forward until they were almost nose to nose. Pressing her head back against the padded leather bench, she was trapped.

"You want to hear what I know? From my lips? I know that you snuck into my office, broke my locks and gave confidential information about my subsidiary to your father. I know that my hated nemesis used that knowledge to hurt a company I am heavily invested in. But you didn't stop there, did you? You kept stealing from me to help your brother, and, most astonishing of all, you have been using a false identity to illegally and fraudulently invest in the London Stock Exchange for years without official membership."

She swallowed hard. "When did you find out?"

"Oh, I've known for quite some time."

"You've been watching me? Why didn't you confront me after you learned what I had done for my father? You must have been furious."

He sighed, then leaned back in his seat. "I *was* furious, but after my initial rage wore off, I was in wonder at what you had accomplished. Without help, you made sense of highly complicated financial statements, purchase orders and legal documents, and accurately reported only the most critical, the most damaging facts. Further, it took genius to invent sick old Uncle Sheldon in order to penetrate that male-dominated Exchange, and it took brains to *successfully* invest in an unpredictable market. Quite simply, I'm impressed with your intelligence, guts and investing savvy."

Victoria sat back, speechless at his words. All her adult years, she had desired a man who would appreciate her for her mind. And here was a man she had hurt, cost thousands of pounds, and yet he could look past her treasonous deeds to admire her "investing savvy."

"I'm sorry for what I did," she whispered. "If it is any consolation, I felt horrible doing it. I regret any loss of money you have suffered and don't blame you for your anger."

"Foolish girl! You think I'm angry over money lost? I already told you I got over that. I would have done the same if our situations were reversed. No, I'm furious over your putting yourself at risk. I wasn't jesting when I said if you were discovered, you could spend twenty years in Newgate."

"But I have to help Spencer," she explained.

"You enable him."

She opened her mouth to protest, but he held up his hand. "Because I fear your brother is in over his head, that Slayer's men are a real threat to him and you, I paid the blackguard off."

Shock flew through her. "You did that? For Spencer?"

"No, for you."

Reaching over, he plucked her from her seat and placed her on his lap.

Victoria gasped, and her arms went around his neck to steady herself. She was immediately conscious of the heat from his muscular thighs through their clothing, and her body tingled from the contact.

His solid arms encircled her, one hand at the small of her back. His breath fanned her neck; his gaze traveled over her face and searched her eyes before dropping to her mouth.

He looks like he's going to ravish me. Even though Victoria couldn't deny the spark of excitement at the prospect, she pressed her palm against his chest.

"You swore not to force me into your bed."

Blake allowed her to push him back only as far as it took to meet her stare with his own. Desire had darkened his cobalt eyes to near black.

"All promises became null and void the moment you broke my locks and turned into a thief. Make no mistake, you *will* be mine tonight, Victoria."

Chapter 22

Blake's powerful words crashed down upon her, and with the age-old wisdom of Eve, Victoria knew she would lie with him tonight.

She felt no fear, no outrage at his boldness. But instead, the smoldering flame she saw in his eyes, and the knowledge that he desired her, sent her spirits soaring.

All too quickly her resistance toward him drained from her body. Unable to deny the truth any longer, she realized she was falling in love with him. It was not the adolescent infatuation of her youth but instead the fully blossomed love of a grown woman. Here was the type of man she had been searching for—a man confident enough in his own masculinity not to be intimidated by her intelligence and independence.

Hadn't she always known there was something special about Blake Mallorey from the beginning?

Victoria was no longer willing to deny herself his touch. Every moment in life was precious, and she refused to always wonder what it would have felt like to be loved by Blake.

Cocking her head to one side, she traced his hard jaw

with a finger. "No words of seduction, my lord? No promises of pleasure? Have you lost your touch?"

Blake's pupils dilated, and he looked at her in utter disbelief. It was clear that he was taken aback at her response,
her acceptance of him.

"Are you challenging me? I'd perish before I'd disappoint you," he said, a teasing light in his eyes.

He captured her hand in his larger one, peeled back her
satin glove and placed a hot kiss on the center of her palm.

A tingling of excitement raced through her fingers at
the grazing of his moist lips. She lowered her eyes, suddenly shy.

"I have no experience, so I may pose a greater challenge
than you believe."

He raised her chin, his handsome face fierce, and gazed
into her eyes. "The knowledge that there has been no other
pleases me greatly, Victoria. You are a treasure, a woman
to be worshiped and initiated into the act of lovemaking
with great attention."

It was her turn to be surprised, and her jade eyes widened
with astonishment.

"I want you, Victoria," he said huskily. "I want to make
love to you."

"I'd like that very much," she whispered.

Blake's eyes gleamed with victory. His lips took possession of her mouth in a fiery kiss that sent shivers of desire
racing through her. She rested a trembling hand against his
solid chest and felt his heart pound. When he sucked on
her bottom lip, she moaned and pressed closer.

He raised his dark head to look into her eyes, letting her
see the raw need that burned inside him. "I've imagined
this for so long. Despite what I said, I would never force
you. Are you sure, sweetheart?"

When she nodded, he grinned and banged on the

coach door with a fist, signaling the driver to begin the journey home.

The coach began to sway a steady rhythm, and she rocked gently on his lap.

Blake traced her swollen lips with the rough pad of his thumb. "My only fear is that we will not arrive home fast enough. I don't want to make love to you inside a coach for your first time."

"Our second time, then?" she taunted.

"You'll drive me mad." He cupped her face with both hands and reclaimed her lips.

Their mouths became greedy and the kiss more intimate. When his tongue touched hers, her breath caught, and she eagerly responded—touching, tasting, nibbling until her flesh quivered from arousal.

Her fingers inched their way up to bury in his dark hair and hold him close. She squirmed in his lap, and the heat from their bodies scorched her buttocks and thighs. It was as if by granting herself permission to be with him, her defenses crumbled, and she was free to respond with all the pent-up passion that had risen inside her.

Blake's hand slid up from her waist to cover her breast. His fingers circled a sensitive nipple through the fine silk gown, and it hardened instantly beneath his touch. Pleasure radiated outward, and she panted between parted lips. Arching toward his palm, she wondered what it would feel like for him to touch her naked flesh.

As if he heard her thoughts, he unfastened her gown. Deft fingers untied her chemise and he slid both garments off her shoulders, down her arms, baring her full breasts to his hungry eyes. He reached out to reverently cup the globes with his large hands.

"Do you know how long I've wanted to touch you like this?" Lowering his head, he sucked the tip of a breast into his mouth and swirled his tongue around a diamond-hard nipple.

The wet, rough texture of his tongue sent liquid tremors shooting between her thighs. Her body erupted to life, and she clawed at his shirt and kneaded the slabs of muscle beneath.

She stiffened as he raised the hem of her gown and his hand slid up her stockinged leg. When his fingers traced the smooth skin above her garter, she shivered. He caressed the insides of her thighs, inching higher, until he barely brushed the nest of curls covering her woman's center.

She felt her face grow hot from his brazenness, yet at the same time, her blood soared, and she writhed against his hand.

"Easy, my little tigress," he murmured against her lips. "We're almost home. I promise to touch you like this and more once you are in my bed."

Victoria raised her head, a dazed expression on her face, her mind foggy with newly discovered passion.

Blake rearranged her clothing and hooked the tiny clasps of her gown before she fully comprehended his words.

At the sound of springs squeaking and the driver jumping down from his seat, Victoria snapped out of her trance.

"Oh!" She jumped off Blake's lap and smoothed her skirts a moment before the door opened and the driver lowered the step.

With a firm grasp, Blake took her arm and escorted her into his town house. They flew past Mr. Kent, whose impassive expression never once cracked, and rushed up the stairs hand in hand.

As she struggled to keep up with Blake's brisk pace, she stole a glance at his face. His profile was strong and rigid, and a strange, eager look flashed in his eyes. Her gaze swept from his broad chest to his narrow hips to a definite bulge in his trousers.

Her eyes widened in wonder. *He's not as detached as he would like me to believe.*

Excitement and a trickle of fear ran down her spine at the knowledge that such a physically powerful male was so anxious to be with her.

They reached the top of the stairs. Blake swept her into his arms and carried her into his suite. He kicked the door shut with a booted foot and walked to the enormous canopied bed which dominated the room. Not bothering to pull back the coverlet, he placed her in the center of the mattress and loomed above her.

"I can't wait to have you in my bed a second longer." Pulling the pins from her hair, he spread the inky mass across the bed and raised a shiny tress to inhale its fragrance. "Your hair is stunning, like shining midnight."

She reached up to cup his head and urged him to kiss her. With a low growl of approval, he claimed her lips in a mind-numbing kiss.

He was not satisfied for long with kissing, and soon his hands caressed her throat, then lowered to stroke the side of a breast and the curve of a hip.

He nuzzled her throat and the tops of her breasts which swelled above her low neckline. "I want to see you without your clothes. I want to see all of you in the full light of day."

Her pulse skittered. The gruffness of his voice and the smoldering flame in his eyes unlocked her heart and soul.

Rising slowly, she sat on the edge of the bed beside him and watched through lowered lashes as he unhooked her gown. When her silk dress and chemise lay loose on her shoulders, she pulled them down to her waist until her breasts were bared to his hot stare.

Blake groaned. "You are perfect—molded for my hands."

When he reached out to caress the globes, her nipples were already pebble-hard, seemingly crying out for his touch. He pushed her down gently, and stretched his long length beside her. Instead of removing the rest of her clothes as she expected, he raised the hem of her gown once more. As in the coach, his hand slid up her stocking to the top of her garter. But this time, she knew his goal, and she was eager to feel his fingers on the flesh of her bare thighs.

She arched her hips against his hand, and he hissed. He unfastened the garter and slowly drew off her stocking. The heat from his hand warmed her skin. She desperately wanted the other stocking off, and she sighed with pleasure when he was quick to peel it down her leg and toss it on the floor to join its mate.

The silk gown and chemise bunched around her waist. Through a haze of passion, she realized she wanted him to remove them too. She felt no shame, only urgency as her body hummed and felt more alive than ever before. She pushed the garments over her hips, and he was quick to pull them down her legs. With a rustle, they fell to the floor.

"You're so beautiful," he whispered.

His dark eyes swept over her intensely, and through his trousers, his rigid manhood burned against her thigh.

The realization flashed through her mind that her beauty enraptured him. *He desperately wants to possess me. Maybe he will come to love me.*

He stroked her inner thighs and brushed against the tight curls between her legs. She gasped as he separated the curls and eased the tip of one finger inside her. He stroked her gently until dewy moisture made his finger slick.

"I want your first experience to be all pleasure without a trace of pain. There is a sensitive nub I ache to touch." When his wet finger slid across it, her breath caught and her eyes flew open.

"Yesss," he hissed.

He slid one finger inside her hot sheath, and when she bucked against his hand, he eased a second inside. Slowly, he ran one finger back and forth across her nub as the other slid in and out of her body.

The sensations were so unexpected and intense, she grasped fistfuls of his shirtsleeves. She writhed beneath his touch, panting through parted lips, urging his fingers to quicken their pace. Her body began to vibrate with liquid fire, until a delicious torment built. With one last bold stroke, her feet dug into the coverlet and her hips arched off the bed while waves of exquisite agony rocked her.

Victoria lay sprawled across the bed as Blake smoothed the hair away from her forehead. She stared up at him in wonder. "Is that what all the fuss is about?"

He laughed. "There's more."

"More?" she asked, amazed. Her languid gaze slid down his fully dressed form stretched beside her. She was naked, and he still wore all of his clothes. "I want to see you too."

"My pleasure, sweetheart." Blake sat up and began to unbutton his shirt.

"No. Let me."

She rose to push away his hands. She had a strong urge to touch him, to get closer to him. Even though she had just experienced ecstasy at his expert hands, she sensed she was missing the cataclysmic event that would bring them together as one.

Victoria's fingers trembled as she undid his buttons and helped pull the shirt free of his trousers. Muscles in his broad shoulders flexed beneath her hands. His chest was sprinkled with dark hair that ran down his tight stomach into the waistband of his trousers.

She willed herself not to look lower, knowing the difference in their bodies would frighten her.

Passing her tongue over her lips, she reached out to stroke his chest. With great daring, she leaned forward and licked his flat nipples, then kissed her way down the corrugated muscles of his abdomen.

"Victoria," he groaned. "I do not know how much more I can stand."

She raised her head, black hair cascading over her breasts and down her back. "Then teach me. I want to experience everything."

Blake stood, and his hands went to the fastening on his trousers. Breathing heavily through parted lips, she stared at him with rounded eyes. He removed his trousers, and his cock sprung free, bold and forceful, from a nest of black hair.

"Ohh," she gasped as a ribbon of fear ran down her spine.

As she watched fascinated, it moved, growing harder.

She raised her eyes to his. His dark gaze was so hungry and full of raw need that her heart lurched in her chest.

She swallowed, and pushed aside her trepidation. "Make love to me, Blake."

He swept her up off the bed, turned back the coverlet and laid her on the sheet. He kissed her long and thoroughly, urging her to surrender completely to his masterful touch.

Victoria felt her breasts crush against the hardness of his chest, felt his hands move downward, skimming both sides of her body to her thighs. When his hand moved between her legs, she parted them eagerly for his exploration.

"Ah, you're ready for me."

His mouth closed off any reply, and he moved over her. The head of his hardness traced across her slick bud. He slipped his hands beneath her and pressed the tip of his rock-hard shaft against the opening of her body. Victoria arched upward, needing him to finish what he had begun. With one bold thrust, Blake plunged forward. Her scream was muffled by his mouth.

"I'm so sorry, my love. Hold still and the pain will pass."

Seconds passed and she didn't breathe, didn't move. She was aware of his hot breath against her nape, of his hard length inside her, completely still, yet stretching and possessing. Then slowly, miraculously, Blake began to thrust in and out. A burning, then an aching sensation leapt to life within in her.

She began to move with him and soon matched his rhythm with an urgency of her own until her body exploded in a fiery climax. Once, twice more he plunged within her, and then he stiffened and spilled his white-hot seed inside her.

He rolled to the side and pulled her against his heated length. "Are you all right, sweetheart?"

"I'm fine," she murmured, then laughed at her answer. "I feel more than fine, I feel wonderful."

She leaned back to study his face and caught his broad grin. She reached out to touch the ruffled dark hair that clung damply to his brow.

He caught her hand and planted a gentle kiss on her palm. "Thank you. If I knew it would be this glorious, I would never have promised not to ravage you at will."

"And I would never have waited this long to demand you carry me to your bed."

She nuzzled her face in his chest and inhaled his masculine scent. He stroked her hair, lulling her to relax against his warm flesh. His heart beat rhythmically beneath her cheek, and she yawned, thoroughly exhausted.

Completely satiated, they slipped into a deep sleep.

Blake woke before dawn, instantly aroused by the delicious female flesh pressed against him. Opening his eyes, he found Victoria asleep beside him. Skeins of ebony hair curved over her shoulders and traced the tips of her breasts. Rosy nipples thrust through the dark strands, and his mouth watered at the sight.

He lay still, not wanting to disturb her peaceful slumber. She slept like an angel. Long dark lashes lay like delicate fans against her cheeks. Entranced by her peaceful beauty, he reached for a silky tendril of hair and raised it to his face. He inhaled deeply of her scent.

Sighing dreamily, she slipped a slender leg between his and parted her lips in contentment when their flesh touched.

Lust, commingled with a strange possessiveness, ripped through him.

He had been convinced that once he had possessed her body, the tightly coiled need inside him would ease. But instead, it was keener than before, driving him to madness. He had made love to her the night through, yet he wanted her again, desperate to impress the memory of their shared passion in her mind forever.

Why did he feel this way?

He told himself it was because Victoria was a beautiful woman who responded like fire to his slightest touch. What man wouldn't want to taste such pleasure again? Or maybe it was because she had been a childhood friend he had always admired and looked after. Uncertain of his feelings, he leaned back, rested his head on his palm and studied her features.

Charles Ashton had sold his daughter for what he believed was a few months' reprieve on several business loans. Victoria's mother had done nothing to stop her tyrannical husband. Spencer Ashton was a selfish pleasure-seeker, a habitual gambler and drunk, who used his sister for money. And Jacob Hobbs, the corrupt businessman who proclaimed to love and want to marry Victoria, had conceded out of fear that he too would be sent to the poorhouse.

Not one person in Victoria's life had considered her feelings or desires, or had tried to protect her. Even though it had been to Blake's advantage that Victoria had come to him, he was still irked by her family's selfishness.

Amongst such a vile environment, Blake was amazed that Victoria had survived unspoiled. Instead of withering beneath her father's dominance, she had used her keen intelligence to accomplish the unthinkable: penetrate the male arena of the London Stock Exchange.

Charles Ashton had never discovered her secret. As far as Blake knew, no one had learned of her clandestine activities except Spencer, in whom she had confided.

Blake's original plan had been simple and based entirely on hatred and a burning need for revenge. He would destroy Charles Ashton economically, and he would use Victoria to ruin Charles socially.

Blake had all but achieved his original goals. Charles's greed had assisted in his own downfall. By abusing his position in his official capacity as a Junior Lord Commissioner of the Treasury including stealing from the Crown, Charles Ashton could be stripped of his position and wealth, and possibly tried for treason.

But making love to Victoria had complicated Blake's well-laid plans, for it was an experience he did not want to soil with thoughts of vengeance.

A public scandal would hurt Charles, but it would destroy Victoria. If Charles Ashton was accused of treason, then Victoria would never again be able to show her face amongst society. The mere thought made bile rise up Blake's throat. He knew of society's cruelty firsthand, and he did not want Victoria to suffer such a fate.

Yet the painful memories of his father's suicide, his mother's painful death in filthy conditions, and the fate of his sister haunted him still.

How could he let Charles Ashton go unpunished?

Victoria shifted in her sleep, her lips brushing against his throat.

Blake's swollen shaft jerked in response. He had known for some time, hadn't he, that he could never throw her to the wolves? Her innocence and intelligence had enraptured him and changed his goals, and he found himself in an impossible position.

He had to find a way to punish Charles Ashton for his past sins, yet protect Victoria from the taint of scandal afterward.

Chapter 23

Victoria woke alone in Blake's large bed. She stretched her limbs against the cool sheets and moaned when the sore muscles in her thighs and groin protested. Her mind burned with the memory of last night, and she smiled a secret smile.

Even though her muscles ached, she would never regret the ecstasy of being held against Blake's strong body.

Her lips tingled in remembrance of his masterful touch. Once she had made up her mind to be with Blake intimately, she refused to be ashamed of her actions. He was an incredibly handsome man whom she had been enthralled with ever since she was a girl. And this morning, she considered herself fortunate to have experienced what it felt like to be loved by him as a woman.

Now that she knew, could she ever be satisfied with another man?

She found the thought disconcerting. Sitting up, she wrapped the sheet around her and cautiously slipped off the high bed.

Just then, the door opened, and Blake swept inside, carrying a large bathing tub.

"Good morning, sweetheart. I'm glad you are awake. How do you feel?"

She glanced at him, suddenly shy. "Sore all over."

He set down the big tub on its ornately clawed feet and strode toward her. "I apologize for any discomfort, but I can't say I regret last night." Taking her hand in his, he kissed her palm. "A hot bath will help ease all your aches and pains. Don't move an inch. Cook is heating water as we speak. I'll be right back with steaming buckets."

"You're going to carry them yourself?"

He smiled. "Of course. I didn't think you'd want the servants to see you naked in my bed, even though I find you quite delectable this way."

She blushed to the roots of her hair.

He teased her with a slow wink and left the room.

Must his every movement remind me of his sexual attractiveness? Victoria sat still on the edge of the mattress and clutched the sheet to her breasts.

Allowing him to make love to her only strengthened her infatuation. Despite their families' pasts and Blake's thirst for vengeance, she was fascinated. Her feelings had nothing to do with reason, for her normally rational brain seemed to shut down whenever he was present. Her only hope was to believe that Blake felt something more than mere lust for her and that lying with him last night would not end his pursuit.

A low knock at the door signaled his return. Blake entered carrying four large buckets of steaming water, two in each hand. He set them down and began to fill the porcelain tub.

When the last bucket was emptied, he turned to face her, a cake of soap and a sponge in his hands. "Consider me your lady's maid for the morning."

"You mean to watch me bathe?"

"No. I mean to help you."

Again she blushed. But the smile in his eyes contained a sensual flame she could not resist, and her wicked woman's juices bubbled forth. She pushed away from the bed and slowly let her fingers go. The sheet slipped down her body to pool at her feet.

Placing one dainty bare foot before the other, she walked to the tub. "I've never had a man bathe me before."

She felt his stare burn into her back, then drop to her buttocks. When she turned around she nearly gasped out loud at the savage, lustful look in his dark eyes.

"I had better be the only man to lather you up."

She felt a thrill of excitement race through her veins at his possessiveness. Easing into the steamy water, she tied her long black hair in a knot at her nape. Her arms relaxed on both sides of the large tub, and she rested her head back. With a deep sigh, she closed her eyes and allowed the hot water to ease her sore muscles.

"This feels wonderful," she said dreamily.

In a flash, he was by her side. "This will feel even better." Taking the soap, he lathered the sponge and gently scrubbed her neck and shoulders.

"Hmmm. I smell lavender."

"It's your favorite fragrance."

She opened her eyes to study his face. "How did you know?"

"I've smelled your hair, and the scent lingers whenever you leave a room."

Again his attention to detail caught her by surprise. She never dreamed he would notice such things as the scent of her soap, but was pleased and flattered that he had.

Closing her eyes again, Victoria tipped her head to one side so that he could lather her neck and shoulders. The soapy sponge gliding over her skin was mesmerizing.

The highly attractive and virile male kneeling above her, bathing her, was erotic.

When the sponge slid over her breasts, she gasped and looked up.

"Your skin is like velvet," he said, his voice gruff with need. "I want to touch you all over."

With a soft splash, he dropped the sponge in the water, and his hands cupped her breasts. His soapy thumbs flicked her hard nipples. His hands disappeared beneath the water, caressing her taut stomach and skimming her thighs. He lifted a slender leg from the water and with great care massaged her toes and arch, then slid up her calf and thigh.

Victoria held her breath, wishing his fingers would delve in between her legs, but that he did not do, choosing instead to wash her other leg with the same attention. She lay drowned in a floodtide of need, aware of every fiery stroke of his sleek, soapy hands.

When he moved around and touched his lips to hers, she clung to his neck and kissed him back greedily. She didn't care that she was soaking his fine linen shirt. Or that the bath water sloshed over the side of the tub, wetting his trousers. She didn't care, and neither did Blake, for in the next instant, his arms swept around her and lifted her from the tub. She let out a startled gasp and clung to his damp shirt, fearful that she would slip from his arms.

He laughed. "I shall not drop you. Once I have a hold, I'll never let go."

He carried her to his bed, but this time, instead of laying her fully on the soft mattress as she had expected, he placed her buttocks on the edge of the bed and left her legs dangling. He kissed her mouth, her breasts, then down her flat stomach. Then he sank to his knees, spread her thighs apart and planted a hot kiss above her pubic bone.

Victoria rose up on her elbows, confused by his actions.

His heated gaze met hers. "Trust me. I want to taste you here . . . taste your passion."

She wasn't sure what he meant, and she watched in disbelief as he lowered his dark head.

He cupped her bottom cheeks and raised them to his mouth, his hot breath blowing on the curls between her parted legs. When his lips touched her soft core, she moaned and collapsed back on the bed.

He took his time, kissing and laving her most intimate parts. His tongue slid across her sensitive nub, and she grasped fistfuls of his hair and panted. Then his tongue boldly plunged into her tight sheath, and she trembled and arched mindlessly beneath him, urging him on.

Sensations built to a frenzied peak inside of her, and she felt her body quiver and convulse, and then explode as the honeyed liquid inside of her burst forth.

Blake stood and brushed damp tendrils of hair from her face. "You're beautiful in your passion."

She lay sprawled on the end of the bed, her legs hanging limply, her hair a wild tangle around her. She thought that she would slip onto the floor, a thoroughly satisfied creature. Then he did no more than lick the rosy tips of her breasts and the wanton inside of her leapt to life yet again.

Blake moved above her, pulled off his trousers and thrust into her with a spurt of hungry desire. He clenched his teeth, never taking his eyes from her. She drove him wild with the arching of her slender hips and her throaty moans. His ardor mounted when he felt the beginnings of her release. He wanted to prolong the moment, savor the gusts of desire that now shook her, but he was too far aroused. He plunged deeply in and out of her tight sheath. He couldn't get deep enough, possess enough. Then he exploded, shouting out hoarsely as he spent.

His heart was hammering in his chest as he lowered his head to her breast.

Victoria ran her fingers through his hair. "I never knew a man could do such things to a woman."

"I've longed to touch you, to taste you since the day you came to Rosewood."

"Really? I had no idea."

He traced his fingers down her cheek. "I know. You drove me to near madness."

They lay entwined until the midmorning sun rose high and bathed them in warmth. Blake was the first to rise. He covered Victoria with the sheet, kissed her forehead and then donned his trousers.

He moved to the door, and said, "I told Cook to prepare some sustenance and, knowing Mr. Burke, a tray is outside my door."

Blake opened the door, bent down and returned with a silver tray in hand. A variety of sliced cheeses, fresh bread, a flask of wine and two crystal goblets weighed down the silver.

Victoria sat up, suddenly ravenous. "It looks delicious."

She reached for a slice of cheese and chunk of crusty bread, still warm from the oven. As they ate, sitting naked with legs crossed in the center of the wide bed, a disturbing notion occurred to her.

Blake had thought of everything after their lovemaking. The bath. The food. What if he was playing a well-practiced role, and she was nothing more than one of many actresses on his private stage?

Victoria sipped from her glass of wine, but the expensive liquor did not go down smoothly.

Scowling, she looked him in the eye. "How many times have you done this?"

"Pardon?"

"This. Your bed. The bath. The food. How many times?"

He looked at her warily. "I never professed to be a virgin."

She threw down a piece of cheese she had been holding. "So you've brought many women here before . . ."

He raised his hand, cutting her off. "I've never brought a woman into this room, into this bed. In fact, no other woman has spent the night under my roof before. I've always been careful to avoid—how shall I say it?—commitment . . . before, and have had no desire to be with the same woman more than once. Until you."

Stunned at his admission, her mouth gaped open.

He picked up the piece of cheese she had recently discarded and stuffed it in her mouth. "I've never known you to be speechless, Victoria, so I'll assume you are still hungry."

Feeling suddenly foolish, she chewed the food and glanced at his profile as he lifted the wine flask to refill the two goblets.

What did he just confess? That he wanted a commitment? Or that his feelings for her were growing?

Both notions made her skin prickle pleasurably.

"I have something for you." He rose and walked to the wardrobe in the corner of the room. He opened the large doors and returned to the bed carrying a brown package tied with string. Handing her the mysterious bundle, he said, "Open it."

Victoria untied the string, curious as a child about what the package contained. Ripping open the thick paper, she found a pair of breeches, striped silk stockings, a high-buttoned waistcoat, a ruffled starched shirt and a double-breasted jacket. At the bottom of the package lay a pair of leather pumps with buckles. The clothing was of fine quality and material but was obviously too small for Blake's large frame, and seemed more suited for a young boy. The shoes were no exception.

She looked at Blake in confusion. "I don't understand."

"Do you like them? I had to revisit Madame Fleur's dress shop to get your measurements and had a most difficult time convincing her to make me these garments for you. As for the shoes, I borrowed a pair of your slippers and took them to the shoemaker's to ensure the proper fit. He also thought me mad."

"You had these garments made for me? But why?"

He gave her a devilish grin. "Because I'm taking you with me to the Stock Exchange. And not just the lobby like you're accustomed, but inside, on the trading floor."

She looked at him blankly. "But how? I don't need to point out to you that women aren't allowed."

"But as my guest and distant young cousin named Victor, you are more than welcome." He nodded toward the clothing she held in her limp hands. "Thus the attire."

"You think to pass me off as a boy?"

"I do. We'll have to be creative about your hair, of course. But I think a hat with a curled brim ought to do it. You're shorter than most men so it shouldn't be hard to look down and avoid eye contact. Besides, everyone is so busy with their own agenda on the floor, no one pays attention to anyone's appearance, let alone a boy."

Victoria's heart thundered. A seductive excitement raced through her at the thought of actually standing on the trading floor. But she was not convinced Blake's masquerade would work or that she could carry it off. And then there was the fact that Blake had scolded her, had even threatened to tell the magistrate about her scheme of concocting her Uncle Sheldon so she could make money in the market.

What had changed his mind?

"I thought you disapproved of my activities. What happened?"

"Like I said, I was angry. It took time to forgive that you stole information from me to help your father. And then I learned that you were at it again because of Spencer's involvement with the bloodthirsty, unethical Slayer, and my fury exploded. Eventually Spencer would have revealed your secret to Slayer just to buy himself time, and you would have been in great danger. But I looked past that as well, knowing you were only trying to aid your brother."

"But why would you do this for me?"

"I know it's your dream, and I have an ache to do something for you, to make you happy. And because I admire your intelligence and think it unfair that you're denied what others have based on nothing but their birth status. And because I like to thumb my nose at the aristocratic snobs that turned their backs on my family and never offered a scrap of aid when we came upon hard times."

His explanation, no matter how simplistic and convoluted it sounded at the same time, satisfied her. She told herself it was because she ached to have what he offered a thousand times before—to step foot on the trading floor. But she knew the truth was that, at this moment, she would follow him no matter where he led. And that every time he mentioned that he valued her brain, a bit more of her heart was lost to him.

She sat up on her knees and hugged him, the sheet dropping and her bare breasts crushing against his chest.

"Yes. Yes, a thousand times yes. I'd love to go to the Stock Exchange with you."

Chapter 24

Victoria had walked through Capel Court many times before, but never like this.

The slim-fitting breeches and silk stockings felt indecently decadent against her skin. They lent a freedom of movement she had never experienced. Her skirts had always inhibited her movements. But the breeches she now wore encased her legs and gave her the feeling she was walking *naked*. The short cut of the front of her double-breasted jacket left little to the imagination below the waist. With the masculine style being so suggestive and open, no wonder men were obsessed with their nether parts.

"You look quite fetching, my dear," Blake said, walking beside her. "Don't fret. No one is paying us any untoward attention. Just remember what I told you—don't forget to breathe easy and follow my lead."

Victoria glanced at Blake's profile beneath her brimmed hat. He looked striking in his trousers, tailored jacket and snowy cravat. He exuded an air of confidence that told all that he was sure of himself and his rightful place in the universe.

Of course no one would question him.

Victoria frowned. "I would feel calmer if you did not call me 'my dear.' At least not until I'm out of these clothes."

He gave her a lazy wink. "I promise not to slip."

They came upon the doorman, who immediately opened the ornate doors upon seeing Blake, and they entered the building.

It was the same sparsely furnished lobby Victoria had walked across, either alone or with Spencer, countless times. Many hours had been spent waiting for the portly Mr. MacDonald to finish with his more important clients before meeting with her. It was the same lobby, yet now it felt immensely different.

Today she would go inside the sanctum, the prohibited temple. Yes, she would step foot on the trading floor of the London Stock Exchange. Her pulse beat in her throat at the prospect.

As they proceeded to walk across the lobby, past brokers meeting with their clients, Victoria paused to catch her breath. Nervousness slipped back to grip her.

Could she carry off this ruse?

Back at the town house, after she had tried on the masculine attire, she had come close to backing out of Blake's scheme. But he had assured her that she looked like a respectable young man, and that it was not uncommon for a member of the Exchange to bring along a guest.

Now that she was here, she was not so certain. Her tightly bound breasts felt as if they would burst within the confines of her jacket. And her long hair was crammed so firmly beneath the hat that she feared it would pop off without warning.

Several well-dressed gentlemen stood to the side conversing. One in particular caught her eye—an attractive dark-haired man, whose tall frame rivaled Blake's. The intriguing stranger stood out from the group of gentlemen not so much due to his height but because of his rugged profile, which gave him a predatory look. Black curling hair framed his face, and his dress—navy blue jacket and buff waistcoat—was simple but rich.

The stranger spotted Blake, and Blake nodded in return. The man then gave Victoria his undivided attention. She met a pair of sinfully dark eyes that were sharp and assessing.

Anxiety spurted through her, gnawing away at her fragile confidence. She felt a terrible tenseness in her body, certain the stranger saw through her ridiculous disguise.

Blake's fingers curled around her wrist and held her still when she was tempted to flee. "Let me introduce you."

Blake stepped forward, toward the man, and she had no option but to follow.

"Good afternoon, Mr. Hawksley."

"Good day, Lord Ravenspear," the man said, his eyes briefly leaving Victoria's face to glance at Blake, then returning to examine her.

"I see you've noticed my relative, Victor Mallorey. The boy is visiting and expressed an interest in the Exchange. I thought it worthwhile if he saw it firsthand."

Victoria smiled and nodded in agreement to Blake's statement and prayed that she wouldn't have to speak. Even a boy as old as she was supposed to be had a deeper voice than she could feign.

"Ah, I see," Hawksley nodded, seeming to accept Blake's explanation for Victoria's presence. "I was wondering why your man, Mr. Woodward, did not advise me of your visit to the Exchange today. I wouldn't want you to find fault with my services, Lord Ravenspear."

"Marcus Hawksley conducts business for me, Victor," Blake explained to Victoria.

So this was Blake's stockbroker. She was stunned,

expecting Blake's broker to be older, stuffier, more like the numerous fogies she had seen meeting with their wealthy clients in the lobby.

Hawksley broke into a leisurely smile, and his bold features softened. She could only hope that his prior scrutiny upon seeing Blake at the Exchange without notice was from fear of losing a wealthy client.

"You are fortunate indeed to have Lord Ravenspear take you under his wing," Hawksley told Victoria, "for he is indeed the craftiest, most knowledgeable client I have had the honor to work for."

Victoria smiled and nodded, lowering her eyes beneath the curled brim of her hat. Marcus Hawksley may not be like the other stockbrokers she had witnessed, but he was shrewdly observant and exuded an undercurrent of dangerousness.

Perhaps that's why Blake used him.

"Let's be on our way, then, Victor," Blake said, his hand at her back. "Justin Woodward will be in touch with you soon," Blake told the stockbroker, then turned to leave.

As Blake steered her away, Marcus Hawksley gave her a conspirational wink.

Victoria gasped. She reached up to wedge a finger between the tightly knotted cravat and the skin of her throat. The fabric, however soft, felt like it was closing off her air supply.

"Don't," Blake warned. "Your skin is too smooth. It will draw the eye."

Swallowing the excess saliva in her mouth, she whispered back, "I swear I saw recognition in that man's eyes."

Blake chuckled. "That's why I use Marcus. As the younger son of a titled family, he's not as old or established as the other brokers most members utilize. But he is not as conceited either, nor does he charge exorbitant commissions, and he knows the market better than anyone. If he suspected the truth about you, he wouldn't whisper it to a dead man. His confidentiality and ethics are beyond reproach."

"His family holds a title, and he became a stock-broker? I thought trade was looked down upon by the upper classes."

"It is. After Marcus became a stockbroker, his father, the earl, and his older brother, the heir, wanted nothing to do with Marcus. It doesn't matter that he's become extraordi-narily wealthy and successful."

"How sad," she said. She wanted to ask more questions about Blake's mysterious broker, but she lost her train of thought when the swinging doors leading to the trading floor came into view.

Before she could mask the anticipation on her face, Blake pushed through the doors, and together they stepped inside.

It was nothing like she had expected. The massive room was striking—stunning, but in an odd way. The trading floor consisted of an immense elongated hall, wider in some areas than others. The climax was a large central area covered by a gilt dome and arched glass roof. Sturdy stone columns upheld the structure, and Victoria wondered if they were meant to symbolize the solidness and stability of the Exchange. The artistry of the dome reminded her of pictures she had seen of St. Paul's Cathedral.

But it was the huge crowd that soon captivated and held her attention. The scene was mass pandemonium, from packs of men bellowing at each other to individuals dart-ing across the room to destinations that appeared com-pletely random. The floor was littered with paper, and she wondered what poor soul had to clean the mess at the end of the day. The roar of the voices was deafening, and it took her a full minute to become accustomed to the volume.

The chaotic arena radiated power and vitality that drew her like a magnet. Her breath caught in her throat and her hands trembled.

"Let's stroll the perimeter," Blake said.

"I'd love to."

As they walked through the crowd, the tension in her muscles eased. There were so many people, immersed in their own heated conversations, that no one paid them any attention.

The noise level escalated as they passed certain groups, the men gesturing wildly to communicate when shouting in each other's faces failed.

They stopped at the central area beneath the dome, and Blake pointed to a cherry wood hat rack that spanned its perimeter. "You can always tell the jobbers from the stock-brokers by their headgear. That hat rack is for the jobbers who never wear hats outside since they are constantly walking back and forth from their offices nearby. But the brokers mostly stay on the trading floor and are never without their hats."

Victoria found the information fascinating. She had never had contact with a jobber before. She knew their role in the Stock Exchange was critical. Only the broker had contact with the public, but it was the jobber who did the actual buying and selling of the shares behind the scenes.

"When the broker receives an order from his customer," Blake explained, "he seeks out the jobber. Contrary to popular belief, the price of shares is not decided by the Stock Exchange, but can be influenced by supply and demand, war, political unrest, and even severe weather conditions.

"When the broker speaks with the jobber, the broker does not reveal whether he wants to buy or sell and thus the jobber gives two prices; the lower is the buying price and the higher his selling price. The jobber earns money for his services by inflating the price he offers the broker. This is called the jobber's 'turn.'"

Victoria watched, awestruck, as brokers made snap decisions agreeing to prices offered by the jobbers. As far as she could see, business was transacted and shares bought in a matter of seconds.

No formal documents were signed or exchanged. A jobber would merely scratch a note of the deal in a small notepad he carried in his coat pocket.

"A verbal contract is sufficient," Blake explained. "The trade will be verified tomorrow morning by the broker's clerk at the Exchange Clearing House and the appropriate transfer deeds drawn up. On settlement day, usually a fortnight ahead, the broker pays for the shares. Only after he receives the deed is he paid by the customer. The shares can then be officially filed with the applicable company."

A slight attendant with a particularly solemn expression caught Victoria's eye.

He had a limp which became more pronounced as he mounted the steps of a rostrum beneath the dome and moved to a podium. The attendant licked dry lips, picked up a hammer and proceeded to rap a wood block three times. Clearing his throat, he cried out, "Gentleman, Mr. Carlton begs to inform the House that he cannot comply with his bargains."

The cacophonous noise was instantly stilled. The awkward silence and a sudden tenseness in the room made all the occupants feel as one.

"Jobbers and brokers must pay on settlement day. It does not matter the reasons their investors have not paid, even if they are bankrupt," Blake whispered in her ear. "Thus, they do not look kindly upon defaulters."

The attendant climbed down the steps in an awkward manner, all eyes in the room following, and pinned a sheet of yellow paper on a cork board mounted behind the rostrum.

Victoria suspected the yellow paper declared Mr. Carlton a defaulter who was now expelled from the Exchange.

A moment later, the crowd went about its business, the volume returning to its previously noisy level as if nothing untoward had occurred.

Blake and Victoria resumed their walk around the perimeter, and Victoria continued to observe the people conduct their business.

An outsider viewing the scene might consider the methods of the brokers and jobbers haphazard, inefficient, almost reckless. But as she watched them conduct their transactions, she thought it an artful dance, well choreographed, almost *graceful*.

Blake lowered his mouth to her ear and raised his voice to be heard above the noise. "Jobbers deal in specific markets. The markets are stationed in certain vicinities on the trading floor. See if you can identify them as we pass by."

Of course, she thought. How efficient for the jobbers to trade in certain stocks and have their own spots on the floor. That way, brokers wouldn't waste time soliciting the wrong people.

Victoria kept her ears open, and sure enough, she overheard the jobbers buying and selling different types of goods.

They strolled past those specializing in the West India trade companies, haggling over share prices based on the latest sugar, rum and coffee costs. Then there were those dealing in the Russian and Baltic trade with timber, oil, hemp and tallow. Opposite these were jobbers specializing in the East India Company and its competitors and those dispensing goods from the Americas.

She stared agog. "The place appears as disorderly as a city tavern on a busy Saturday night, but there is a rigid structure behind it, isn't there?"

Blake flashed a white smile, and Victoria's heart skipped a beat at his attractiveness.

"It's as well planned as an experienced general's battlefield and runs smoother than the Regent governs England," he said.

"Comparing it to the Regent's ability isn't much of a compliment."

Blake arched an eyebrow at her treasonous remark. "What I mean to say is that the Exchange runs efficiently and smoothly."

Victoria nodded, her lips twitching with the beginnings of a smile. She knew Blake had no love for Prinny.

A man carrying a tall stack of papers crossed directly in front of her. Victoria jerked back to avoid colliding with him. A jobber beside her was not so observant and bumped into the oblivious man. Papers flew through the air like New Year's confetti.

The man yelped and dropped to his knees, scrambling to gather his lost stack. His ink-stained fingers were a blur as he rushed to pluck the pages from the floor.

Victoria suspected he was a clerk whose sole duty was to record transfers all day, a mundane task.

No one paid the struggling clerk the slightest attention and went about their business, stepping on the papers as they passed by.

"Oh, my," Victoria said, "will no one help him?"

"I'm afraid for all its glory, the people that work here care naught about a clumsy clerk. They are too busy making money to assist one another."

"How awful!"

Victoria bent down, reaching for a loose sheet, intent on helping the clerk. She panicked when a group walked by, filling the space, nearly trampling her.

Blake grabbed a fistful of her waistcoat from behind and yanked her to her feet. "Be careful," he warned. "There's an old saying here: don't get in the way of a businessman and his money. People here can be cutthroat."

Immediately, Victoria thought of her father and Jacob Hobbs. Either would step on the clerk's hands before helping him. The notion to aid someone less fortunate wouldn't enter their self-absorbed brains.

"Shall we continue?" Blake asked, studying her face.

She hadn't realized she had stopped, her lips pursed as she thought of her father and Hobbs.

"Of course," she replied, forcing a smile. She refused to allow thoughts of home to sour her previously jubilant mood.

When they finished, and she had seen everything she had ever dreamed of seeing there, Blake escorted her back through the swinging doors into the lobby.

She felt a sense of loss, knowing she would never again experience what she just had. At the same time, she was overwhelmed with gratitude for what Blake had done for her.

She maintained appearances until she sat across from him in his crested coach. Waiting until the footman shut the padded door and they were shielded from the rest of the world, she leaned toward him and placed a hand on his knee. "Thank you for today. You brought my most vivid fantasy to life."

"Just as you did mine last night," he murmured, reaching out to pluck her hat from her head.

Freed from restraint, thick waves of ebony hair tumbled across her shoulders and cascaded down her back.

Victoria's scalp had begun to itch beneath the snug hat, and she was glad to have it off. She shook her head and ran her fingers through her unruly curls.

Blake's blue eyes darkened and, this time, she recognized the desire that burned within their depths.

"Do you have any idea how luscious you look in breeches?" he asked, his voice husky, earthy.

The question should have shocked her as it would have any proper English lady, but she was no longer one of those females. A sliver of warmth rushed through her breasts and belly.

"I could see the outline of your slender legs, and when you bent over to help that clumsy clerk . . . I had to restrain myself from touching you."

She gasped at his erotic words. "If my appearance caused such a reaction, then maybe others knew of my gender."

"No. One sees only what one expects to see, and none would have suspected a woman amongst them. Only I knew the truth, and it has been near torture having you beside me without touching you. I've decided I can wait no longer."

In a flash, he swept her from her seat and settled her on his lap.

Just like last time, she thought. *Only now I know what pleasure can be found in his arms, and he has me quivering with anticipation.*

Their lips met in a fierce kiss, tongues exploring as greedily as their roaming hands through the confines of their clothing.

The tight, thin material of her breeches allowed her to feel the full extent of his arousal. She rubbed her bum cheeks against his hardness, and he groaned.

"Victoria." The word wrapped around her like a caress.

His large hands encircled her waist and lifted her up. "Straddle me."

Without hesitation, she wrapped her legs around his waist and lowered herself. The breeches allowed her to spread her legs, and she took full advantage, squeezing her thighs to hold him close.

"You'll drive me crazy," he moaned.

"Good," she teased. "'Tis only fair."

Running her fingers through his silky black hair, she leaned forward and kissed him. Even though her legs and feet were wedged awkwardly against the leather bench, she refused to let that prevent her from touching him.

With a hand low on her bottom, Blake drew her close. The kiss escalated from playfulness to fiery passion in mere seconds. The interior of the coach grew hot and steamy, and his cotton shirt grew damp beneath her hands.

He plucked at the buttons of her breeches, then at the tie of her drawers, tugging and pulling until the material parted in a gaping *V*. He banged his elbow against the side of the coach and swore as he wrestled with her clothing, but he did not hesitate in his movements.

"I never knew masculine attire could be so arousing." He cupped her exposed mons, and the heat from his palm melted her body against his. His fingers threaded through her tight curls and found her aching cleft. He stroked her sensitive bud until she was slick with desire.

Passion pounded the blood through her heart, chest and head. Moaning against his lips, she abandoned herself to his skillful hands.

"I need you now, Victoria. I need to be inside you."

"Yesss," she breathed. "Oh, yes."

With trembling hands, he tugged at her breeches, but because she still straddled him, they would not slide down far enough.

"Rise up on your knees," he commanded, his voice rough with need.

She obeyed, and with considerable effort inside the confines of the coach, her breeches, drawers and stockings were drawn off and haphazardly discarded onto the opposite bench. She still wore her shirt, waistcoat and jacket.

Together they reached for the buttons on his trousers, and his manhood was freed to her hungry gaze. The space was too confining to remove his trousers altogether, and their need was too great to bother.

She reached for him herself, marveling in the contrasts of his hardness and length and the satiny texture of his marble-hard tip. As she stroked him, a pearly drop of liquid appeared on the head, and she swirled it with her thumb.

"Victoria," he groaned. "I'll spill."

Instinctively, she knew what they both craved. Victoria straddled him again, naked from the waist down, and slowly lowered herself upon him.

He hissed when her hot cleft first touched the tip of his arousal.

She met his fierce gaze as inch by delicious inch she encompassed his throbbing manhood into her hot sheath. His hardness electrified her, and her desire flowed like warm honey. She writhed on top of him, and Blake moaned at the slow, teasing movement.

He grasped her hips and taught her how to ride him and give them both pleasure. She was quick to learn, soon meeting him thrust for thrust, tightening her thigh muscles around him.

Sensation built upon sensation until reality ebbed away. Roused to the peak of desire, a cry of ecstasy slipped through her lips as she was hurled beyond the point of return.

Blake went rigid with her cry, his expression taut with need, as he spurt his seed inside her. For a heartbeat, she sensed his defenselessness, and she gripped his shoulders, heart lurching as he found his release.

Victoria collapsed on top of him, gasping for air, her lips pressed against the glistening flesh of his throat.

Blake made no move to slip out of her body, his hands tracing the lines of her back and stroking her hair. Gradually she became aware of the cramped muscles in her spread thighs and hips. The steamy air inside the coach made it difficult to breathe, but she loved the closeness.

"What am I going to do with you?" he murmured against her neck.

You can love me like I love you.

The unspoken thought jolted her, then filled her with despair. She bit her lip until it throbbed like her pulse.

When had she fallen in love with Blake Mallorey?

She had always been enamored of him, but that had been a girlish infatuation. Hadn't it? When had it turned into a woman's love? What made her think, even in her wildest fantasies, that this man—who had been nothing but forthright in his demands for revenge—could love her?

If nothing else, she had never lied to herself. The moment she had decided to share his bed, she had known there was no future for them together. She had wanted to experience the man, and she had.

She pushed aside the anguish that hovered over her heart.

The carriage hit a large rut in the road, and they bumped heads. Laughing like children, they rubbed their temples and reached for their clothes.

In that instant she knew that every moment with Blake was precious, and she would continue to experience all she could before returning to her father's home and her former life.

Chapter 25

Robert Banks Jenkinson, Second Earl of Liverpool and First Lord of the Treasury, resided at 10 Downing Street. Blake had previously met with Jenkinson at his business offices, but this was Blake's first visit to the public official's private residence.

Less than three months ago, Blake would never have dreamed that he would be making today's visit. He would have bet his entire fortune against it. But that was before Victoria had entered his life . . . had changed his plans.

A dour-faced butler escorted Blake to a parlor to wait. Blake was struck by the room's lack of opulence. With no artwork on the walls and its sturdy furnishings, the parlor was as unassuming as any commoner's. Blake's admiration for Jenkinson grew. The treasurer was an ethical and hard-working public servant with no need for false pretenses.

Jenkinson entered the room and extended a hand in greeting. A tall, thin man with an air of seriousness, he had deep frown lines between his brows, a testament to his stressful position.

"Good afternoon, Lord Ravenspear," Jenkinson said. "I was surprised to see you on my appointment list this morning. My financial secretary, William Padgett, said you had important business to discuss."

Blake was not fooled by Jenkinson's apparent innocence as to the reason for his visit.

"Lord Treasurer, I trust Mr. Padgett informed you that one of your commissioners has helped himself to the Regent's pot of gold," Blake said.

Jenkinson's brows furrowed further, a feat Blake had thought impossible.

"Which commissioner do you speak of? There are four others on my commission other than Nicholas Vansittart, my Chancellor of the Exchequer."

Blake knew Jenkinson was testing him. He looked the older man squarely in the eye. "I speak of Junior Lord Commissioner Charles Ashton. I suspect Mr. Padgett informed you of Ashton's covert activities as soon as they had occurred."

"And who informed you, Lord Ravenspear?"

"I am heavily invested in Treasury bonds, and I do not want an internal scandal to cause my investments to plummet." Blake knew he failed to directly answer Jenkinson's question, but he was unwilling to reveal that William Padgett was Blake's spy as well as Jenkinson's financial secretary and chief assistant.

"You are an interesting man," Jenkinson said. "My instincts tell me you are not here to try to bribe me for money or political gain. Then why?"

"I assume a magistrate has not issued a warrant for Commissioner Ashton's arrest because you desire to keep the thefts private. The reputation of the Treasury Commission is at stake, and the Regent must seek to avoid a public spectacle like a trial. Such would result in the people's distrust of one of the most important branches of the government."

The shrewd Lord Treasurer looked at Blake with open interest. "What are you suggesting, Lord Ravenspear?"

"That it is in the best interest of the Regent for the missing money to be returned to the Treasury without disclosing any information to the public. Commissioner Ashton can then be disciplined and removed from his position privately, and the integrity of the government preserved."

"Your logic is most sound, Lord Ravenspear," Jenkinson said, "but how do you propose to achieve such lofty goals?"

"If Commissioner Ashton was led to believe you suspected his thefts, he would be forced to flee London or stand trial for treason. He would undoubtedly choose to abandon his country and take his stash of monies with him. If you had him followed, you could easily detain him and retrieve the money. A public scandal would be avoided."

Blake knew the moment Jenkinson agreed to his plan. The man's dark eyes sharpened, and then he nodded his head in approval.

"I'll speak with Junior Lord Commissioner Ashton myself and let him know I'm suspicious of his activities. I'll lead him to believe that as a fellow public official I am willing to give him the benefit of the doubt. Rest assured, Lord Ravenspear, your Treasury bonds will remain stable and secure."

The following two weeks passed by in a blur. June blended into July and the whirl of the Season continued.

As Earl of Ravenspear and one of the most eligible bachelors in London, Blake received a tremendous number of social invitations. There were masques, balls, teas, house parties, wedding breakfasts and christenings, but he declined them all, wanting to spend his time with Victoria and all too aware that she could not attend on his arm.

They fell instead into a pleasant routine, enjoying each other's company as much as possible. They spent their mornings reading numerous papers Blake subscribed to and had delivered to his London home. There was *The Morning Post, The Times, The Saint James's Chronicle, New Lloyd's Evening Post, The Observer* and *Cobbett's Weekly Political Register,* each a wealth of information on the current status of the market. Such a pastime would have bored other ladies to tears, but Victoria was thrilled, remembering when she had to hide *The Times* beneath her pillow at her father's home.

When Blake met with Justin to conduct his business affairs, Victoria was no longer banished from the room but was welcomed if she chose to attend. Blake would ask for her advice concerning his investments, and she would beam with pride.

They weren't complete hermits and occasionally left his home. He took her to famous dining establishments and inns, not the type where she would be recognized, but to institutions she had heard of, mostly where the brokers and jobbers ate.

Her identity was not questioned here, and Blake was careful to reserve a table in a dim corner or in a private room altogether.

She tried turtle soup at the Ship and Turtle in Leadenhall Street, juicy steaks and chops at Joe's off Cornhill and at Dolly's off Paternoster Row. She feasted on famous beefsteak pudding at the Cheshire Cheese and sampled the unusual wines at the Rainbow Tavern on Fleet Street.

Then, in the middle of her first week back in London, there had been a shocking visit from Spencer.

Victoria's brother had learned of Blake's dealings with

Slayer and had shown up on the doorstep to question Blake. Blake had not been as stunned as Victoria was at Spencer's sudden appearance and had welcomed him into his home.

Things between the two men had been tense at first, but Spencer had acknowledged that Blake had not harmed Victoria's reputation, and no one was wiser as to her whereabouts.

Victoria suspected that her brother's change in attitude was due largely to the fact that Blake had paid off all of Spencer's debts to Slayer. She loved her brother, but she was not ignorant of his weaknesses.

Thereafter, Spencer visited Victoria daily, and brother and sister spent time discussing affairs back home. It appeared that Charles Ashton and Jacob Hobbs were so engrossed in making money to pay off their debts to Blake that they didn't concern themselves with where Spencer spent his time.

It was during one of Spencer's visits, when Victoria was serving her brother tea in the parlor, that Blake strode in with an embossed invitation in hand.

"Lady Howard is having a masque," Blake said, repeatedly tapping the invitation in the palm of his hand.

Victoria set down the teapot and looked up at Blake. He appeared agitated, shifting from one booted foot to the other. "Is there a problem with Lady Howard?"

"A problem? No. Except that this is one invitation that I cannot decline."

"I see," Victoria said, except she didn't understand at all.

Since Blake declined all his social invitations, they spent their evenings talking and playing chess or cards in the library. And their nights . . . ah . . . well, their nights were spent in passionate splendor, and she was loath to give even one up.

"I believe I can explain," Spencer spoke up. "Lady Howard is generous to a fault. And she was the only titled lady not to turn her back on the Ravenspear family when they fell upon hard times."

Victoria turned to Spencer. "How do you know this?"

"I overheard father cursing the woman years ago."

She swallowed hard. Another damning fact against Charles Ashton.

Was there not one redeeming quality to be found in her father's character?

Blake dropped the invitation on the table. "Lady Howard did more than refuse to cut my family socially. She donated money to provide my mother medicine in the workhouse."

"Did it ease her symptoms?"

"No. The taskmaster stole the money and pocketed it for himself."

An awkward silence permeated the parlor air.

"How awful," Victoria whispered, breaking the stillness in the room. "You must attend Lady Howard's party, of course."

Blake nodded. "Yes. The masque is this Saturday. You may spend the evening with your brother if you wish."

Despair washed over her, but she pushed it aside, anger rising to her defense.

What did she expect? That she could accompany him as a wife would be able to?

Ridiculous.

"Our family received an invitation as well," Spencer said. "Victoria can go with me. Everyone believes she has been spending time in the country visiting a friend. They will think she is newly returned."

"She may go if she wishes," Blake said.

Victoria watched Blake struggle with his emotions,

seeing worry and anxiety and disappointment cross his face.

She was caught off guard by his reaction. Why didn't he want her to attend Lady Howard's masque?

"Of course my sister wants to go." Spencer touched her sleeve, oblivious to the tenseness in her arm.

Victoria gave Spencer a sideways glance. She had never told her brother that she and Blake had become intimate, and judging by Spencer's behavior, he had not suspected.

No doubt if he knew his sister and Blake Mallorey had shared a bed, Spencer would not be so amicable.

"We shall see, Spencer," Victoria said. "I have not been out and about of late, and I need time to decide if I would like to attend."

The truth was, Victoria had no desire to attend a masque. Since her coming out years ago, she had attended countless parties and found most of them tedious. But the fact that Blake did not want her to go aroused her suspicions and brought forth a defiant streak.

They had both carefully avoided the topic of her father, of Blake's reason for bringing her to his residence in the first place. She had not wanted to ruin their time together, no matter how much she had to dissuade herself from thinking about the true nature of their relationship.

But it seemed time had run out, and a confrontation was long due.

That night, Victoria swept into the library like a soldier prepared for battle.

Mr. Kent, in his usual efficient manner, had delivered dinner, and silver-hooded platters awaited on a table covered with snowy-white linen. Delicious aromas drifted from the trays. Candles were lit around the room and illuminated the vast volumes of books lining the oak shelves.

Blake stood behind his desk, arms crossed, gazing out the window. He turned when she entered the room, a frown creasing his dark brow.

"Why don't you want me to attend Lady Howard's masque?" she demanded, dropping all pretense of civility.

He sighed and hesitated before answering. "I apologize for my initial reaction."

"Do you plan on continuing with your mad scheme to ruin my reputation, then?"

He walked forward, stopping in front of her, and clasped her hands. "How can you ask me that after all we've been through?"

"You've made me no promises, my lord," she said, her voice hollow and emotionless. "It's been two weeks since you brought me back to London without a whisper from you of your plans. Nor have you led me to believe you have forgotten your feud against my father. I cannot reside with you in London for the remainder of the year with no one the wiser. Surely the secret will eventually come out. What else am I to think?"

Blake's hands dropped to his sides. "You're right. I have not told you of my feelings. I had thought you would know by my actions, by my touch."

Tell me. Tell me you have fallen madly in love with me as I have with you. Her heart beat erratically in her chest as she gazed up at him.

"I could never hurt you, Victoria."

"And my father?"

Blake's expression hardened, lips thinning into a tight line. "My plans toward Charles Ashton have not changed."

The false hope that had momentarily seized her heart deflated like a punctured lung. "I don't understand. Are you saying you no longer plan to reveal our living arrangements in order to disgrace my father, but you still seek revenge against him in other ways?"

Blake nodded. "Charles Ashton cannot escape his past crimes unpunished."

"Then I can leave here—" Her voice broke off in midsentence. "I mean . . . there's no reason for me to stay anymore."

He moved so abruptly that she squealed in surprise. Gripping her upper arms, his fingers caressed her naked shoulders above the neckline of her gown. Blue eyes stared down at her, probing her soul.

"You promised me a year, remember? It has been less than half that time, only four months. I never thought you were the type of woman to go back on her word."

Her spine stiffened at his words as she tried to ignore the soft, rhythmic stroke of his fingers on her flesh. She was assailed by a terrible sense of bitterness. He made no declaration of love, mentioning only her coerced consent to stay the year.

What did she expect?

Victoria stood motionless, fearing her voice would crack if she spoke. She rigidly held her shameful tears in check.

"You don't believe me, then, that I don't want to harm your reputation?" he asked.

He actually sounded hurt, and she nearly laughed at that.

"How can I trust a man who still swears vengeance against my parent?"

His fingers stopped kneading her shoulders, but he did not release his grip on her arms. "I've had opportunities, my dear. Remember Mrs. Taddlesworth?"

She twisted out of his grasp then, and folded her arms across her stomach.

"Please," he said, "let me prove myself to you. I want

you to go with Spencer to Lady Howard's masque. I promise to act the perfect gentleman, a mere acquaintance and no more. Do you trust I'll keep my word?"

Did she believe he wouldn't stand on the table in Lady Howard's dining room and shout to the crowd that Victoria Ashton had been living with him at his country estate for months and in his London home for two weeks, and that she had willingly slept with him?

Yes, she did, but not because of his vehement promise. She believed him because he had had numerous opportunities to ruin her reputation and had passed each by—the annoying Mrs. Taddlesworth being only one.

"Why? Why would you do this for me?" she asked.

"Because I can't bear the thought of you not trusting me, of disliking me."

She did laugh out loud then. The sound had a sharp edge, half-hysteria, half-cynicism.

Waiting until she had regained some semblance of control, Victoria raised her chin and met his eyes. "Then do something else for me. I want you to cease your crusade against my father."

"I cannot." His voice was quiet, yet held an undertone of cold contempt.

"But why? The past can't be changed. Loved ones cannot be brought back. Even if my father did what you accuse him of—" Then before he could speak, she rushed to add, "And I am even willing to concede that he may have, the clock cannot be turned back."

"We've discussed this before."

That was before we made love and I lost my heart completely. "Things between us have changed."

There was a softening of his face, a slight slackening of his mouth. "You're right, Victoria. Our relationship has changed, and that's why I will do everything in my power to protect your reputation, but I cannot make any concessions regarding Charles Ashton. He must suffer, and it must be by my hand."

Damn him. She had dared hope that he had grown to care for her even a little, that he might want to have a real courtship, a real future together. If only he would relent on his obsession with revenge, if he would only meet her halfway, perhaps things would be different.

She swallowed hard and bit back tears of disappointment. She dared not speak, afraid her trembling voice would reveal her traitorous feelings for him. Turning on her heel, she fled the room.

Chapter 26

"Don't be nervous, Victoria. It is just a silly party, like many of those you have attended in the past."

Victoria gave Spencer a sideways glance before she adjusted her black velvet half mask and stepped into Lady Howard's mansion with unease.

Wearing an expensive silk evening gown of deep blue trimmed with silver that boasted a scandalously low neckline, she knew she looked attractive. Her dark hair was piled high in an elegant style with loose curls brushing her bare shoulders. A tiny black patch in the shape of a heart was pasted by her full lips, inviting a kiss.

To all appearances, she was a mysterious society lady set out to enchant the opposite sex.

The problem was, the only male she desired to dally with was determined to crush her heart for something as hollow as spiteful retribution.

Spencer and Victoria entered the drawing room, where as guests they would normally be announced by Lady Howard's staff. But tonight was a masque, a party contrived to be mysterious, and the masked guests mingled about, holding glasses of bubbly champagne as they attempted to discern their fellow revelers' identities.

A stunning blond woman approached, carrying two glasses of champagne. The lady wore a full silver mask that matched her exquisite gown of silver tissue. The dress had an even lower bodice than Victoria's, which managed to be scandalous and stylish at once. Fat platinum curls crowned her head, and a brilliant-cut diamond the size of a walnut glittered in the deep valley between her breasts.

The woman extended a bubbling flute toward Victoria. "Drink up, darling, it looks like you can use one of these."

"Lady Samantha!" Victoria cried out, recognizing the baroness's voice. A warm glow flowed through Victoria as she met the twinkling blue eyes behind the silver mask. "What are you doing back in London?"

"I got bored after you left." Samantha took a long sip from her glass. Leaning close, she whispered, "And I missed my Justin terribly too."

A cough at Victoria's side alerted her to Spencer's presence. Turning toward her brother, she was amused to find his face flushed, his eyes round disks as they feasted on Samantha.

"May I introduce my brother, Mr. Spencer Ashton," Victoria said. "Spencer, this is Lady Devon."

Spencer bowed gallantly. "A great pleasure, my lady."

Samantha's teasing laughter rippled through the air. "I see that daring, attractive looks run in the family."

Spencer's chest puffed with masculine pride.

The baroness gifted him with a seductive smile as she led Victoria away. "I'll return your sister later, Mr. Ashton."

"He'll have that silly smirk on his face all evening, you know," Victoria pointed out.

Lady Samantha gave a low, throaty laugh. "I'll save him a dance this evening. Hopefully, Justin will be watching."

"Oh, Samantha, I've missed you."

They strolled arm in arm around the room, when suddenly the lady grabbed Victoria's hand and pulled her into an empty alcove away from prying ears.

"I want to apologize to you, Victoria," Samantha said. "I have worried myself sick after the awful debacle with Mr. St. Bride in my home. I can't tell you how sorry I am for leaving you alone with the man. I had no idea that he would act so . . . so dishonorably. I caused trouble between you and Ravenspear that day. How have you fared with him since?"

Suddenly the room went silent. All heads turned toward the entrance of the drawing room, and Victoria's eyes followed.

There stood Blake Mallorey, Earl of Ravenspear. He looked devastating tonight in simple black-and-white evening wear. He was unmasked, and his blue eyes shone fiercely in the candlelight. His strong features held a certain sensuality, and Victoria understood why so many women found him deliciously appealing. There was an air of isolation about his tall figure as he stood at the top step staring at the guests below that only added to his allure.

The females in attendance began to whisper. Victoria overheard excited murmurs that the realm's most eligible bachelor had finally decided to come out of solitude and attend a society function.

Lady Howard, short with a full figure and a head of thick gray hair, came forward to greet him.

Blake kissed the elder lady's wrinkled hand, and his grin flashed briefly, dazzling against his dark skin. It was clear that he held the lady in high regard.

"Ah, you've been with him intimately."

Victoria started at Lady Samantha's remark. "Is it that

obvious, just by looking at me?" She did not try to lie; she needed Samantha's guidance now more than ever.

"It's not clear to the world, but I know you, darling. I also know what to look for. When a woman's first experience is with an attractive and sexually skilled man, she looks sated and tortured at the same time."

"Yes, that is an accurate description for how I feel when I am with him."

Samantha's eyebrows drew together above her mask. "I understand why you feel sated, but why are you suffering? Are you afraid he will reveal the truth tonight? Or is he playing with your heart like a typical, selfish rogue?"

"The latter, I confess. He refuses to budge on his plans for retribution against my father, no matter what we share together. And even though he has sworn not to humiliate me, he will not allow me to return home before the year is over."

Lady Samantha reached out, lacing her fingers with Victoria's. "I believe he is more tormented than you, darling. He cannot contemplate giving you up."

Victoria watched as Blake roamed around the room at a leisurely pace, then stopped to lift a glass of champagne off a servant's tray. Sipping the alcohol, his eyes skimmed the hall until they spotted her in the isolated alcove. One corner of his mouth pulled into a slight grin, and he raised his glass in salute.

The smile was without malice, almost apologetic, and it warmed Victoria.

"I see that Ravenspear is still the charmer," Samantha said.

As they watched, a beautiful brunette approached Blake and engaged him in conversation. The woman's figure was voluptuous, and Victoria swore she saw peeps of nipple from her low-cut bodice.

Blake smiled at the lady and plucked a glass of alcohol for her from a passing tray.

The brunette batted dark, enticing eyes at him and touched his sleeve suggestively.

"That's Lady Walgrave," Samantha explained. "A whore who has no qualms about seducing a man, married or not, right beneath her husband's bulbous nose."

Victoria glared at the pair with burning, reproachful eyes. Jealousy—unexpected and unwanted—welled within her breast.

"And where is Lord Walgrave?" Victoria asked.

"No doubt in the gaming room or stinking drunk at his club." Samantha pulled Victoria away from the scene. "Come. Dinner is being served."

Dinner turned out to be hell.

With a stroke of bad luck, Victoria and Spencer were seated across from Blake.

Lady Walgrave had somehow managed to arrange a seat next to Ravenspear, and like any good opportunist, she flirted outrageously with him throughout the entire meal.

Lord Walgrave must have indeed been drinking at his gentleman's club tonight.

If Victoria had any fear Blake would go back on his word and humiliate her in public, she need not have worried. Other than a polite nod of acknowledgment as she took her seat, he completely ignored her.

So Victoria was forced to watch the immoral female cast Blake seductive glances and whisper in his ear.

The brunette laughed and feigned interest in whatever the topic of conversation was between them, her dark eyes widening in invitation. Growing bold, Lady Walgrave leaned close and traced elegant fingers down his sleeve to his bared wrist, then her hand disappeared altogether beneath the snowy-white tablecloth.

A moment later, Blake stiffened, but he made no move to distance himself from the lady.

The shock of the woman's actions held Victoria immobile. Her temper then rose in response, and she clenched her teeth until her jaw began to ache. She turned her head and her attention away from the disgusting scene, fearing she would have no control over her anger if she did not.

How dare he? What made him think he could flirt with another woman beneath her nose?

Yet, she had no claim on him. They were neither engaged nor married. He was not her suitor. Still, he should have some respect for what they had shared, enough not to seek out his next mistress in her presence.

At long last, dinner ended, and Victoria was one of the first women to rise from her chair and depart the room. The men remained to enjoy their port and cigars. If Blake cast her a departing look, she did not bother to glance back at his face in her haste to leave.

The ladies wandered into the ballroom where the musicians began to play. The music flowed through the acoustically designed room like sweet wine, but Victoria did not stay to enjoy it.

She sought out Lady Samantha with hopes that her friend could take her mind off Blake and the curvaceous Lady Walgrave, but found the baroness in a private corner engaged with Justin Woodward.

Though the pair talked at a proper distance, the way their eyes clung to each other, the way their smiles were alive with affection and delight, made it clear they were in love.

Victoria turned away, feeling the nauseating sinking of despair. She should have known this would happen. Blake Mallorey was a virile man with strong sexual needs who craved the conquest as much as he desired the prize. She had allowed herself to be seduced, seized and captured by the ultimate hunter. He was now stalking his next prey. But still, Victoria had hoped that he cared more for what they shared than he did for the rush of the game.

If only she was not Charles Ashton's daughter, perhaps things would have been different . . .

Seeking solitude, Victoria headed for the open French doors in the rear of the ballroom. Fresh air wafted through the curtains, and she breathed in deeply, like a drowning victim whose lungs had been starved of oxygen. Her head cleared, and she gazed down on the beautiful gardens below.

A full moon illuminated the well-tended evergreens and freshly potted plants. It was an usually cool July evening, and the sweet scent of blooming flowers wafted up to her. A delicate waterfall with the statue of an angel pouring water from a casket was lit by a dozen outdoor lanterns.

"I've been hoping to get you alone."

Victoria jumped at the sound of the familiar yet eerily distant masculine voice.

"Jacob!" she cried out. "I had no idea you were here."

Jacob Hobbs walked forward, stopping in front of her. He had changed since she had last seen him. His silver hair had thinned, revealing the shiny scalp beneath; there were a few extra pounds on his belly. But the shrewd, pale-blue eyes were the same, as well as his expensive choice of dress. As he drew close, she realized he was only an inch or two taller than she, not the foot she had thought.

But then, standing next to Blake's six-foot-two-inch height had made her aware of how tall a man could be.

"I've been present all evening, Victoria. You were preoccupied with your conspicuous attempts to ignore Ravenspear's sickening display with Lady Walgrave."

She stiffened, unsure if it was the truth of his words

that bothered her or the terse tone in which he had delivered them.

"You should be happy, dearest," Jacob said. "If Ravenspear is consumed with that harlot, then perhaps he has tired of you. Of course, he could be putting on an act, intending to protect you from the wagging tongues of the ever-present gossips." He cocked his head to the side, studying her. "If I had to place a wager, I'd say it was the latter."

"Why are you telling me this?" Her mind whirled at Jacob's presence, trying to comprehend what she was hearing.

"Because I want to know what you gave Ravenspear in exchange for him not to reveal your shame. Or, maybe I should ask, what did you do for him?" Jacob leered at her, his eyes roaming over her figure. "You must be very good in bed. Or is it that you follow instructions well? I admit I'm full of curiosity. But the truth is, I still want you, Victoria. No matter how foolish on my part. I'm willing to have you, even if you are soiled and used by that filth."

She glowered at him, her lips thinning in anger. "I'm not sure if I'm flattered or insulted."

"No matter. Your father has promised you to me. You have no choice."

Her temper flared and her memory returned. Jacob Hobbs had never been willing to consider her wishes. As if things became suddenly clear, she saw him for the first time. He was an exact replica of her father. No wonder Charles Ashton wanted her to marry Jacob. It was a testament to himself.

"There are better ways to court a woman than to call her used goods, then tell her she has no choice in the matter," she spat.

Jacob ignored her sarcastic tone. "Use your time with

Ravenspear wisely, Victoria. Your father and I are close to paying that devil off, but we need more from you to speed things up a bit."

"You want me to spy again?" she asked in disbelief. "I cannot. It was dumb luck that I had discovered the truth behind Illusory Enterprises. There is nothing else I can give you. Ravenspear's files are too . . . complicated for me."

"I would expect no less of a woman. But what we now need does not involve rummaging through his papers."

"What, then?"

"We will be in touch. Either your father or me." Jacob leaned close, intending to kiss her.

Victoria shrunk back, aghast at the thought of his lips touching hers.

Jacob stiffened at her rejection. "You should be nice to me, dearest. After all, who will want you after Ravenspear is finished with you?"

Chapter 27

The night had been a disaster.

Leaning against the doorjamb of his bedroom, Blake stared across the hall at Victoria's closed door. She had ignored him from the moment they had both separately arrived home, and had fled to her room.

One thing was certain: she was furious with him.

Her green eyes had clawed him like talons when she thought he wasn't looking. She had held her rage in check and had shut herself in her room to avoid conversation with him. At first he had thought she was mad from the cross words they had exchanged in the library regarding her father. But now he was not certain.

Something else irked Victoria.

Her behavior was uncharacteristic. The Victoria he knew would not back down from a challenge or an argument.

He realized he wanted a fight. He wanted to see her throw her head back, place her hands on her hips and eye him with defiance. He missed her using her keen intelligence to spar and spat with him.

He wanted *his* Victoria back.

He tugged off his cravat, ripped off his evening jacket

and dropped both carelessly to the floor. He strode across the hall, and without knocking turned her doorknob.

Locked.

He stared at the keyhole, feeling his temper rise in response.

What was under her skin? Hadn't he kept his word? Hadn't he protected her reputation and not whispered a word about her living with him? Hadn't he tolerated the clinging Lady Walgrave in order to misdirect the ton's attention from Victoria?

And her response was to ignore him, then lock him out?

Logic fled. He stepped back and then crashed his shoulder against the door like a battering ram. Wood splintered, the hinges gave way, and the door slammed against the wall with an ear-deafening crash.

Victoria jerked upright in bed with a startled screech and clenched the coverlet on her lap. She hadn't yet put out the candles on the night table, and he could make out the curve of a full breast beneath the sheer silk nightdress.

"You forgot to say good night, sweetheart."

"You're crazy, Ravenspear!"

"Perhaps. But I find you have that effect on me."

He swaggered forward, resting his large hands on the footboard of the bed. She squirmed back, like an animal caught in a trap, and he grinned.

"You're pouting, Victoria. Now, tell me, what did I do to offend you?"

"I'm not offended, but repulsed, my lord," she spat.

"Repulsed?" Whatever he had expected, it was not *that*. "Last I recall, you were scratching my back like a wildcat, moaning my name with your pleasure."

Her emerald eyes darkened, dazzling with fury. "Get out. Now."

"This is my home, mistress," he said, pointing a finger at the splintered door. "No one tells me what to do here."

"Go to your cheap whore."

"What!"

"Return to the hussy you were panting over all night."

"Lady Walgrave? Is that what this is all about?"

"You all but dove down her bodice with your fork in your haste to sample her flesh. I'm sure she'll welcome you."

"You don't think I enjoyed her attentions?"

"Why wouldn't I, or anyone else present tonight, for that matter?" She stared at him with haughty rebuke. "I sat across from you the entire meal watching that woman drape herself all over you. And when she . . . when she reached for you beneath the table, you made no attempt to push her away."

He threw his head back and laughed. He couldn't help himself. But the combination of outrage and jealousy on her beautiful face made his blood roar in his veins.

"What you didn't see, my dear, was me crush Lady Walgrave's greedy hand before she could reach her intended target."

He pushed away from the footboard and strode forward to gaze down at her in the bed.

Victoria jumped to her knees and dragged the sheet upward to cover her chest. Scrambling to the opposite side of the mattress, she eyed him warily.

Blake spoke before she could flee further. "I was pretending to be interested in Lady Walgrave. It was an act, nothing more."

Victoria looked dubious. "Why would you do that?"

"For you, sweetheart. I promised not to taint your reputation. You must realize that one stray rumor among the ton could have destroyed my honorable intentions. I feigned interest in Lady Walgrave to mislead them. If tongues wag in the wrong direction after tonight, it will not be the first time."

Bloodless fingers released and clenched the white sheet, and then she froze, perched on the edge of the bed.

Silence lengthened between them, and he wanted nothing more than to sweep her into his arms and assuage her doubts.

"I trust that you did not want to reveal our relationship," she conceded. "However"—she raised a hand to hold him off—"I don't believe you were not interested in Lady Walgrave. No one can act *that* well."

He imagined wrapping his hands around her tempting neck and throttling her. Frustration welled within him, and he experienced a sudden, overwhelming urge to wound her.

"Perhaps you're right," he snapped. "It is difficult for a flesh-and-blood man to resist dangling fruit."

A shadow of distress flickered across her face before it vanished beneath a cool, aloof mask. "There's no need for you to resist, my lord. As you've reminded me, there's no commitment between us, only your sworn oath to destroy my father. My year with you will soon be half over. You are free to pursue other interests, as am I."

"So you are condoning other affairs—for both of us now? And you have no objection to my bringing other women here for a rendezvous?"

She nodded tersely. "And I am free to do the same, at another bachelor's home, of course."

His temper flared, his anger becoming a scalding fury. He had never been so injured, so devastated, by a woman. He had sworn she felt something for him, that her heart had battled her head and near won, as his had.

"Are you saying you no longer feel anything for me?" he asked. "That your body does not burn beneath my touch?"

Her chin raised a notch, challenging him. "Nothing. I feel nothing."

"Liar."

Without warning, he leapt across the mattress and seized her by the waist. With a squeak, she tumbled on the bed, and he was on top of her in a blink of an eye.

Struggling wildly, she beat against his chest. "Get off! How dare you!" she hissed as she tried to knee him in the groin.

"Stop it, Victoria."

He secured her flailing fists and pinioned her wrists above her head with one large hand. He ignored the curses she threw at him and his guilt over physically overpowering her.

She was magnificent in her rage. Skeins of shiny black hair curled around her head and gleamed against the bright-white pillows. The green flame of her eyes burned with outrage. Her breasts heaved, rising and falling beneath the sheer gown until he thought he would go mad from the need to bury himself deep inside her.

He bent to take her mouth in a demanding kiss. She lay pinned between his thick thigh muscles, and his free hand slid down her full breasts and her taut belly, then explored her silken thighs. Deft fingers untied the ribbons at the neckline of her gown, and he parted the silk to reveal her lovely breasts to his hot gaze. Dipping his head to her beckoning flesh, his lips teased a dusky pink nipple until it became diamond-hard. He licked and then sucked the full globe exactly the way he knew would make her frantic with need.

She whimpered beneath his onslaught, yet still there was resistance in her body. His thigh pressed between hers, and he separated her legs until his hardness rubbed against her sensitive core.

He rocked back and forth, the silk becoming hot, then slippery, from the warmth of their bodies. As he aroused her passion, his own grew stronger, and his manhood jerked and strained against his confining trousers.

His lips recaptured hers, more urgent this time. Her nails dug into his restraining hand pinned above her head, and he knew her defenses were crumbling. He kissed her neck and traced her earlobes with the tip of his tongue in remembered patterns until her soft body squirmed beneath his. When he cupped her private center, his desire flared higher to discover it was slippery-wet with her need.

Hoarse with passion, he whispered, "Let yourself go. Don't fight me."

At last, reluctantly, her struggles ceased, and she began to squirm beneath him. He immediately released her wrists, and her arms slid around his neck and pulled him close. She kissed him back with abandon and strained against him in her need.

"Yes," she moaned. "Touch me, Blake."

Her plea shattered his remaining restraint. He tugged on the nightgown until it rent down the center, parting to reveal her naked glory to his hungry eyes. His roughness aroused her further, and she wrapped her limbs around his waist. She tugged impatiently at his shirt until it pulled free from the waistband of his trousers.

More than eager to help her, he jerked up and tore off his shirt, popping the buttons in his haste.

She reached up to claw his chest and drew blood. "Hurry, Blake."

He sat back on his knees. His cock jerked at her urgency, at the thought of driving deep within her wet, hot sheath. He could take her now, swiftly and violently, with the force of his passion. In her desperate need, she would welcome him.

But how would she feel about him tomorrow? He had broken down her bedroom door, physically overpowered her and then seduced her without a thought to her wishes.

She had wounded him where no other woman had. She had challenged his manhood, dared to tell him she felt nothing for him.

She lay panting, her chest heaving as he slid off the bed and picked up his discarded shirt. His movements were slow and painful as his engorged groin rebelled against his mind's decision. Perspiration formed on his brow, and he knew that the image of Victoria sprawled naked and aroused on the sheets would taunt him all night.

She pushed herself up on her elbows as he donned his shirt. "What are you doing?"

"I needed to know that you still desire me . . . that the passion that rages through me every time I look at you consumes you as well."

He turned from her, and walked past the broken door into the hallway. "Good night, sweetheart."

Seconds later, he heard the crash of an object against the wall of her room accompanied by a loud curse.

Chapter 28

What was she supposed to say to Blake this morning?

Victoria stepped past what remained of her chamber door and avoided the splintered wood scattered on the plush carpet.

God only knows what the servants will think.

Across the hall, Blake's door was open, and she prayed he had risen early and had left the town house for the day.

Thoughts of last night intruded her mind no matter how hard she tried to push them away. He had used her, simply to prove a point: that she could not resist his skillful seduction. He could have easily taken her, she had begged him to do so, yet he had not. She had seen, had felt, the evidence of his desire. His restraint had cost him, she was certain.

A war of emotions raged within her. She felt furious and miserable at the same time. She was sick with the struggle within her. She needed answers from him—clear, sensible answers. But Blake continued to be a complex man, more a mystery to her than ever before.

Victoria descended the grand staircase and approached the dining room with caution. The smell of fried bacon alerted her to someone's presence. Masking her face into one of cool appraisal, she walked into the room.

Blake sat at the table, a full plate before him, reading the business section of *The Morning Post*. All she could see of him were his fingers, tapered and strong, as he held up the newspaper, immersed in an article.

"Good morning, my lord."

The paper lowered, and Justin Woodward smiled in greeting. "Good morning, Miss Ashton."

She looked at him with surprise, caught off guard. "Justin . . . I thought you were—"

"Ravenspear sends his apologies this morning, but he had business which could not wait." Justin stood and politely waited for her to sit before he returned to his chair.

"Does Ravenspear's business have anything to do with avoiding me?"

Justin stared at her in utter disbelief. "Why would you say that?"

"Come now, Mr. Woodward. After having spent months beneath Ravenspear's roof at Rosewood, I know you share his every confidence. I also know you were at Lady Howard's masque last night. Let's be honest with each other."

"Are you referring to Lady Walgrave's behavior?"

"It's not entirely Lady Walgrave's behavior to which I refer."

At that moment, a maid entered carrying a plate of steaming eggs, bacon and rolls. She placed the food before Victoria, then turned to leave as quietly as she had come.

Justin waited until they were alone once again. "Lady Walgrave means nothing to Ravenspear. He was protecting your reputation."

"Why bother?"

"He cares for you more than any woman he has ever known. You must know that."

"If that were true, then why can't he forget . . . let the past lie . . . live for the future?"

"You don't understand. He is not an ordinary man. His past includes great suffering that has carved his character."

Biting her lip, she looked away. "I know about that."

"Not all of it," Justin said. "You know of his father's suicide, his mother's contraction of consumption from the poor conditions in the workhouse, but you do not know the truth about his sister, Judith."

"Then tell me." She spoke with quiet but desperate firmness.

"Blake was a boy when his family was sent to the workhouse. Judith was the eldest, and she felt she held the fate of her family in her hands. You see, she had an alternate means of earning money aside from laboring longer hours. Conditions were pitiful. The taskmaster—a man by the name of Herman Mutt—was brutal, and he forced inmates to work fifteen-hour days to earn six ounces of bread and two ounces of cheese for supper. The work itself was incredibly tedious. Women were expected to launder, cook and sew. The men were forced to saw logs and crush stone for use on the roads. Bones were also crushed by hand to make fertilizer. It was not unusual for hungry inmates to pick scraps of flesh off the bones to eat. The bones weren't all animal bones, either."

Victoria swallowed a lump in her throat. "I thought bone crushing had been banned." Her hands, hidden from sight, began to shake, and she pressed them flat against her thighs to still them.

Justin merely shook his head at her incorrect assumption and continued with the story. "Herman Mutt had an eye for the pretty inmates and Judith was exceptional.

After witnessing her mother cough up blood and Blake injured in a commonplace riot, Judith sold her body to Mutt. She believed Mutt when he promised special treatment for her younger brother and ill mother, but they received nothing more than an additional potato a day, without a decrease in labor hours.

"Once Judith chose that path, her life spiraled out of control. After Mutt had finished with her, she was forced into a life of prostitution and was sold out to the highest bidder. You see, the workhouse turned into Mutt's brothel at night with his select group of girls laboring in the laundry during the day and laboring on their backs in the evening. Other than a few 'working dresses,' Judith received nothing, not even a shilling.

"When Blake discovered the truth, he turned into a raging bull and attacked Herman Mutt. Outnumbered by Mutt's lackeys, Blake was restrained, beaten and put in solitary confinement for months. He had managed to hurt Mutt badly, though, and Blake made a terrible enemy. It was when Blake was in confinement for over two months that Mutt paid him a visit. By then Blake was immersed in his own bodily filth, his muscles lethargic, and his eyes straining against a mere sliver of light. Mutt had waited until conditions had physically weakened him. With cruel anticipation, Mutt told Blake his mother had succumbed to her disease, and his sister, now worthless as a whore, had contracted syphilis and had been transferred to the Wakefield Asylum to die. Only after Mutt had closed Blake's cell door did Blake finally break."

"I had no idea." The blood siphoned from Victoria's face, and she pushed away her plate, her stomach revolting at the smell of food after hearing such a tale. "How did he get out?"

"He later killed Mutt with his bare hands and escaped."

She swallowed hard. "I see."

"I told you the truth because you need to know Blake's past to comprehend his actions now. He has survived over the years for one reason: justice. He had witnessed great evil from an early age, and swore to avenge his family when he had acquired the power to do so. He believes evil cannot go unpunished. He sees everything as black or white, right or wrong, there is no in between. He cannot let the man he holds responsible walk away, nor can he forget the past. He believes utmost in his cause and will always put it ahead of even his own desires or needs."

She swallowed the despair in her throat. "Then there is no room in his life for me."

"I have told you what he *thinks,* but that is not necessarily the *truth.* Ravenspear needs you more than life itself. You have the power to heal him, to change his course. You are his conscience."

"Why are you with him?" Victoria asked. "You are a talented man. You can work for anyone."

Justin smiled. "Ravenspear may be merciless with his enemies, but he is loyal unto death. He is fiercely protective towards the weak and vulnerable."

"I don't understand."

"Ravenspear saved my life. In my family I was the younger son, born into wealth and luxury. But I had the misfortune of having an elder brother who gambled away the family fortune, then died of a weak heart. My brother left behind a mountain of debt without a means for me to repay it. The debt collectors had me arrested and delivered on the doorstep of the poorhouse—the same institution where Blake had labored."

A long-buried image focused in Victoria's memory. "Yes, I remember you now. The first time I was introduced to you as you boxed Ravenspear in Rosewood's west wing,

I had thought you looked familiar. Now I remember your family. I had wondered what had happened. How did you escape the workhouse?"

"Unbeknownst to me, Ravenspear had returned from the East Indies a rich man," Justin said. "First on his list of business was to purchase the poorhouse and tear it down stone by stone. It was there that he found me, with a broken nose and two black eyes after refusing to do the current taskmaster's books. He paid off my debts, then hired me. I've been with him ever since."

"I now understand your loyalty to him," she said.

"I owe him my life. That's why I'm speaking frankly with you now. I believe you are what he needs, and that your love can heal him, can free him of his demons."

"I'm the daughter of his sworn enemy. How can I free him?"

"He loves you. He just doesn't realize it. Once he does, he will be able to forget the past and live for the future with you. You have to force him to acknowledge his feelings."

She laughed. "*Force* Blake Mallorey? Could you have given me a more difficult task?"

Justin winked. "Trust me."

For the first time, Victoria saw how Justin Woodward had charmed Lady Samantha.

Chapter 29

Hyde Park was a stunning expanse of tended lawns and old oak trees. But Victoria noticed little of nature's beauty as her feet flew along the sun-washed bank of the Serpentine River.

She had come here to clear her head, to contemplate the disturbing information Justin Woodward had given her.

A few well-dressed ladies, strolling together with their parasols open, stopped to stare at Victoria, who dared to boldly walk without her own parasol, exposing her white skin to the evils of the sun. She paid them scant attention and continued with her brisk pace, her mind racing along with her feet.

Justin's smooth voice drummed about in her head. Blake's suffering had far surpassed what her father had told her and what she herself had imagined.

Judith. Poor Judith. Feeling responsible to ease her remaining family's suffering, Judith had tried to help them, only to fall victim to a flesh peddler like Herman Mutt, a man without a conscience.

A heinous thought intruded the recesses of Victoria's mind and corrupted the fabric of her being.

Did Blake seek to make her his whore as part of his retribution for Judith's fate? Were his sweet words, his blood-stirring kisses a well-planned act?

The idea was like a blow to the stomach. She abruptly stopped walking, leaning heavily against an ancient oak by the riverbank.

Justin was convinced that Blake loved her but didn't realize it. Victoria found such logic hard to believe.

How could Blake not know if he loved another?

No matter how hard she had fought against it or tried to deny it, in the end she couldn't lie to herself: she loved Blake Mallorey with all her heart. And the thought of living without him in her life tore at her insides.

She looked up, blinking to clear the tears in her eyes. The park's well-traveled track came into focus. The cobblestone path was littered with carriages and phaetons of high society, their occupants intent on being seen rather than on enjoying the park's beauty.

Victoria's nails scratched the hard bark of the old oak in agitation. She had once been part of that group. How shallow and empty her past life seemed to her now.

"It's good to see you again, daughter."

Victoria stiffened as the all-too-familiar voice sent tremors of alarm down her spine. She turned slowly, gathering her composure, and looked her father in the eye.

"Good afternoon. How did you find me?"

Charles Ashton wasn't alone. Jacob Hobbs was by his side, a smile on his thin lips that did not reach his pale-blue eyes.

"I had you followed, of course," Charles said.

"Of course," she repeated dumbly as if it were the most natural thing for a father to do.

"You do not look well, Victoria. Has Ravenspear been mistreating you?" Charles asked.

"I am quite well," she lied.

He stepped forward, and her eyes traveled his form. Even though Charles Ashton was well over sixty, he was an imposing, impressive figure with shrewd green eyes, a sharp nose and fleshy jowls. As usual, he was exceptionally dressed, with a tailored navy jacket and matching striped waistcoat and trousers. His cropped hair, mostly gray, matched his steel-gray brows. His bearing and costume bespoke the strict disciplinarian that she had grown to resent as a child.

Victoria sensed the importance of revealing nothing more about Blake's finances to the men standing before her. They reminded her of a pair of vultures circling a corpse—except she wasn't dead. And she was fully in charge of her faculties.

She mentally shook herself. This was her father, not an assassin sent to kill her. Yet he was also the man that forced her to live with Blake Mallorey in dishonor just to delay the debt collectors by a few months.

Victoria glanced at her father's stern-faced expression. She was suddenly anxious to escape his overbearing presence.

"Forgive me for not reaching out to you sooner upon your return to London, Victoria," Charles said. "I have been working hard to find a way out of Ravenspear's trap."

"Have you the money, then? To pay off Ravenspear's loans?"

Charles frowned, his eyes level under drawn brows. "Not yet."

"That's why we have come to see you," Jacob Hobbs said, speaking for the first time.

"I don't understand," Victoria said. "I've done what you have demanded. I've gone to live with Ravenspear despite my wishes. I've passed on his most sensitive secrets to you. There is nothing left for me to do."

Jacob eyed her with a calculating expression. "We need more—"

Charles raised a hand. "We appreciate your sacrifice, Victoria. I know it must not be easy for you, living with that whoremonger, the threat of ruin hanging over your head. But we are close to having the money and to freeing you from his grasp."

"What else do you need?" she asked.

"Ravenspear has numerous warehouses on the London docks, each containing different goods for export," Charles said. "These goods are moneymakers for him. We have managed to learn what merchandise is in each warehouse, save one, Warehouse Thirteen. We need you to gain us entrance into this remaining warehouse so that we may find out what is stored there. We will then invest in the same commodity. The profit we earn should be enough to pay off Ravenspear's entire loans, not just the interest."

Victoria suspected they bribed longshoremen to learn what was in Blake's other warehouses.

"Isn't there another way?" she asked.

"We have tried, but our sources have failed," Charles said. "We believe Ravenspear has secret items stored in this warehouse. Since he is often ahead of the market, we trust there is considerable profit to be made if we beat him to the punch."

"What makes you think I can rummage through his belongings for something as small as a key and go unnoticed?" she asked incredulously.

"You must. I shudder to think what would happen with my position on the Treasury Commission should *your* disgrace become public knowledge."

Her mouth gaped. Her father spoke only of *his* position, *his* embarrassment, and cared naught for the cost to her.

Yet he expected her to risk her safety to aid him once again. The thought tasted like gall.

"I cannot help you," she said. "If I could get my hands on the key, which I probably could not, I would be putting myself in great jeopardy."

"Surely you have learned how to manipulate Ravenspear by now," Jacob said. "There's no sense pretending you have not shared his bed. Seduce the man and steal his key. Deception is what women do best, is it not?"

Victoria stood stunned, unable to speak.

Charles, more tactful, placed a heavy hand on her shoulder. "I do not blame you for what you have had to endure to survive. Ravenspear forced you to do things you would not otherwise think to do."

No, she thought. *You did that, Father.*

At her continued silence, Charles squeezed her shoulder and smiled.

She was not fooled by his display of false sympathy. Though he thought the same as Jacob, Charles hid his disgust behind a smooth, polished façade of an experienced politician.

"I'm . . . sorry," she spoke in a broken whisper. "You will have to find another way."

Charles dropped his hand from her shoulder. "We have thought of everything. There are no other options."

When she hesitated further, Charles blinked, then nodded as if in understanding. "Ah, I see," he said. "You have feelings for Ravenspear and have foolisly allowed yourself to fall in love."

His expression grew hard and resentful, and Victoria was immediately reminded of the parent that had raised her. Her comfort level rose; she was now on familiar ground, dealing with the mean disciplinarian that loathed to be denied instead of the fake politician.

"Why should I help you again?" she asked coldly.

"Because," Charles said, a satanic smile spreading across his thin lips, "things are simpler now. You fancy yourself in love with Ravenspear, but he has not expressed his feelings for you, has he? No, my dear, my guess is he has still sworn to destroy our family. His rage and vengeance consume him. In fact, they are the only emotions you are certain he has. Am I right, Victoria?"

His smug grin was intolerable, and she looked away swiftly, only to catch Jacob's face, hardened with contempt.

Charles stepped forward to grasp her chin with firm fingers and forced her to look him in the eye. "You will help us because once the loans are paid and we are free from Ravenspear's yoke, then you will be free as well. Only then will you learn how he truly feels about you."

Her mind whirled at the truth behind his words. No matter how selfish her father was, he was remarkably intuitive. She was uncertain how Blake felt about her, and her doubt left her vulnerable, even desperate. She wanted, no, *needed,* to learn whether Blake cared for her, for the woman she was. Her need had escalated after learning about his sister's fate.

Did Blake insist she live with him because the thought of her leaving would break his heart? Or was he convinced her presence in his household would cause Charles suffering? Worse still, did Blake want her to suffer like Judith had, a lady forced by life's cruel circumstances into bartering her body?

Victoria honestly did not know, and she was willing to sell her soul to discover the truth.

Her father and Jacob Hobbs were giving her the opportunity to learn Blake's true feelings. Even though her helping them would serve their interests, her actions—as her father was quick to point out—would serve her concerns as well.

And what harm would come to Blake?

She would not be stealing, just borrowing his key for a few hours. It would be returned to its rightful place with none the wiser as soon as the deed was done. She would not have to rummage through his desk drawers, copy confidential documents or steal stock information. Blake's warehouse goods would not be touched, damaged or moved, and he would be able to sell them for a profit as planned.

Her decision made, she looked up to see both men studying her.

Charles nodded, his expression holding a note of mockery. "I knew you would come to your senses." Turning to Jacob, he said, "My daughter would never choose Ravenspear over her own blood."

Blood has nothing to do with it, Father. You taught me that long ago.

As she walked away, Jacob placed a restraining hand on her arm. "Tomorrow night, then, at eleven o'clock. I'll be waiting for you on the docks."

Blake was waiting for her when she returned to St. James Street.

He rushed forward to greet her as soon as she stepped inside the marble vestibule. "I was worried. Mr. Kent told me you went for a walk in Hyde Park hours ago. Are you well?"

Still feeling awkward about the previous night's events, she searched for a plausible explanation. She must not let on that anything was amiss, that she had just met with her father and Jacob Hobbs.

She looked at Blake innocently, surprised to see that

he appeared so concerned, his expression serious, his brow furrowed.

"I'm quite fine, really," she said. "The park is so pretty this time of year, I must have taken longer than I thought."

She walked past him, farther into the vestibule. A dozen long-stemmed peach roses in a crystal vase rested on a pedestal table. A delicate fragrance filled the room, and she was amazed she had not noticed the blooms earlier.

"Beautiful flowers." She reached out to touch a silken petal.

"They're for you." He came close, looking down at her intensely. "An apology gift for my behavior last night."

She swung her head around to look up at him. "Your behavior was barbaric. It will take more than roses to make up for it."

"You have every right to be furious with me. I lost control when you told me to take another lover . . . and that you planned to do the same. Your words inflamed me, and I reacted the only way I knew how. I can only hope you will accept my apology today."

She had a maddening urge to slap him and kiss him at the same time. Her fingers itched to stroke his chiseled jaw until his brows unwrinkled and he grinned once again. Yet, she wanted to scratch at his eyes until he cried as much as she had when he left her lonely and craving in her bed last night.

He reached out and took her hand in his. When she showed no resistance, he tucked her limp hand beneath his arm and led her toward the main part of the house. "Come. Mr. Kent has arranged tea in the library. I want you to join me."

She followed, conscious of his possessive touch on her arm and the heat emanating from his large body.

Tea had indeed been waiting. A sparkling silver service,

with a teapot, creamer and sugar bowl, was arranged on a tray set on the sideboard.

Blake strode forward, removed his frock coat and tossed it on the desk.

It was then that she noticed he had been dressed for the outdoors. "I thought you had been waiting for me. It looks like you came home soon before me."

His expression stilled and grew serious. "I never bothered to take off my coat. When Mr. Kent told me how long you had been gone, I feared the worst—that you had left me and returned to your father. I was going to go after you. But then, you wouldn't break your promise to stay the year, would you?"

Not if you said you loved me, she thought, *and that you would willingly give up your ludicrous plans for revenge rather than risk losing me.*

"I wouldn't be breaking a vow if my father manages to pay off your loans." She held her breath, hoping his response would reveal a crack in his emotions.

"That's not likely anytime soon," he said matter-of-factly. "And if you leave before then, be warned that I will come after you."

The force of his reply took her off guard.

Why? Why was he so determined to keep her with him? Did he think Charles Ashton lost endless hours of sleep over the knowledge that his daughter was under Blake Mallorey's roof? Or was there another reason?

For the hundredth time that day, she thought of her father's plans. There was truth behind her parent's logic, however corrupt. Only when she was freed from her one-year commitment would Blake be forced to reveal his true feelings for her.

Would he ask her to stay out of love, or watch her walk away?

Blake reached inside his pocket and pulled out a large ring of keys. The heavy keys clanked noisily as he opened a desk drawer and dropped them inside.

Her attention was immediately piqued. "Justin said you went out this morning for business."

"Yes. I had to attend to several of my warehouses on the docks. It seems thievery is on the rise. I needed to speak with my guards."

He poured tea at the sideboard and handed her a steaming cup and saucer.

Taking the edge of a chair, she balanced her cup and saucer and strived not to appear too eager. "Whatever do you mean?"

"My head guard came to me the other day. He said a thief attempted to break into one of my warehouses by bribing the guard to gain entry. I've taken precautions by changing the locks and doubling my guards."

"I see," she said. "I hope your problems are solved."

A knock on the door drew her attention. Justin Woodward entered, a frown marring his handsome face.

"Pardon my intrusion, Miss Ashton, but I need to speak with Ravenspear." Turning to Blake he said, "Your solicitor is here, waiting in the parlor. He mumbled something about one of your companies."

"Damnation. My morning was so busy that I forgot about my appointment." Setting down his teacup, Blake strode from the library with Justin close on his heels.

Chapter 30

After Victoria knew where the keys were, it had been a simple task to identify the key marked *W13* for Warehouse Thirteen. She had removed the brass key from the ring and dropped it in her pocket when Blake and Justin were distracted with the lawyer.

The more difficult part was stealing away in the dead of the night to meet Jacob Hobbs on the docks.

Donning a black cape, she covered her hair and shielded her face with its hood. Beneath the cover, she wore a dark dress, wool hose and black leather riding boots. She waited until all the occupants of the house were asleep before slipping from the town house on St. James Street. She walked several blocks before she felt safe enough to wave down a hackney cab.

The driver barely gave her a glance, looking at her only long enough to see the coin in her upturned palm before slapping the reins on the horse's back to start the coach.

She should not have been surprised. A lady of good virtue did not wander the streets of London alone at night. Only a prostitute or a married woman of loose morals seeking her lover would be out roaming the district.

A storm hovered over the city, making the air feel as heavy as a wet blanket. Her breathing, already shallow from her nervousness, was even more stifled by the humidity.

Pushing aside the curtains of the rented cab, she looked outside the narrow window. Dark clouds gathered above, partially obstructing the brightness of the moon, but through the haze, she could still make out the tall masts of the ships that had docked at the wharves.

The coach jolted to a stop. Victoria, not bothering to wait for the driver to hop down and open the door, jumped out herself. Her nerves were raw, her mind congested with doubts and fears. She needed to finish the deed before she changed her mind and ran back to St. James Street.

Rain began to fall, wetting her face and hands. She pulled her hood more tightly around her face and headed for the docks. As she got closer to her destination the foul odor of the river sharpened. She kept onward at a steady pace until she came upon large warehouses, all shuttered and dark from the outside. Only a few streetlamps were lit here, for the price of oil was too high to waste on buildings unused at night.

Victoria caught herself glancing uneasily over her shoulder at the slightest sound. She knew she put her safety at serious risk. She was well aware that thieves, pickpockets, drunken sailors looking for whores, or, worse still, murderers, could be lurking behind a building waiting for easy prey.

But she had made up her mind; she couldn't afford to return to the town house now.

She came up to the first warehouse and wondered how she would be able to discern which one was Blake's. There was no sign on the tall building which identified its owner. It was too dark to see the warehouse numbers.

A thought froze in her brain: Blake had said he'd

increased the number of warehouse guards. Possibly they'd be armed.

She spotted the building soon after. Two large torches illuminated the entrance and the muscular man that stood by. From this distance, she could see a large number thirteen on the door. She guessed a second guard would be stationed at the back of the building.

Taking a deep breath, she ventured forth.

Rain had saturated the cracks between the cobblestones, and her leather boots squished as she walked. For the first time, she was grateful for the shroud of darkness and the patter of the rainfall which both concealed her figure and muffled her footsteps.

A cold knot formed in her stomach as she approached the unguarded side of the building. She looked for Jacob, her mind a crazy mixture of fear and anxiety. When a heavy hand landed on her shoulder and spun her around, she bit her lip to keep from screaming.

"Jacob! You nearly scared me to death."

"So it's true. I did not think you would come. I doubted what your father said, but I was obviously wrong. You do care for Ravenspear and would do anything to learn if he reciprocates your feelings." His mouth twisted. "You're wasting your time, Victoria. The only man that will have you when this is all over is me."

She raised her chin and gave him a cold stare. She refused to give him the satisfaction by responding to his insulting comment.

"Let's get this over with," she said. "How do you plan to get past the guards?"

"My man is taking care of that as we speak."

"Your man? I thought we were going inside the warehouse by ourselves."

"We are," Jacob said in a nasty tone. "I hired him as a precaution only."

Victoria could only imagine what type of person Jacob had paid. A vagrant or criminal wandering the streets, no doubt. She only hoped Blake's guards were not murdered before the night was over.

"Matters should be dealt with by now. Let's go." Jacob pulled her behind him.

With her arm trapped in his iron fingers, Victoria had no choice but to follow. They reached the front of the warehouse, and she immediately spotted the prone form of the guard lying unconscious against the side of the building. Undoubtedly the guard out back had met the same fate. If a passerby should notice the man, it would appear as if he had fallen asleep on duty. Jacob's hired lackey had not bothered to extinguish the torches, and they continued to burn brightly.

Victoria recoiled at the sight of the guard. "Is he dead?"

Jacob chuckled. "I didn't pay the man enough to kill."

"How reassuring," she said, her voice laced with sarcasm.

Jacob dragged her to the solid iron door and tried the handle. "It's locked. Give me the key," he demanded.

She hesitated only a moment before reaching into her skirt pocket to pull out the heavy brass key.

Jacob snatched it from her hand and inserted it into the lock. The iron hinges creaked as he pushed open the heavy door with his shoulder.

It was pitch-black inside. The air was colder than outside, and Victoria pulled her cloak tighter about her. The strong smell of straw and sawdust permeated the cavernous space.

A moment later, she heard the sound of a match striking a rough surface, and then she squinted against the brightness of the lamp Jacob held in a raised hand. He must have carried the lantern with him; she hadn't noticed it earlier.

"Let's get to work. We haven't much time," Jacob said, walking forward.

Her eyes adjusted to the limited light and she followed, staring in amazement at the mountain of wood crates stacked on both sides of the aisle. She counted over ten aisles, each stacked neatly with just as many crates. As for the depth of the warehouse, she was stunned when they walked ten minutes before reaching the back wall.

The building was gargantuan. She had not anticipated the extent of the goods Blake imported. And he owned two more of these warehouses besides.

"This is a good place to start," Jacob said, startling her.

Setting down the lantern, he reached into his pocket. He withdrew a chisel and used it to pry open the lid of a nearby crate. Puffs of straw burst forth as Jacob plunged his hands beneath to pull out a porcelain vase.

"Chinese," he explained. "You wouldn't believe what the bon ton would pay for one of these."

Jacob opened several other crates, each holding different exotic items. There were handwoven Indian rugs, fragrant spices and Caribbean rum.

"I expected only one or two types of goods to be stored here," Victoria said. "And I had no idea there would be so many crates. You can't expect them to all hold Chinese vases or expensive rum."

"Of course not." Jacob looked at her as if she were a simpleton.

"Then what good is my bringing you here? How will you and my father be able to discern the bulk of what Ravenspear has imported without opening every box?"

A malicious expression crossed Jacob's pale face. "We never intended to, Victoria. There are more efficient ways to harm Ravenspear's interests than to discern what he imports."

Her mind refused to register the significance of Jacob's words. And yet she watched in fascinated horror as he grasped a handful of hay, touched it to the flame of the lantern and tossed it into an open crate.

The remaining straw in the crate instantly burst into flames, blinding Victoria with its brilliance.

"Jacob!" she screamed. "What have you done?"

Within seconds, the entire wooden box was an inferno, the heat scalding her face.

She staggered backward, panic rioting within her.

"This is what we planned all along." Jacob's face was flushed, his normally dull blue eyes shone with fervor.

The acrid scent of smoke filled her nostrils and burned her eyes. She wanted to shriek at Jacob, but when she opened her mouth to yell she coughed instead, her lungs protesting from the thick smoke.

A deafening crack rent the air as the torched crate collapsed, igniting the box beneath it. Sparks leapt like fireworks, landing on nearby crates and feeding the ravenous fire. It reminded Victoria of an enraged beast voraciously consuming everything in its path.

"This place is better than dry tinder. All will be ashes soon!" he shouted above the destructive noise of the roaring flames. "We'll leave by the rear exit." Jacob reached for her, but she evaded his grasp.

"You're crazy!" she screamed, a thread of hysteria in her voice. Backing away, she bumped into stacked crates, a corner jabbing painfully into her hip.

"Don't be a fool," Jacob hissed. "You must come with me now before you burn with everything inside here."

She turned in the opposite direction and ran, fleeing recklessly down the narrow aisle. All rational thought flew from her head. She focused on one goal: to escape from Jacob and the evil deed that she had helped him accomplish this night.

Without Jacob to guide her to the back of the building, her only hope to escape the all-consuming flames was by the front door. But the farther she ran from the inferno, the darker it became, until all she could make out before her were the large shapes of shipping containers and crates.

And then she heard the scraping of heavy footsteps on the wooden floor, and she knew Jacob was in pursuit. She gasped, panting in terror. She had been certain he would save his own hide rather than chase after her.

She continued to run, praying that when she neared the exit, the torches left burning by the door would be enough light to lead her outside. Stumbling, she fell to her knees, scraping her hands and tearing her dress. She scrambled to rise and bolted forward, only to lose her sense of direction in the blackness and slam headlong into a stack of crates.

Blood, wet and sticky, trickled down her hairline.

A hand seized the back of her cloak and violently jerked her backward. Still dazed—she felt like her skull had split open—she tumbled into Jacob's cruel grasp.

"Ungrateful bitch." His breath was hot on her throat. "I should let you burn. But I want my leftovers after Raven-spear is finished with you."

She flew into action, clawing at his hands and slamming her foot against his instep.

He howled in pain and she spurted forward. Her cloak rent about her neck and the garment fell from her body, freeing her from Jacob's hold.

His curses bellowed after her, but she did not stop her flight. The dim light of the torches finally came into view. Victoria darted outside and gulped the night's fresh air. She hesitated only long enough to glimpse back inside.

The voracious orange flames had spread; the beast's fingers leapt high to the rafters and engulfed all in its path.

With a gush of strength and energy fueled by panic, she pushed the solid steel door closed. Jacob carried the lantern, but it would take him longer to find his way out without the aid of the torches.

The rest of the evening was a blur. When her initial fear subsided, she became numb with shock. She trotted through the rain, oblivious to her drenched clothing. Without her cloak and hood, her hair dripped in wet cords around her face, and her skin puckered from the cold.

Somehow she managed to hail a cab and find herself on the front steps of Blake's town house. Careful not to awaken anyone, she removed her sodden boots, and, barefoot, climbed the grand staircase and shut the door—newly repaired—to her bedroom.

She collapsed against the door and sank to the carpet. Only then did she allow herself to cry. She wept aloud, rocking back and forth on her haunches.

How had things gotten so out of control?

What was supposed to be a simple task had turned into a nightmare. She should have suspected the worst from Jacob and her father—should have known that their plan sounded too simple. After all, she prided herself on her business smarts.

Why hadn't she seen the idiocy in their plans?

A raw and primitive grief overwhelmed her. Blake's warehouse and all the goods inside were a total loss. Nothing could have survived that fire. He had forgiven her betrayal once before despite the fact that her actions had aided his enemy. Blake had seen past the destruction of his sham corporation, Illusory Enterprises, to recognize her intelligence. He had even acknowledged that he would have acted the same way if he was in her position.

But she knew he would never forgive tonight's betrayal even if she had been tricked herself.

Guilt welled within her breast, and she felt an acute sense of loss. She had caused him to lose thousands of pounds tonight. And she had conspired once again with her father and Hobbs. Blake would not understand. Even if she laid her heart at his feet and confessed her love for him, how could he see her as anything other than the liar she was?

Her only hope was that Blake would not discover her involvement. No witnesses saw her and Jacob enter the warehouse. The guards were unconscious. Any evidence left behind had turned to ashes. She would never willingly confess.

She rose and walked to the cheval glass mirror in the corner of the room. She looked a fright, and she gave a choked, desperate laugh at her appearance.

Her dark hair was plastered to her scalp and hung limply down her back. Blood trickled from her scalp onto her forehead.

Gingerly, she parted her hair to see a nasty gash. She became aware of a pounding in her head and stinging in her scalp as if seeing the injury firsthand brought on the pain. Her dress was torn and tattered and stunk of smoke. She had to get rid of it and any other evidence of her guilt.

She stripped quickly, noting the cuts on her hands and knees, and the bruise on her hip where she backed into a sharp corner of a crate.

But it was the raw scrape across her neck that held her attention. She had no recollection of what had caused it. Her cloak had torn when she escaped Jacob's clutches, but the garment was made of soft wool that would not leave a mark. A sudden realization occurred to her as her hand clutched the red welt.

Her emerald necklace was gone. In her nervousness tonight, she had foolishly forgotten to take it off, and the clasp must have broken when the cloak was ripped off.

Dear God. Would the jewelry Blake gave her be found among the ashes?

She prayed the gold chain would melt from the heat of the fire. Or that none would notice an emerald among the debris.

A sudden sinking feeling gripped her stomach. Tonight had changed everything for the worse; she knew what she had to do.

Ripping a pillowcase off her bed, she put her wet garments inside. They reeked of smoke and betrayal. She opened the window and dropped the sack into the bushes below. She would retrieve her clothes tomorrow and properly dispose of them.

Next, she sat at her desk and penned a note to her brother.

Spencer,
    Things have changed. I must leave Ravenspear, but I cannot go home. I plan to see Mr. MacDonald at the Exchange two days from now, on Monday, to withdraw all my funds. Please meet me there at ten o'clock.
                                                    Victoria

Chapter 31

Black ashes swirled around Blake's Hessian boots as he stepped through the debris. Reluctantly, he pressed onward, his movements stiff and awkward as his mind comprehended the overwhelming damage.

"I'm afraid all is a total loss."

Blake stopped in midstride and turned to see Justin. A glazed look of despair spread over the younger man's face as he surveyed the destruction.

"Nothing is salvageable," Justin said. "I don't believe it's even safe to be in the building. The rafters are mostly cinders."

"How much did we lose?"

Justin looked away hastily, then shifted his feet. "It's difficult to estimate. Warehouse Thirteen held your exotic imports from the Far East. Several thousand pounds, at least."

Blake closed his eyes, his mind languid, still recovering from the shock of discovery. "And insurance?"

"Lloyds of London has sent out an investigator. Our policy covers natural disasters—flood, lightning, wind, fire—but not arson."

"We both know this fire was not the result of a natural disaster."

Blake's shock at seeing the devastation firsthand yielded quickly to fury. He had interviewed the hired guards himself, and he had learned that both men had been rendered unconscious by an assailant. They were fortunate enough to awaken before being burned alive.

No, this was no accident, no natural disaster, but was a targeted attack instead. It was an act of war, designed to strike at Blake and cause the most harm. Blake's mind raced with a list of possible suspects, but only one name rang repeatedly in his mind.

Charles Ashton.

Who else would hate Blake enough to take such drastic measures? But why would his nemesis attack now, when Blake held the upper hand? Nothing could stop Blake from calling in Charles's loans tomorrow.

Unless Charles had managed to steal sufficient funds from the Crown to cover his outstanding debts.

But that still didn't explain how Charles Ashton or Jacob Hobbs had managed to break into the warehouse. The doors, constructed of steel, had not been damaged. That meant the intruder had to have a key.

And where would one get the key?

"Lord Ravenspear, may I have a word?"

Blake swung around to see a short, wiry man dressed in a cheap suit waiting expectantly. His spectacles, whose lenses were the thickest Blake had ever seen, were perched high on the bride of his bulbous nose.

"Can I help you?" Blake asked.

"This is Mr. Stevens, the investigator from the insurance company," Justin explained.

Mr. Stevens cleared his throat, and his chest puffed with self-importance. "I have completed my investigation, Lord

Ravenspear, and have concluded the fire was the result of arson. I'm sorry to say your policy doesn't compensate for acts of malice."

"I see," Blake said. "What evidence have you uncovered?"

"There was the testimony of your guards," Mr. Stevens said, "and then I found this." The investigator raised a hand to show an oil lamp, tarnished to almost black with a thick layer of soot. "I found it on the floor near the front of the warehouse, although I believe the fire was started in the rear. The arsonist must have utilized the lantern to start the fire, and then used it to exit the building. Does it appear familiar?"

"It does not," Blake said.

"I shall report my findings to Lloyds immediately. Again, I'm sorry for your loss." The gaunt investigator turned to leave, then stopped. "I almost forgot. There is something else I discovered in the debris. I don't know if it is of any consequence." He reached into his pocket and handed a small object, badly blackened, to Blake.

Blake stared at the item in his hand, disbelief crashing down on him. His fist clenched tight around the object until it bit into his flesh. He was suddenly furious at his vulnerability.

How could he be so gullible?

His heart hardened, erecting barriers of anger. He kicked a half-torched crate, and the wood splintered and scattered across the blackened floor. He cursed, and then looked up to see Justin and Mr. Stevens watching him curiously.

"Have the building torn down," Blake ordered sharply. "The guilty party will pay for the damage."

Victoria brushed her dirt-stained hands on her worn skirt. On her hands and knees, she tended the small herb garden behind Blake's home. She had no real interest in gardening, but had used the excuse of needing fresh mint for a homemade facial-cream recipe in order to dispose of the bundle of clothing beneath her bedroom window. She worked furiously, digging and then burying the damning evidence of her betrayal.

In contrast to her dismal mood, birds sang gaily and the fresh scent of herbs filled the air.

"What have we here? I never knew your talents included horticulture."

Victoria jerked to her knees at the familiar male voice. "Good morning, my lord. You startled me."

At the sight of Blake, impeccably dressed in tan breeches and a brilliant-white shirt, she struggled to control her rioting emotions.

He doesn't know of your betrayal. You mustn't act differently until you can meet Spencer. It was Saturday, the day after the fire, and the Exchange wouldn't be open until Monday morning. She had to survive the weekend without succumbing to her overwhelming guilt and confessing all. Even if she begged for forgiveness, she knew Blake would never accept a second betrayal.

He took her hand and helped her rise to her feet. At the sign of her old gown, dirt-stained and frayed, he arched a brow.

"I borrowed it from the gardener's daughter," she explained. "I didn't want to ruin one of my own dresses."

"You look as I did this morning after I returned from the fire at the warehouse."

She blinked rapidly. He spoke as if she already had knowledge of the event. "What fire?"

His eyes were sharp and assessing. "Why, the fire that was purposely set to destroy every last item that I had stored inside. Justin estimates the loss to be several thousand pounds."

"I'm sorry, I had no idea." Bending down she scooped up a handful of fresh mint, and made to move past him.

"Of course you know about it, my dear. There's no sense continuing to act innocent."

Blake cut off her escape by gripping her arm, and the freshly cut herbs scattered at her feet.

Icy fear twisted around her heart. She whirled to face him, and struggled to keep her face blank. "Whatever do you mean?"

"Tsk-tsk. I would think you would have perfected your charade by now. Are you actually shivering?" There was a lethal calmness in his eyes as they lowered from her face to her imprisoned arm.

In a heartbeat, she knew she had been caught. Yet she refused to confess and held herself rigid, like a bird caught in an elaborate snare.

"Ah, so you require proof."

He released his viselike grip and reached inside his pocket. Slowly, he pulled out a gold chain, roughly cleaned and still showing signs of soot. Dangling from the chain was her unmistakable large emerald. A ray of sunlight glimmered off the gem's faceted surface, as if pointing a guilty finger at her. "My gift to you was found among the ashes."

He reached into his other pocket and pulled out a ring of heavy keys, with the key to Warehouse Thirteen ominously absent. "There is also the missing key. Thinking back, you did see where I stored these. Shame on me— I never thought to lock them away from you."

There was a hard bite to his words now, and she felt the fight drain out of her body. A wave of guilt overtook her, and unbidden tears came to her eyes.

"I'm so sorry," she blurted out. "The truth is Jacob Hobbs and my father fooled me. They asked me for the key so that they could get inside your warehouse to discover what goods were stored there. They claimed other attempts to determine its contents had failed. They swore that once they knew what your 'secret' commodity was, then they planned to invest heavily in it and use the profits to pay off the money they owe you."

"And you believed them?"

"Yes."

"Why? Why did you agree to help? I trusted you—trusted that you would not betray me again."

She lowered her dark lashes, fighting back tears. Here was the moment of truth, more terrifying than admitting she allowed Jacob to torch Blake's property.

"I agreed because I have come to care for you," she said, "despite everything—our families' horrific past, my coming to live at Rosewood and my own efforts not to feel anything for you other than resentment. My father sensed how I felt, and in his usual manner, he exploited my emotions for his benefit. You see, he knew that if the loans were paid off and I was free to leave, then it would force you to confess your true feelings for me. Either you would allow me to walk away, or you would ask me to stay of your own free will, without the incentive of revenge."

She wiped her tears with the back of her dirt-splotched hand and then raised her eyes to find him watching her intently. Taking a deep breath, she plunged onward, "I agreed to help them because I've fallen in love with you."

He blinked, unmoving, and she sensed the tension in his body. Then he laughed harshly, eyes narrowing. "Bravo, Victoria. Such a fine performance should be reserved for the theater. And to think, for a mere heartbeat, you had almost convinced me. But then a woman that loves a man wouldn't betray him with her ex-fiancé, now, would she?"

Her heart plummeted at his hostility. "I swear, every word I said was the truth! I could never lie about my feelings."

"*You* could never lie?" he asked, disbelief written on his handsome face.

He didn't believe her. She had bared her heart and soul, and he thought her a liar. Could she blame him? She closed her eyes, feeling utterly miserable. She couldn't bear the sight of him without breaking down herself.

"I'm truly sorry. I shall leave your household immediately if that is what you want."

"Leave?" Reaching out, his fingers bit into the tender flesh of her shoulders. "I've bought a whore for a year, it's about time I got my money's worth."

Her breath caught in her lungs. She stood before him, blank, amazed and shaken.

"Despite everything, Victoria, I still want you." Unspoken pain was alive and glowing in his blue eyes. "I'm a damn fool, for I cannot trust you, but I refuse to allow you to go home to *him*."

Jerking her toward him, he took her mouth with savage intensity. The stubble of his unshaven chin scratched her sensitive skin. Her palms pressed against his solid chest in resistance.

It was not a loving or tender kiss, but a kiss intended to bruise and punish. Crushing her struggles with his powerful arms, he forced open her lips with his thrusting tongue and ravaged her mouth. She squealed in protest. He released her abruptly, and pushed her away like she was a leper.

His chest rose and fell with exertion. "That's how I should have treated you from the beginning."

"You mean as retribution for your sister?"

He stiffened, and his fists clenched at his sides. "You spoke with Justin. There is no other way you could have learned about Judith."

"I would have found out eventually," she argued. "You now have an incentive to treat me the way Judith suffered. You must have planned it that way all along, but your conscience could not allow you to use an innocent woman in such a manner. But now that I'm not so innocent, you won't suffer from guilt."

"Since you have it all figured out, there is nothing else for me to say. I expect you in my bed tonight, Victoria, willingly or no."

Without another word, he turned and stalked out of the garden.

Victoria stood in stunned tableau, watching his broad back disappear around the corner. Slowly, she became aware of the birds chirping and the afternoon sun heating the bridge of her nose. But still she found it difficult to move. Her throat ached with defeat, and her sense of loss was beyond tears.

Blake despised her. How had it come to this when what she had intended was to prove he cared for her? Ah, yes, he desired her. But lust and love were two entirely different emotions. His forceful embrace alone had shown her that. The kiss had been full of hate and bitterness, and had been used to punish.

She could live with him as a loved and cherished mistress. But could she tolerate life as a despised and distrusted whore?

Never.

"Miss Ashton? Are you well?"

Victoria's reverie was broken by the approach of Mr. Kent. The butler's normally impassive expression was touched with concern. She realized she must look a fright, dressed in a soiled gown and standing in the middle of the garden as pale and still as a marble statue.

"I'm fine, Mr. Kent. Were you searching for me?"

"I had your note delivered to your brother's household as you requested this morning. The messenger returned with a missive for you," Mr. Kent said, holding out a sealed envelope. "I thought you'd like to read it as soon as possible."

"Yes, thank you." She took the envelope from his hand, frowning at the unfamiliar handwriting on the front. Why hadn't Spencer written it?

When the butler was out of sight, Victoria tore open the envelope. As she read the message, her body stiffened.

My Dear Victoria,

I regret to inform you that your brother is seriously ill and has been asking for you. The physicians are not hopeful. Please return to your father's home at once so that you may sit at Spencer's bedside.

Devotedly yours,
Jacob Hobbs

Spencer was gravely ill? What mysterious ailment was Jacob speaking of?

Had Spencer been trapped in Slayer's web once more?

Enough time had been wasted. Grabbing her skirts, she ran for the back entrance into the house. She had already conveniently packed most of her belongings.

The time to return home had come.

Chapter 32

Victoria pounded on her father's front door. She no longer had a key. There had been no need to take one when she rode away in Blake's coach months ago.

The door swung open; a dour-faced butler glared down at her. Victoria wasn't surprised at the man's complete lack of recognition of her. Servants had never lasted long in her father's employ.

She pushed past the new butler and was already halfway up the staircase before he could call out, "Miss, wait!"

Hurrying down the hall, she headed straight for Spencer's bedchamber. Not bothering to knock, she pushed open the door and rushed inside. Her eyes immediately swept to the four poster, expecting to see her brother lying deathly still and pale beneath the sheets. It took her a moment to realize the bed was empty, neatly made.

A rustle of movement in the corner of the room drew her attention. She strained to see in the dimness, the heavy velvet curtains drawn against the daylight.

"Spencer?" she called out.

Charles Ashton stepped forward, his stocky frame half-hidden by the shadows. Behind him, Victoria could make out the shorter figure of Jacob Hobbs. He reminded her of a circus monkey at her father's shoulder, always eager to please his master.

"What a loyal sister you are to come so quickly," Charles said. "I only had Jacob send the message an hour ago."

Victoria was puzzled and more than a little nervous at her father's and Jacob's presence in Spencer's chamber.

"Where's Spencer? I was told he was ill."

"Oh, your brother is sick," Charles said, a cold edge of irony in his voice. "But not in the sense that you were led to believe. I gave the boy twenty pounds. He's probably in Cheapside at the gaming hells as we speak. An illness, to be sure."

Jacob chuckled in amusement, drawing Victoria's attention to his pinched face.

A primitive warning sounded in her brain. She had already learned the hard way not to trust the pair. What were they up to now?

"Why send a message scaring me to death, leading me to believe Spencer was . . . dying?"

"To get you to leave Ravenspear quickly, of course." Charles turned around and pulled on the tasseled cords of the velvet curtains. They sprang open, and Victoria was momentarily blinded by the brightness of the afternoon sun.

"I don't understand." Victoria said. "I've done everything you have asked. I even helped Jacob into the warehouse. Had I known the true reason behind your insistence to gain entry into the building, I never would have agreed."

"I regret deceiving you, my dear," Charles said. "But the truth is, we have taken risks trying to obtain the funds to pay Ravenspear off."

"What kind of risks?"

Charles waved his hand in the air. "As one of the Lords Commissioners of the Treasury, I took the liberty of bor-

owing money from the Crown in order to pay off the
dreaded loans. I had every intention of replacing the funds,
of course, but I fear my actions have been discovered
before I can do so. Fortunately, Robert Jenkinson, the First
Lord of the Treasury, told me one of the Lords Commissioners is under suspicion for theft of government monies,
and that the authorities will soon issue a warrant for an
arrest. I fear Jenkinson knows I'm the culprit, and as a professional courtesy, he gave me notice."

Victoria stared at her father in shock. She couldn't believe her parent was so bold and unscrupulous as to steal
from the country's Treasury.

"After everything that has occurred," she whispered,
"you have still managed to destroy yourself. But I still
don't understand why I am here. You committed treason,
embezzlement from the Crown. There is nowhere to run;
you have doomed us all."

"Ah, but that's where you're wrong, daughter. I'll be
damned if I'm going to allow Ravenspear to ruin my life,
deprive me of my freedom and my power, and not harm
him in return." His mouth twisted into a thin-lipped smile.
"You may not be certain of Ravenspear's feelings for you,
but I am. The moment he failed to reveal you to society
as his mistress, I knew. You silly chit, a man wouldn't protect the daughter of his enemy unless he fell in love with
her. I'm going to use that love to lure him into a trap, and
when he comes, I'm going to kill him."

Spittle flew from Charles's hard lips and sprayed her
face. She cringed and backed away until she bumped into
the bedpost.

Her father was insane. With a warrant for his arrest imminent, his mind had snapped. Charles Ashton had always
been intensely focused and rigidly self-disciplined to
achieve his goals of amassing wealth and status. He had

never been an affectionate parent to either her or Spencer
and by exercising strict control of and obedience from
them as children, the less time he had to spend dealing
with them.

But his obsessiveness had turned into insanity, and only
a crazed and desperate man would commit treason and
then plot murder.

When had things spun out of control?

Her father discussed luring and killing Blake, an earl of
the realm, as if the plan made perfect sense. Charles didn't
seem to comprehend the fact that the Bow Street Runners
would be pounding on his front door at any moment.

Victoria mentally retraced her steps. One, two, three
paces until she could reach the door . . .

Predicting her thoughts, Jacob stepped forward and
grabbed her.

"Not this time, Victoria," he said, twisting her arm
painfully. "You may have escaped me in the warehouse,
but I'm quick to learn a lesson. You're coming with us. I
prefer if you were willing, but if not, I'm prepared to use
force."

His breath smelled of onions, and she crinkled her nose.

Jacob's face went grim, and he pushed her out of the
room and down the hallway. Charles followed, muttering
under his breath.

They passed the morose butler, who stood rigidly
against the wall and who had obviously overheard the conversation in the room. She knew better than to ask him for
aid. A prerequisite to working for her father was a cold
heartedness and willingness to turn a blind eye to unsavory
dealings. This man was obviously no exception. Having
just learned that his master would soon be a fugitive, the
servant would think only to save himself.

Victoria found herself hoisted into her father's private

carriage. With Jacob sitting beside her and Charles on the opposite bench, she was trapped. Her mind raced furiously, and she knew she must appear calm so that she could learn precisely what was planned.

Jacob struck the roof of the coach with his fist and barked at the driver.

The conveyance jolted forward, and Victoria banged her head against the side of the coach. The horses traveled at a high speed, reckless among the city streets.

"Where are we going?" she demanded.

"Del Rey." Charles gazed at her with a bland half smile.

"Del Rey!"

The hunting lodge was two hours from London, a remote cabin in the middle of the forest, named after the Spaniard who was the original owner. Charles had taken over the foreigner's company and seized the lodge as part of the Spaniard's debts. Del Rey had been her father's favorite escape when she was a child, and often he had returned home with unpleasant stories of bloody hunts that had given her nightmares.

"Surely you don't believe Ravenspear will travel the journey to Del Rey," she said.

"Of course I do," Charles said. "I predict it will take him less time than us."

Victoria prayed not. She thought about her confrontation with Blake in the gardens this morning. He had looked at her with disgust—but also with unwanted hunger, clearly resenting her for feeling such emotion after her betrayal. She had been devastated, but now she felt grateful. Perhaps if Blake truly hated her as much as she still believed he did, he would not come for her, and so he would not be in any danger.

Glancing at her father, she noted his brittle mouth and

fixed eyes. "It's true, then. Everything Ravenspear claims you did to his family is true."

Charles drew his lips in thoughtfully, then shot her a twisted smile. "Old man Ravenspear was a fool. I needed to borrow money for several investments, but he deemed them too risky and refused me. So I arranged to export guns and ammunition to France despite our country's embargo. I was desperate, you see. As tensions grew with France, lucrative trade became nonexistent, and I needed money. When our company came under suspicion, I cried ignorance and blamed Blake's father. I had no choice. It was his neck or mine. What happened to young Blake, his mother and sister was an unfortunate circumstance."

"An unfortunate circumstance!" she cried out incredulously. She sat forward and gripped the edge of her seat so as not to slap the grin off her father's face. "Because of your actions, the earl committed suicide and his family was thrown to the wolves in the workhouse. Blake's mother died from the filthy conditions and his sister . . . Do you know what became of her?"

"She became a whore."

Victoria gasped. "Have you no conscience?"

Charles rolled his eyes, as if dealing with a temperamental child. "Old man Ravenspear was titled, and I was not. I was the brains behind our partnership. I made him rich. He *owed* me, and when the time came that I needed to borrow money, he turned his back. They all got what they deserved."

Her father's eyes were bright with fervor, and focused on a spot behind her head. He was reliving the moment savoring his enemy's destruction. His madness was clearly written in his eyes, and when he turned his attention back to her, it took all her willpower not to cringe.

"You knew the truth all along, and you sent me into Ravenspear's home unsuspecting and naïve."

Her father shrugged dismissively. "I needed you to delay the loans."

She jerked as if he had slapped her. She had hoped that her father had loved her all along. But his love of money and power dominated.

She lowered her gaze, swallowing the lump in her throat. It was then that she noticed the bag at his feet. Without a doubt, she knew it was full of money. With an outstanding warrant for his arrest he could never return to London. He would use the money to flee the country and leave her and Spencer behind to deal with the scandal.

"What will happen to Mother?"

"I sent her to France to stay with your aunt. When all goes as planned, I will join her there. I do not intend to return to England." He bent down, opened a corner of the bag and pulled out a pistol.

Victoria instantly recognized the gun, and her eyes widened at its deadly double-barrels. The pistol was from her father's private collection, a coveted prize from his entrepreneurial importing days. She'd vividly recalled the gleam in her father's eye when he had explained that the weapon had been invented by Gribeauval, Napoleon's gunsmith, and produced later in 1806 in St. Etienne, France. Even though that was over six years ago, the pistol was still difficult to find, and its side-by-side double-barrels gave its user a distinct advantage over an opponent wielding a single-barreled gun.

Charles noted her interest. "Ah, I see you recognize the weapon."

"It's a bit unnecessary, don't you think?"

Charles lovingly stroked the two triggers, one for each barrel. "No, my dear. One shot for in between Ravenspear's eyes and the other for his black heart." He handed the pistol to Jacob. "Hold this for me, Hobbs, until Ravenspear pays us a visit."

Jacob placed the weapon on his lap, and a satanic smile spread across his thin lips.

Their plans tore at her insides, but she forced herself to remain silent for the remainder of the journey. She knew that her anxiety would serve only to amuse them and upset her already-tenuous position. By the time the horses pulled up before Del Rey, Victoria knew she had to keep her wits about her and seek out every opportunity for escape.

One thing she knew for certain: Blake must not die. If he did come after her, then she had to save him.

Chapter 33

Blake was in the library, nursing his wounded pride with a fine glass of brandy, when Justin knocked on the door.

"Perfect timing, Woodward," Blake said, raising an empty decanter. "I'm afraid the library's out of brandy. Be a good fellow and have Mr. Kent bring me more."

Justin closed the door behind him and walked forward. Ignoring the decanter in Blake's outstretched hand, Justin handed him a sealed envelope.

"This just arrived. I took the liberty of taking it from Mr. Kent so that I may deliver it to you. I recognized the messenger as one of Charles Ashton's." Justin frowned, his eyes level under drawn brows.

Blake looked at the envelope, his dark face set in a vicious expression. "What could the blackguard have to say? Maybe he stole enough from the Crown to pay off my loans."

Slamming down the crystal decanter on his desk, he ripped open the message and began to read. His expression stilled and grew serious.

Ravenspear,

By the time you read this letter, Jacob Hobbs and I will have left London. After some persuasion, Victoria has decided to travel with us. I'm sure you realize we have no intention of returning to England. My daughter is stubborn and does not agree with our plans, but we have managed not to harm her as of yet. If you wish to see Victoria again, then I strongly suggest you meet us at my hunting lodge outside of London. I assume you are intelligent enough to locate Del Rey. Come alone.

Charles Ashton

"Well? What does he say?" Justin asked.

Blake shot out of his chair. A thread of panic formed in the pit of his stomach. "Where's Victoria?"

Justin shrugged. "Probably in the dining room for luncheon. I think we should join her."

"No. Charles Ashton claims he has her."

Blake threw Justin the note, then ran from the library. He swept up the grand staircase, three stairs at a time, and pushed open Victoria's bedroom door.

Empty. The bed was neatly made, the top of the bureau bare, save for a lace runner and a washbasin. Rushing to the wardrobe, he yanked open the doors to find it empty. Not one gown or dressing robe hung within.

He felt as if a hand had closed around his throat. She was gone. She had left without a word, not even a note.

His mind turned to the morning. He had been cold and cruel, wounding her with words. His pride had been stung, and he had taken out his rage on a vulnerable young woman.

Good God, he had called her a *whore,* had led her to believe he wanted to use her as Judith had been used.

The memory of his punishing kiss came back. Her face haunted him, shocked and hurt.

What had he done? He had refuted her story, hadn't believed her when she told him her father and Jacob had tricked her about their reason for gaining access to his warehouse. And worse, he had laughed at her when she told him she loved him and was desperate to learn how he felt about her.

What if she had told the truth?

And now it may be too late. He hated to think what Charles Ashton would do to Victoria, regardless that she was his daughter, if he learned that she loved Blake.

Panic like he'd never known before welled in his throat. A vision of Victoria concentrating over her next chess move sprang to his mind—glossy dark hair tumbling down her back, bewitching green eyes shining and focused.

With stunning clarity, he realized that he loved her. That his fierce desire to keep her with him, to not let her return to her father, had nothing whatsoever to do with revenge, but everything to do with the fact that he couldn't bear to part from her. And he had buried his true feelings, kept them from her, not as a form of punishment, but because he had been too frightened to admit the truth to himself.

Since his mother's and sister's death, he had refused to rely on anyone; he had learned not to trust or to need. He had thought such reliance was a form of weakness, and after escaping the workhouse, he had sworn never to be weak again.

And then along came Victoria, and he had fallen helplessly in love, not just with her beauty but with her intelligence and keen wit. The truth was: he *needed* her. Needed her as much as he needed air to breathe and water to drink.

And now it may be too late to tell her.

"It could be an elaborate trap."

Blake swung around to see Justin standing in the doorway. "I expect no less from Charles Ashton."

Justin nodded. "Mr. Kent told me that Victoria ran from the gardens after receiving an urgent message supposedly from her brother this morning. I suspect it was from her father or Hobbs rather than Spencer. Your horses are being readied as we speak. Del Rey is one of Charles Ashton's properties. It's close to a two-hour ride."

Blake was already halfway down the staircase. "I've been a fool. We must reach her before harm befalls her."

The rope binding her wrists was unbearably tight. Her fingers were numb, and she flexed them in a vain attempt to get the blood to circulate.

Victoria sat on a bed, gagged and bound to a bedpost. Suspecting Blake was less than two hours behind them, her father had taken no chances, ordering Jacob to secure her.

A cold knot formed in her stomach. Each minute that passed could draw Blake closer into her father's trap. And here she sat helpless to prevent a possible murder.

She felt panic riot within her, threatening to rob her mind of logic. She shook her head, and stray wisps of hair fell from her bun into her face.

She mustn't succumb to her terror, mustn't lose control.

Victoria took a deep breath and tried to relax. She was never the type of woman to fall into hysterics or faint. Looking around the room, she catalogued the furnishings and loose items that could help her.

The lodge was clearly designed to be a man's escape to nature, there being very little in the way of luxury. The room was large, with a table at one end for eating, playing cards or drinking, and a bed in the opposite corner. Two windows, one above the table and the other above the bed, were all that allowed the sun to illuminate the large space during the day. There was a night table, two rustic-looking chairs and a fireplace. A porcelain jug resting on the night table caught her eye. If she could reach it, then she could smash the jug and use a jagged piece to cut through her bindings.

She tugged against her bindings in frustration.

How could she help Blake if she couldn't move? With her mouth stuffed with Jacob's cravat, she couldn't even scream a warning.

Her fingernail caught and ripped on the edge of the bedpost. Her hands were bound behind her so she could not turn around. Feeling the decorative wood with a finger, she found a rough edge the woodworker had missed.

She feverishly began to rub her bindings against the unfinished surface. Her numb fingers wouldn't always cooperate, and she slipped and gashed her hands several times. But she persisted, and soon beads of perspiration formed on her brow. Her shoulders ached from the strain; her hands were slippery with fresh blood, but her efforts were finally rewarded when the rope grew hot, and it began to unravel bit by bit.

Slowly, ever so slowly, the bindings loosened until all that secured her to the bedpost were a few strands.

A movement outside the window above the bed caught her eye. Her hands froze in midmotion.

It had been a colorful blur, nothing more. And yet, the hair on her nape stood on end. Blake was here, she was certain, and he had had the sense to approach the lodge from the back.

He had come for her. Despite what had happened between them, he had come. That could mean only one thing: Blake cared for her.

Despite her fears, her heart sang with delight.

She immediately set to work, cutting through her remaining bindings. Time was of the essence now.

The front door swung open, crashing against the wall, and Jacob Hobbs stood in the doorway.

Victoria stiffened, as guilty as a child with a stolen piece of candy in her pocket.

Did Jacob suspect she was about to untie herself? Or, worse, did he know of Blake's arrival?

She kept her hands, now free, behind her back, and shot him a withering glance.

Jacob slammed the door shut and strode arrogantly forward until he reached the bed, towering above her. With an angry jerk, he ripped the cravat out of her mouth.

She licked her dry lips and met his stare. "I never realized how much you are my father's lackey."

Resting a knee on the mattress, Jacob clenched her chin with his fingers. "You should know better than to irritate me right now. I thought you were smarter than that."

She tried to shake off his hold. Her palm itched to slap him across the face, but if she succumbed to the urge, then of course he would realize she had freed herself. She would end up tied more tightly the second time. Where would that get her?

It was obvious he had no notion that Blake was approaching the lodge, and she needed to keep Jacob from finding out.

"This is insanity," Victoria said, grinding out the words between her teeth. "What are you going to do with me afterwards?"

Jacob cocked his head to the side. "Why, make you my mistress, of course. Although I fancied marrying you at one point, Victoria, you must realize that those plans were crushed the moment you rode away to live with Ravenspear. You're nothing but tarnished goods now. I was furiously jealous at first, but then I came to the conclusion that a year of training how to please a man in bed would be useful for your future profession in my household."

"You're as crazy as my father if you think I'd ever become your mistress," she hissed.

"I told you already, don't provoke me."

His face hardened, and his mouth came crashing down upon hers. She fell backward on the bed beneath his heavy weight, her fists pinned behind her. His lips were smothering, and she could not breathe. His heavy weight lay on her chest, preventing her lungs from filling with air.

Panicked, she wriggled her hands from beneath her back and smacked Jacob hard on the ear.

Raising his head, he stared at her in amazement.

"How the hell—"

Victoria seized the moment of his shock and lunged for the porcelain jug. The porcelain was unexpectedly heavy, and she almost dropped it in her haste. But the blood pounded in her veins, and her fingers clamped down on the smooth handle. Raising the jug high above Jacob's head, she smashed it down upon his skull with all her might.

A loud crack rent the air. For a heart-stopping moment, Jacob gazed at her in complete astonishment. Then his eyes rolled back in his head, and he collapsed fully on top of her.

Victoria flew into action, pushing and shoving at his barrel-shaped chest until his body rolled to the side. Scrambling off the bed, she stared at Jacob's unconscious form for several seconds, not believing what she had done. For a moment she feared she had killed him, but then she saw his back rise and fall and knew that he still breathed.

Turning away, she ran for the door, her only thought

now to warn Blake of the imminent danger. But as her hand touched the doorknob, it turned of its own volition.

Victoria stepped back just in time before the door opened forcefully, and her father towered above her.

Hard, cold eyes scanned the room, missing no detail and coming to rest upon Jacob's still form on the bed.

"What have you done, Victoria?" Charles asked. "Jacob is to be your savior when all this is over."

Charles pulled her to where Jacob lay and forced her to kneel. He turned Jacob over and slapped the younger man's face.

"Jacob!" Charles shouted. "Wake up, man."

Jacob roused, grasping his head. Gingerly, he touched his hairline and when he brought his fingers away, they were covered in blood.

"Bitch!" Jacob's eyes clawed her like talons. He raised an open palm to strike her when Charles stopped him.

"Now is not the time," Charles said. "Ravenspear has arrived ahead of schedule."

Charles stood and headed for the door. "Bring Victoria, Jacob. Ravenspear must pay for his sins."

"No!" Victoria cried. "Listen to yourself, Father. Something has changed within you. You're not acting rationally."

"You're right," Charles said. "Ravenspear has destroyed all that I hold dear—my position and my power. Now it's time for me to take something of his."

Jacob rose and wrenched Victoria's arm painfully. "You've tricked me twice so far, but no more." He pulled the double-barreled pistol from his jacket pocket and aimed it at her head. "Come. It's time to kill your lover."

Jacob dragged her outside, her heels scraping in the patch of dry dirt beyond the door.

Victoria's eyes focused on the pistol pressed against her temple, its smooth black surface ominous and terrifying.

Would Jacob shoot her? Would her own father permit it? They were two desperate men trying to escape the law—one insane and the other his protégé.

Would she die, or were they bluffing?

As if sensing her thoughts, Jacob jerked her close and cocked one of the two triggers. "Come out, Ravenspear!" he shouted. "I know you've come for Victoria. If you want her back alive, do as I say."

Chapter 34

They stood in the center of a large clearing, the lodge behind them. Victoria's breath stalled in her throat as they waited for a response, each searching the thick woods ahead.

A flurry of movement weaved between the trees, and then Blake stepped out of the woods into the clearing, a small pistol in his hand.

Drops of moisture clung to his damp forehead, and his skin was pulled taut over the ridge of his cheekbones.

He stood there, tall and angry, and was the most wondrous sight she had ever witnessed.

Blake's eyes shifted to the deadly weapon pressed against Victoria's temple, and a swift shadow of rage swept across his face.

"Let her go, Hobbs."

Jacob laughed, his chest rumbling against her side. "You're not in a position to give orders, Ravenspear. Throw down your weapon."

"Don't listen to him!" Victoria screeched. "He will kill you!"

Jacob twisted her arm, and Victoria cried out.

"Drop the gun, Blake," Charles said. "I know how you feel about my daughter."

Blake lowered his pistol and threw the weapon ahead of him. It landed with a *thud* and a puff of dry dirt.

"Let her go *now*," Blake growled.

Jacob shoved her aside, the gun never wavering in his hand.

Charles cackled, an eerie sound of a crazed and possessed man. He stepped forward and took the gun from Jacob.

"I must have the honor," Charles said as he aimed the gun at Blake's chest. "You're truly a fool, Ravenspear. You fell in love with your enemy's daughter. The mistake will cost you your wretched life."

"No!" Acting on instinct, Victoria lunged forward and grasped her father's outstretched arm. The pistol aimed upward and discharged, jerking her father's wrist back and simultaneously releasing an ear-deafening explosion.

Charles shrieked and swung out at her in a black fury. Victoria jumped back to avoid the harsh blow, and then tripped and fell to the ground.

"There's another shot!" she screamed, desperate to warn Blake.

But he must have known, for Blake immediately dove onto Charles. Squealing in alarm, she scrambled away on all fours.

Clouds of dirt rose in the air as the two men wrestled for control of the gun. Over and over they rolled, fists flying and curses spewing, until Blake finally pinned the older man to the ground and threw aside the gun.

Out of the corner of her eye, Victoria saw Justin Woodward rush from the woods to tackle Jacob.

Blake dragged her father to his feet, both men covered with dirt from their struggle. Justin stepped forward and tied Charles's hands behind his back with a leather belt. Jacob Hobbs once again lay sprawled unconscious. Justin Woodward's boxing lessons had paid off.

As Justin led Charles away toward the lodge, Charles jerked and strained against his bindings. Disheveled gray hair stood on end, and his eyes blazed in his dirt-stained face.

"I had nothing to do with this, Ravenspear!" Charles cried out. "Hobbs put me up to everything. It was his idea to use Victoria to lure you to your death, and his idea to steal from the Crown to pay off our debts."

As he was led farther away, Charles became more desperate to save himself, and further elaborated his story of innocence to Justin.

Ignoring the crazed man's ranting, Blake ran to Victoria's side and helped her to her feet. "Are you all right?"

The panic in his voice thrilled her. She blinked, then opened her mouth to answer, but her mouth felt like old paper, dry and dusty.

Blake didn't wait for her reply. He turned her head this way and that, looking for signs of obvious injury. Then he held her small hands in his, frowning as he examined the raw marks on her wrists and ugly gashes on her arms.

Finding her voice, she asked, "You came for me. Why?"

Intense blue eyes met hers, and her heart soared at the depth of emotion she saw written there.

"My sweet, sweet, Victoria. I've been a fool. Can you ever forgive me?"

"Forgive you?" she asked in astonishment. "Have you forgotten that just yesterday I made it possible for Jacob Hobbs to burn down your warehouse? Or that I rummaged through your private documents and gave sensitive information to my father? Information that hurt you?"

"It is of no consequence." Raising her hand to his lips, he placed a fiery kiss in the center of her open palm.

She shivered. "The threat of death has made you emotional, my lord. I have heard of such things from the wives of soldiers that have returned from the war against Napoleon."

He gave her a smile that sent her pulses racing. "No, Victoria. It is the threat of harm to *you* that has made me come to my senses and beg your forgiveness."

"What of the past? I know the truth now . . . what my father did to you . . . to your father, mother and sister. It's unforgivable."

"I was wrong to blame you for the ugly deeds of others. My actions have been intolerable, forcing you to come live with me out of wedlock. I wanted to punish your father with the scandal, but when you walked into my life that fateful day at Almack's, I was already falling under your spell. And when I got to know you, to realize your intelligence and fierce spirit, I was lost. My pride prevented me from seeing the truth. You are my salvation, the only person that can make me forget the past and live for the future. You have saved my soul, and the thought of you not in my life terrifies me."

Dropping to his knees, Blake looked into her eyes. "I love you, Victoria Ashton. I need you by my side. Will you have me as your husband?"

Shocked and afraid to breathe lest the dream evaporate, she stood still. "What of my father?"

"I have found someone more important to focus my energies on. He is your father, your flesh and blood, and because of that fact I no longer wish him harm. I admit, I may not lovingly embrace him as a father-in-law, but I will not go out of my way to cause him injury. As far as I'm concerned, I will have the best part of him with me."

A cry of joy broke from her lips. She threw herself at him. Strong arms immediately enveloped her, and a warm glow flowed through her. "Oh, Blake. I thought I had lost you forever."

He murmured sweet words against her neck. Tears slowly found their way down her cheeks. Blake gingerly brushed each tear away as if they were precious diamonds. Rising to his feet, he led her toward the front of the lodge where Justin and her father were waiting.

The rumble of hoofbeats on the dry earth drew their attention to the road. Four armed horsemen, wearing the uniform of the private police of the Regent, rode into the clearing. Another single rider, a tall, older man who sat uncomfortably in the saddle, accompanied the guard. Whoever he was, he clearly was not one of the police.

The captain jumped down from his horse and strode forward. "Junior Lord Commissioner Ashton, you are wanted for questioning by the Crown."

The older man, whose brows were heavily creased, dismounted and held off the captain with a wave of his hand.

"It's good to see you again, Lord Jenkinson," Blake said. "I trust your plans remain intact."

"Aye, Lord Ravenspear. I will abide by our agreement." The First Lord of the Treasury spoke to Blake, and then turned his attention to Charles.

"Where's the money, Commissioner Ashton?" Jenkinson asked.

Charles's face paled. "For obvious reasons, Lord Jenkinson, we were not planning on returning to London. You will find a bag in my coach."

With a wave of Jenkinson's hand, the captain of the guard was sent to search Charles's private coach. Within minutes, the man returned with a heavy bag.

"You are fortunate indeed to have Lord Ravenspear as an ally, Charles," Jenkinson said. "He has saved your neck from the noose. You must leave England, of course, but exile is a small price to pay for treason. The captain here will escort you to a ship. I trust you will join your wife in France."

Charles looked at Blake. He was clearly stunned. "After all that has passed, why did you help me?"

Blake's expression darkened with an unreadable emotion. "Because I have found something else to live for that's more important than avenging you."

Charles's hand dropped, and he looked at his daughter. "I'm sorry, Victoria. I never thought it would come to this."

Victoria nodded, unable to speak with the lump in her throat. Despite all that had happened, he was still her parent, and knowing he was off to France never to return to England was shocking.

The remaining officers escorted Charles to his coach. There was a moment of hesitation as to what to do with Jacob Hobbs, who was now rousing. It was decided that they would transport him back to London, where he could then be interrogated to determine the extent of his knowledge regarding Charles's illicit activity and prosecuted.

"Thank you for your cooperation, Lord Ravenspear," Jenkinson said. "The missing money will be returned, with none the wiser and the integrity of the nation's Treasury preserved. The Regent will be most appreciative that a scandal was avoided."

Blake stood beside Victoria as the authorities escorted Charles's coach away.

Victoria waited until Justin disappeared in the woods to gather their own mounts before turning to Blake.

"Was Lord Jenkinson serious about your aiding my father?"

Blake took her hands in his, his eyes full of promise. "As serious as I am about marrying you, Victoria. Life is too short to spend it seeking vengeance. I'd much rather spend it loving you. I'm sorry your father is forced to leave

England. Even though it will devastate me if you choose to follow him to France, I shall understand. I won't force you to stay with me ever again."

Tears found their way down her cheeks. She was struck by the thought of how much Blake was sacrificing by giving up his near-lifelong crusade of avenging his family. He had the opportunity to let her father hang for treason but had saved his life instead. Charles Ashton's insane greed had almost destroyed any chance of happiness she could have had with Blake. Her father was alive and had escaped prison. Victoria had no doubt he would flourish in France, and that she could see her parent again if she chose. God had given them all a second chance.

Reaching up, she caressed the stubble on his cheek. "I love you, Blake Mallorey. I have always loved you since I was a clumsy girl of ten."

He cradled her in his strong arms. "Does that mean you will allow me to make an honest woman out of you?"

"Oh, yes," she whispered breathlessly against his neck. "Let's really give the ton something to talk about."